T0374926

DUMBARTON OAKS
MEDIEVAL LIBRARY

Jan M. Ziolkowski, General Editor

SATIRES

SEXTUS AMARCIUS

EUPOLEMIUS

DOML 9

Satires

Sextus Amarcius

Translated by

RONALD E. PEPIN

Eupolemius

Edited and Translated by

JAN M. ZIOLKOWSKI

DUMBARTON OAKS
MEDIEVAL LIBRARY

HARVARD UNIVERSITY PRESS
CAMBRIDGE, MASSACHUSETTS
LONDON, ENGLAND
2011

Library of Congress Cataloging-in-Publication Data

Amarcius, 11th cent.

[Sermones. English & Latin]

Satires / Sextus Amarcius, translated by Ronald E. Pepin. Eupolemius,
edited and translated by Jan M. Ziolkowski.

p. cm.—(Dumbarton Oaks medieval library ; 9)

Includes bibliographical references and indexes.

Latin with facing English translation.

ISBN 978-0-674-06002-9 (alk. paper)

1. Satire, Latin (Medieval and modern)—Translations into English.
2. Latin poetry, Medieval and modern—Translations into English.
I. Pepin, Ronald E.   II. Ziolkowski, Jan M., 1956–   III. Title.
IV. Title: Eupolemius.

PA8250.A2S4713 2011

877'.03—dc22   2011010433

Contents

Introduction

Satires

Respue opes falsas, fuge ceca negotia mundi.
"Reject false riches, flee the blind business of the world."

Amarcius

This refrain, repeated six times in the final book of Amarcius's *Sermones,* signals a monastic theme: contempt for the world. It supports the view that the poet was a monk. Little else is known with certainty about the author whose grandiose name, Sextus Amarcius Gallus Piosistratus, is surely a pseudonym. There are scant notices of his work in the medieval period. One is found in Hugh of Trimberg's *Registrum multorum auctorum* (ca. 1280), "Register of Many Authors," where he is described as "a teacher of truth, catholic, a satirist, a lover of honorableness, born in the province of Zurich *(Turiaca)* near the Alps, an imitator of Horace in his own satires." Hugh concludes by calling Amarcius "a rare author." All other information concerning his identity must be gleaned from his writing. Internal evidence of the texts suggests that he flourished in the late eleventh century, in Germany; that he was well-educated in classical literature, especially Roman poets, and sacred scripture; knowledgeable in medicine; a polemicist against Jews in their denial of Christ as Messiah; a disciple of Prudentius; a gifted poet in the satirical tradition, whose penchant for classical allusions and rare words sometimes shrouds his meaning in obscurity. These points, and his relationship to the author of *Eupolemius,* with whom he shares this volume, will be discussed below.

The prevailing scholarly view today is that Amarcius was Germanic. This consensus is based not only on Hugh of Trimberg's statement that he was born in *"Turiaca provincia secus Alpes,"* but also on the frequent naming of Germanic peoples and places in the *Sermones:* Saxons, Swabians, Teutons; Sigambria, Rhine, Rhone, and more. The third book includes the story of Beradon, a young man enfeebled by famine and seemingly dead, thrown in among corpses in a mass grave at Speyer, where, Amarcius puns, "a breath of air *(spiritus aure)* is heavy." This and other references have led to the inference that he had connections with Speyer. In his text, this anecdote is linked to high praise for a compassionate ruler and "virtuous patrician," Henry III, German king of the Salian dynasty (1039–1056) and Holy Roman Emperor (1046–1056), whose reign did indeed witness a terrible year of famine (1043) that produced many corpses.

There also seems to be universal agreement among scholars that our poet was an ecclesiastic, probably a monk. Christian themes, apologetics, and polemics dominate many sections in the four books of *Sermones.* For example, Amarcius specifically rails against several of the deadly sins in

Book 1, devotes much of Book 2 to the Incarnation and the "hardness" of the Jews who deny this doctrine, assails the lack of self-restraint in priests and the venality of bishops in Book 3, and advocates contempt for the world and acceptance of human suffering for heaven's sake in Book 4. The prohibition of marriage for priests is taken up at length, and counsels of sacerdotal behavior are advanced. Into all these passages, Amarcius laces lines from the Old and New Testaments and reveals his impressive acquaintance with the Prophets, Psalms, Gospels, and Epistles. These themes and a pervasive *contemptus mundi* corroborate the theory that our poet was himself a monk, one who could observe:

> The monk willingly withdrew from worldly pomp.
> To reprove him does not concern me much,
> Nor do I wish to. Yet this I say firmly, that he is
> A miserable monk who does not want to know what it
>   means
> To be a monk and to be a monk by living a holy life.
>   (3.739–43)

Amarcius was steeped in the classics, and he demonstrates his knowledge of Roman authors through frequent allusions and borrowings. Verbal echoes of Virgil, Ovid, Statius, and Lucan abound in his verses. His citations include Ennius (3.792), Gallus (3.268), and Terence (3.527), whom he knew only by name. He read the ancient satirists and hailed Juvenal (3.268) and Horace (4.299). The latter was his favorite. Although the title *Sermones* is not attested in the manuscripts, Horace's work by this name clearly suggested a form for the satires of the medieval poet, and it is understandable that Amarcius's poem was designated by this name in medieval manuscript catalogs and elsewhere. Indeed, traces of Horace's entire corpus—*Odes, Epodes, Epistles, Sermones,* and *Ars Poetica*—are found in ample supply in the poetry of Amarcius, an author so drawn to classical models that his satires often mock contemporary foibles not in their medieval forms, but in terms reminiscent of imperial Rome. This pattern, of course, lends a scholarly air to his work, but it also leads to annoying obscurity, such that one literary historian declared: "It cannot be denied that he is obscure, so obscure at times that it is difficult to seize his meaning."[1] This difficulty must have alienated readers of his day, who might have been attracted to his themes but who would have been baffled by his arcane examples and expression.

In addition to the ancient Roman writers, Amarcius was well read in postclassical Christian Latin authors. He called Augustine "a wise teacher" (3.427), referred to the renowned reputation of "Severinus" Boethius (3.110), quoted Jerome (1.77–78), and employed an allegory of "wise Gregory" (3.225). He praised Alcimus Avitus (450–ca. 520), Arator (fl. 544), Sedulius (5th century), and Juvencus (fl. 330), Christian poets who had composed epic poems based on biblical texts. Of these writers and their narratives, he declared: "I don't dare to find fault with them" (3.270–73).[2] Moreover, close reading of his satires reveals the influence of other unnamed poets on his work, such as Abbot Odo of Cluny (d. 942), whose *Occupatio* "found one of its only certain admirers" in Amarcius and left "substantial echoes" in his *Sermones*.[3] In short, our poet may have had access to the library of one of the Cluniac convents favored by Henry III and loyal to the memory of Abbot Odo.

Among the Christian poets, Prudentius was the "special favorite" of Amarcius.[4] Although this prolific author is named only once (2.383) in the *Sermones,* his influence is clearly detected in a host of phrases, examples, doctrines, and other borrowing from all his works: hymns, satires, and dogmatic texts. For example, Amarcius's attack on various vices owes much to the *Psychomachia,* an epic account of the combat between personified vices and virtues, while his lengthy discussion of Christ's Incarnation in Book 2 depends heavily on the *Apotheosis,* in which Prudentius set out to refute heresies concerning the Savior's divine and human nature. His refutation of pagan beliefs and practices draws substantially on the two books *Contra Symmachum,* in which Prudentius assailed Roman cults and idols. Some of his scenes from the Old and New Testaments are expressed in terms similar to the *Dittochaeon,* a collection of inscriptions or titles composed to accompany pictures in a church, and his description of the Fall reveals a dependence on the didactic *Hamartigenia.* The moving hymns which constitute the *Cathemerinon* and *Peristephanon,* the longest of Prudentius's works, influenced the language of Amarcius's verses. In notes to his text, Karl Manitius, the most recent editor of the *Sermones,* cited the works of Prudentius as sources over 170 times. Clearly, Amarcius was strongly attracted to the fervent zeal and poetic charms of this "Christian Horace."[5]

The *Sermones* of Amarcius are also connected closely to the narrative poem known as *Eupolemius.* Numerous verbal parallels suggest that the author of one work had surely read the other or that both pieces were composed by the same person. The closeness between the two extends to their common use of pseudonyms, reliance on the same sources (especially Prudentius), probable Germanic nationality, and even manuscript tradition. The standard edition of both was published by Karl Manitius, who, after sifting all available evidence, remained uncertain about the identity of the poet. A complete prose translation of *Eupolemius* by Jan Ziolkowski, with an introduction that includes discussion of this question, accompanies this translation of Amarcius. For my own part, I am convinced that "Eupolemius" and "Amarcius" are the same individual.

The impressive erudition displayed in Amarcius's *Sermones* also embraces the field of medicine to such an extent that Max Manitius, his first editor (and father of Karl), suspected the author to be a physician. In fact, most of the passages cited by Manitius to support his claim prescribe certain herbs whose curative powers overcome specific ailments, such as horehound for a cough, celandine for mange, and danewort to dispel goiters. Some speak of distasteful remedies such as burnet for heartburn, chalk for jaundice, radish for lice, and so on. The poet describes surgery once (4.416–18: "a man . . . who must be cut by a scalpel probing his belly"), and mentions one specific doctrine of Hippocrates. In a few places, Amarcius chides those who do much to promote bodily health but who care not at all for the health of the soul. As his poem draws to a close, he underscores his point that heaven cannot be gained without suffering by reminding readers of harsh cures undertaken for coughs, consumption, catarrh, and gout. Taken together, these examples surely bespeak the poet's interest in medicine and herbal cures, but they hardly prove that he was a physician. In fact, his knowledge of these remedies could have been gained from a manuscript herbal, a common book in medieval libraries.

Amarcius was an apologist for certain doctrines being discussed and debated in the church of the eleventh and twelfth centuries. The *Sermones* argue vigorously for the observance of practices being advanced by some in the church at the time, e.g., celibacy for priests (3.695–821), tithing (3.847–65), avoidance of simony (3.882–905), and the doctrine of good works (4.1–86).

SUMMARY

The *Sermones* of Amarcius are in four books of unequal length that total 2,684 lines. Book 1 (573 lines) opens with a "letter" of eleven elegiac distichs addressed to Candidus Theophystius Alchimus, who is hailed as a former teacher of the poet ("your pupil of tender youth"). The true identity of the person concealed by this pseudonym is unknown, but Amarcius salutes him for his virtues, and puns (twice) on his name *(candidus; candidior)* in praising his "radiant" service to God. He declares his intention to write about the lofty morals of their ancestors, now subverted, and appeals to his mentor to accept a poem created by the "dull little light" of his mind. He asks Theophystius not to be deterred by its "rustic quality."

The remainder of Book 1 is divided into six sections, all composed in dactylic hexameters; indeed, this is the meter of the whole of the *Sermones*. The first section begins with a general lament for the moral decline of a topsy-turvy world, one where vices are rampant again, especially avarice. Amarcius contrasts the virtuous ways of old with the corrupt practices of his day and grieves that "the whole world now races to hell." The second section continues to expose the prevalence of avarice, the dominance of silver and gold, in a land where robbers roam, and bishops with "ravenous maws" are whirled about by insatiable greed, "just as whips whirl a hoop." Even stingy priests shamefully neglect their offices unless they receive "at least four pennies."

Amarcius turns his attention to lust and pride in the next two sections. The former vice, he complains, changes men into beasts and causes such perversions that women don men's clothes, young men adopt feminine fashions, clerics and monks turn away from chapter houses and cloisters because of "fire in the loins." Pride, too, is censured and linked to Lucifer and Adam. The union of "raving pride and the insane desire for possessing" is illustrated in the words and deeds of rich and poor alike, and in the boasting of the "new man" who refuses to imitate the humble Lord who entered Jerusalem seated on "a lowly ass."

In the final sections of Book 1, Amarcius assails luxury, or excess *(luxuria, luxus)*, and envy *(invidia)*. He creates amusing scenes of debauchery, where gluttons wallow in lavish banquets reminiscent of Nasidienus's feast in Horace's *Sermones* (2.8), musicians and jesters revel in exotic entertainments, and lords spur on their horses to the hunt for wild game. The poet's pledge to treat of envy, that "plague from hell," is not realized in the closing portion of Book 1, for tracing this vice to its source, "the ghastly serpent [which] enticed our first parents with cunning deceit," leads him to discuss at length the continued delusion of "the hearts of the Hebrews." Amarcius blames envy for preventing the Jews from accepting Christ as Messiah, in spite of the prophesies of their own scriptures. These are detailed and supported by numerous New Testament examples marshaled by our poet to overcome their doubts and hesitations (though the Jews, of course, would hardly be persuaded by reference to that source).

The second book (674 lines) of *Sermones* continues the polemic against the Jews' failure to acknowledge Jesus as Messiah. Amarcius punctuates his arguments with verses from the Old and New Testaments, and he addresses the specific question of the Incarnation: the Eternal Son of God became flesh to instruct us and to redeem us. The poet paraphrases biblical examples to portray Christ as a humble teacher of mankind: he subjected himself to parents, deigned to be blessed by aged Simeon, submitted to baptism and to temptation, washed the feet of his disciples, and died on a cross. Amarcius proceeds to confirm the Lord's Incarnation from testimony of the scriptures, including prophesies of Isaiah, Micah, and the book of Daniel.

Next, Amarcius devotes a lengthy passage (2.279–476) to the "hardness of the Jews," a theme he underscores with repeated epithets ("hard race of Judah") and vehement direct address ("most wretched Jew"; "wicked nation, lost nation"). He invokes the ancient accusation that Jews are "unspeakable" *(infandos)* because "they killed Christ." He supports his condemnation of their stubbornness and hard nature with quotations from the prophets who rebuked the children of Israel in times past, such as the words of Isaiah (1:3): "The ox and the ass recognize their master's manger, but my people Israel refuses to know me." The ox and the ass, Amarcius asserts, represent the gentiles who abandoned their superstitious cults to become believers in Christ. In a vivid, detailed passage, he catalogs a number of deities and their primitive rites. These once-brutish pagans, now converted, he contrasts with the Jews who are unwilling to accept Christ despite the compelling evidence of his miracles, which the poet enumerates at length.

In the closing sections of Book 2, Amarcius returns to his discussion of specific vices. He resumes his attack on "biting envy," and reiterates the point that the "ancient serpent" still employs this vice to delude the hearts of the Jews, but it also ensnares all mankind and propels people toward "shadowy Orcus." Our author again mingles scriptural examples of envy with amusing instances drawn from folklore. He likens an envious person to a spiteful stepmother glaring at a stepson, a cat watching a mouse, or a dog lying on hay and snarling at oxen just to keep them from eating it. Finally, the poet addresses discord and anger. In fact, he traces the concatenation of vices and their consequences as he describes how discord leads to anger and rage, and in turn to shame, regret, and despair. The book ends with an appeal to resist despair by clinging to the hope of heaven. As encouragement to the reader, Amarcius offers the New Testament examples of the "restoration" of Peter and the "rescue" of the woman taken in adultery. He also relates the story of a group of Jews in Beirut who desecrated an image of Jesus and "cut open its side," from which, miraculously, came forth blood and water. This mixture, saved in a jar, cured people suffering from all sorts of illnesses and infirmities and led directly to the conversion of those Jews to Christ. The second book closes with the following:

> . . . and with a remorseful heart seek the Lord. To be guided by his reins is the greatest freedom; to be subject to his gentle yoke is the highest dominion!

Book 3 of the *Sermones* is the longest (967 lines). At its outset, Amarcius announces his purpose: "to draw those recalled from the path of vices toward virtues." In particular, he counsels a life of sobriety and charity. The first section constitutes a call to moderation. The poet mocks lives of excess: the wealthy, prodigal in spending, gluttonous, and bestial in behavior; the greedy, preferring money to life and living sparingly to amass it. These ways are contrasted to the prudent life of sobriety and charity by which Christians lay up treasures in heaven. As models, Amarcius praises the almsgiving of St. Lawrence and the compassion of King Henry III. As a specific example of "the pious deeds of the virtuous patrician" [Henry III], the poet relates the story of Beradon of Speyer, and then urges all Christians to imitate the actions of the glorious ruler.

The second section of Book 3 is devoted to another rampant vice: lust. In order to resist "obscene lust" and its "fierce flames," Amarcius recommends traditional monastic responses: fasting, avoidance of idleness, toil, and prayer, including recitation of the Psalms. Our model of innocence and cleanliness is Christ, a virgin born of a virgin, and thus unique among all men who ever lived, Amarcius declares, for no one among the ancients was so born, not Plato, Achilles, Caesar, or the heroes and "ridiculous gods whom a brutish people worshipped." Our poet asserts that "shitty Jove," the seducer of so many mistresses, should by no means be called a god. Before closing this passage, he admonishes readers again to avoid excess, for "drunkenness ruins chaste men," and Daniel taught us to eat in moderation. As a final exemplum of modesty, Amarcius tells a story derived from St. Jerome about a chaste monk (St. Malchus) and a pure woman saved from violent pursuers by a lioness when they hid in her den.

In the next section of Book 3, Amarcius contrasts pride and humility. He reminds readers of Christ's embrace of little children, his condemnation of arrogance, his call to be "meek and humble of heart." Warning that "pride is more aggressive than all the vices," our author cautions against vainglory and urges contrition. As a model of humility, Amarcius cites St. Macarius, "a venerable abbot," who taught his followers by example, just as in war a brave general rallies his spirited troops in battle, but a timid or downcast leader inspires no one. He includes an anecdote about a confrontation between Macarius and Apollyon, "a hideous angel of the lower regions, wielding a sharp sickle and snarling," who conceded that the saint's greatness resulted from his virtue of humility.

After a brief discourse on the nature of the soul, our poet proceeds to a discussion of the highest virtue, true love, "the commandment greater than all commandments." He observes that everyone cares for the body and learns "a thousand forms of healing," but rarely do men care about the soul or seek "to adorn the soul with brotherly love." He emphasizes the supreme place of love in a Christian life by quoting St. Paul's famous declaration in 1 Corinthians (13) and St. John's commendation of love in his first Epistle (4:16). Amarcius notes that the enemy of love is envy, which must be cast aside, just as love of neighbor and tearful remorse for sin must be cultivated. These lead to heaven, "the shining city" whose earthly exemplar is the church "made visible by continual lights" and adorned with paintings of the four living creatures (man, ox, lion, eagle) praising God in the celestial city.

To explain how all things are founded on and depend on love, Amarcius turns to the teachings of Euphronius, of whom, he declares, "men used to say that true love resided in his heart." Who, exactly, is concealed by this pseudonym remains unknown, but Amarcius recalls that when he was a small boy, he saw this renowned teacher. The doctrines of Euphronius that follow amount to a paraphrase of the creation story in Genesis. This passage is reminiscent of the biblical epic of Avitus, while the catalog of trees it includes imitates Ovid (*Met.* 10.90–105). It concludes with the affirmation that God's immortal creature, mankind, was made to look heavenward, to the abode of eternal light, but that no one can reach the celestial city without love, the "true salvation," "the perfection of life."

The closing sections of Book 3 concern priests: their lack of restraint and what practices they should observe or avoid. This theme is incorporated into the extended discourse of Euphronius on love, when he distinguishes between true love that comes from heaven and "love of a woman." Although the last mentioned was divinely created and is lawful in marriage, no one should wallow in adultery or attach himself to harlots. This holds especially true for priests, to whom marriage is forbidden. Satire is then directed toward priests who do not fear to approach the altar "with impure hands" and unclean heart, men who think that they are made holy by reliquaries and incense, by chasubles and cruets, even though they neglect morning vigils and "arise damp and reeking after shameful acts in the warm lap of a wife."

Euphronius thus enjoins priests and pastors to banish marriage from their minds. Moreover, he cautions them to avoid gluttony, drunkenness, babbling, gambling, and such pursuits in order that they might criticize vices among the populace "like a sounding clarion." They ought to live plainly, purely, teaching the faithful with a mild manner, just as a groom gently strokes the nape and wipes the haunches of an untamed horse until the steed is subdued. They should teach by example, visiting the sick, praying for the dead, and they must insist on the payment of tithes. Euphronius calls for discernment in priests and decries the fact that blameworthy bishops "very often" elevate ignorant, vicious men to holy orders. This they do because of bribes. He devotes the remainder of his discourse to a denunciation of simony and venality and to a summation of the proper behavior for priests. His final words renew the call to "true love," the love that must belong not only to priests, but to all the faithful.

At the outset of Book 4, Amarcius reverts to his own voice. He takes up the theme of brotherly love and expounds on the doctrine that faith without works is dead. He remarks that men of faith might be illustrious for different virtues, but neither many virtues nor a single one makes a man holy without true love. Through this, one gathers all virtues together and secures "a staircase to the stars," to the hall of heaven composed of twelve different gems, according to St. John (Apocalypse 21:19–20). Then he proceeds to describe the colors and properties of these precious stones in the next passage, and he includes an allegorical interpretation for each, as, for example, the green jasper signifies those who thrive in steadfast faith, or the purple amethyst stands for saints who suffer martyrdom.

The third, lengthy section of this book encourages contempt for the world by illustrating how deceptive are its delights, and how transitory. Amarcius introduces the *ubi sunt?* (where are they?) topos, naming Caesar and Herod specifically, to underscore the fleeting nature of earthly power and pleasure. He cleverly satirizes young men's attraction to fashion and fame, the vainglory of the rich, and the excessive demands of fastidious gluttons. As an antidote to such folly, he urges a life of moderation and issues the reminder that:

> . . . the delights of this fluid world remain with us for a short time. The Elbe will be weary of wars, the Athenians of studies, the French will be loath to wheel about their brown stallions.

The section closes with the reiterated call to "reject false riches, flee the blind business of the world," and to do so without delay, for after death there is no time for reform, no place for flight. The blissful halls of celestial life are surely worth our efforts.

The last portion of Book 4 argues that the kingdom of heaven cannot be gained without suffering. Amarcius reminds readers of the toil and travail of Job, of saints (Stephen, Maurice, Vincent), and of Christ himself, who suffered scourges and death on a cross. Though we cannot equal his sacrifice, we should deny ourselves and bear our crosses in imitation of him, just as lowly shrubs imitate lofty oaks. Among the various tribulations of human experience to be borne patiently, Amarcius specifically cites false detraction and reproachful insults. We should endure these, he writes, just as a sick man accepts bitter remedies for a cough or consumption, or as he tolerates lancets and cautery to heal gout, "for no one gains joys except through sorrow."

A prayer of thirty-nine lines to the Holy Trinity closes the poem as an epilogue, not a continuation. In it, Amarcius begs to reach the celestial shore one day and to share in the court above. After acknowledging the fame of Lucan, the praise owed to Statius and Sallust for their accounts of secular glory, he asks that his own pen and tongue might resound with God. He offers a confession of faith and pleads that on the last day "Stygian Charybdis not swirl about me," but that God's kindness and pity will preserve him. His final appeal is to be snatched from the gaping jaws of Leviathan and taken up "to your dwelling place, where the sonorous assembly of the just sing worthy songs to you without end."

A few words on Amarcius's name and other pseudonyms in the text seem appropriate before concluding this introduction. First, we should recognize that pseudonyms are part of the satirical tradition, often employed to disguise the actual names of enemies or powerful figures held up to ridicule. Amarcius invented several, which he used to conceal the identity of mentors and friends, as well as his own. Most of them are based on Latin, but some are rooted in Greek, and this has led to speculation that his education included study of that language.

The pseudonym that he chose for himself is recorded by Hugh of Trimberg (cited above): Sextus Amarcius Gallus Piosistratus. Perhaps "Sextus" was intended to suggest that our author was a follower of Quintus Horatius, or "sixth" after him (Quintus means "fifth"). "Amarcius" might be derived from *amarus,* "bitter" or "caustic," to indicate a satirical outlook. Karl Manitius linked the name to *(h)amartia,* "error" or "sin," from the Greek verb *(h)amartanein,* "to miss the mark," and he pointed out that Prudentius, a favorite author of Amarcius, had titled one of his polemical poems *Hamartigenia,* "The Origin of Sin."[6] Max Manitius offered two possible interpretations for "Gallus": that the name referred to the monastery of St. Gall or that it implied that the poet was a native of Gaul.[7] Karl Manitius traced it to C. Cornelius Gallus, the friend and fellow poet whom Virgil named in his *Eclogues* (10 and 6.64), and whom Amarcius himself cited in the *Sermones* (3.268). He suggested that Pisistratus, the tyrant of Athens praised for his eloquence by Cicero (*De Oratore* 3.34.137), might be the source for "Piosistratus." In a fine paper, "Horace as a Preacher: The Sermons of Sextus Amarcius (*De sermonibus Horatianis Sexti Amarcii*)," presented at the 2009 International Medieval Conference in Leeds, Kurt Smolak pointed out that Sextus Amarcius Gallus and Quintus Horatius Flaccus have the same rhythm and number of syllables. He argued that "Sextus" was intended to indicate the medieval poet's succession to the place of the Roman satirist. He linked "Amarcius" to the aforementioned didactic poem of Prudentius, "Gallus" to the poet's homeland, and "Piosistratus" to *pietas,* with its connotation of dutiful conduct and faithfulness to God.[8] All attempts to account for our poet's name are, of course, speculative, and they fail to bring his true identity to light.

So also, the pseudonyms employed for Amarcius's former teachers and mentors leave us puzzled, except that all have positive connotations. They are meant to signify praiseworthy individuals. For example, the *Sermones* are prefaced by a letter to Candidus Theophystius Alchimus. The first of these names, from Latin, means "radiant" or "bright." Theophystius may be from the Greek *theopeistos,* suggesting obedience to God, while *alchimos* means "strong" or "brave" in Greek, and could allude to the *praenomen* of (Alcimus) Avitus, whose work Amarcius knew. A long discourse on "true love" in Book 3 is attributed to a great teacher, "Euphronius," whose name might be translated from Greek as "understanding well," or even "well-disposed." But again, we are no closer to actual identities, or, for that matter, to the conviction that there are real persons behind these names, rather than mere literary inventions.

In 1888, Max Manitius published the editio princeps of Amarcius's *Sermones* based on a single, thirteenth-century manuscript (Dresden A. 167a). Eighty years later, his son, Karl Manitius, produced a new edition and introduction to the *Sermones* (MGH, 1969), amply annotated and based on two manuscripts (Dresden A. 167a and Copenhagen, Konigl. Bibl. MS Fabr. 81). The Dresden MS had once belonged to the Benedictine monastery of St. Peter in Merseburg (founded in 1091). The Copenhagen MS contains forty-six lines from the *Sermones* (4.87–133) written in an early thirteenth-century hand. Originally, it belonged to the Benedictine cloister of Sts. Cosmas and Damien in Liesborn (Westphalia) and later to the famous philologist, J. A. Fabricius (1668–1736), compiler of the *Bibliotheca latina mediae et infimae aetatis.*

Despite the generous claim of Max Manitius that Amarcius was "the oldest of the extant great satirists of the Middle Ages,"[9] our poet achieved neither great fame nor influence. Although he might not have been widely read owing to a difficult style and a penchant for obscure allusions and expressions, he is an important source for eleventh-century satirical themes and ecclesiastical controversies. He is an outstanding representative of the classical tradition in his time, a disciple of the Romans, and a precursor of the medieval satirists who would proliferate in the twelfth-century renaissance, including monks such as Bernard of Cluny and Nigel of Canterbury. His *Sermones* are worth reading for their historical insights, numerous proverbs, and amusing scenes of human folly. In the ancient manner, they offer a *satura lanx,* a full platter of wit and wisdom from a learned monk of long ago.

On the Translation

My prose translation of Amarcius's *Sermones* is as faithful to the Latin original as it can be with an author noted for obscurity and odd syntax, but I have tried to avoid a rendition that is wooden or stilted. In the translation and accompanying notes, I have not attempted to cite the poet's numerous sources (for which one can turn to the extensive apparatus in the editions of Karl and Max Manitius) or to record his debt to them for countless phrases and paraphrases. Suffice to say here that his verses are replete with echoes of ancient and early medieval poetry, and sacred scripture as well. Amarcius was clearly a man of vast reading, strong convictions, and sardonic wit, and I am glad to make his satiric views more accessible to scholars and students of medieval life and letters.

With deep gratitude, I acknowledge the warm welcome and expert guidance given to my translation of Amarcius by Jan Ziolkowski, Danuta Shanzer, and the editorial board of the Latin Series of Dumbarton Oaks Medieval Library. I am indebted to Professor Robert G. Babcock, who first introduced me to Amarcius and who fostered my interest in his work with many insights and helpful suggestions. My thanks go to Professor Michael Winterbottom for arbitrating several difficult passages and offering superb solutions. For invaluable assistance with computer technology, I thank, once again, Matthew P. Pepin.

Ronald E. Pepin

Eupolemius

Contra Messyam violenti prelia Caci / Detestanda cano
"I sing of cursed battles of violent Cacus against Messiah"

The *Eupolemius* is a Latin epic of 1,463 dactylic hexameters, divided into a first book of 683 verses and a second of 780. Written in the late eleventh century, it offers an extraordinary recasting of salvation history, from the fall of Lucifer through the Resurrection of Christ. Transposing the conflict between God and the devil into social terms that would have resonated well with a learned audience in the Middle Ages, the poem recounts a struggle between on the one hand the forces of King Agatus (meaning "good" in Greek) and his son Messiah and on the other those of the rebellious Duke Cacus ("evil" in Greek) of Babylon. In particular, the epic concentrates upon the efforts of Agatus and Messiah to free the brothers Judas and Ethnis, who stand for the Jewish people and the gentiles, respectively. Their father, Antropus (whose Greek name points to his role as the archetypal "man," Adam), was led astray from Agatus. In turn, the brothers became captives of Cacus. As even this superficial sketch makes apparent, the *Eupolemius* fuses Greek and Hebrew components within a framework that is uniquely medieval. It is at once heroic, biblical, and allegorical.

If compared with postmedieval literature, the *Eupolemius* could be characterized as an exceptionally early and adventurous expression of the same impulses that led to later religious epics. The foremost example would be John Milton's seventeenth-century *Paradise Lost,* which narrates in blank verse the story of the Fall of man, presented as a confrontation between divine providence and human free will, from the temptation of Adam and Eve by the fallen angel Satan through their expulsion from the Garden of Eden. In second place would come a direct successor of Milton's, the eighteenth-century poet Friedrich Gottlob Klopstock, who composed a religious epic in German hexameters, *Der Messias* (The Messiah). The poem, twenty cantos in its final form, is devoted half to the Passion and death of Christ and half to his Resurrection and triumph. It portrays the redemption as resulting from a battle fought between the forces of heaven, under the command of God, and the powers of hell, under Satan.

From another perspective the poem deserves a place alongside other literary experiments in verse narrative produced by medieval German authors who wrote in Latin. One such specimen would be the *Waltharius* (Poem of Walter), dated variously in the ninth and tenth centuries, a heroic epic of 1,456 dactylic hexameters that personalizes legendary struggles among Huns, Franks, Burgundians, and Aquitanians by focusing on an individual hero (Walter of Aquitaine) and heroine (Hildegund of Burgundy) and that deserves a place beside *Beowulf* in the annals of early medieval Germanic epic. A second case in point is the *Ruodlieb,* a fragmentary poem, probably of the mid-eleventh century, of which more than two thousand internally rhymed (or "leonine") hexameters survive, which has sometimes been considered the first courtly romance. A third and final example is the *Ecbasis cuiusdam captivi per tropologiam* (Escape of a Certain Captive, Told Allegorically), an anonymous poem of 1,229 hexameters, many of them wholly or partly quoted from earlier poetry, most likely composed between 1043 and 1046, and regarded by some as the first beast epic in the lineage that led ultimately to Renard the Fox and his fellow characters.

Mapping such disparate compositions in relation to one another is complex. The challenge is compounded when we seek to situate the *Eupolemius* with regard to the relatively small deposit of vernacular literature extant from the eleventh century or earlier that grapples with biblical narrative in Old Germanic epic forms. For instance, the early ninth-century Old Saxon Bible epic known as *Heliand* relates the life of Christ in six thousand alliterative lines, accommodating the synoptic Gospels to the style and values of Germanic poetry. Old English literature includes ninth- and tenth-century poems, such as *Christ and Satan,* that cast Christ as a poetic hero, as well as others, such as *Genesis B* and *Judith,* that have figures from the Hebrew Bible as protagonists and antagonists. Although unlike the *Eupolemius* in many aspects, all of these poems in the spoken languages respond to the same pressures to merge the language and ethos of the established Greco-Roman epic tradition with the alien content of the scriptures.

Almost everything that we can state about the boldly idiosyncratic *Eupolemius* rests on inference. Even the title provokes uncertainties. The incipit and explicit of the older manuscript refer to the poem as *liber Eupolemii,* "the book of Eupolemius." The Graecizing name could designate the epic itself (Good War), perhaps with reference to its protagonist (Good Warrior). Alternatively, it could characterize behind the veil of a pseudonym the author, as the person who put together the poem of the Good Warrior or who served as a Good Warrior by undertaking it. Jerome singles out a Hellenistic historian named Eupolemos among "writers against the gentiles who like Josephus make the case for the 'antiquity' of Moses and the Jewish people."[10] It typifies the independent outlook of our poet that, if he holds responsibility for the title, he did not calque it on Virgil's *Aeneid* by making it *Eupolemeis* (or, better yet, *Messias*) or on Prudentius's late fourth-century Christian Latin *Psychomachia* (Soul-Fight) by calling it *Eupolemos* (or *Eupolemia*). Instead, we must grapple with two constituents, both recognizable, but one modified just enough (from the bona fide Greek *polemos,* "battle" or "fight," to what would seem to be an adjectival *polemius*) to make confidence elusive.

Until the mid-twentieth century the poem was preserved in two codices of German origin, one written in the second half of the twelfth century and the other copied from it around 1200. During the Second World War the apograph was destroyed. In the Middle Ages the poem left no signs of influence beyond the two manuscripts. In the earlier of the two someone (and his occasional misinterpretations confirm that he was not the author) took the trouble to gloss the poem extensively. Yet no subsequent Medieval Latin writers mention it outright or can be proven through quotations to have read it. It is not cited in any medieval library catalogs or curricular lists.

During the Middle Ages both codices containing the *Eupolemius* belonged to the Benedictine cloister of St. Peter in the town of Merseburg. Slightly to the east of the center of present-day Germany, Merseburg lies on the river Saale, in the south of the state of Saxony-Anhalt. The nearest major city is Halle an der Saale ("Halle on the Saale," to distinguish it from other places with the name Halle), with Leipzig being the next closest. Like the manuscripts, the author of the poem has been most often presumed to be of German origin. More narrowly, it has been hypothesized—although the hypothesis is only one of several—that he came from the region of the Upper Rhine, where the river stretches from Basel in Switzerland to Bingen in Germany, near Mainz.[11] He evinces an ethnographic and geographic interest that embraces Germanic peoples and bodies of water, such as the Main, Elbe, Ill, Mosel, and Lake Geneva.

The anonymity of the poet (or pseudonymity, if we call him Eupolemius instead of or as well as the poem), if it was an expression of modesty, could support the supposition that he was a monk. In theory he could have been a brother in the monastery of St. Peter in Merseburg, although its foundation date of 1091 would put him very late in the eleventh century, unless (as is likely) a less formal community preexisted the establishment of the monastery proper. What would his audience have been? The glosses in one manuscript may indicate that the poem was employed, if only at St. Peter's, in schooling. Slight underpinning for the idea that the epic originated in a scholastic milieu can be found in the vignette of music instruction in a schoolroom within the *Eupolemius* itself.[12] With its many quotations and echoes of earlier "classics" (including postclassical "classics"), the poem would have been well suited for use as a complement to the reading and study of Virgil, Lucan, Prudentius, and others. Yet it must be admitted that with many levels of reference to classical poetry and myth, the Bible, and allegory, the poem could have lent itself equally well to *lectio divina,* the usually private reading for meditation and study that was incumbent upon Benedictine monks.

Among the many puzzles about the creator of the *Eupolemius* is the enigmatic connection between him and the poet of the Latin hexameter satires that circulate under the pseudonym of Sextus Amarcius Gallus Piosistratus.[13] Most obviously, the two poems differ in genre. Nonetheless, both texts betray a reliance on many of the same literary sources. Furthermore, they evidence close resemblances in verse technique, such as their avoidance of leonine rhyme and the extent to which they permit elision and hiatus.[14]

Likewise, they display many similarities in language and especially in lexicon, such as a propensity for words built upon Greek elements. Finally, they share some common ground in content, ranging from a preoccupation with the opposition between virtue and vice down to a fascination with medicine.

The *Satires* of Amarcius and the epic of *Eupolemius* are bound together intimately in their transmission, since the only complete manuscript of the *Satires* also belonged to the monastic library of Merseburg. Both the manuscript of the satires and the later one of the *Eupolemius* were donated to the library by an otherwise unknown monk named Alexander.[15] In fact, the same scribe may have penned portions of both the Amarcius manuscript and the more recent of the *Eupolemius* manuscripts.[16]

In sum, the poets of the *Satires* and the *Eupolemius* were at a minimum closely related, as teacher and pupil, fellow students, or members of the same small coterie; possibly they were identical. Amarcius refers glowingly to Henry III, the German king (1039–1056) and Holy Roman Emperor (1046–1056), but in a way that suggests he is looking back in time. Thus there need be no friction with passages in the *Eupolemius* that have been seized upon to date the epic to the time around the First Crusade (1095–1099), in the last few years of the eleventh century.

Although the poet of the *Eupolemius* was probably a monk, his purview was not claustrophobically monkish. Medieval society was famously distributed across three social orders, the praying class, the warriors, and the peasants. Whatever his own social position in the church, the poet excludes from the *Eupolemius* much overt discussion of the praying class. In contrast, he incorporates into the poem passing attention to both warriors and peasants. On the one hand, Cacus and his henchmen, the Apolide, constitute a court, with knights (*equites* and *milites*), dukes *(duces),* counts *(comites),* and princes *(principes)*. All members of Cacus's retinue, except Ethnis and Judas, qualify as noble. These noblemen are mounted on horseback, dandies in their attire, puffed with pride, hungry for power, boastful, greedy, and gluttonous.[17] On the other hand, the adherents of Agatus, designated as the Agatidae (Agatide, in medieval orthography), are not flagged with titles becoming the highborn. From humbler stock, they are craftsmen and peasants—but though mocked for being of base blood and poorly equipped, they prevail.[18]

To move from social to historical context, the *Eupolemius* makes such scant reference to contemporary circumstances that it has been hard to fix with any specificity either the date or the context of the poem. Nevertheless, the atmosphere in the poem can be shown to partake of the aura that surrounded the First Crusade.[19] In a very loose way the epic can be grouped provocatively with literary utterances of Crusade fervor that were set down in the spoken languages of medieval Europe. The foremost model of such Crusade literature would be the Old French verse *Chanson de Roland* (Song of Roland), also composed shortly before 1100, which tells first of the death of Roland, Emperor Charlemagne's nephew, in an ambush while retreating from Spain, and then of Charlemagne's revenge on the Saracens and punishment of the traitor Ganelon. Resemblances can be pushed only so far between an allusion-packed Medieval Latin text in dactylic hexameters and an Old French *chanson de geste* (song of deeds) rooted in legend and oral tradition, but it must still be said that those committed to understanding the backdrop to the Crusades would do well to pay attention to the Latin epic as well as to the Old French song.

The *Eupolemius* could be seen as a one-of-a-kind manifestation of the eleventh-century reforms that helped to channel the violence of the nobility from sinfulness toward salvation, in defense of Christianity. It bears a certain likeness to early histories of the First Crusade, in that both likened the achievements of the warriors they depicted to those of the Israelites in the Hebrew Bible.[20] Furthermore, the poet ventures suggestively into the borderland between pilgrimage and Crusade when he describes the military use of a pilgrim's staff: one of the Agatide named Doxius carries a staff of polished wood that turns out to be a "sword-stick" with a knife inside and that serves to slay his opponent.[21]

Underlying the poem is the general assumption that combat between divine and satanic forces plays out in holy war on earth. More specifically, the holy war between the forces of Agatus/Messiah and Cacus is presented as a campaign of liberation that focuses on Jerusalem. In this case, the freeing of Ethnis and Judas would correspond to the liberation of Jerusalem. Yet these traits of what could be called a "Crusade perspective" do not necessarily verify that the *Eupolemius* poet meant to tie the poem to any specific time or events in the late eleventh century. It would be futile to build a case on the basis of phraseology. Many key terms in discussions of the Crusades surface repeatedly in the *Eupolemius,* such as *miles, fidelis, liber (liberare, libertas),* and *servitium (servus, servire),* but these nouns, adjectives, and verbs are all common and even ubiquitous in Latin literature throughout its long history and carry multiple valences that can be impossible to differentiate. Furthermore, much of the case for the First Crusade was advanced in preaching that does not come down directly. We have nothing of the words of Peter the Hermit, and even the sermons of Pope Urban II have come to us only second- or third-hand.

Beyond the strictly verbal, Cacus and the Apolide characterize Messiah and his fellows as boors and peasants and taunt them about their humble footwear, clothing, and occupations—but do the references suffice to peg the composition of the *Eupolemius* to the first half of 1096 and to perceive the poem as a reaction to the so-called Peasants' Crusade or People's Crusade of Peter the Hermit?[22] Similarly, it is difficult to detect firm grounds on which to infer that the poem originated precisely in the stretch between the summers of 1099 and 1100. The Latin phrase *sic voluit deus* has been construed as a deliberate transposition into the perfect tense of the Crusader motto in Old French *Deus lo volt* (God wills it).[23] A sermon in favor of taking Jerusalem from the Muslims that was delivered by Pope Urban II at the Council of Clermont on November 27, 1095, is supposed to have stirred the large audience to make this exclamation in French. But although the words appear in a passage of the *Eupolemius* that makes this interpretation attractive, their appearance earlier in an altogether different context—to describe the attitude of God toward the harlot named Rahab whose family was kept safe when Jericho fell—argues that the resemblance between the Latin and the French is coincidental.[24] Even when the formulation appears in the *Eupolemius,* it does not function as an exclamation.

Whatever consensus develops concerning the hypotheses that argue for specific dates based on alleged internal references, the *Eupolemius* is an allegory, but it is certainly not a historical allegory in the sense of being a roman à clef and even less a historical epic.[25] In the initial invocation the poet tellingly declines to invoke either Clio or Calliope, the muses of history and epic, respectively, and instead appeals to the highest wisdom of God. By the same token, in the conclusion he first challenges the reader to get at the inner truth of the narrative and then voices appreciation to God for having supported him in his effort:

> Let the person who wishes to train his mind in a deep understanding scrutinize the battles that we have recorded, and in examining the battles with constant skill (for what is not learned through practice?) he will find, once the bone has been broken, the marrow, which has a good taste.
>
> Highest wisdom, as your writer I render thanks to you; through you I began this task and finished what was begun, that it might be milk to those tender of age and strong meat to those strong of age.[26]

In the closing metaphor the poet enlists terms familiar from the Bible, a signal that his allegory is essentially scriptural.

The richest context for the *Eupolemius* is literary, since the poet proves himself to be extremely well versed in the Vulgate Bible, the whole gamut of Latin literature, and much more. His knowledge of Latin literature encompassed, alongside poets who could be considered classical in the strictest sense (Virgil, Ovid, Lucan, Horace, Statius), those

Christians of late antiquity whose poetry became canonical in the Middle Ages (such as Alcimus Avitus of Vienne and Prudentius).[27] His command of Medieval Latin poetry appears also to have been broad and deep, although it is harder sometimes to demonstrate definite familiarity with individual poems. One unquestionable source is the *Ecloga Theoduli* (henceforth, Theodulus's *Eclogue*), a poem probably of the tenth century by an author who took the Greek pseudonym Theodulus ("servant of God"), in which miracles of the Bible are compared with episodes in pagan literature; the juxtapositions take place in a dialogue between the characters Alethia (Greek for "truth") and Pseustis (Greek for "falsehood"). The familiarity with earlier literature of all periods results in both a dense allusiveness and a rich vocabulary. The poem contains hundreds of quotations, allusions, and references to other literary works, and many of its words and phrases carry associations from earlier contexts in which they were deployed.

The author was steeped in dactylic hexameters, the verse form that had been customary for epic, first Greek and later Latin, at the latest since Homer. Since the *Eupolemius* owes more in its language to Virgil than to the Bible, the discovery comes as no surprise that the poem is shot through with compositional elements and structures that reflect the classical epic heritage. Thus it contains the extensive descriptions of such objects as shields and drinking vessels that are known formally as ecphrases.[28] In equally good epic fashion it furnishes detailed astronomical information relating to the times of days and seasons and a lengthy catalog of peoples, packed with nearly one hundred ethnographic and geographical names, that relies heavily upon Lucan.[29]

Along similar lines, it is studded with nearly two dozen of the extended similes that are characteristic of classical epic, and five stand in a particularly close relationship with predecessors in Virgil.[30] Similar epic traits are passages with runs of one-on-one combats, close treatment of a decisive duel, frequent application of particular epithets to identify particular characters, proverbs and sententious statements, number symbolism, and genealogies.[31]

Beyond matters of wording and rhetorical components, at a grand level of narrative structure the events are laid out in what is sometimes called an artificial order *(ordo artificialis)* comparable to that in the first five books of Virgil's *Aeneid.* The poet first throws the reader *in medias res* and then provides background by having a main character retell the vicissitudes of an earlier war. In the first book of the *Eupolemius* Moses informs Judas about the war in which Abraham and Anphicopas engaged, just as in the second and third books of the *Aeneid,* Aeneas relives his earlier experiences for Dido and her court. Even the very fact of having a book division heightens the resemblance of the *Eupolemius* to classical epics, while setting it apart even from other tenth- and eleventh-century Latin poems of nearly identical length, such as the *Waltharius* and *Ecbasis captivi.* Yet the division into books also distinguishes the content of the *Eupolemius* from that of its ancient forebears, since the first book corresponds to the Hebrew Bible and the second to the New Testament. The first book deals with the formative story of the Jews, namely, the Exodus under Moses, while the second develops the foundational story of the Christians, to wit, the Incarnation and Crucifixion of Jesus.

The twentieth-century German philologist, Ernst Robert Curtius (1886–1956), stated categorically in his *European Literature and the Latin Middle Ages,* which remains foundational in medieval literary studies more than sixty years after its publication in 1948 (English translation, 1953): "The Christian story of salvation, as the Bible presents it, admits no transformation into pseudo-antique form."[32] As we have seen, the *Eupolemius* gives the lie to this assertion in many regards. But in other respects the poem bears out Curtius's sweeping generalization. Most obviously, the epic features many references to Greek mythology, often introduced in conjunction with comparable narratives in the Hebrew Bible from which the poet contends that they derived. Most of these parallels are drawn from Theodulus's *Eclogue,* which was a widely used textbook for a few centuries after its composition. The effect of the parallels is to call into question the very originality and integrity of the myths that underlie the classical epic tradition in which the *Eupolemius* apparently aspires to participate.

Indeed, the poem is shot through with the equivocation about classical epic that typifies much of Medieval Latin literature. In its exordium the poet spurns the Muses typically invoked in classical poetry to call instead upon the highest wisdom of God for inspiration.[33] In its peroration the poet asserts with the help of a Bible reminiscence that those who have the right training in hermeneutics will win ample Christian spiritual returns by explicating the fine points of his poem.

On the basis of its opening verses, the *Eupolemius* has been called a Messiad, a narrative about Jesus, understood as the expected king and deliverer of the Jews. The pervasive soteriological scheme would be impossible to deny, since the salvific qualities of both Moses and Joshua (as Soter, "savior" in Greek) receive considerable emphasis. Yet Messiah, the character who plays the role of Jesus Christ in the *Eupolemius,* does not step on stage until just more than two hundred lines remain in the poem. Even then, the Resurrection and Assumption are barely touched on.[34] The redemptive powers of Messiah, perhaps because so assumed, are left unspoken.

The *Eupolemius* has also been labeled, even on the cover and title page of the only full-scale edition that has been produced, a Bible poem: *Eupolemius: Das Bibelgedicht,* edited by Karl Manitius, Monumenta Germaniae Historica (Weimar, 1973). This tag classes it with the four so-called canonical Latin Bible epics or, less misleadingly, Bible paraphrases, retellings of biblical narratives that were composed from the early fourth through the sixth century. The debts of the poet to the two Bible epics that are devoted exclusively to the New Testament, Juvencus's *Evangeliorum libri quattuor* (Four Books of the Gospels, based mainly on the Gospel according to Matthew) and Arator's *De actibus apostolorum* (On the Acts of the Apostles), are scant to nonexistent. In contrast, the *Eupolemius* poet drew heavily upon two other Bible epics, Avitus's *De spiritalis historiae gestis* (On the Deeds of Spiritual History, ca. 500), which deals with five episodes in the Hebrew Bible (Creation, Fall, Punishment, Flood, Moses and Pharaoh), and Sedulius's *Carmen Paschale* (Passover Poem, fifth century), which sets forth miracles in both portions of the Bible, with a typological emphasis on the relationship of those in the Hebrew Bible to those in the New Testament.

In any event, the *Eupolemius* purveys far more than a mere paraphrase of events in scripture, far more than a reordering and synthesis of salvation history as revealed in scattered fashion through the Hebrew Bible and New Testament, and far more than a running commentary on those events or that history. In fact, the poet warns us explicitly and repeatedly against aligning his characters and events in his poem exactly with their apparent equivalents in the Bible. He assigns biblical names to less than half of the characters and places in his poem. Furthermore, on four occasions he compares the chief actors in his poem pointedly with ones in the Bible in such a manner as to mark the two apart.[35] For the rest he coins names based mainly on Greek elements.

The epic of the *Eupolemius* poet is immeasurably more elaborate than any simple taxonomy of classicizing epic, Messiad, or Bible paraphrase could begin to convey. Viewed most generally, it relates the contention on a cosmic scale between good and evil that has been called "the combat myth."[36] This element comes out in the opening lines too. The so-called myth centers upon a struggle between God and Satan over the fate of humanity. The myth was adumbrated already in the Dead Sea Scroll, often entitled *The War of the Sons of Light and the Sons of Darkness,* but it spread beyond Jewish apocalypticism to secure a niche in Christianity as well.[37] Christianity is a unitary religion that has swung periodically in the direction of dualism. Although not presented organically in the Bible, the myth transmits the story of an angel who rebels against God, seizes earth and humankind as his dominion, and subjugates it through sin and death. When later his subjects crave freedom, the son of God achieves their liberation through the simultaneous victory and defeat of crucifixion.

In the hands of the *Eupolemius* poet, the myth boils down to a war over man—initially equated with the Jewish people—waged with conventional epic weapons between the partisans of God/good and those of devil/evil, from Adam through Christ. The struggle of the leaders and prophets to release the Jewish people from idolatry, heathenism, and sin that culminated in the self-sacrifice of Jesus Christ to liberate Jews and gentiles alike from the sway of evil is conveyed as a war that is unfolded in conventional epic fashion. The war is reduced to a few decades of one generation that is torn apart by bloody battles between the followers of God/good, Agatidae, and those of Cacus/evil, Apolidae.

There has long been speculation that the poet may have been conditioned by Jewish and apocalyptic traditions, but to date no specific use of such a source in the *Eupolemius* has been pinpointed.[38] The poet's awareness of Hebrew etymology gives the impression of being markedly less profound than his acquaintance with Greek word elements, and his portrayal of the Jewish people lacks the vitriol that comes to the fore repeatedly in the *Satires* of Amarcius. In terms specifically of dualism, the general conception that overarches the *Eupolemius* is Augustinian, especially Augustine as he gave voice in *De civitate Dei* to the notion that the human race split into two branches, one predestined to reign with God and the other to suffer eternal punishment with the devil.[39]

Among the sources that could have inspired the poet, Prudentius's *Psychomachia* is one of the most important. In both it and the eleventh-century epic, virtues and vices engage in combat, real characters and sites from the Bible rub elbows with personified abstractions and imaginary places, and allegory, symbol, and typology interact intricately. The chief difference is that personification allegories in the mold of *Psychomachia* involve dramatis personae who are almost exclusively female characters, since abstract nouns in Latin are preponderantly feminine in their grammatical gender and hence of necessity female characters when personified. Among the many strokes of genius for which the *Eupolemius* poet deserves recognition, one was to have coined many names for his characters on the basis of Greek elements. Thus God is Agatus and his followers, Agatide, while Satan is Cacus and his henchmen, Apolides. Again and again these Greek names enable the poet to sidestep the obligation to have a largely female cast that he would have accepted if he had resorted to Latin nouns. The advantages of his approach stand out in the case of names such as Leuconous (glossed as *alba mens,* "white mind") and Nomus (as *lex,* "law").[40] Even when characters bear Greek names that coordinate them with Virtues and Vices, they can often also be related to specific personages in the Bible.

The *Eupolemius* poet undertook an arduous mission. He trained his sights on three of the most prestigious poetic traditions that were available to Latin poets of his day: Virgil's *Aeneid* and other classical epics, Bible epics, and personification allegories such as Prudentius's *Psychomachia* and Theodulus's *Eclogue.* Yes, he imitated them—but he transcended mere mimicry to achieve genuine emulation. His poem honors the trappings of these three epic traditions in lovingly expert fashion. At the same time, it goes beyond all of them. The *Eupolemius* adopts many features of classical epics, but in the service of Christianity. It covers much of the same ground as the Bible, but it is no mere paraphrase. It contains personifications, but it depends just as much on real personages and incidents taken from salvation history. Its poet, like his hero, fought a good fight in attempting to devise a coherent poetic system with which to rival multiple traditions of Latin epic. His *Eupolemius* may not have caught the fancy of the decades to follow him. The Crusades brought new influences from outside. In some areas of culture, momentum may have passed from Germany to the Anglo-Norman and French orbits. In intellectual life, first the cathedral schools and then the nascent universities captured energies that had once been attracted to the monasteries. In literature, the very nature of Latinity as well as its relations to vernacular literature transformed as the efflorescence known now for roughly a hundred years as the twelfth-century renaissance took shape. The *Eupolemius* sits uncomfortably alongside the texts that became canonical a century later. Alan of Lille's allegorical epic, the *Anticlaudianus,* bears the imprint of a Platonism that is altogether absent from the late eleventh-century poem. Bible epics such as Matthew of Vendôme's *Tobias* and Peter Riga's *Aurora* lack the complex interplay with personification allegory, Latin epic, and Greco-Roman myth that contribute to the distinctiveness of the *Eupolemius.* Whether any or all of these factors affected the reception of the earlier epic, the reality is that the author's poor luck in timing has no bearing on the intrinsic quality or significance of his poem. The *Eupolemius* may not be a total success; even if judged a partial failure, it is an audaciously imaginative one.

ON THE TRANSLATION

For those who wish to shuttle between the text and the translation or vice versa, I have matched the two as closely as possible in punctuation and capitalization. Without the fanfare of brackets I have incorporated into the English small expansions, usually in the form just of names, to gloss designations that might otherwise be cryptic and to clarify antecedents. Like many other Latin poets, the author of the *Eupolemius* switches freely from past to present tenses. I have not standardized all verb forms to the one or the other temporal frame, but I have endeavored within paragraphs to impose substantial uniformity.

In choosing words, I have subscribed to a common school of thought by avoiding in most cases translating the Latin with an exact cognate in English. One large and problematic exception, to which I have adverted already, is that in most cases I have translated *miles* as "knight" and not as "soldier," *dux* as "duke" and not as "leader," *comes* as "count" and not as "companion," and *princeps* as "prince" and not as "chieftain." Absolute uniformity has not been feasible or desirable. For example, at 1.11–12 consistency would have required taking *te duce* as "under you as duke" and *te presule* as "under you as bishop." The phrases may indeed carry those connotations, but only in part. Accordingly, I opted in this early instance for the less socially specific "under your leadership" and "under your charge."

My thanks go out to three individuals for looking at the text and translation while the present volume was in gestation. The first was Thomas Miller, who made the suggestion for emending 2.688, among other things. The second was Danuta Shanzer, who gave me generously a weekend of her time and expertise so that we could allay my anxieties about specific textual problems. The last, and definitely not least, was Julian Yolles, who reviewed the Latin and English judiciously and who proposed the improvement in 1.464–65. To this troika I am much beholden. In addition I owe appreciation to the *Journal of Medieval Latin,* which published my first version as the opening piece in its inaugural issue and which has permitted me to print a thoroughly revised form in this book. Finally, I am grateful to those associated with the present volume, both Ronald Pepin and my colleagues at Harvard University Press, for their collaboration. In the last throes Anne Marie Creighton paid meticulous attention to the proofs. Most broadly, the excellence of colleagues in Medieval Latin studies makes me feel very fortunate in my choice of specialization as a scholar, and I hope that the Dumbarton Oaks Medieval Library will contribute in at least a small way to maintaining or even enhancing the well-being of the field in times to come. For reasons both economic and cultural, the variety and distinction of the Latin literature written in the Middle Ages have yet to receive the recognition they merit, perhaps especially in the Anglophone world, and my dream is that this series of publications will help improve the situation by furnishing prospective readers with both well-known classics and lesser-known mysteries and masterpieces.

Jan M. Ziolkowski

Notes

1 Raby, *History of Secular Latin,* 402.

2 Michael Lapidge, "Versifying the Bible in the Middle Ages," in *The Text in the Community: Essays on Medieval Works, Manuscripts, Authors, and Readers,* eds. Jill Mann and Maura Nolan (Notre Dame, Ind., 2006), 11–40.

3 Christopher A. Jones, "Monastic Identity and Sodomitic Danger in the *Occupatio* by Odo of Cluny," *Speculum* 82 (January, 2007): 49.

4 Raby, 403.

5 Edward K. Rand, *Founders of the Middle Ages* (Cambridge, Mass., 1928), 192.

6 K. Manitius, *Sermones,* 10–11.

7 M. Manitius, *Sexti Amarcii,* ix.

8 I thank Professor Smolak for providing a copy of his Latin oration at Leeds. His paper makes a convincing case for the view that Amarcius intended his title, *Sermones,* to be taken in the double sense of "satires" and "sermons."

9 M. Manitius, *Geschichte der lateinischen Literatur,* 571.

10 Richardson, *De viris inlustribus,* chap. 38, p. 27.

11 Borst, *Der Turmbau,* 597.

12 1.537–40.

13 Erdmann, *Forschungen,* 130, saw the poets as being one and the same, whereas Karl Manitius took a more tentative stance in his edition of the *Eupolemius,* pp. 10–11. Ratkowitsch, "Der Eupolemius," 262–71, concludes on the basis of her philological analysis that the authors of the *Eupolemius* and Amarcius were different poets, with the first likely dependent on the second, as already Max Manitius maintained in "Zu Amarcius," 195–96.

14 Orlandi, "Metrica e statistica," 31, tabulated the frequency of spondees in the first four feet of sample swatches from both the Satires and the *Eupolemius.* The results are extremely close:

Foot	1	2	3	4	Total
Amarcius	98	96	120	122	436
Eupolemius	84	90	117	124	415

Similarly, his figures for the number of syllables and *morae* (the length of time required to enunciate one short syllable) in the two poems come very near to each other:

	Syllables	Morae
Amarcius	2.36	3.82
Eupolemius	2.44	3.93

The only data that could occasion anxiety relate to the numbers of words and verses included in periods:

	Words	Verses
Amarcius	12.61	2.00
Eupolemius	17.71	2.90

Yet it must be pointed out that the counts depend on editorial decisions in punctuation that can be somewhat arbitrary. To be concrete, the periods in the present edition are shorter than in Karl Manitius's edition.

15 Babcock, "Alexander Monachus."

16 K. Manitius, *Sermones,* 36n76, and "Dresdner Handschriften," 256 and 259.

17 On clothing, see 2.668–69; on gluttony, 1.517–40.

18 2.111–12, 2.123–24, 2.207–35.

19 For review of the older scholarship, see K. Manitius, *Sermones,* 10.

20 Riley-Smith, *The First Crusade,* 91–92.

21 2.213–19.

22 The references to peasant status appear at 2.10–13, 107–21, 180–90, 207–10, 667–74. For the theory that the *Eupolemius* is propagandistic text written in 1096, see Ratkowitsch, "Der Eupolemius," 253–62; rebutted by Smolak, "Epic Poetry as Exegesis," 243n42.

23 Smolak, "Epic Poetry as Exegesis," 243.

24 Compare 2.660 with 2.85.

25 A third theory, that the poem treats of wrangles between Emperor Henry IV (r. 1056–1106) and Rudolf von Rheinfelden (slain in 1080), rival claimant to the throne, was advanced by Jacobsen, review of Karl Manitius's edition, 306–7.

26 2.774–80.

27 The starting point is the index of authors in K. Manitius, *Eupolemius,* 111–17. Specifically on Avitus, see Gärtner, "Zum spätantiken," 194–96, and "Zu den dichterischen Quellen," 549–62; on Prudentius, Ratkowitsch, "Der Eupolemius," 241–43.

28 For ecphrases of shields, see 2.67–74, 2.82–89, 2.271–81, 2.605–10; of drinking vessels, 2.617–20, 2.623–25.

29 For astronomical information, see 2.1–3, 2.315–18, 2.352–54, 2.654–56, 2.743–44. The catalog of peoples is 2.488–550, to be compared with Lucan 2.583–95 and 3.171–82.

30 Compare 1.592–97 with *Aeneid* 9.59–64; 2.146–50 with 10.454–56; 2.384–88 with 2.496–99; 2.400–401 with 2.310–11; and 2.292–97 with *Georgics* 1.201–3.

31 For one-on-one combat, see 2.37–45; for a duel, 2.696–732, modeled on Virgil's *Aeneid* 12.887–952. Examples of epithets include *acer* ("fierce") for

Cacus in 1.136–37, 2.696–97; *inclitus* ("renowned") for Eleimon in 1.416, 1.637–38, 2.573; *torvus* ("grim") for Amartigenes in 1.200, 2.238; and so forth. Proverbs and sententious statements appear at 1.139–41, 286–87, 300–301, 484–85, 665–66; 2.194–96, 224–25.

32 Curtius, *European Literature,* 462.

33 1.5–6.

34 2.766–770.

35 1.236–44, 2.44–48, 2.76–79, 2.740–42.

36 Forsyth, *The Old Enemy.*

37 For the text, see Yadin, *The Scroll of the War.* For discussion, see Collins, "The Mythology of Holy War."

38 Lehmann, "Judas Ischarioth," 231.

39 15.1, Dombart and Kalb, *De civitate Dei,* 57–59.

40 2.629 and 1.419.

SATIRES

Virtutum norma, Theopysti, fulte decora,
    Inque dei vernans candidus obsequio,
Ut cum corporea superes albedine cygnos,
    Gemmis interius candidior niteas.
5 Si magnum te parva iuvant, hoc excipe carmen
    Contextum crasso pectoris igniculo,
Oblitus tenerae quod pubertatis alumnus
    Confisus domino caelitus ausus eram.
Et si noscere amas, quo pacto trusus ad hoc sim,
10 Cordis luminibus perspice, quod sequitur.
Perverti mores habitos maioribus hoc in
    Tempore pertractans vix tenui lacrimas.
Hinc carptim priscos intendi scribere ritus
    His qui nunc degunt ferre volens reduces.
15 Sed cum talis adhuc titubaret mente libido,
    Publicus herentem scribere iussit amor.
Non ergo te rusticitas deterreat eius,
    Versibus altisonis non opus omne viget.
Cumque superborum pigeat fastigia semper
20 Inspicere, huc oculos flecte aliquando tuos.
Israhel qui venit oves revocare celebres,
    Manzeribus nobis contulit ille manum.

Theophystius, supported by the fair model of the virtues, you are radiant, flourishing in the service of God, so that although you surpass swans in bodily whiteness, you shine within more radiantly than precious stones. If small things 5 delight you in your greatness, accept this poem composed by the dull little light in my mind, and forget what I dared as your pupil of tender youth who trusted in the Lord in heaven. And if you would love to know how I was pushed toward this, examine what follows with the light of your 10 heart. Studying how the morals held by our ancestors are subverted in these times, I scarcely held back my tears. Hence I intended to write selectively about the old ways, wishing to bring them back again to those who are living now. But since such a desire still wavers in my mind, love for 15 the people bids me, though hesitant, to write. And so, let its rustic quality not deter you; not every work excels in its sublime verses. And since it is irksome to look always at the heights above, turn your eyes this way sometimes. He who 20 came to recall the renowned sheep of Israel has offered his hand to us, his illegitimate sons.

3

I

Epilogus de virtutibus patrum et posteriorum viciis

Quem bis natorum, semel ex genitrice, secundo
Pneumate de sancto regni celestis amore,
Corrugare genas et eas conspergere fletu
Non deceat, quod que quondam fortissima pugna
5 Virtutum stravit munimine rursus in hostes
Surrexisse sacro letisque vigere triumphis
Fataque victricum vicia irridere videmus?
A patrum vita tantum distare videmur,
Occasus quantum rutilanti distat ab ortu.
10 Cana venenose secura libidinis etas
Lumbos constrinxit zona succincta pudica,
At nos hircosum molli oblectamine flatum
Ructantes auras suffundimus atque canino
Ore remordemus; tento inspicere aera collo
15 Est amor, et cupido nummos abradere rostro:
Illud more gruis, hoc corvi more voracis.
Inservire iocis avium libet et catulorum,

I

A Discourse on the Virtues of Our Fathers and the Vices of Their Descendants

Which of the twice-born, once of a mother, a second time
of the Holy Spirit through love of the heavenly kingdom,
ought not to furrow his cheeks and moisten them with tears
because we see that the vices which the most vigorous battle
of the virtues once laid low have risen again from their ac- 5
cursed fortification against their foes, and flourish in happy
triumph, and laugh at the doom of their conqueresses? We
seem to be separated as far from our fathers' way of life
as the setting of the sun is separated from its red-glowing
rising.

The secure age of old, girt about with a chaste girdle, 10
bound the loins of poisonous lust, but, belching forth a go-
atish breath, we fill the air with a soft delight and bite again
with a dog's tooth; with neck extended we love to look at
money and to scrape away coins with our greedy snout: the 15
former in the manner of a crane, the latter like a voracious
raven. We are pleased to pay attention to the sport of birds

Et vana extolli scurrarum laude vafrorum,
Turbidulasque modis variis conpescere curas.
20   Inter avariciam constat via luxuriamque,
Quam raro incultam—namque his divina voluntas
Grata fuit, nec eos domini precepta gravarunt—
Dimisere patres renovantes passibus illam
Crebris. Mendicos victu cassos et amictu
25   Fulcibant et non marcarum pondere fiscos
Stipabant aut mole gravi granaria frugum.
Illi etiam heroas virtute evoque verendos
Constituere duces, primates atque tribunos.
Tunc qui vilis erat, quamvis centena talenta
30   Palma porrigeret tremula gemmasque nitentes
Proferret titubante vola, non ulla potestas
Concessa est illi. Sed nunc qui vendit opellas,
Discissas senio, byrsas qui tendit olentes
Dentibus inpressis, tereti qui lignea torno
35   Vasa rotat, multo si scrinia faenore farta
Exspolians nitidam portabit ad atria massam,
Ille tribunus erit, quodcumque affectat habebit.
Nemo tunc scalprum, nemo tunc scruta paterna
Inproperat, dat gaza genus, formam, probitatem.
40   Nummatis pars prima favet, laudantur amantur.
      Consulibus quondam Romanis mos erat iste
Non nisi discretis committere pontificatus,
Utpote morosis scripturarumque peritis;
Illis agricolas brutos ratione carentes
45   Presbiteris formare probis, nec poscere soldos.
Immo sedulius ipsi petere ac peterentur.
Quis et quot claris tunc pollens terra sophistis

and puppies, and to be extolled by the empty praise of cunning buffoons, and to repress our confused cares in various ways.

Between avarice and excess there is a path that our fathers rarely left neglected, for they renewed it with frequent steps—indeed, to them the divine will was pleasing, and the precepts of the Lord did not weigh heavily upon them. They supported poor beggars with food and clothing, and they did not stuff their treasuries with masses of money or cram their granaries with heavy heaps of corn. They also appointed heroic men revered for virtue and age to be their leaders, magnates, and tribunes. Then no power was granted to a man who was contemptible, even if his trembling palm held forth hundreds and hundreds of dollars and he offered glittering gems in the hollow of his quaking hand. But now one who sells little services interrupted by old age, one who holds out stinking purses with teeth [marks] pressed into them, one who spins wooden bowls on a smooth lathe, if he carries home a glittering mass while polishing his chests stuffed with much gain, will be a tribune, and he will have whatever he strives after. No one made fun of a chisel then, no one then reproached a father's junk, but now riches grant character, beauty, and probity. The first rank favors those with money; they are praised and loved.

Formerly it was the custom for Roman consuls to entrust priesthoods to none but the discreet, on the grounds that they were exacting and well acquainted with scripture; for those honest priests it was the custom to mold the character of brutish peasants who lacked reason, and not to demand money. But today, they zealously ask for money more than they are asked for it. What renowned wise men, and

20

25

30

35

40

45

Fulsit, quotque animae regna obtinuere beata!
Heu nunc posteritas contempto more parentum
50 Omnia pervertit, pietas heu funditus omnis
Destruitur, pauci sunt qui ad caelestia tendant.
Quere fidem, non invenies, fraus regnat, et ipse
Cui bona tu facis aspergit rumore malo te.
Simpliciter quis agit? "nichil est," malus intonat omnis,
55 Quique lupum vivit, cunctos similes sibi credit.
Ei mihi! ad infernum totus modo cursitat orbis.
Felix cui dabitur Stigias non ferre latebras,
Et Flegetonteos evadere caelitus ignes!
Felix quem tristem manes Acheronta colentes
60 Non detentabunt nec lurco vorabit Avernus!
Circa momentum mundanus abit dolor, illic
Eterni luctus, nec cessant stridere dentes.

2

De eo, quod avaricia leges
et sanctiones subvertat

Quo terre reges, argenti splendor et auri,
Precipitas? Quid rectores mundi illice forma
65 Hortaris nescire deum? Quid lucis alumnos
Perpetuis cecas tenebris? Te regia caeli

how many, did our mighty land shine with then, and how many souls gained the blessed kingdom! Alas, now posterity perverts everything and despises the ways of our fathers; 50 alas, all piety is utterly destroyed. There are few who strive for the things of heaven. Seek faith and you will not find it; deceit reigns, and one to whom you do good spatters you with evil rumors. Who behaves innocently? "This means nothing!" every wicked man roars, and one who lives like a 55 wolf believes that all are like him. Ah me! The whole world now races to hell. Happy the man who is allowed by heaven to escape the Stygian recesses and to avoid the fires of Phlegethon! Happy the man whom the shades dwelling in gloomy Acheron will not detain, nor will gluttonous Avernus 60 devour! Worldly grief disappears in a moment, but there eternal affliction and the gnashing of teeth do not cease.

2

Concerning the Fact That Avarice Subverts Laws and Sanctions

O luster of silver and gold, where do you drive headlong the kings of the earth? Why with your alluring beauty do you urge the rulers of the world to ignore God? Why do you 65 blind the children of light with perpetual darkness? The

Verarumque locus precellit deliciarum,
Mellifluo rutilans per tempora cuncta nitore!
    Unde modo incipiam de mundi principibus qui
70 Turpis avariciae vexillum ferre videntur?
Pene potens omnis temerarius agmine facto
Dedere munificam leto gliscit rationem.
Nec trutinam iudex aequo discrimine librat:
Illinc iusticiae sedes, hinc sessio gemme,
75 Sed toto obtutu gemmarum ad gaudia fixo
Naso suspendit camiro iusti stationem.
Illud pertractans animo Hieronimus inquit:
"Omnium avaritia est mater radixque malorum."
Quam recte intonuit! namque hac suadente magistra
80 Abiciunt domini decretum sepe fideles,
Ut victis quondam Ierichenis perfidus Achan.
Sordent Christicolae, nisi quis est copia gaze,
Diraque barbaries auro sociante fovetur.
Si pauper christus Iudeo dixit "Apella,"
85 Proclamant cupidi nil nil cruce dignius esse.
At si cristatus Iudeus et excoriatus
Ex nostris inopem percellit strage profana,
Excusso querulis obpeditur ore propinquis.
    Quid loquar in tribulis latrones more ferarum
90 Palantes cecosque specus et lustra colentes
Nil differre feris? Non illos arcet ab antris
Ianus et horrifico ramalia candida nimbo,
Pendula non glacies, sitis augens dira calorem.
Quid memorem regum rimantes tecta scelestas
95 Raptorum furumque manus? quos non pudet auri
Instimulante fame vagina stringere sicam,

palace of heaven and place of true delights glowing for all time in mellifluous brilliance surpasses you!

Where now shall I begin [to tell] about the princes of the world who seem to bear the banner of shameful avarice? Almost every powerful man with his troops arrayed rashly desires to surrender his generous reckoning to death. And the judge does not balance the scales in equitable judgment: on that side the seat of justice, on this side the site for a gem, but with his gaze fixed entirely on the delights of the gems he turns up his hooked nose at the position of a just man. Contemplating that in his mind, Jerome declared: "Avarice is the mother and the root of all evils." How rightly he cried out! For with this mistress urging them on, men of faith have often forsaken the Lord's decree, as faithless Achan once did when the men of Jericho were defeated. Worshippers of Christ are despised, unless they have abundant wealth, and savage barbarism is cherished, if gold accompanies it. If one of Christ's poor says "Apella" to a Jew, the greedy cry out that nothing, nothing is more worthy of a cross. But if a crested, circumcised Jew strikes down one of our poor people in an impious slaughter, he farts violently in the clean faces of the complaining relatives.

Why should I say anything about robbers wandering among thorns like wild beasts and inhabiting hidden dens and woods who differ not at all from wild animals? January and its branches white with awful rainstorms do not keep them from their caves, nor does ice hanging down, or dreadful drought intensifying the heat. Why should I mention the wicked bands of plunderers and thieves ransacking the palaces of kings? When the hunger for gold urges them on, it does not shame them to draw a dagger from its sheath and

Et non speratos vibrare proteruiter ictus,
Aut conto cerebrum aut seva mulcare securi,
Ut mutilatorum stellata veste fruantur
100 Ignitaque auro trabea, proh ceca cupido!
     Pontificum tedet coruinos promere rictus,
Quos, ceu flagra trocum, rotat insaciata cupido.
Non tam avide pandit stomacho latrante palatum,
Quando errare pecus per prata recentia cernit
105 Sopito pastore lupus, quam pontificum mens
Pluribus ecclesiis hiscit rectoribus orbis,
Se nitidum sperans corradere posse metallum
Quod multi ignavi protendant divite palma.
Cui cuius casus quaerenti verbera "Neutri"
110 Reddit apudque probos stat muto inglorius ore
Et fronte obstipa; non presulis horret adire
Atria, distentas rutilanti fasce crumenas
Apportans, vernas ambit dominumque serenat;
Nam frendens viso subridet episcopus auro.
115   Hic ubi ruricolis nummo fautore sacerdos
Est datus, infirmis audet subducere corpus
Divinum, nisi dentur ei vel quatuor asses.
Quin et si infantum subitus dolor appetit artus
Nondum tinctorum sacrato in fonte, malignus
120 Absterret querulos prolis de morte propinqua;
"O quantus labor est!" plus insistentibus illis.
"O si bis senis rotulis mihi palma gravetur
Argenti, puto sic posset labor iste levari."
Sicque mori plures linquit sine crismate, gazam
125 Illicite expensam sibimet persolvere querens,
Duriter ille stolam calicemque miser luiturus.

boldly threaten unexpected blows; they are not ashamed to bash in brains with a pole or a cruel battle-ax in order to enjoy the star-studded clothing of the mutilated and a royal robe afire with gold. Oh blind desire!

It disgusts me to tell about the ravenous maws of pontiffs whom insatiable desire whirls about just as whips whirl a hoop. A wolf with a growling stomach does not open his mouth so eagerly when he sees the flock wander through fresh meadows while the shepherd sleeps as the minds of bishops gape at many churches, the guides of the world, hoping to be able to scrape away the shining metal that many ignoble men stretch forth in their rich palms. To the man asking for which fault a flogging [should be imparted], the bishop replies "Neither," and among honest men, one without glory stands with a silent tongue and head hanging down; he is not afraid to approach the bishop's great hall carrying money bags filled with their red gold burden. He bribes the homebred slaves and cheers up the lord, for though he gnashes his teeth, the bishop smiles at the sight of gold.

Here, where a priest is given to the country folk when money aids the process, he dares to withhold holy sacraments from the sick unless at least four pennies are given to him. Why, even if a sudden affliction assails the limbs of infants not yet washed in the holy font, the stingy priest scares away those protesting about the imminent death of their child. "It's so much work," he says to them when they keep on insisting. "O, if my palm were loaded with twelve little silver coins, that toil, I think, could thus be eased!" And so, while seeking to pay himself a treasure unlawfully expended on him, that miserable priest leaves many to die without

100

105

110

115

120

125

13

Preterea si qui sua plebibus ora resolvunt,
Promulgare sacras sic intendunt omelias
Ut plus pro nummis quam pro mercede tonantis
130 Ultro prebendam videantur pandere sanctam.
    Quid de conuersis, quos recto et nomine vero
Appellare volens perversos dicere debet,
Christe, feram? Sed enim tenebrosis vestibus artus
Frenantes tumidos et amantes abdita claustra
135 Primitus, inter se paulatim nobilis auri
Argentique struem, quanta est cuiusque facultas,
Secreto conferre student, quo limpida coram
Succina prodentes consciscere singula sensim
Rura queant. Hic fulmineus cupit esse decanus,
140 Alter egenorum provisor flagitat esse,
Ille peni curam petit, alter preposituram;
Ille cupidineum, novitatis amicus, amaro
Sollicitans rancore iecur moderamine fratrum
Enodi res cunctorum decernere gestit.
145   Continuo nactus, quod mens exusta sitivit,
Ad regem si forte means signavit ocellis,
Pontifices Pario lapidi aequos ferre bacillos,
Mordacem ex imo gemitum pulmone remittit
Et natat in curis quo more vitellus in albo,
150 Atque haec intra se: "Que te detrusit in artum,
Sors tam dira locum candente satellite cassum
Vestitumque toga residi, roseos ubi stulti
Aut niveos viciant tunicis nigrantibus artus
Denormantque caput ferro? Quid fiet? in illis
155 Degener obscuris numquid versabere semper?
Absit ut hoc, fieri nummus sinat induperator!

chrism; he will atone severely for the stole and chalice! Moreover, if any open their mouths to preach holy sermons to the people, they do so in such a way that they seem of their own accord to offer the sacred gift (of grace) for money 130 rather than as a reward from God.

Christ, what shall I say about lay brothers ["converts"], whom one wishing to name rightly and truly ought to call perverts? But indeed, restraining their swollen limbs in gloomy garments and loving remote cloisters first, among themselves little by little they strive to gather a heap of no- 135 ble gold and silver, as much as each one can, in a secret place where, while openly bringing forth clear amber, they are gradually able to decide on individual country estates. This man seeks to be a thundering dean, another demands to be 140 the provider for those in need, that one seeks the care of the storeroom, another the office of overseer; that one, a friend of novelty, stirring the covetous liver with bitter rancor by his smooth direction of the brothers, desires to determine the affairs of all.

One who has gained straightway what his inflamed mind 145 thirsted for, if by chance he indicated it with his eyes while walking near the king, sends forth a carping groan from deep in his lungs because bishops bear crosiers equal to Parian marble, and he swims in cares like a yoke in a white egg, and 150 within himself says these words: "What lot so cruel has thrust you into this narrow place without a dazzling retinue and clothed in a leftover toga where fools mar their rosy or snowy limbs with black tunics and disfigure their head with an iron blade? What will happen? Surely you won't remain, 155 forever ignoble, among those obscure ones? God forbid that money, our ruler, might allow this to happen! On the con-

Immo hanc lacteolo baculus volo candidiorem
Dente manum repleat; quid convenientius hoc est?"
Hinc fit ut egroti medicamen ubique salutis
160 Querentes errent, ut oves quas perdidit altor,
Et pereant, fido dum non fotore iuvantur.

3

De eo, quod libido maxime dominatur in hominibus

Sunt inmundarum quos semper more ferarum,
Quod dictu scelus est, obvolvit feda libido.
Inde Severinus negat esse homines viciosos,
165 Sirenumque sonos et Circe fingit Homerus
Pocula collegas Ythaci fecisse canes et
Setigeros verres, canibus quod dignaque porcis
Fecerunt. Et sic homines mutasse Medusa
Fingitur in lapides, quos stare in sorde coegit.
170 Sorde pudiciciam vicisti tempore nostro
Insigni pridem redimitam timpora lauro,
Feda lues. Populum babtismate nobilitatum <. . .>
Annon degeneris victores quo patre creti
Percensere decet? Iam desine, tolle catenas
175 Tolle, tuas, priscique furens reminiscere fati!

trary, I wish that a crosier might fill this hand brighter than a milk-white tooth. What is more fitting than this?" Hence it happens that the sick wander everywhere seeking the 160 healing of salvation like sheep which the shepherd has lost, and they perish when they are not supported by a faithful helper.

3

Concerning the Fact That Lust Especially Holds Sway among Men

There are men whom foul lust always envelops after the manner of unclean wild beasts, which is a wicked thing to say. Thus Severinus [Boethius] denies that vicious men are men, and Homer imagines that the Sirens' songs and Circe's 165 potions made the Ithacan's companions hounds and bristly boars because they did things worthy of dogs and pigs. And thus Medusa is thought to have changed into stones men whom she forced to stand petrified in their filth. O foul 170 plague, by your filth in our time you have overcome Modesty whose head was once wreathed with glorious laurel. A people ennobled by baptism <. . .> Is it right to pass in review degenerate conquerors [and ask] who their father was? Cease now! Remove your chains, remove them and in your 175

Bellantesne putas incerta sorte carere?
Nunc hi succumbunt, nunc aequa sorte resurgunt;
Non semper vaga sors in eodem tramite currit.
Dic age, dic, que tanta tuae fiducia palmae?
180 Cum quandoque satus de virgine respiciet nos
Ac nostri clemens miserebitur, interimet te.
    O mater felix, heresim nam perculit omnem,
Quae virgo peperit, post partum virgo remansit.
Virgo deum peperit, non patrem, sed patre natum,
185 Ut quidam cinici voluere, quod ipse Philippo
"Indubitas" inquit "quod ego in patre et pater in me est?"
Sed tamen et soli variae sunt proprietates.
Ergo abscidantur de quorum pullulat error
Robore: Fotinus, Nestorius Elbidiusque,
190 Appellas, Noetus, Sabellius atque Bonosus.
Argumentum etiam frustrata puerpera virgo est:
Femina si peperit, peperit semente virili.
Virgo deum genuit coniuncti ignara mariti.
Quid barbatorum vigilantum corde sagaci
195 Inuestigatus summa certante sophia
Sylogismus agat? quidve arte probata refellens
Contortis arguta modis dialectica possit
Cum, deus, innupte prodires ventre puellae?
Sed quid acumen ego Demostenis atque Themisti
200 Inculcando moror? Summi patris unice fili,
Qui mare, qui terras, qui caelos, Christe, regis, te
Clausa verecundae producit virginis alvus.
Ergo de feda nos solve libidine et omnes
Catholicos igni da sudo fervere facque
205 Astu serpentes, fac simplicitate palumbes!
    Heu quanto interitu vincit cum plebe libido

madness remember your ancient destiny. Do you think that the lot of those waging war lacks uncertainty? Now they surrender, now with equal fate they rise again; fickle fate does not always run in the same path. Tell us, come, tell us, what is this great confidence in your victory? Some day when the   180
Merciful Son begotten of the Virgin looks upon us and pities us, he will destroy you.

Oh the Blessed Mother (for she struck down every heresy) who bore him as a virgin remained a virgin after birth! The Virgin bore God, not the Father, as certain cynics wanted, but the Son born of the Father, since he himself said   185
to Philip, "Do you doubt that I am in the Father and the Father is in me?" But yet there are different properties belonging to him alone. And so, let Photinus, Nestorius and Helvidius, Apellas, Noetus, Sabellius and Bonosus be banished,   190
from whose trunk error sprouts, for the Virgin in labor has proved the argument false, that if a woman has given birth, she [must] have given birth from a man's seed. The Virgin bore God without knowing union with a husband. What does a syllogism traced out with the highest wisdom striv-   195
ing in the sagacious hearts of watchful philosophers accomplish? Or what can keen dialectic do, rebutting proofs with its art, in twisted arguments when, oh God, You come forth from the womb of an unmarried girl? But why do I waste time treading on the subtlety of Demosthenes and Themis-   200
tius? Christ, you who rule the sea, the earth, the heavens, only son of the Almighty Father, the closed womb of a modest virgin bore you. Therefore, free us from foul lust and allow all Catholics to glow with a bright flame. Make them serpents in cunning, and make them doves in simplicity!   205

Alas, how great is the destruction with which savage lust

Inportuna duces! Amor instat conubiorum,
Sed tamen ante omnes Lamia atrox cecat eburnos
Heroum thalamos, que vel Samsona Ididamque
210 Cecavit quondam. Cursare per atria dicunt
Cyrris truncatis masclorum more puellas,
Ut dum primatum lectis verniliter assunt,
Obscenos coitus, quantum facinus! paciantur.
Obtutus haec externos vesania carpit,
215 Ut larvae pueros fallunt tragicique coturni,
Ebrius aut petus numerat plerumque lucernam.
Non est qui, facili quamquam discrimine sollers,
Sexu inmutato verum perpendere possit,
Supara dum spernens bracis caligisque virago
220 Crura tegit tunicasque exerto poblite findit.
Haut aliter quam si vesca lanugine nec dum
Crinitus invenis linquat de fronte virili
Femineas pendere comas et eas caliendro
Constringat parvaque genas obnubat aluta
225 Ac celante pedes incedat sirmate fusos
Aut colum usurpet, verum inspectare queamus.
Nos glaucos latet hoc, occulto fallimur actu.
Lama viae similes deludit sero viantes,
Meiit et in stratum dum potum somniat infans.
230   Hoc et pontifices vicium, si creditur, atque
Abbates premit, ah, documentum flagiciosum!
Clericus hinc canones avertitur et Benedicti
Monachus iniuncta claustrumque chorumque perosi
Pharmacopolarum male olentia tecta frequentant.
235 Proh dolor! et sceleri si compta iuvencula desit,
Succumbit veteres ululans edentula cantus.

conquers leaders along with their people! The love of wed-
lock urges them on, but yet above all [others] the fierce en-
chantress blinds the ivory bedchambers of heroes; she once
blinded even Samson and Solomon. They say that girls run 210
here and there through the halls with their curls cut like
men so that, when they first fawningly approach the beds,
they might submit to lewd intercourse. What wickedness!
This madness enjoys strange sights, as masks and tragic bus- 215
kins deceive boys, as a drunken or squinting man generally
sees one lamp as two. There is no one, even if he is skilled
in making facile decisions, who can assess the truth when
the sex has been altered, while the manly woman, spurning
women's garments, covers her legs with breeches and boots, 220
and parts her tunic with her bare knee. No differently than
when a youth not yet long-haired with fine down on his
cheeks lets feminine locks hang down from his manly coun-
tenance and holds them together with a headdress of false
hair, and covers his cheeks with a little beauty patch and 225
marches forth with a long train concealing his feet, and takes
up spindle or distaff, are we able to see the truth. This is
concealed from us in our blindness; we are deceived by this
secret act. A bog in the road tricks us like those traveling
late at night, and, while an infant dreams of drinking, he
pees in his blanket.

If one can believe it, this vice even afflicts bishops and 230
abbots. Ah, the shameful example! On account of this the
cleric turns away from the canons, and the monk from the
commands of Benedict; hating the cloister and choir, they
frequent the houses that reek badly of drug peddlers. Oh 235
grief! Even if a beautiful young girl is lacking for their evil
deed, a toothless hag howling old songs submits to it. Now

Visere nunc discunt meritoria feda scolares;
Sanctarum fugiunt habitacula relliquiarum.
Non turpis flatus, non illos polipus arcet,
240 Non unce nares, non dependentia labra.
Cordibus humanis ceu flamma insistit ofellis
Saevus amor, qui nos confundere iura fidemque
Conpellit; renum nil importunius igne!

4

Invectio in superbos

Nunc mihi de sacro perstringere pauca tumore,
245 Quire, deus, presta, qui certo tramite lunam
Dirigis obscuram, quae prima nitore bicorni
Paulatim crescens pleno secat orbe tenebras,
Maior eis quae sunt in signum classibus astra
Plyades, Artofilax, Cinosura, Arcturus, Orion,
250 Regnorumque statum solitus mutare cometes,
Ac Tytane minor, qui lumen ei dare fertur,
Officio distans ab ea distans quoque cursu.
Stellarum numerum scis atque vocabula solus
Inque tuis oculis ut heri sunt secula mille,
255 Nilque deo vetus est. Relegamne ab origine cana
Antiquum Satanae scelus, an replicare recusem?

scholars learn to look upon shameful rooms for rent; they flee from the dwelling places of holy relics. Foul breath does not keep them away, nor a nasal polyp, nor hooked noses, nor lips that hang down. Fierce passion, which forces us to confound laws and faith, pursues human hearts as a flame pursues bits of meat. Nothing is more troublesome than the fire in the loins!

240

4

An Invective against the Proud

Now, O God, grant that I might be able to say a few things about accursed pride, you who direct on its fixed course the dim moon which, first waxing little by little in two-horned splendor, cuts through the darkness with a full orb, greater than these constellations which are lodestars for ships— Pylades, Arctophylax, Cynosura, Arcturus, Orion, and the comet accustomed to alter the status of kingdoms—and less than Titan who is said to give light to [the moon], standing apart from it in function and also in its course. You alone know the number of the stars and their names, and in your eyes a thousand ages are as yesterday, and to God, nothing is old. Shall I relate again from its ancient beginning the old sin of Satan, or shall I refuse to repeat it? Why should I

245

250

255

Quid repetam infaustum, domino dum cedere nescit
Factori factus, dum se illi turgidus equat,
Ut subitum fulgur libratum cardine celi
260 Luciferum, culpae simul assensoribus actis,
Et sic fuscatum viciosi crimine nevi
Ut focus obducit cacabum fuligine cupreum?
    Quid repetam domini formatum pollice plasma
De limo et limum subito incaluisse tumore,
265 Dum domini iniunctum servare exhorruit Adam?
Pomum manducans vetitum culpamque superbus
In dominum torquens sibi et omni posteritati
Aeternum inpendens aeterna morte laborem,
Ni rex excelsus, virides qui gramine terras
270 Lucentemque globum lateque sonantia stagna
Fecit, mortali dignatus carne operiri
In cruce pro nobis mortem libasset acerbam?
    Vitam signat adhuc mediam tamen atra cicatrix.
Nunc Adae factum pauper locuplesque sequentes,
275 Quamquam dissimiles, buccas inflare solent et
Naribus excussis suspendere cuncta nisi aurum.
Nempe tumor demens et habendi insana cupido
Convenere fide dextrasque dedere vicissim.
Nam cum paupertas rebus plerumque secundis
280 Pollet postque sagum lugubre effulget in albis,
Cernere tedet humum priscamque reducere sortem
Inflaturque genas, ut onustae tubere turpi
Assurgunt scapulae, velut uncis unguibus olim
Haurit tabifluum pellis lacerata liquorem
285 Aspiratque novo sanies exotica folli,

revisit that ill-starred deed when one created does not know
how to yield to the Lord, his creator; when one swollen with
pride equals himself to him, as Lucifer endured the sudden
thunderbolt hurled from the height of heaven, together 260
with the assenters to his crime, and thus he was blackened
by the guilt of a vicious fault as a fireplace makes a copper
cooking pot black with soot?

Why should I repeat that a creature was formed from
mud by the Lord's thumb, and that the mud suddenly glowed
with swelling pride when Adam dreaded to observe the 265
Lord's injunction? The haughty man ate forbidden fruit and
directed his crime against the Lord, paying the price of eter-
nal suffering through eternal death for himself and all future
generations, except that the Most High King who made the
earth green with grass and the shining orb [of the moon] 270
and the waters resounding far and wide, deigning to be
clothed in mortal flesh, tasted a painful death on the cross
for us.

Yet a dark scar still marks our midlife. Now poor and rich,
following the deed of Adam, though dissimilar, are wont to 275
puff up their cheeks and to turn up snooty noses at every-
thing except gold. Indeed, raving pride and the insane desire
for possessing have united in trust and clasped their right
hands in turn. For generally when poverty grows strong in 280
prosperous circumstances and shines forth in white af-
ter [wearing] a pitiable coarse cloak, it is distasteful to look
upon the ground and to recall the old condition, and it puffs
up its cheeks as shoulders burdened by an ugly swelling rise
up, or as a hide once torn by curved claws drinks in decaying
putrefaction, and a strange gore blows into a new bladder, 285

Aut ut caenosae brumali tempore lamae
Declivesque viae nimbo turgent tenebroso.
    Et sublatus inops quivis haec corde volutat:
"Hem, quis ego sum! quisve mihi par? Hercule nullus!
290 Namque fruor simila plus Caucasea nive cana,
Nec porro cogor gingivas urere, quippe
Cui passer visco capiturque timallus ab hamo.
Stragula palla mihi est et iuncto purpura cocco.
Quid dubitem tortos cidari cohibere capillos,
295 Aut cur me nitidus non cingat balteus auro?
Nam et totum corpus gemmis velare coruscis
Et margaritis possum, mihi si placet illud.
Si libet, ut magnos gestat me reda Quirites.
Hactenus indulsi nec vindice dente remordi,
300 Si quis 'rauce culix' dixit mihi 'fetide cimex.'
Iam qui dicet idem mihi, bubo scrofave fiet.
Si soleas quondam et phaleras in paupere tecto
Conpegi aut molles fiscellas vimine lento,
Nunc mea me virtus et cista referta lucello
305 Extulit. Absistat, cui populus alba mapale
Dat fruticesque breves qui pisa procurat et omnis
Non bene vestitus, scabiosus, iners, strabo, varus."
    Hec novus aut paria his elato pectore iactat.
Nec minus hoc errant primates et generosi,
310 Qui de tesauris, titulis statuisque tumentes
Christum contempnunt, gemmae byssique datorem,
Suffocantque bonos ut Nili pessimus olim
Arbiter obpressit sanctos Moysen et Aaron;
Doctoresque pios stantes ad pulpita abhorrent
315 Ut scabiem, lendes quam sulcant atque peducli,

or as muddy bogs and sloping paths grow thick with dark clouds in the winter season.

And any poor wretch, now raised up, turns over these words in his heart: "Ah, who am I? Or who is equal to me? No one, by God! For I enjoy flour whiter than the snow on the Caucasus, and I'm not forced to chafe my gums any longer; in fact, a sparrow is caught for me with birdlime and a grayling with a hook. My garment is purple with scarlet trim. Why should I hesitate to confine my braided locks with a tiara, or why should a belt gleaming with gold not encircle me? For I can cover my entire body with glittering gems and pearls, if that pleases me. If I like, a four-wheeled carriage bears me like the mighty Roman citizens. Up to this time I made allowance and did not bite back with an avenging tooth if anyone called me 'noisy insect' or 'stinking bug.' Now let one who says this to me become an owl or a sow. If I once made house slippers and horse trappings in a humble house, or fashioned delicate little baskets of pliant willow, now my virtue and my money box stuffed with small gains have raised me up. Let him go away, that one to whom the white poplar gives a hut and little shrubs, one who takes care of peas, and everyone poorly dressed, mangy, idle, squinting or bowlegged."

The "new man" from his proud heart utters these words, or ones like these. No less than this do magnates and noblemen go astray, men who puffed up by treasures, titles and statues, despise Christ, the giver of gems and gauzy fine linen, and suffocate good men as once the evil lord of the Nile oppressed the holy men, Moses and Aaron; pious teachers standing in the pulpits they abhor like the mange which nits and lice furrow through, while barking with abominable

Talia latrantes infanda voce: "Quid hoc est,
Quod populo inponunt grave et inportabile pondus?
Nempe per hystorias nos annichilare severas
Querunt ypocritae, religant anathemate quosvis,
320 Cauponas theatrumque vetant, a rege Gehennae
Haec docti potum regerunt ut hirudo cruorem."
Sed rogo, quos adeo iactantia frivola tollit,
Ut quid inaccesso genitum patre non imitari
Nituntur miseri? qui tectus carne caducas
325 Tempsit delicias, qui Iherusalem introiturus
Sprevit equos, mulos, humilemque insedit asellum,
Et proficiscenti pubes Iordanica laete
Obvia palmarum ramos oleaeque virentis
Stravit humi et puerum clamavit "osanna" caterva.

5

De diversis luxurie illecebris

330 Nec tu tyriacae labes deterrima pennae,
Tu quae blandiciis diversicoloribus omne
Evum hominum, pueros, iuvenesque senesque, triunca
Fuscinula rapiens patulo detrudis Averno,

voice words such as: "What is this? What heavy, unsupport-
able weight do they impose on people? Surely through their
austere narratives these hypocrites seek to annihilate us;
they bind all sorts of people with excommunication; they   320
prohibit taverns and theaters, and, taught by the king of
hell, they persist in these things like a leech after its drink of
blood." But I ask, whom does worthless boasting so raise
up? Why do wretched men not strive to imitate the Son
since the Father is unapproachable, the One who, clothed in
flesh, scorned perishable pleasures and who, as he was about   325
to enter Jerusalem, spurned horses and mules and sat upon a
lowly ass, and whom as he proceeded the people of the Jor-
dan joyfully met, and strewed upon the ground branches of
palm and of budding olives, and a crowd of children shouted
"Hosanna"?

5

On the Diverse Enticements of Luxury

Nor are you absent, O Luxury, most wicked cause of ruin   330
on serpentine wings, you who with your allurements of vari-
ous kinds, carry off human beings of all ages—children and
youths and the aged—and with your three-pronged fork
thrust them into wide-gaping Avernus. Tradition says that

Luxuries, aberis; tibi tot quot Prothea vultus
335 Fama habuisse refert, sed maxime aplestia mentes
Dissicit et venas distendit et incitat inguen.
   Nunc de missilibus diversis accipe luxus!
Huius flammifera lumbos transverberat hasta
Blandius effusum detentans vulnere caeco.
340 Palpitat ille cadens coituque avertere pestem
Cogitat inmissam; vulnusque ita curat ut ille
Qui lippo suadet varias spectare figuras,
Aut qui fomentis credit parere podagram,
Aureaque incassum dispendit frusta chirurgis.
345 Ast alium caeso de silva mille saporum
Appetit hastili viribusque premit duplicisque
In miserum iuris truculentos depluit imbres.
   Ille labans nec iners iaculo stridente repugnans:
"Si mihi perdicum nidore adolere supinas
350 Contingat nares nec non pipere atque piretro
Irritare gulam gratoque rubore Falerni
Proluere et stomachum monstris placare marinis,
Que fluviis aiunt ignota minoribus ut sunt
Renus, Arar, Rodanus, Tanais, Padus, Hister, Araxes:
355 Hoc equidem, reor, hoc medicamen reddere sanum
Me queat; i, puer et propolas perspaciare
Venit ubi vinum, moratum, sicera, medo.
Consummat Cererem sine Dacus Saxoque potu,
At bonus et tenuis mea pernatet exta Lieus!
360 Tu fora percurrens obsonia cara macelli
Huc eme, fer panes et edules adde placentas!
Vinctis deinde levem scopis abradito limum,
Ut cum narcisso dempto obice lilia vernent.

you have as many faces as Proteus, but insatiable desire es- 335
pecially scatters minds and distends veins and arouses the
groin.

Now from these diverse missiles, learn about excess! The
fiery shaft [of excess] pierces the loins of this person with a
hidden wound while gently holding back the flux [of blood].
That one convulses as he falls, and he plans to avert by co- 340
ition the pest sent against him; he cares for his wound like
the man who encourages a bleary-eyed person to look at
various shapes, or one who believes that gout yields to poul-
tices, and in vain he pays out pieces of gold to surgeons. But 345
excess attacks another with a javelin cut from the wood of
a thousand delicacies and overwhelms him with force, and
rains down upon the wretched man fierce showers of double
sauce.

That one, wavering but not inert, fights back with a shrill-
sounding spear: "If it happens that my nostrils grow wide at
the aroma of partridges, and also I provoke my palate with 350
pepper and chamomile, and wash it down with the pleasing
blush of Falernian, and placate my stomach with monsters
of the sea which they say are unknown to smaller streams,
like the Rhine, Saone, Rhone, Don, Po, Danube, and Aras,
this medicine truly, I think, can make me healthy. Go, boy, 355
and walk about among the hucksters' stalls where wine,
blackberry brandy, cider, and mead are. Let the Dacian and
the Saxon devour their bread without drinking, but let a
good, subtle wine swim through my entrails! When you pass 360
through the markets, buy expensive victuals in the provision
market, bring loaves here, and add cakes to eat! Then with
a broom, sweep away the light mud so that when the hin-
drance has been removed, lilies may bloom with the narcis-

Iam picturato proscaenia pegmate vela
365 Fulcraque gemmatis scobe rasa thoralibus orna!
Nescio an esuriam vel non, tabulam tamen abta!
Rumpe moram! Quid stas? Quid hiantem, pessime, vexas?"
Dicit et adducto procumbit cernuus armo,
Perpetuo opperiens leti discrimina morbo,
370 Nam cibus inmodicus facit egrotare gulosum,
Dum certant elixa assis, mansueta ferinis.
Isti cyaneo purganti flumine palmas
Astat devote villoso gausape verna.
Dein nitidus malas distendit panis edaces;
375 Tunc, quia vulgaris ventri sordet cibus albo,
Aggravat ingentes patinas rombusque lupusque.
Lancibus in pandis culter coclearve moratur.
Aurea blandito portantur cymbia potu,
Chia ciphum tingunt abiecto vina Falerno.
380 Poma refutantur nisi, que dat Medica tellus.
        Quid loquar astantes ficta ditescere laude
Mimos? hi dominis astu per verba iocosa
Plurima surripiunt, etiam scalpente datore
Sinciput, exhausto decrescit copia cornu.
385 Alterius molles perturbat harundine Erinis
Auriculas resona, tenui volat illa susurro
Diffinditque cito cerebrum vitale volatu
Ocior ac tigris rapidis agitata molosis,
Nec tam pernici quassatur machina choro.
390 Tum sese in sponda vovet ut lasciva puella:
"Cur in avaricia tantum plerique laborant?
Vellem ori dulcis blandiretur cibus, aures
Mulcerent moduli, brevis hic quia mansio nobis.

sus. Now cover the stage with painted scaffolds, and with
jeweled drapes adorn the bedposts that have been scraped 365
and rubbed smooth! I don't know whether I'm hungry or
not, but set the table! Break off delay! Why are you standing
still? Why torment me as I gape, wicked one?" He says this
and, inclining, he falls forward with his shoulders drawn in,
awaiting the moment of death from continuous illness, for 370
excess food makes a glutton sick when boiled [meat] vies
with roasted, and tame with wild. For this fellow washing
his hands in a sea-blue stream, a house slave stands by faith-
fully with a plush towel. Next, fine bread swells out his glut-
tonous jaws; then, since common food is filthy in his white 375
belly, turbot and pike weigh down his huge serving dishes. A
butcher's knife or spoon waits on curved platters. Golden
bowls with pleasing drinks are carried in, and Chian wines
bathe the cup after the Falernian is cast out. Fruits are re- 380
fused, except those which the Assyrian land produces.

Why should I mention the mimes standing around grow-
ing rich on false praise? By their cunning they snatch away
many things from their lords through droll words, even
while the giver scratches his head and his abundance de-
creases as the horn [of plenty] is emptied. The Fury con- 385
founds the tender ears of another with her resounding reed;
she flits about with her subtle whispering, and in her swift
flight she splits open the life-giving brain more quickly than
a tiger chased by swift Molossian hounds, nor is a platform
shaken by so brisk a band of dancers. Then she promises 390
herself like a wanton girl in bed: "Why do many men suf-
fer so much from avarice? I want sweet food to please the
mouth, music to soothe the ears, since our stay here is brief.

'Ve mihi' cur dicam, si morbo non agitar, si
395 Turgentes papulae, si torquens pleurisis absit?
Non talis mihi mens. Puer, o puer, ales adesto!
Scin aliquem liricum, dic, aut gnarum chitaristam
Aut qui casta cavo concordet tympana plectro?
Scito quidem, si non mulcebit Lidius aures
400 Has—sed curre, ardet mea mens in amore canendi,
Ut torrela foco vel adunca cremacula igni."
   Ergo ubi disposita venit mercede iocator,
Taurinaque chelin cepit deducere theca,
Omnibus ex vicis populi currunt plateisque,
405 Affixisque notant oculis et murmure leni
Eminulis mimum digitis percurrere cordas,
Quas de vervecum madidis aptaverat extis,
Nuncque ipsas tenuem nunc raucum promere bombum.
Si quis ab externo dimotus climate caeli,
410 Sol roseus vastos ubi rura per Afra vapores
Evomit, aspiret terris qua frigida clausis
Omnibus hybernas exercet zona pruinas
Obcalletque tenax emuncto stiria naso.
Secum miretur caelum constare duabus
415 Unum naturis, estate geluque trementi.
   Ille fides aptans crebro diapente canoras,
Straverit ut grandem pastoris funda Goliath,
Ut simili argutus uxorem Suevulus arte
Luserit, utque sagax nudaverit octo tenores
420 Cantus Pytagoras, et quam mera vox Philomelae
Perstrepit. Interea motus clangore tubarum
Urget herus celerem calcaribus ire caballum
Per saltus, nemora et spissos caligine lucos.

Why do I say 'Woe is me' if I am not troubled by disease, if I   395
don't have swelling pustules and torturing pleurisy? Such is
not my intention. Come, boy, come, O winged boy! Tell me,
do you know some lyric poet or skillful cithara player, or one
who harmonizes chaste timbrels with a hollow plectrum?
Indeed, know, if the Lydian mode will not delight these ears
—but hurry, my heart is aflame with the love of singing,   400
like a burning brand in a fireplace or a curved kettle hook on
a fire."

And so when a minstrel arrives after his salary has been
arranged, and starts to remove his lyre from its ox-hide case,
people rush forth from all the neighborhoods and streets,
and with eyes fixed on him and with low murmuring observe   405
the minstrel with the tips of his fingers stroke the strings
which he furnished from the moist entrails of wethers, and
now they put forth a gentle sound, now a harsh one. If any-
one were removed from the outer region of the heavens
where the rose-colored sun sends forth vast warmth over   410
the African countryside, he might desire to reach lands
where the cold zone employs its wintry frosts when all are
shut in and a persistent frozen drop grows thick on a nose
just wiped. He might marvel that one sky exists with two
natures, with summer heat and with quivering cold.   415

Frequently adjusting the melodious strings a fifth of an
octave, that minstrel [tells] how the shepherd's sling once
laid out mighty Goliath, how the sly little Swabian with sim-
ilar skill tricked his wife, and how shrewd Pythagoras laid
bare eight tones of music, and how pure the call of the night-   420
ingale echoes forth. Meanwhile, moved by the blaring of
trumpets, a lord spurs on his speedy horse to proceed
through forest passes, groves and woods thick with mist. He

Hic tilias, fagos reboare inpellit et ornos
425 Procerasque feras ferro sulcante trucidat,
Sed teneros pullos annexo fune domandos
Venari atque plagis vivos innectere fervet,
Ut muscis letum molitur aranea tela.
Precipitique capit volucres indagine cervos,
430 In qua conveniunt linces, capreae, ursus aperque.
Post haec irretit assuetos vivere rapto
Accipitres pedicis et captos sepe coronat
Suppeditatque cibos tuguri clausos ut in arce
Umbrosa videat pluma candente novari.

6

[Untitled]

435 De viciis memorans non te, Cocytia pestis,
Transierim, invidia, te, per quam luridus anguis
Arguta primos pellexit fraude parentes.
Per te Hebreorum nunc ludit pectora, libris
Ne credant propriis, Iacob patris utpote dictis:
440 "Sceptrum de Iuda numquam tolletur et unctus
Donec is adveniat qui demittendus ab alto est,"
Subiunxitque "et eum gentilia corda manebunt."
Sic etiam vates de Christo iunior inquit:
"Cum sanctus veniet sanctorum, desinet unguen."

makes the lindens, beeches and mountain ashes resound, and with slashing steel he slaughters grown wild beasts, but 425 he eagerly desires to hunt young animals to be tamed when they are tied with a rope, and to catch them alive with nets, as the spider's web contrives death for flies. By a rapid encircling he captures swift stags where lynx, wild goats, bear, 430 and boar meet. After this, with snares he catches hawks accustomed to live by plunder and he often crowns them once they have been captured and provides food for them mewed in their hut, so that in this shadowy citadel he may see them renewed with shining plumage.

6

[Untitled]

While telling of vices, I should not omit you, Envy, plague 435 from hell, you through whom the ghastly serpent enticed our first parents with cunning deceit. Through you he now deludes the hearts of the Hebrews so that they do not believe in their own books, namely, in the words of father Jacob: "The scepter and the anointing will never be taken 440 away from Judah, until he comes who must be sent down from on high," and he added, "And the hearts of the nations will await him." So also the younger prophet said of Christ: "When the Saint of Saints comes, the ointment will cease."

445 Olim namque suos reges Iudea solebat
   Unguere, quod Regum liber attestatur aperte.
      Ast ubi de caelis mittendus erat genitoris
   Filius excelsi, cui compar cuique coevus
   In deitate manet, servilem assumere formam,
450 Stirpis Iulee cretus de sanguine Caesar
   Augustus celsum tenuit tunc Romulidarum
   Imperium, sibi qui preclarus belliger orbem
   Subdidit; ipsius dono iussuque senatus
   Excluso Hyrcano Iudeam sumpsit agendam
455 Barbarus Herodes. Cuius sub tempore Christum
   Catholicus populus natum de virgine credit.
   En bene concordant adolescentisque senisque
   Verba: Palestinis paganus prefuit arvis
   Rex et inunctus, ubi rex summus ab aethere venit.
460   "Messiam" dicunt "venturum credimus." Hic non
   Venit adhuc, ergo dicant, ubinam unctus eorum.
   Quem si non possunt ostendere, credere tandem
   Incipiant Christum, de quo non hi duo tantum,
   Verum cunctorum cecinere oracula vatum.
465 Iam nunc nobiscum conpuncto pectore dicant:
   "Est pater, est natus, sacer una spiritus his est
   Coniunctus, tres hi deus unus." Num sine nato
   Quis pater esse potest vel iure pater vocitari?
      Nonne duos libro Genealogus indidit almus
470 Personas quando dixit "Cum sulphure flammas
   Depluit a domino dominus Sodomam super urbem"?
   Hinc etiam David: "Deus unxit te tuus," inquit
   Premisitque: "Deus sedes tua"; dicit et alter:
   "Exulta Syon, iubila satis, en ego namque
475 Tecum habitaturus venio, dominus deus inquit,

For indeed, Judaea was once accustomed to anoint its kings, 445
which the book of Kings clearly attests.

But when he was to be sent from heaven to assume a ser-
vile form, the Son of the Most High Father, to whom he
is equal and to whom he remains coeval in divine nature,
Caesar Augustus, sprung from the blood of the Julian stock, 450
a celebrated warrior who subjected the world to himself,
then commanded the mighty empire of the Romans;
through his gift and by order of the senate, after Hyrca-
nus was removed, the barbarous Herod assumed the gover-
nance of Judaea. Catholic people believe that during his 455
time Christ was born of a virgin. See, the words of the young
man and the old are in harmony: a pagan king, and one un-
anointed, ruled the land of Palestine when the Highest King
came from heaven above.

They say: "We believe that Messiah will come." He has 460
not yet come, and so let them say where their anointed one
is. If they cannot point him out, let them at last begin to be-
lieve in Christ, concerning whom not only these two, but re-
ally the pronouncements of all prophets have foretold. Now, 465
at this time, with contrite hearts let them say with us, "There
is a Father, there is a Son and together with these is joined
the Holy Spirit; these three are one God." Without a son
who can be a father or rightly be called a father?

Did not the kind author of Genesis introduce in his book
two persons when he said "The Lord rained flames and sul- 470
fur from the Lord upon the city of Sodom"? After this David
also said "Your God has anointed you," and he first said
"God, your seat [is forever]"; and another says: "Exult, O
Sion, rejoice enough, for behold, I come to dwell with you,
says the Lord God, and you will know that the Lord your 475

39

Et nosces quia me misit dominus deus ad te";
"Me dominum" dominus. Quid adhuc dubitatis, inepti,
Christum hominem atque deum venerari? Quid dubitatis
Virginis ex vulva Christum prodisse Mariae?
480   Contra naturam qui fari iussit asellam
More hominum, intactam iussit generare puellam.
Quem generare? Deum, per quem pater omnia fecit.
Hic est verus homo, verus deus; accipe, num sit:
Esurit et dormit, tristis dolet. Hec hominis sunt.

485   Nunc quae sint, adverte, dei, Iudee, retexam:
In vinum convertit aquas; bibit architriclinus
Et vinum servasse bonum pincerna putatur.
Siccis ceruleas plantis peragrat deus undas.
Stans panda in puppi tumidas Aquilone procellas
490   Conterit et pelagus depulso mitigat Euro.
Piscando tota nequicquam nocte laborans
Petrus ut in verbo domini sua retia laxat,
Vix effert multo distentas pisce sagenas.
Dum pergit dominus Iayri revocare puellam
495   Suprema de sorte, retro bene femina credens
Accedit tangitque manu pendentia fila:
Nec mora, tacta rubrum constrinxit fimbria fluxum.
Quis neget esse deum qui demones eicit et cui
Spirituum humano glomerata in carcere tetra
500   Exclamat legio: "Quid vis nos perdere, Ihesu?"
Quis pulsis olidae concedit harae pecus hocque
Grunnitu rauco se mergere per freta currit.

        Ipsa deum plane testantur facta: duos sic
Augentem pisces, sic panes quinque sacrantem ut
505   Milia quina hominum saturans auferre refertos
Bis senos micis cophinos iussisset, eas ne

God has sent me to you"; the Lord [meant] "me, the Lord."
Oh foolish ones, why do you still hesitate to worship Christ
the man and God? Why do you doubt that Christ came
forth from the womb of the Virgin Mary? The One who   480
commanded a little ass to speak as men do, contrary to na-
ture, commanded an untouched girl to procreate. To procre-
ate whom? God, through whom the Father made all things.
He is true man, true God; hear whether he is [both man and
God]: he hungers and he sleeps, he is sad and grieves. These
are actions of a man.

Now, oh Jew, pay heed. I shall repeat what are actions of   485
God: he changes water into wine; the chief steward tastes it
and thinks that the waiter has reserved the good wine. God
walks on the blue waves of the sea with dry feet. Standing at
the curved stern of a boat, he crushes the tempests swollen   490
by the north wind and calms the sea, with the east wind dis-
pelled. Toiling for the whole night in vain to catch fish, at
the word of the Lord that he let down his nets, Peter can
scarcely haul up the nets distended by many fish. While the
Lord is proceeding to recall Jairus's daughter from her final
fate, a woman of great faith approaches from behind and   495
touches the hanging threads of his garment with her hand:
without delay, when the hem is touched, it stops her red
flux. Who would deny that he is God, who casts out demons
and to whom a foul legion of spirits gathered in a human
prison cries out "Why do you wish to destroy us, Jesus?" Af-   500
ter these are driven out, the herd leaves its smelly sty and
with raucous grunting runs to drown itself in the sea.

These works testify clearly that he is God: multiplying
two fishes and blessing five loaves so that after feeding five   505
thousand people, he ordered them to take away twelve bas-

Sorex vel limax tardus vel talpa vorarent.
Regulus eius opem pro nato postulat egro,
Ad quem "Vade, tuus iam vivit filius," inquit.
510 Ille abit et sanum reperit quem liquerat egrum.
Hec inter pascenda cibis celestibus assunt
Agmina, conspectum speciosi visere Christi
De quo sic quondam cecinit rex atque propheta:
"Gratia digna tuis diffusa est in labiis, qui
515 Pre pueris hominum forma pollente renides."
    Nonnullos Christi facies gratissima visu
Allexit, quosdam vitae doctrina perennis,
Et circumfusam videas stipare cohortem,
Sicut apes circa flores densantur in Ybla,
520 Suavia quando petunt thyma convolitantque gregatim
Ad cithisum, unde favos generent et dulcia mella;
Utque ferae Hyrcanis coeunt in montibus, utque
In parvis stipant formicarum agmina cellis.
Quis non estimet hoc magnum visuque stupendum
525 Atque deo dignum, quod Christus milia multa
Panibus ex paucis saturavit, fragmine panum
Bissenos pridem qualos et denuo septem
Accumulans; qui invisibilis sine carne farina
Pavit inexhausta Sareptensem viduam atque
530 Inconsumpti olei non deficiente lagena
Arida frugiferis caruit quo tempore tellus
Imbribus Helia sic exorante beato?
    Nunc carne assumpta panes paucos benedicens
Innumeras hominum saciat turbas et ob hanc rem
535 Dumtaxat plures ad eum venere, sed illos
Ipse piis monitis miti de pectore sumptis
Instituit: "Solam ne querite corporis escam,

kets filled with morsels lest a mouse or sluggish snail or mole should devour them. A ruler asked his help for his sick son; to him he said: "Go, your son now lives." The man went and 510 found him well, whom he had left sick. Among these to be nourished with heavenly food come multitudes to look at the sight of the beautiful Christ about whom the king and prophet once sang thus: "Fitting grace is poured forth on your lips, you who shine with great beauty beyond that of 515 the children of men."

The most pleasing face of Christ attracts some men by its appearance, the doctrine of eternal life attracts certain ones, and you might see a dense throng crowded about him just as bees are thick around the flowers in Hybla when they seek 520 sweet thyme and fly in swarms to clover from which they produce their honeycombs and sweet honey, and just as wild beasts gather in the Hyrcanian mountains, and as trains of ants pack [themselves] into their cells. Who would not consider this a great and stupendous sight, and one worthy of 525 God, that Christ filled many thousands from a few loaves, once heaping up twelve baskets with fragments of bread and a second time seven baskets; (the same God) who unseen, without flesh, supplied food for the widow of Zarephath from undepleted flour and an unfailing flask of undimin- 530 ished oil at the time in which the arid earth lacked rains that produce crops, when blessed Elijah entreated him thus?

Now after he assumed flesh, blessing a few loaves, he sat- isfies countless throngs of people, and on account of this 535 deed at least, no matter how many came to him, with kind admonitions taken from his gentle heart he taught them: "Seek not only food for the body, but rather desire that your

Quin immo dictis vestras petitote cibari
Divinis animas; tales epulas operari
540 Non cessate, quibus valeatis vivere semper!
Manna patres vestri, cum per deserta mearent,
Atque coturnices deplutas aere denso
Ederunt et non potuere evadere mortem.
Panis ego vivus sum. Quique comederit ex me,
545 Esuriet numquam, numquam vitalis obibit."
Pani confertur domini et dilectio fratris,
Et bene, namque epulum pane est elucius omne,
Et tam dulce nihil tibi torretur coquiturve.
Si modo pane cares, vilescunt fercula cuncta.
550 Sic si sola tibi desit dilectio Christi,
Quicquid agis, nichil est; virtus prodest tibi nulla.

EXPLICIT LIBER PRIMUS.

souls be fed with divine maxims; do not cease to toil for such
meals, by which you might be able to live forever! Your fa- 540
thers ate manna when they wandered through the desert,
and quail that rained down from the dense air, and they were
not able to escape death. I am the living bread. Whoever
eats of me will never be hungry; alive, he will never die." 545
Love of the Lord and one's brother is compared to bread,
and rightly, for all sumptuous food is more insipid than
bread, and nothing so sweet is roasted or boiled for you. If
you do not have bread, all dishes of food are worthless. So 550
also, if only the love of Christ is lacking to you, whatever you
do is nothing; no virtue profits you.

HERE THE FIRST BOOK ENDS.

I

De eo, quod incarnatio Christi predicta sit in Veteri Testamento

Incipe amare deum, Iudae stirps dura! Quid a te
Prognatum refugis venerari? quippe prophetam,
Qui de gente tua surrexit, uti tibi legis
Promisit lator, quem clausum in virginis alvum
5   Venturum David typica ratione spopondit:
Ut pluvia in vellus descendet et ut super herbam
Ros cadet, inque eius pax aurea tempore fiet.
Tunc gens queque teret reseratis ocia portis,
Vectibus amotis urbes et castra patebunt;
10 In toto dominabitur orbe potens et ab Indis
Extorres penitus regnabit ad usque Britannos.
Eius in aspectu gens procidet Ethiopum atque
Parthorum, et nullus stabit contrarius illi;
Adducent et quos spaciosus continet orbis.
15 Reges atque duces illi sua colla verenter
Flectent, et gentes credent in eum simul omnes.
Hoc etiam psalmus notat hic, qui proximus astat

I

Concerning the Fact That the Incarnation of Christ Is Foretold in the Old Testament

O hard race of Judah, begin to love God! Why do you re-
fuse to worship one born from your own stock? Indeed, a
prophet who arose from your people, as the bringer of the
law foretold to you, the one enclosed in a virgin's womb
whom David in a figurative manner promised would come: 5
as the rains come down upon the fleece and as the dew falls
upon the grass, and in his time there will be golden peace.
Then every nation will spend time in leisure with its gates
unlocked, cities and castles will stand open with their door
bolts removed; the mighty one will rule the whole world, 10
and he will reign from India all the way to the exiled Brit-
ons. At the sight of him the race of Ethiopians and Parthians
will fall prostrate, and no one will stand opposed to him;
and they will lead to him those whom the wide world holds.
Kings and dukes will bend their necks reverently before 15
him, and all peoples together will believe in him. That psalm
also indicates this, the one that stands next after the six-

Post sextum decimum, divina ubi vox ita fatur:
"Quem non cognovi, populus servire mihi atque
20 Auris in auditu parere libens properavit.
Sed qui filioli fuerant mihi nunc alieni;
Mentiti mihi sunt et sordibus inveterati.
Omnino claudi cessere a tramite veri."
    Cum domino quondam Iacob patriarcha beatus
25 Luctari aggressus nervo crepitante recessit
Claudus, premonstrans sub imagine carnis, Hebrei,
Errorem vestris in cordibus esse futurum.
Nam cum scripta patrum sacra vobiscum et rata vatum
Pagina luctentur, non vultis credere Christum
30 Venisse, inque fide Iudeus claudicat amens.
Iam tandem fidei callem, Iudee, requirens
Christum crede tuae causa advenisse salutis.
Crede, miser, quod sit genitori filius. Aut cur
Appellas patrem, cui prolem subtrahis? Et cur
35 Ipse tuis libris contrarius esse videris?
Stans, ut vestra refert scriptura, sub ilice Mambre
Abram ad se pueros tres aspexit propiantes.
Quis ait, "O domine, mecum tibi gratia si qua,
Pauxillum huc limphae ferri sine." Cum hoc ait ad tres,
40 Scilicet, "O domine," tres est fassus manifeste
Personas unum esse deum. "Deus est mihi" dicis
"Astra creans terram mare; non est filius illi."
    Nil credis, nec enim me plus istud capit ac si
Dedalon alatum credas dextraque Promethei
45 Humanum fecisse genus, vel vivificatos
Deucalioneos lapides et, quicquid in hortis
Plantatur Pelusiacis, divos fateare:
Abrotanum, rutam, laphatum, cepe, allia, anetum.

teenth, where the divine voice speaks thus: "A people whom
I knew not hastened to serve me and as soon as they heard   20
freely hastened to obey me. But those who were my sons are
now strangers; they have lied to me and have grown old in
their own filth; utterly lame, they have withdrawn from the
path of truth."

Once Jacob, the blessed patriarch, began to wrestle with   25
the Lord, but he departed lame, with his sinew creaking,
presaging, O Hebrews, under the likeness of flesh, that error
would be in your hearts. For when the sacred scriptures of
your fathers and the established page of the prophets wres-
tle with you, you are unwilling to believe that Christ has
come, and the foolish Jew is lame in his faith. Now, at last, O   30
Jew, as you seek the path of faith, believe that Christ has
come for the sake of your salvation. Believe, wretch, that he
is the Father's son. Or why do you call him Father, from
whom you take away offspring? And why do you seem op-   35
posed to your own books? Standing under an oak at Mamre,
as your scripture says, Abraham saw three boys approaching
him. He said to them, "O Lord, if your favor is with me at
all, allow a little water to be brought here." When he said
this to the three, namely, "O Lord," he clearly acknowledged   40
that three persons were one God. You say, "My God is the
creator of heaven, earth and sea; he has no son."

You believe nothing, for this does not win me over more
than if you were to believe that winged Daedalus and the
right hand of Prometheus made the human race, or the   45
stones of Deucalion came to life, and you should acknowl-
edge as gods whatever is planted in the gardens of Pelusium:
artemisia, rue, sorrel, onion, garlic, and dill; if you were to

Pana deum Archadiae venerere eiusque lupercal,
50　Et fatis credas balat que corniger Hammon
Aut in Dodona fallax bachatur Apollo.
　　"Quid si concedam quod summo sit genitori
Filius? Idcirco non concedo tibi quod sit
Ille incarnatus." Causam dic! cur? "Quia qui nos
55　Condidit et nullius eget, super omnia rex est.
Cur de celestis descendens culmine regni
Sese ergasterio carnis committeret et cur
In mortis legem properaret vita perennis?"

2

De eo, cur Dei filius
incarnari voluerit

Ausculta mihi nunc rationem concipe cur sit
60　Perdicio summi si non fateare parentis
Gnatum hominem factum et genitum de carne Mariae
Virginis ut culpam lascivae tolleret Evae.
Nam legis ut viridi duo mansere in paradiso,
Utque elusit eos serpens nequissimus, hoc est,
65　Demon verba vomens serpentis ab ore gravati.
Quippe gravatus erat serpens nec quid loqueretur,
Possessus norat veluti fanaticus omnis

worship Pan, the god of Arcadia, and his sacred grotto, and 50
you were to trust in the oracles that horned Ammon bleats
at or which deceitful Apollo rants about in Dodona.

"What if I concede that the Supreme Father has a son? I
do not on that account concede to you that he became in-
carnate." Why? Tell the reason! "Because the one who made
us and who lacks nothing is the king over all things. Why in 55
descending from the height of his heavenly kingdom would
he entrust himself to the prison of the flesh, and why would
everlasting life hasten to the law of death?"

2

On the Topic: Why the Son of God Willed to Become Flesh

Now listen to me and understand the reason why it is dam- 60
nation not to acknowledge that the son of the Supreme Fa-
ther was made man and born of the flesh of the Virgin Mary
to take away the guilt of lascivious Eve. For you read how
two [people] dwelled in a verdant paradise, and how the
most wicked serpent, that is, the devil, deceived them while 65
spewing words from the mouth of a crushed serpent. In-
deed, the serpent was crushed and, possessed, it did not
know what it was saying, just like every pagan and all who
are possessed by a demon. Believing him as he spoke, (she

Demonioque omnes obsessi. Cui rudis Eva
Dicenti, per quem cavisse satis sibi posset,
70 Si saperet, credens edit vetitum sibi pomum
Porrexitque viro, qui captus et ipse comedit.
　　Et quia primus homo per lignum corruit, ipse
Per lignum reparandus erat, quoniamque tumoris
Ex vicio cecidit, contrito corde redire
75 Instituendus erat, namque Ypocrate docente
Morbos per paria aut contraria novimus esse
Pellendos. Hoc aeterni veniens genitoris
Filius aeternus de caelis atque caduca
Sese carne tegens homo mansit humillimus inter
80 Inplacidos tumidosque homines, et vivere sancte
Exemplis sanctis nos inbuit. Ut bonus omnis,
Cum bonus et iustus sit, quod facit, estimet in se
Esse parum, Christus docuit, cum purus et insons
Ad templum ferri voluit geminoque piari
85 Turture, quique facit sanctos sanctissimus ipse
Decrepiti est ulnis contrectari Simeonis
Dignatus verbisque sacris ab eo benedici.
Utque suos sancto vereatur amore parentes
Quisque, suis dominus subiectus erat. Sed et ut nos
90 Per fontis lavacrum sacrati sive salubrem
Per cordis gemitum mundandos esse doceret,
Ipse vir annorum triginta venit ad undam
Iordanis subiitque manus felicis amici,
Quem strophio donavit ovis, pavere locuste.
95 Quo baptizatus detersit crimina nostra,
Ipse carens menda nec peccato oblitus ullo.
　　Quin et ab hoste volens temptari nos docuit, ne,
Temptamur quociens, dicioni subiaceamus

could have been sufficiently wary concerning him on her own account, if she were wise) ignorant Eve ate the fruit forbidden to her and offered it to the man, who was seduced and consumed it.

And since the first man perished on account of a tree, he had to be redeemed through a tree, and since he fell by reason of the vice of pride, he had to be taught to return with a contrite heart, for as Hippocrates teaches, we know that diseases must be expelled by like forces or by contrary ones. Hence, the Eternal Son of the Eternal Father, coming from heaven and covering himself with perishable flesh, dwelled as a most humble man among savage and haughty men, and he instructed us with holy examples to live a holy life. That every good man, although he is just and good, should think that what he does is in itself little, this Christ taught, when he was willing to be borne to the temple and to be purified with [an offering] of two turtledoves, and the Most Holy One who makes men holy deigned to be held in the arms of aged Simeon and to be blessed by him with holy words. And so that everyone might honor his own parents with holy love, the Lord was subject to his. But also, to teach that we must be cleansed through the washing of the holy font or through the salutary groaning of the heart, he came as a man of thirty years to the waters of the Jordan and submitted to the hands of his blessed friend, whom a sheep provided with a girdle and whom locusts fed. Baptized by him, he wiped away our offenses, he who lacked fault and was not stained by any sin.

Indeed, willing to be tempted by the enemy, he taught us that as often as we are tempted, we should not submit to the

Temptantis, sed ab illicitis desideriis nos
100 Flectentes illum pellamus pectore forti.
Ipse etiam quo nos humiles faceretque benignos,
Qui solo poterat nutu necuisse malignos,
Saxa malignorum fugiens se abscondit ab illis.
Discipulisque pedes doctor bonus abluit unda
105 In pelvim missa nec Iudam excepit iniquum.
Hunc quoque convivam pius inque parapside secum
Tingere non rennuit digitos, patientia mira!
    Post haec a vobis summi patris hostia sese
In cruce permisit perimi. Caput, inpie, quid nunc
110 Quassas? Nempe cruor te credere non sinit eius.
Cedo. Tui quando Pharium fugere tyrannum,
Morsibus infestas prius evitare cerastas
Num potuere patres, quam serpentem aere politum
In cruce prefixit ductor? Sic nemo, licebit
115 Alter erat Moyses, evadere quivit eos, qui
Pulsi de superis habitant latebrosa chelidri,
Donec plectendum se tradidit in cruce Christus.
Utque olim Iezi baculo revocare magistri,
Quem sibi defunctum Sunamitis femina planxit,
120 Non potuit puerum, donec vates Heliseus
Vivificavit eum, sic vestrae virgula legis
Non valuit salvare homines sub lege manentes,
Donec iter faciens animae custos quadriformis
Nostra coaptavit sibi membra deus stabuloque
125 Inpositus. Moriens hominem de clade levavit
Seminecem, septena sui munuscula flatus
Curato tribuens. Hoc quisquis credere non vult
Nil a vittatis senibus distare potest qui
Liba ferunt turpi et sinum cum lacte Priapo,

control of the tempter, but directing ourselves away from illicit desires, we should banish him with a brave heart. Also, to make us humble and kind, he who could have killed wicked men with a nod alone, fled from the stones of those malicious ones and hid himself from them. And with water poured into a basin, the Good Teacher washed his disciples' feet, and he did not leave out Judas, his foe. Also, the Kind One did not reject him as a table companion or refuse to dip his fingers into the dish with him. Oh wondrous patience!

After this he allowed himself to be killed by you on a cross as a sacrifice to the Supreme Father. Why now do you shake your head, impious one? Really now, does his blood not let you believe? When your forefathers fled the Egyptian tyrant, were they able to avoid the bite of dangerous serpents before their leader fixed on a cross a serpent adorned with bronze? Thus no one, even if he were another Moses, could escape those snakes which, driven from the upper world, now dwell in hidden places, until Christ handed himself over to suffer punishment on a cross. And just as in time past Gehazi could not call back to life with his master's staff the dead son for whom the Sunamite woman lamented, until the prophet Elisha revived him, so also the rod of your law was not able to save the people who remain under the law until, making his journey, the guardian of the four-formed soul, God, took our limbs upon himself and was placed in a stable. By dying he raised up half-dead mankind from destruction, imparting the seven little gifts of his spirit to one who has been healed. Whoever is unwilling to believe this cannot differ from old men bound with fillets who carry cakes and a bowl with milk to shameful Priapus,

130   Alcidae Bromioque litant Ianoque bifronti
Et tibi, qui vaccas Admeti, o Cinthie, pascis.
     "Credere non possum fabricae quod conditor omnis
Caeli, terrarum, maris et quecunque in eis sunt,
Femineam intraret matricem carne gravandus.
135   Nempe mei similem, non abnuo, gignere natum
Morti subiectum peccatoremque marito
Mixta suo potuit tua tam preciosa Maria.
Filius ille dei proprius mage non fuit ac tu
Aut ego." Quid mihi vis illudere, callida vulpes?
140   "Si vis proficere, de nostris conice libris!
Dic habeatur ubi quod amena palatia caeli
Qui regit et Sabaoth vocitatur factus homo sit.
Quod mihi si certa scriptum ratione probabis,
Ad tua, ni fallor, poteris me cogere sacra,
145   Et via celsus Athos erit, et segetes dabit Ahtlas."

3

Confirmatio incarnationis dominice
ex prophetarum testimonio

Fiat ut optasti; litem conferre tuorum
Aggrediar patrum de libris. Psalterium qui
Composuit, regem David dixisse negare
Non potes, "Ad callem currendum more gigantis
150   Exultavit, et a summis egressio celis

who offer sacrifice to Hercules and Bromius and two-faced 130
Janus, and to you, O Cynthian Apollo, who pasture the cows
of Admetus.

"I cannot believe that the founder of every work, the
maker of sky, lands, and sea and all things in them entered a
woman's womb to be burdened by flesh. Certainly that pre- 135
cious Mary of yours, I do not deny, after she was united to
her husband, could bear a son like me, one subject to death,
and a sinner. But he was no more God's own son than you
or I." Why do you want to mock me, you sly fox? "If you 140
want to make progress, draw conclusions from our books!
Tell where it is said that he who rules the pleasant palaces
of heaven and is called Sabaoth was made man. If you prove
to me with unerring reason that this is written, unless I am
wrong, you will be able to compel me to your holy rites, and 145
lofty Athos will be a highway, and Atlas will yield crops."

3

Confirmation of the Lord's Incarnation from the Testimony of the Prophets

Let it be as you have chosen. I shall undertake to contend
from the books of your forefathers. You cannot deny that
King David, who composed the Psalms, said "He has re-
joiced like a giant to run the path, and his going forth is from 150

Illius et rursum summam est occursus ad arcem,
Et non est homo qui se subtrahat eius ab estu."
   "Non nego." Quandoquidem consentis, altius illud
Scrutemur, licet hoc tibi sit nichil et videatur
155 Vile. Gigas terra genitus sermone Pelasgo
Dicitur, et quando pepulit de sede virenti,
Ne vitae de ligno esset, quod flammea nunc et
Anceps custodit romphea vetatque nocentes
Aspirare, reum deus Adam, sic ait illi:
160 "Terra es et in terram solvendus es." En homo terra
Dicitur; inde gigas salvator nomen habet, quod
Filius est hominis. Super omnes arbiter ipse
Nonnullos differt sontes multosque flagellat,
Ut convertantur; neutra flexis pietate
165 Ipse vices equa reddet quandoque statera.
   En optata tenes, vati modo credere si vis!
Idem duriciae vestrae non inscius huius
"Numquid" ait "dicet Sion: homo, natus in illa est
Hic homo, pre cunctis celsus fundaverat ipsam?"
170 Ac si dixisset "Numquid Iudea fateri
Sponte volet, quod concipiens de pneumate sacro
Intemerata suum generavit filia patrem?"
Partem pro toto posuit, Iudee etenim pars
Est Syon; quondam Iudea fuit, modo non est.
175 Tunc habitatorum sortita est patria nomen.
Illam proselitus populus nunc incolit, ex quo
Infandos Titus huc illuc dispersit Hebreos,
Infandos, quia natum ex se Christum necuere.
   Factori servire suo quicumque recusat
180 Mancipium domini merito fit deterioris.
Accipe quod Christi mortem scripturus Ysaias

the highest heavens, and his meeting again is at the highest point, and there is no man who removes himself from his heat."

"I do not deny [it]." Since you agree, let us examine that more deeply, even though this is nothing to you and seems worthless. One born of the earth is called a giant in the Greek language, and when God drove guilty Adam out of the verdant dwelling place lest he should eat of the tree of life, which now a flaming, two-edged sword guards and forbids the wicked to approach, he spoke to him thus: "Earth you are and into earth you must be dissolved." See, the man is called earth; hence the Savior has the name giant, because he is the Son of man. As the judge over all, he separates some of the guilty and scourges many so that they may be converted; to those persuaded by neither mercy he will at sometime assign recompense with an equal balance.

See, you have what you wished for, if you are now willing to believe the prophet! Not unaware of this hardness of yours, the same [prophet] says: "Will Sion not say: a man, this man, is born in her; the Highest One of all has established her before all others?" As if he had said, "Surely Judaea will not be willing to acknowledge of her own accord that her undefiled daughter, conceiving by the Holy Spirit, has brought forth her own father?" He cited the part for the whole, since Sion is part of Judaea; once it was Judaea, but now it is not. At that time the fatherland was allotted the name of its inhabitants. Now a strange people dwells in it, ever since Titus scattered the abominable Hebrews here and there, abominable, because they killed the Christ born of themselves.

Whoever refuses to serve his own maker deservedly becomes the slave of a worse master. Accept that Isaiah, about

155

160

165

170

175

180

59

Dixerit: "O here mi, quis dictis credidit almis
Aut consensit eis, quae nos percepimus a te?"
Atque quibusdam interpositis, quae tota referre
185 Non opus est, sub persona patris addidit ista:
"Stravi grande mei populi propter scelus illum;
Hic pro morte sua penis tradet locupletem,
Proque sepultura dabit ignibus inpietatem.
Quatenus in mundo degens non egit inique
190 Nec dolus est ullus sacro eius in ore repertus."
Cui non est fraus ulla deum fateamur oportet.
Nam rex et vates David testatur aperte
Quod gnatos hominum de siderea deus aula
Contemplans omnes ivisse per avia vidit.
195 Idem alibi affirmat quia mendax omnis homo sit.
Ergo qui numquam declinavit deus apte est.

Quod sit homo constat, qui sevos sustinet ictus,
Nam res nulla potest cedi nisi corporea; ergo
Est deus, est et homo. Sed iunctus homo deitati
200 Non peccat, quia non culpam deitas capit ullam,
Nec lux admittit pallentes vera tenebras.
Hinc sic per quendam de se deus ipse prophetam
Inquit: "Ego dominus non commutabor in evum."
Hinc quoque sumptus aqua vester dux, filius Ambrae,
205 Quem deus archano legitur mandasse sepulchro,
"Iustus," ait, "deus est rectus, merus atque fidelis."
Factus homo deus est nec ob hoc a limite veri
Discessit, namque est vir de quo psalmographus sic
Libri in principio "Vir felicissimus" infit
210 "Qui se consilio non miscuit inpietatis

to write of Christ's death, said: "O my Lord, who has believed my life-giving words or consented to those things which we have learned from you?" And after interposing certain verses, which there is no need to repeat wholly, in the person of the Father he added these: "I have laid him low on account of the great wickedness of my people; for his death he will hand over the rich to punishments, and for his burial he will give ungodliness to the flames. As long as he lived in the world he did not act unjustly nor was any deceit found in his holy mouth." We ought to confess that he is God, in whom there is no deception. For David, the king and prophet, declares openly that God, looking upon the children of men from his heavenly palace, saw that all had gone through trackless ways. The same [David] affirms elsewhere that every man is a liar. Therefore, he who has never gone astray is properly called God.

It is evident that he who endures cruel blows is a man, for nothing can be struck unless it is corporeal; thus, he is God and he is man. But the man united to divinity does not sin, because divinity is not capable of any fault, nor does true light grant admittance to pale shadows. Hence God himself, through a certain prophet, speaks thus of himself: "I, the Lord, will not be changed for all time." Hence also your leader who was taken from the water, the son of Amram, whom, we read, God entrusted to a hidden sepulcher, said: "God is just, upright, pure, and faithful." God was made man and did not depart from the way of truth on this account, for indeed he is a man about whom the psalm writer begins thus at the outset of the book: "Most blessed is the man who has not shared in the counsel of impiety and has not stood

Inque via peccatorum non substitit inque
Pestifera non est visus sedisse cathedra."
    Haec si tu sic esse negas, similaris eis qui
Naiades, Driades, Nimphas Satirosque verentur.
215 Cur adamante tuum cor durius esse videtur?
Non stirps est de rupe tibi; non te peperere
Ismarus aut Rodope. Tu vere germinis almi
Progenies, nec adulor in hoc. Gens dura, memento,
Qui quondam fuerint abavi tibi quique parentes
220 Ante dies quibus in terras descendit ab alto
Omnipotens et pro nobis verbum caro factum est!
    Verbum quo genitor firmavit celica summus,
Hoc verbum deus est, hoc et sapientia summi.
Que se in principio natam anteque tempora cuncta
225 Affirmat de patre deo genitamque priusquam
Luciferum faceret, montes et stagna crearet,
Et se presentem cum conderet astra fuisse
Cumque parente suo sese omnia conposuisse.
Filius hoc domini est, quem natum in tempore scimus
230 In mundum, verum penes eternum genitorem
Ante satum quam lux fieret seu tristis abyssus.
Illud Micheas bene pertractans ait: "Et tu,
Bethlem, parva quidem Iudeae in milibus es tu,
Et tamen Israhel qui presit prodiet ex te,
235 Primevosque dies egressus prevenit evis."
    "Quando tuum non credo deum, cur non pereo mox?"
Ulcio currentem capiet claudo pede sontem.
Num, miser, ignoras quid rex Babilonius inquit
Quando tres pueros tepida in fornace vagari
240 Vidit: "Nonne viros in furnum misimus amplum
Tres tantum, o proceres?" "Tres, princeps optime, tantum."

on the path of sinners and has not been seen seated on the chair of pestilence."

So if you deny that these things are so, you are like those who revere naiads, dryads, nymphs, and satyrs. Why does your heart seem to be harder than adamant? You don't have your lineage from rock; Ismarus or Rhodope did not beget you. In truth, you are offspring of a bountiful seed, and in this I am not fawning [on you]. Remember, hard race, who your forefathers once were, and your parents, before the days when the Almighty descended to earth from on high and the Word was made flesh for us!

The Word by which the Supreme Creator made celestial things firm, this Word is God, and this Word is the Wisdom of the Highest. This [Wisdom] declares that she was born in the beginning before all time and begotten of God the Father before he made the morning star, before he created mountains and waters, and she was present when he formed the stars, and that she, with her Father, set all things in order. This [Word] is the Son of the Lord, who, in time, we know, was born into the world, but begotten with the Eternal Creator before there was light or the dismal abyss. Exploring that [subject] well, Micah says: "And you, Bethlehem, you are indeed small among the thousands of Judaea, and yet the one who will rule Israel shall come forth from you, and his going forth precedes the earliest days."

"Since I don't believe in your God, why don't I perish right away?" Vengeance with her lame foot will catch a guilty man as he runs. Don't you know, wretched one, what the Babylonian king said when he saw three young men walking in the tepid furnace: "Did we not cast only three men into the great oven, O nobles?" "Only three, excellent prince."

63

"En ego non iam tres, sed quatuor ire potenter
Huc illuc video flamma cedente, deique
Quartus non dubia portendit imagine natum.
245 Sydrac et qui sunt tecum servi omnipotentis,
Ocius ite foras; magnus vester deus est et
Filius eius, eisque potest obsistere nullus,"
Dixit et inmani iussit clamore silere
Diversos strepitus: sambucas, organa, sistra.
250   Ipse eciam in somnis, dictu mirabile, vidit
Scilicet absque manu lapidem de monte recisum.
Quid fuit hoc, nisi quod de vestrae stirpis alumpna
Messias satus est sine crimine concubitoris?
Hic lapis est quondam reiectus ab edificantum
255 Insensatorum manibus; nunc angulus illum
In capite ostentat pariesque coheret eidem
Parte ab utraque. Quid hoc sibi vult, nisi quod reprobatus
Gentibus est olim? Sed nunc compago duorum
Sedis in etherae muro dominus populorum,
260 Iudeis etenim gentes coniunxit amicas.
Hinc est quod catus hoc Barachie filius infit:
"Exulta, Syon. Tuus ecce tibi veniet rex
Pauper eumque rudens ad te gestabit asellus;
Gentibus optatam pacem pius ipse loquetur.
265 Occasus quod habet, quod in eois manet arvis
Oceanusque ingens circumfluit, hoc regit ipse."
    Et quod non solum lapsura regat, sed et illis
Que sine fine manent nec torpor detinet ullus,
Presit, si dubitas, stipulare librum Danielis,
270 Inquid enim: "Vidi per visum noctis, et ecce
Spectanti nubes hominis quasi filius est mi
Visus. Is antiquum pervenit ad usque dierum

"Look, now I see not three, but four walking mightily here and there with the fire yielding, and the fourth with a definite likeness foretells the Son of God. Shadrach and the servants of the Almighty who are with you, go forth quickly; great is your God and his son, and no one is able to oppose them," he said, and ordered the diverse sounds with their wild din to be silent: sackbuts, [other] instruments and rattles. 245

Also, in dreams he saw clearly—a wonder to tell!—a stone cut away without a hand from a mountain. What was this, except that from a daughter of your race Messiah was born without the sin of a bed companion? This is the stone once rejected by the hands of the foolish builders; now it is the cornerstone, and the wall clings to it on each side. What does this mean, except that he was once rejected by the nations? But now the Lord is the bonding of two peoples in the wall of the heavenly abode, for he joined the gentiles to the Jews as friends. Hence it is that the wise son of Berechiah says this: "Rejoice, O Sion. Behold, your king will come to you as a pauper, and a braying little ass will bear him to you; he will compassionately declare the hoped-for peace to the nations. What the West has, what abides in the lands of the East, and what the vast ocean flows around, this he will rule." 250 255 260 265

And if you doubt that he will rule not only perishable things, and is also in charge of those that endure without end and that no torpor holds back, cite the book of Daniel, for he says: "I saw in a vision of the night, and, behold, as I looked at the clouds, one like the Son of man appeared to me. He came even to the ancient of days into whose sight 270

Cuius in aspectu nequam gens obtulit illum.
Sed pater omnipotens, a quo processerat ipse,
275 Magnificavit eum regnoque et honoribus amplis
Sic ut ei populi quos orbis continet atque
Cum tribubus linguae famulentur, sitque potestas
Eius in eternum, regnetque perenniter ipse."

4

Quod ineluctabilis sit
Iudeorum duricia

Sed quid tot prodest exempla inducere? Dudum
280 Os obpilassem de vobis, ni moveat me,
Quod lusor dubio perdens absistere pirgo
Non vult nec dubitat, dum perdit, perdere multum.
Sic nec me quamvis que vobis scriptito perdam
Perdere plura piget. Sed me nisi opinio fallat,
285 Veros ob monitus vestrarum in sede domorum
Nec rubrica meum nomen nec creta figuram
Exprimet, immo niger nigrum me carbo notabit.
    Fors et risus ero vobis et fabula. Quippe
Utile suadentem qui non sapit efferus odit;
290 Assentatores ut veros stultus amicos
Diligit. Hoc animas vicium ligat; hoc procul absit
Doctorum a lingua qui presunt aecclesiae, nam

a vile race presented him. But the Almighty Father, from whom he had proceeded, glorified him with a kingdom and ample honors so that the peoples whom the world contains and their tongues along with their tribes would serve him, and his power would be forever, and he would rule always." 275

4

That the Hardness of the Jews Is Inevitable

But what does it profit to bring forth so many examples? I would have shut my mouth about you before, except that I'm inspired that a player, while losing, does not want to desist from the dubious dice box, nor does he hesitate, while he is losing, to lose much. Thus, although I might lose what I keep on writing for you, it doesn't trouble me to lose more. But unless my expectation deceives me, because of my true admonitions neither red chalk nor white will express my name in the meeting places of your homes, but in fact black charcoal will mark me black. 280 285

Perhaps I'll be an object of laughter and a conversation piece for you. Indeed, a savage who has no sense hates one who urges what is useful; a fool loves flatterers as true friends. This vice binds souls; may it be far from the tongue of the learned who rule the church, for one who applauds 290

Qui favet artato pede non est mundior illo
Qui crus denudat detracto tergore, sicque
295 Non minus est turpis qui consentit facienti
Turpia quam faciens. Quocirca, dummodo vera
Suadeat et doceat, stulti non cesset ob iram
Doctior. Hoc dominus vult. Hoc se velle notavit
Quando ait Ezechiel: "Peccantem corripe, quo te
300 Illicitas pravasque vias monitore relinquat.
Quodsi te non audierit, certe ipse peribit.
At pro doctrina merces dabitur tibi digna."

Hoc quantum valeo sequor, est etenim mihi curae,
Ne quem commisit dominus mihi mantica censum
305 Servet inutiliter. "Nauci tua verba videntur,
Nam solet esse tibi sus qui non ruminat esca;
Nec cum lactucis agrestibus azima sumis,
Nec mactas agnum." Gens inproba, gens peritura,
Littera te perimit! Nos vitae spiritus aptat.
310 Que tu carne colis, nos mente. Quid obicis agnum,
Insignem postquam cunctis virtutibus agnum
In cruce mactasti Christum? Non proderit ultra
Tingere vestibulum seu postes sanguine caesi
Agniculi niveae vestiti vellere lanae.
315 Ire per ambages multas exemplaque patrum
Plura queam, nisi quod fabellam dicere surdo
Nil iuvat. Helchia satus ista profecto notavit
Cum de duricia vestra indignatus ait: "Si
Horribilis nigram Maurus deponere pellem,
320 Aut pardus varios valet inmutare colores,
Certe ego confiteor vos recte vivere posse,

[you] with his foot bound is no cleaner than one who bares
his leg with the leather removed, and likewise he who con- 295
sents to one doing shameful things is no less shameful than
the one doing them. For this reason, provided he exhorts
and teaches the truth, the more learned man should not
yield on account of the fool's wrath. The Lord wills this. He
indicated that he wills this when Ezekiel says: "Reprove the 300
sinner, so that with you as his admonisher, he may abandon
his lawless and wicked ways. For if he will not listen to you,
surely he will perish, but a worthy reward will be given to
you for your teaching."

I follow this as much as I am able, for I am concerned
that my pack not uselessly preserve the riches that the Lord
has entrusted to me. "Your words seem worthless, for the 305
swine, which does not chew the cud, is wont to be your food;
you do not eat unleavened bread with wild lettuce, nor do
you sacrifice a lamb." O wicked nation, O nation destined
to perish, the letter kills you! The spirit prepares us for life.
What you honor in the flesh, we honor in the mind. Why do 310
you reproach us with a lamb, after you sacrificed Christ, the
Lamb outstanding for all virtues, on a cross? It will do no
good any more to sprinkle the entrance or doorposts with
the blood of a slaughtered lambkin dressed in a fleece of
snow-white wool.

I could go through many digressions and more examples 315
of the Fathers, except that it is no benefit to tell a story to a
deaf man. The son of Hilkiah certainly noted this when, dis-
pleased at your hardness, he said: "If the monstrous Moor
can put aside his black skin, or the panther change its varie- 320
gated colors, surely I acknowledge that you are able to live
rightly, although your chief inclination is to learn [to live]

Cum sit precipuum studium male discere vobis."
Et rursum brutis vos esse minus sapientes
Conquestus summi sub persona patris inquit:

325 "Cum turtur milvusque rapax sua tempora norint,
Adventusque sui peregrina ciconia servet
Tempus, quaeque hominum est convictrix, mitis hirundo,
Iudicium domini nescit populus meus." Illud
Urbanis dictis proles eciam notat Amos:

330 "Caeli, audite, et humus, quid vestri dixerit auctor!
Filiolos ego nutrivi fecique potentes,
Econtra ingratis ego sum contemptus ab illis.
Bos asinusque sui domini presepia norunt,
At populus meus Israhel me scire recusat."

335 Qui bos aut asinus? Gens Christo credula nunc, sed
Dedita sacrilegis fanorum cultibus olim.
Parnasus Phebo statuit sacra, Tracia Marti,
Gnosiades coluere bovem, Mynoida, laudes
Latranti cecinit populus Memphitis Anubi,

340 Deprensae Veneri Paphos, oblatisque corimbis
Boeciae Bacho celebrarunt orgia gentes,
Teutonici humanum Diti fudere cruorem.
    Eneas Asiae post diruta Pergama ab oris
Ausoniam veniens Vestam attulit atque Penates

345 Iliacis raptos ex ignibus; is Tyberina
Stagna et Aventini iocunda cacumina collis
Religione coli magna docuit. Numa post hunc
Auguria et sortes et Tessala carmina, ut aiunt,
Instituit primus Romae; cuius pronepotes

350 Innumeras divum sibimet finxere catervas,
Inter quos multas habuit Thirintius aras.
Gerionem stravit, cessit quoque Cerberus illi;

wickedly." And again, when he lamented that you are less wise than brutes, in the person of the Highest Father he said: "Although the turtledove and the rapacious kite know 325 their seasons, and the sojourning stork observes the time of her coming, and likewise the gentle swallow that is the companion of men, my people do not know the judgment of the Lord." The son of Amoz also noted with these elegant words that: "Hear, O heavens and earth, what your Creator has 330 said! I have nourished my children and made them strong, but on the contrary I am despised by those ingrates. The ox and the ass recognize their master's manger, but my people Israel refuses to know me."

Who is the ox or the ass? The gentiles now believing in 335 Christ, but formerly devoted to the sacrilegious cults of temples. Parnassus established sacred rites for Phoebus, Thrace for Mars; the Cretans worshipped a bull, a descendant of Minos; the people of Memphis sang praises to barking Anubis, Paphos to Venus caught in the act, and the peo- 340 ple of Boeotia brought clusters of fruit to celebrate festivals in honor of Bacchus, the Teutons poured out human blood for Dis.

After Troy was destroyed, when Aeneas came to Italy from the shores of Asia, he brought Vesta and his household gods, snatched from the fires of Ilium; he taught that the 345 pools of the Tiber and the pleasant peaks of the Aventine hill [should] be honored with great awe. After him, as they say, Numa first established auguries and oracles and Thessalian incantations at Rome. His grandsons fashioned 350 countless troops of gods for themselves, among whom Hercules had many altars. He overthrew Geryon, and Cerberus

Antheum, ut fertur, necuit Cacum quoque et ydram.
Et quot virtutes gessit, tot energima cepit.
355 Flaminibus curae pulvillos atque tapetas
Sternere qua gybsum statuit Iovis et Cithereae,
Et segnes tenui fucos arcere flabello
Qua levis podex omentaque feda iacebant;
Menades astabant, haec compta monilibus aureis,
360 Illa periscelidas iactans, hec molle theristrum,
Clamabantque simul salientes "Euhion! Euhoe!"
    Quid vel Thesiphonem vel manes persequar atros?
Quidve Memallonides verbena et cespite cultas?
Tales ob ritus gens quondam bruta vocata;
365 Nunc, quoniam Christum colit, orthodoxa vocatur.
Sed quia tu Christum, Iudee miserrime, non vis
Credere, credentes te spernunt, Christus et ipse.
    "Vis hominem esse deum credam, sed non licet; et quid,
Dic mihi, tale egit natus genetrice Maria
370 Credendus quod sit deus?" Hoc describere plene
Nemo valet, tamen ex multis paucissima pandam.
Sanat filiolam Phenissae; ydropica membra
Deplet; et incolomem dat centurionis alumnum,
Curvatosque diu longum terrena videntis
375 Ecclesiae in formam muliebres erigit artus.
    Est Hierosolimis piscina probatica quinque
Porticibus discreta, salus ibi certa fit egris.
Hic cernens hominem triginta octoque per annos
Languentem, Christus solidatis precipit illum
380 Surgere membrorum compagibus atque grabatto
Sublato repedare domum monet; otius ille

also yielded to him; as they say, he killed Antaeus, Cacus, and also the Hydra. And as many strengths as he exhibited, so many were the frenzied devotions he received. The 355
priests attended to spreading little cushions and coverlets where he set up plaster [statues] of Jove and Venus, and with a thin fan they kept away the lazy drones from where the smooth anus and loathsome guts lay; the maenads were assisting, this one adorned with golden necklaces, that one 360
shaking leg bands, this one [wearing] a soft turban, and leaping together they cry "Euhoe, euhoe!"

Why should I describe Tisiphone or the gloomy spirits of the underworld? Or why describe the Bacchantes who are honored with a leafy bough and turf? Because of such rites a people were once called brutish; now, since they wor- 365
ship Christ, they are called orthodox. But since you, most wretched Jew, are unwilling to believe in Christ, the believers and Christ himself scorn you.

"You wish that I might believe that a man is God, but it is not lawful; and what so great deed, tell me, did the son of mother Mary do that he must be believed to be God?" No 370
one can describe this fully, yet I shall make known a very few examples out of many. He heals the Phoenician woman's little daughter; he cures limbs afflicted with dropsy; he gives the centurion his son safe and sound, and he straightens into shape the woman's limbs that had long been curved, one 375
who saw [only] the earth [floor] of the church.

There is in Jerusalem a pool for sheep divided by five porches, and there health is assured for the sick. Seeing here a man who was feeble for thirty-eight years, Christ commanded him to arise since the joints of his limbs had been 380
strengthened, and he instructed him to go home when he

Surgit et exultans vacuum cubitale reportat.
Hoc prope piscinam gestum est; Prudentius ipsam
Syloam esse putat. Variis ebullit in horis;
385 Tunc undam tantum solita exsudare salubrem,
Cum caelestis eo demittitur angelus. Illic
Passim captivae quovis languore catervae
Conveniunt et arenoso sub margine stipant
Et manaturum laticem de pumice sicco
390 Exspectant avidi, quia qui descendit in undam
Primus et abluitur sua membra scatente procella,
Abscedit sospes gaudetque adiisse lacunam.
Huc caecum natum Iesus direxit ut inde
Squalentes oculos sputisque lutoque lavaret.
395 It, lavat atque videt prius ignotam sibi lucem.
    Esse deum constat qui cecos lumine donat,
Extinguit febres, lepram fugat, expedit aures
Surdorum gratoque frui dat famine mutos.
Vivificat loculis inposta cadavera mestis,
400 Nec solum loculis, sed et in tellure reclusos
Evocat, et verbo vacuat latebrosa sepulcra.
Bethania hoc novit, qua Lazarus in monumento
Bis duo pene dies exegerat abditus et iam
Rancidus in cinerem dissolvere ceperat artus.
405 Accedit deus omnipotens et nomen amati
Ingenti clamore ciet, redit ille. Quis ultra
Ambigat esse deum, per quem tot signa fiebant?
    Quid dicis, Iudee, modo? Vis cedere vel nunc
Non te permittit cor saxo durius? Atqui
410 Quo nil durius est. Lapidem mollis cavat unda,
Malleus excudit duris de cotibus ignes,
Scintillatque silex duro calibe icta frequenter,

74

had taken up his pallet; the man quickly arose and, rejoicing, he carried off his empty bed. This was done near the pool; Prudentius thinks this was Siloam. At various times of day it bubbles up; only then is it accustomed to exude healthful 385 water, when an angel from heaven is sent down to it. Bands of people seized by any sickness assemble there at random and crowd together on the sandy edge, and eagerly await the water that will flow from the dry rock, because the one who 390 descends first into the water and is washed by the blast of water gushing over his limbs, goes away sound, and is glad that he entered the pond. Jesus sent a man born blind here so that from it he might wash his eyes caked with spittle and mud. He goes, he washes, and he sees the light unknown to 395 him before.

It is certain that he is God who gives light to blind men, who extinguishes fevers, drives out leprosy, opens the ears of the deaf, and allows mutes to enjoy pleasing speech. He restores life to corpses placed on sorrowful biers, and not 400 only on biers, but also he calls forth those shut up in the earth, and with a word he empties hidden graves. Bethany came to know this, where Lazarus had spent nearly four days concealed in the tomb and already stinking, he had begun to dissolve his limbs into ashes. Almighty God ap- 405 proaches and calls the name of his beloved [friend] with a mighty cry, and he returns. Who doubts any longer that he is God, through whom so many miracles happened?

What do you say now, Jew? Will you concede even now or does your heart harder than rock not permit you? Certainly gentle water hollows out a stone than which nothing 410 is harder; a hammer beats fire out of hard flint stones, and flint struck often by hard steel sends out sparks, yet sooth-

Cum neque te sermo valeat perfringere blandus
Ut credas dominum Christum, nec torva minarum
415 Asperitas de te queat ullum extrudere fructum.
Nonne, miser, legis in psalmo? Forsan legis et non
Attendis dominum dulcem rectumque vocatum.
"Cui dulcem?" Qui divertit de limite pravo,
Qui Christum credit sacroque lavatur in amni,
420 Et legem domini meditatur nocte dieque.
"Cui rectum?" Qui nequicia resipiscere non vult,
Inque sua minime trepidat persistere sorde.
Inveniet quod querit homo, nam qui bona quaerit
Inveniet bona, nec mala deerunt qui mala quaerit.
425 Qui mactare iuvat tot tauros totque bidentes,
Ipsum te Christo macta, cui victima nulla
Gratior offertus quam spiritus est tribulatus.
Quod si in duricia districti iudicis atrum
Exspectare diem quam te convertere mavis,
430 Non te grex ovium capiet, iungeris ad hedos
Ignibus eternis qui sunt sine fine cremandi.
Tunc "heu me miserum" dices, sed nil valet; illum
Clamorem dominus non percipiet, sed ut olim
Virginibus fatuis sponsus "te nescio" dicet.
435 "Nil minus hoc vereor, nam vivo rectius ac tu."
Fallere! Quicquid agit stultus, laudabile censet.
Quam felix esses si te cognoscere velles,
Si velles animo perpendere veneris unde,
Tendere si summam velles properanter ad aulam!
440 Silvis innatam volucrem doctus capit auceps
Glutine; et includit caveae, subponit et escas.

ing speech cannot break through you so that you believe
that Christ is Lord, nor can the stern severity of threats ex-   415
tract any fruit from you. Wretched one, do you not read in
the Psalm (perhaps you do read and do not heed) that the
Lord is called sweet and righteous. "Sweet to whom?" One
who has turned aside from the crooked path, who believes
in Christ and is washed in the sacred stream, and who medi-   420
tates night and day on the law of the Lord. "Righteous to
whom?" One who out of wickedness is unwilling to come to
his senses, and who is not afraid to persist in his own un-
cleanness. A man will find what he seeks, for one who seeks
good things will find good, and evil things will not be lacking
to him who seeks evil.

You who delight in sacrificing so many bulls and so many   425
sheep, sacrifice yourself to Christ, to whom no victim more
pleasing is offered than an afflicted spirit. But if in your
hardness you prefer to await the dark day of the severe judge
rather than to convert, the flock of sheep will not receive   430
you, [but] you will be joined to the goats who must be
burned without end in everlasting fires. Then you will say
"Ah, wretched me," but to no avail; the Lord will not hear
that cry, but he will say, as once the bridegroom did to the
foolish virgins, "I do not know you."

"There is nothing I fear less than this, for I live more vir-   435
tuously than you." You are mistaken! Whatever a fool does,
he considers it laudable. How happy you would be if you
were willing to know yourself, if you were willing to weigh in
your mind where you came from, if you were willing to pro-
ceed swiftly to the highest palace! With glue, a skilled fowler   440
captures a bird born in the woods; he confines it in a cage
and places food before it. If perchance it sees a grove, this

Que si forte nemus videt, unguibus improba curvis
Conculcat micas et ticiat anxia silvas.
Dum leo mansuescit Libicus, sufferre magistri
445 Verbera non renuit iussisque obtemperat eius.
Qui si desueto gustaverit ore cruorem,
Nec tutus dux ipse manet. Si pascere temptes
Pane lupum, tandem perdes operam; magis agno
Querit et anseribus pasci. Si denique tollas
450 Inque sinu foveas languentem algore colubrum,
Mox ubi fit calidus, cauda te perfidus angit.
Naturam servare suam norunt animata
Cetera; solus homo quis sit non vult meminisse.
    Haec ad Iudeos dixisse sat est, neque enim istud
455 Tantillum surdi curant attendere; namque,
Ut supra dixi, sic pectora ludit eorum
Antiquus serpens ut prave vivere malint.
Hocce per invidiam facit, ut quia concidit ipse
De superis per fastum et apostata semper in igne est
460 Arsurus, plures habeat socios cruciatus.
Nam contentus eis non est quos iusta tonantis
Depulit ira polo quia consensere magistro.
Demonas appellant. Hi toto quicquid in orbe
Patratur sceleris suadent, et tela furoris
465 Suppeditant: fraternum odium, civilia bella,
Prestigium, fraudes, periuria, furta, rapinas.
Sensibus illudunt hominum numquamque fideles
Absistunt a calle boni seducere mentes.
Concessum tamen his non est penetralia cordis
470 Rimari, sed, dum deluso pectore sensus —
Gustus, odoratus, auditus, visio, tactus —
Blandicias sese iaculantur ad exteriores,

restless bird tramples those crumbs with its curved claws and fills the woods with its twittering. While a Libyan lion is tame, it does not refuse to suffer its master's lash, and it obeys his commands. If this lion tastes blood in its unaccustomed mouth, not even its master is safe. If you try to feed a wolf on bread, in the end you will waste your effort; it wants to be fed on lamb and geese instead. Finally, if you take a serpent listless from cold, and you warm it in your bosom, soon, when it becomes warm, the treacherous snake strangles you with its tail. The other living things know how to preserve their own nature; only man is unwilling to remember who he is.

To have spoken these words to the Jews is enough, but they are deaf and do not care to consider such a small thing; for truly, as I said above, the ancient serpent so deludes their hearts that they prefer to live perversely. He does this through envy, so that in his torment he may have many companions, since through pride he fell from above and will burn forever in fire as an apostate. For he is not content with those whom the just anger of God cast out of heaven because they conspired with their master. Men call them demons. They induce whatever wickedness is brought about in the whole world, and they supply the weapons of madness: fraternal hatred, civil wars, trickery, deceits, perjuries, thefts, and plunder. They make sport of men's senses and never cease to lead faithful minds away from the path of goodness. Yet, they are not allowed to pry into the secret recesses of the heart, but, after the heart has been deceived, while the senses—taste, smell, hearing, sight, touch—hurl themselves toward external allurements, having experienced slumber of

445

450

455

460

465

470

Experti cordis tali oblectamine somnum,
Adveniunt ceptumque malum perducere temptant.
475 Horum sunt socii quos invidiae scelerosa
Est bilis. Mordax bona dissipat omnia livor.

5

De invidia hominum in homines

Quid struis, invidia? Cur illaqueas homines tot?
Cur tot ad umbrosum mortales dirigis Orcum?
Tu quondam in fratrem movisti brachia Cain
480 Quod deus, ut ferri mavult sibi viva, maniplo
Agnum preposuit; tabescis honore propinqui,
Sed neque germano congavisura potenti.
Indignare, reor, quod quisquam te viciorum
Appellet minimam; doleas hinc, dissere, necne.
485 "Non equidem extremis cuneos ad prelia signis
Me ductare decet nec tela levissima mi sunt.
Quid virtutis habent tumor et lascivia vite,
Quamve levis stragem balista libidinis infert,
Sola anima fusa cum ego possim deicere ambo?
490 Cunctas carnales queo sordes vincere fidam
Preter avariciam. Cur ergo novissima, cur, sim?"
    Hac inflammatus furia quicumque lacerna
Nobilium texta precioso stamine serum

the heart because of such pleasure, they [demons] approach and try to prolong the evil they have begun. They are the 475 companions of those whom the accursed ire of envy devours. Biting envy destroys all good things.

5

On Men's Envy Toward Men

Envy, what do you devise? Why do you ensnare so many men? Why do you direct so many mortals to shadowy Orcus? Once you provoked the arm of Cain against his brother because God, as he prefers living things to be offered to 480 himself, preferred a lamb to sheaves; you pine away because of a relative's glory, but neither will you rejoice with a powerful brother. You are indignant, I think, because someone might call you least of the vices; tell us whether or not you grieve on this account.

"Indeed, it is not fitting that I always lead my troops to 485 battle with our standards last, nor are my weapons the weakest. What strength do pride and wantonness of life have, or what carnage does the swift missile of lust cause, since I alone can drive out both once the soul is routed. I am able to 490 vanquish all the filth of the flesh except trusty avarice. Why, then, why should I be last of all?"

Whoever, inflamed by this furious passion, sees a noble-

Primatem splendere videt, deflectit ocellos
495 Tamquam de foveis ubi mingitur atque cacatur,
Vestiri satrapas vulgari canabe malens.
Sic frater fratrem, susceptum patre nepotem
Indutumque stola, rodens convivia, sprevit.
Quem semel apprendit, facit hunc marcescere livor
500 Ac linguam morsu commotae more lisciscae
Debilitare truci. Viso pollente propinquo
Qui pasci artocreis velit apto pollice tortis
Murenis dulcique scaro mulloque trilibri,
Et rigida ex auro pretexta infringere corpus,
505 Inspicit hunc livens privignum ut iniqua noverca,
Ut murem cattus, mustela trucem basiliscum.
    Verum precipue hoc liventem quemque fatigat:
Quod quemquam cernit sese virtute priorem,
Facundum, lenem, lepidum simul atque facetum,
510 Et cum vulgo levis parvi pendentibus ipse
Sit populis, plaudens quam dat plebecula, laudi
Invidet alterius. Faeno canis incubat acer
Inde boum rictus admotis morsibus arcet,
Bubus non cupiens quod sumere non potis ipse est.
515 Invidus infamis populique peripsima cum sit,
Quem non ipse meret, cruciatur honore alieno.
    Quid de pauperibus sublatis stercore dicam?
Hos detestatur sandice crocoque decoros
Emulus ut frater fratrem pro se benedictum
520 Utque viri Ioadem prope ripam Adaris reprobati,
Arcessitque pares et nunc hiat iste remisse:
"Dicite nunc, socii, cur me non vellicet, ohe!
Quod video illum illum tergo pernicis igene

man resplendent in a cloak woven from the precious thread
of the renowned Chinese, turns away his eyes as if from the
ditches where people piss and shit, preferring that rulers   495
be clothed in common hemp. Thus a brother despised his
brother, the prodigal welcomed by his father and clothed in
a robe, while he disparaged their feast. Once envy seizes a
man, she makes him waste away and maim his tongue with   500
savage biting like an aroused bitch. When he sees a powerful
kinsman, the man who wants to feast on meat pies shaped
with an apt thumb, on lampreys and sweet wrasse and a
three-pound mullet, and who wants to bruise his body with
a cloak stiff from gold, the envious one looks upon him as   505
a spiteful stepmother looks at a stepson, as a cat looks at a
mouse, a weasel at a wild lizard.

Truly, this especially vexes everyone who is envious: the
fact that he sees anyone superior to himself in virtue, some-
one eloquent, gentle, charming, as well as witty, and since he   510
is generally of little importance to the people who esteem
him lightly, he envies the praise that the approving populace
bestows on another. A fierce dog lies on hay and keeps the
mouths of oxen away from this with his bites since he doesn't
want the cattle to partake of what he cannot himself. An en-   515
vious and disreputable man, although he be the dregs of the
population, is tormented by another's glory, which he does
not merit.

What should I say about paupers lifted up from the dung?
A jealous rival detests them once they are tricked out in ver-
milion and saffron as a brother hates the brother blessed be-
fore himself, and as the men rejected near the banks of the   520
Adar hated Joash, and he summons his equals and now spews
out carelessly: "Ho! Tell me now, comrades, why should it
not irritate me that I see so and so covering his pleasing

Et lena viridi iocunda obducere membra,
525 Quem caprae turpis membrana prius decoravit?
Nunc quos eiectos huc dira Sicambria mittit,
Aut qui deseruit longinquae menia Thilae,
Seu fullo est aut phyltra parat seu saxifrice vi
Elicit urinam mordentem membra pudenda et
530 Marrubio tussim scabiemque celidonia aufert:
Huc veniat, mox ut fungus surgit vel hibiscus,
Predia dantur ei, fasces alteque curules.
Is nos indigenos deridet agitque retrorsum.
Fibula quanta, pape, quis nectit pallia clavus
535 Istius ignoti patria qui nescio de qua
Huc macer et nudus venit! Quod non bene vertat!
Sed vos quid tanto cessatis symbola questu
Addere vel seriem mihi suggessisse diserti?"
Hec iactando caput male fido pectore quassat
540 Arvinam tenuans evanescente colore.

6

De discordia et ira, et quam utilis sit penitencia

Te quoque subsidium diro furialibus armis
Murmure non dubium est, discordia, ferre bilinguis,
Officiumque tibi concinnum rumpere fedus,

limbs with the hide of a swift hyena and with a green cloak,
a man whom the filthy skin of a she-goat previously adorned? 525
Now those whom frightful Sigambria sends here as outcasts,
or one who abandoned the walls of distant Thule, whether
he is a fuller or prepares love potions, or whether by force of
saxifrage he draws out the urine that stings private parts,
and with horehound he takes away a cough and with celan- 530
dine the mange: let him come here, and as fast as fungus or
hibiscus spring up, manors, high offices and lofty honors are
bestowed on him. He scoffs at us natives and drives us back-
wards. Strange! How great a buckle fastens the cloak, how
broad the stripe of that unknown fellow who came here thin 535
and naked from heaven knows what country! May this turn
out badly! But why, my eloquent comrades, do you cease to
add your contributions to so great a complaint, or to supply
a series [of them] to me?" Hurling these remarks with un-
trustworthy heart, he shakes his head, making his fat waste 540
away as he grows pale with envy.

6

On Discord and Anger, and How Useful Repentance Is

There is no doubt that you also, double-tongued discord,
bring support to raging arms with your dreadful murmuring,
and it is your duty to destroy an agreeable compact, and

Et suadere dolos, convicia, sediciones.
545 Alchimus effecit Numidae quod more Nicanor
Federa que pepigit cum Iuda discidit acer.
Sepe eciam discors dat munera pro nece fratris,
Ut Capitolinus mercede data Menelaus
Prodidit egregium mortique asscripsit Oniam.
550   Sic et detractor (nichil infelicius illo)
Inter germanos rixam serit atque propinquos.
Nos tamen ad vocem talis cuiuslibet ambas
Auriculas quidni causas subrepere ovantes
Litigii arrigimus. Sed ter narrasse citanti
555 Non satis est: instat rabido duplicatque furorem.
Ut si quando olidam nebulosi fornicis orcam
Obsceni subiere sues et feda cloacae
Stercora verrentes halantem auxere mefitim,
Sic patris Achitofel natique diremit amorem.
560 Possem, ni pigeat gravitasque inamabilis acti
Elinguem faciat, bachantis iurgia multa
Eumenidis memorare, leves quibus incitat aures.
      Sed reticere decet non certe cognita, nam nec
Pectora nota hominum sunt nec precordia nobis.
565 Nil ignoranti linquamus operta tonanti,
Et temere incerta de re non iudicet ullus.
Pauca ut homo memini, nam soli plurima nosse
Convenit excelso; cordis penetralia solus
Perspicit et rimas, et non eget indice quoquam.
570 Sacrilegus coram quo non queat inficiari
Crimina que medico vivens nudare fideli
Erubuit, liquitque suam putrescere plagam.
      Ira citus furor est; qua dum quis frendet, ut ovis
Lexiva admixtis spumat revomitque salivas,

to encourage deceptions, contentions, and dissensions. Al- 545
cimus brought it about that violent Nicanor, like the Nu-
midian, broke the treaty which he concluded with Judas.
Indeed, a discordant man often gives gifts for the death of a
brother, as Menelaus the priest betrayed the eminent Onias
and marked him for death after a bribe was given.

So also a detractor (nothing is of worse omen than he) 550
sows strife between brothers and kinsmen. Yet we prick up
both ears at the voice of any such man, rejoicing, naturally,
that the causes of a quarrel are creeping along. But it is not
enough for the rabid one inciting it to have recounted the 555
causes three times: he presses on and doubles his rage. As if,
when disgusting pigs have approached the stinking butt of a
dark brothel and, sweeping along the foul dung in a sewer,
they increase the noxious smell emitted, so did Akithophel
dissolve the love of a father and son. And if the severity of 560
the odious act did not disgust me and render me speechless,
I could cite many quarrels of the ranting Fury, by which she
incites fickle ears.

But it is fitting to be silent about things not known with
certainty, for the minds of men are not known to us, nor are
their hearts. Let us leave such secrets to God, who is igno- 565
rant of nothing, and let no one judge rashly about an uncer-
tain matter. As a man, I recall few things, for to know very
many is proper to the Most High alone; he alone looks into
the recesses of the heart and its cracks, and he does not need
any guide. Before him an impious man cannot deny sins 570
which he blushed to lay bare before his faithful physician
while alive, and thus let his wound putrefy.

Rage is roused by anger; when anyone gnashes his teeth
because of this, just as lye froths and spews foam when eggs

87

575 Alcior assurgit mordaci gutture struma.
Tunc iratus agit subito limphando furore.
Quod fecisse pudet; quod penitet ilico factum
Frustra, nam factum nequid infectum fieri. Sed
Sic confert, quoniam venia conpunctio cordis
580 Non caret erga homines atque equum caelipotentem.
Taliter Ysiades letum deflevit Uriae.
Desperare nocet: vidit Samaria regi
Dilectum calvi renuentem dicta prophetae,
Calcatum in portis miseranda morte perire.
585 Nullus desperet, cum verba salutifer ore
Dixerit ista deus: "Non quero desipientis
Interitum; pravo divertas tramite malo."
Saulus ab erroris discessit calle Damasci
Sedavitque strophas Tuscorum et Cecropidarum;
590 Stoica cessit ei plebs atque academica secta.
     Hinc quoque Christus ait celorum clavigero quem
Victa morte sibi statuit fidum opilionem,
Petro de venia percontanti tribuenda,
Gratia num veniae ter danda quaterque propinquis:
595 "Non tantum tibi, Petre, modo dimittere fratri
Indico vicibus septem cum exorbitat, immo
Undecies septem volo conservare memor sis."
Preterea vos qui spem desperando supernam
Despicitis, quos et vecors inscitia Christi
600 Efficit inmemores, audite, precor, quod in aures
Instillante deo libuit dispergere vestras.
     Est prope Sydonias urbs nomine Biritus horas
Nec longinqua Tyro, sancita lege tributum
Urbis sceptrigero persolvens Antiochenae.
605 Hic sacre quidam purgamine mundus aquai

are mixed with it, a thick swelling rises up in his stinging 575
throat. Then the angry man suddenly does what it shames
him to have done, as rage drives him mad. He instantly re-
grets what has been done, [but] in vain, for no deed can be
undone. But thus it profits him, because remorse of heart is
not without forgiveness before men and the just Lord of 580
heaven. So did David lament the death of Uriah. To despair
does harm: Samaria saw a man, one dear to the king, one
who rejected the words of the bald prophet, die a pitiable
death when he was trampled at the gates. Let no one despair, 585
since the healing God has spoken these words from his
mouth: "I do not seek the death of the foolish; I prefer that
you turn aside from the crooked path." Saul departed from
the path of error at Damascus and ended the artifices of the
Italians and Athenians; the multitude of Stoics and the sect 590
of Academics yielded to him.

Hence also, Christ said to the key bearer of heaven whom,
when he had defeated death, he established as his faithful
shepherd, to Peter, who was asking whether forgiveness
must be imparted, whether the favor of forgiveness should
be given to neighbors three times or four times: "To you, Pe- 595
ter, I say not only to forgive a brother seven times when he
goes astray, but rather I want you to remember to observe
eleven times seven." Moreover, you who despise the hope
of heaven by despairing, you whom senseless ignorance
causes to be unmindful of Christ, hear, I beseech you, what 600
it was pleasing to sprinkle into your ears under the inspira-
tion of God.

Near the shores of Sidon and not far from Tyre, there is a
city called Beirut which pays tribute under a ratified cove-
nant to the ruler of the city of Antioch. Here a certain man 605
cleansed by the purification of holy water purchased meager

(Pauper quando sitit, non aurea pocula querit)
Exile hospicium precio mercatus, in illo
Effigiem Iesu lecti propter stacionem
Fixit, et archanos studuit ructare precatus.
610   Post hec diviciis undantibus arta potenti
Provectoque viro casa pro minimo fuit, ut fit.
Stultus et inconstans inhiat quod non habet; hoc si
Detur ei, spernat. Dominus quoque sive magister
Suspectus presens; bonus est et strenuus absens.
615   Mox utensilibus maiora ad moenia raptis
Inmemor excessit solius virginis. Hoc sic
Disponente deo. Dein contigit ut vacuati
Desertique laris pudibunda in parte minutus
Possessor fieret Iudeus. Non tamen ille
620   Continuo formam procul in caligine fixam
Norat et occultam minime speculamen ad illam
Torserat. Et dudum forsan non visa lateret,
Ni par eiusdem semel invitatus ab ipso
Omnia perlustrans latitantem cerneret illam.
625   Ilicet erumpens, "Unus de Christicolis es
Et nos fallis" ait. Quo magna negante sodales
Ad cameram ille suos qua stabat forma coegit,
Primus in arreptam festinans inpete vasto.
      Hinc hilares alii renovare nefas cupientes
630   Patrum, semiferis peiores Thracibus atque
Deterior crudis generatio prava Gelonis,
(Que pre inmunditia facinus describere duxi),
Aduersus lignum convitia multa latrabant,
Haec tandem dictis mendacibus adicientes:
635   "Si libet et dulce est, forma repetamus in ista,
Quod nostris quondam a tritavis factum est Galileo!

lodgings for a price (when a pauper thirsts, he does not ask for golden cups) and in them he hung up the image of Jesus near where his bed was standing, and strove to utter private prayers [before it]. Afterward, as wealth surged for this pow- 610 erful, exalted man, the cottage became tight and insignifi- cant, as usually happens. A foolish and fickle man gapes at what he does not have; if this should be given to him, he scorns it. Likewise, the lord or master who is present is mis- trusted; the absent one is good and energetic.

Soon, when his furniture had been carried off to larger 615 dwellings, the man departed, unmindful of the virgin alone [Jesus]. Just so did God arrange this. Then it happened that a Jew reduced in his shameful part became the owner of the empty, abandoned dwelling. However, he did not immedi- ately recognize the image fastened far off in the darkness, 620 and did not observe it concealed there. Perhaps it would have remained unseen and hidden for a long time, except that once a fellow Jew invited by him saw it lurking there as he was surveying everything. Bursting out straightway, he said: "You are one of the Christians, and you're deceiving 625 us!" While the other was loudly denying it, he urged his comrades into the room where the image was, hurrying first with great force to snatch the image.

Then the others, joyous and eager to renew the sin of their forefathers, more wicked than half-wild Thracians and a perverse generation worse than bloody Gelonians, (be- 630 cause of this filth, I have adopted [the word] "outrage" to describe it) were barking their many insults at the wooden cross, finally adding these things in their lying words: "If it is 635 pleasing and sweet, let us repeat against this image what was once done to the Galilean by our ancestors! They whitened

Illi fecerunt eius canescere vultum
Sputis et collum colaphis pulsando rubere.
Transfixis demum manibus pedibusque nocentem
640 Affixere cruci quod erat blasphemus et erro
Seque deum natumque deo falso memorabat.
Porrexere eciam sicienti fel et acetum;
Quin et acuta latus patefecit lancea eoque
Elicuit vitream commixto sanguine limpham.
645 Christicolis pascha est, sed nobis ludibrio sit."
      Talia iactantes lignumque cruci sociantes
Derisi secuere latus, sed protinus inde
Ut stabiliretur prius actum, aqua mixta cruori
Exiit, ampulla quam suscepere cadentem
650 Exsortes fidei morboque dedere gravatis.
Tunc divina salus hoc sanguine quosque respersos
Sanavit; cassos carnali lampade luce,
Surdos auditu, mutos sermone beavit;
Multos a lepra retraxit demonibusque.
655 Ante tamen cunctos datur hinc sensisse supernam
Virtutem gravidus membris paraliticus, eger
Ex quo nativa processit matris ab alvo.
His propagatis infirmi convenientes
Passim; concreti stiparunt in synagogis
660 Sanguinis ut sacri conspersio redderet ipsos
Incolomes. Tandem Iudei "Fallimur" aiunt
"Fallimur. Hic certe deus; hic est quem Hieremias
In terris visum et conversatum docet esse."
      Seque catecuminos fieri tingique petebant
665 Abiciendo suas lavacri pro veste thiaras
Nostraque laudando prepucia. Sed quoniam ista

his face with spit and made his neck red by beating with
their fists. At last, after his hands and feet were pierced, they
fastened the criminal to a cross because he was a blasphemer   640
and a vagrant and falsely said that he was God and the son
of God. Also, they offered gall and vinegar to him when he
was thirsty; furthermore a sharp lance opened his side and
from it drew forth clear water and blood mixed together.
For Christians he is the paschal lamb, but for us let him be a   645
laughingstock."

Hurling such words and attaching the wooden image to
the cross, the scoffers cut open its side, but immediately, so
that the former act might be confirmed, from there came
forth water mixed with blood, which they, men deprived of
faith, caught in a jar as it fell and gave to those burdened by   650
illness. Then divine deliverance cured whoever was sprin-
kled with this blood; it blessed those deprived of carnal sight
with light, the deaf with hearing, mutes with speech; it re-
claimed many from leprosy and from demons. However, be-   655
fore all, a paralytic oppressed in his limbs was given to expe-
rience the heavenly power from this [blood], a man diseased
from the time he came forth from the natural womb of his
mother. After these cures were made known, the sick came
together on all sides; thick crowds pressed together in the
synagogues so that the sprinkling of the sacred blood might   660
make them well. Finally, "We are mistaken," the Jews say,
"We are mistaken. This is surely God; this is he whom Jere-
miah teaches about: that he is seen in the land and dwells in
the land."

They were asking to become catechumens and to be bap-
tized by casting off their turbans in return for baptismal gar-   665
ments and by praising our foreskins. But since these things

Non sunt nota satis, sumamus que tenet usus.
Quem non confortet lapsi reparatio Petri?
Quem non soletur deprensae ereptio mechae
670 Gnarum, quod dominus prefert pietatem holocausto?
Quapropter cuncti feralis dogma Novati
Despicite et dominum conpuncto querite corde.
Cuius agi frenis libertas maxima; cuius
Mansueto servire iugo dominatio summa!

EXPLICIT LIBER SECUNDUS.

are not sufficiently known, let us take up what our experience holds fast. Whom does the restoration of the fallen Peter not strengthen? Whom does the rescue of the woman taken in adultery not comfort, knowing that the Lord prefers compassion to burnt offerings? Therefore, may you all despise the teachings of gloomy Novatus and with a remorseful heart seek the Lord. To be guided by his reins is the greatest freedom; to be subject to his gentle yoke is the highest dominion! 670

HERE THE SECOND BOOK ENDS.

I

De sobrietate et elemosinis faciendis

Hactenus infestas infami carmine sordes
Dissuasi flatus sancti karismate functis;
Nunc ad virtutes viciorum calle reductos
Allicere est animus. Sed carmen futile promo
5 Ni tu, rex agye—nec enim tibi deliquium ullum
Corda illustrandi—cui subdita copula rerum est,
Sis inbecilli columen doctorque canentis,
Ut nullus prodest ad sevi seria Martis
Pugio qui dura non cote receperit iram.
10   Quatenus a domino fragilis nobis data vita est,
Noxarumque viam tociens heu! corpore prono
Currimus, et tetri pilis succumbimus hostis,
Clementi domino iugis cerimonia detur
Sepeque ducantur nostrum sub doma carentes
15 Pastu et opermento, venerandi more Tobiae.
Quae corpus ledunt properamus reicere, et cur
Que mordent animam fulvum servamus ut aurum?
Limpha domat prunas; occulta elemosina culpas.
Si dominum vitae veneramur opumque datorem,

I

On Sobriety and Doing Charitable Deeds

Thus far in my infamous poem, through the grace of the
Holy Spirit I have dissuaded those who have engaged in
harmful filth; now it is my purpose to entice those recalled
from the path of vices to virtues. But I put forth a worthless
poem, unless you, Holy King, to whom is subject the joining 5
of all things (for you do not fail in illuminating hearts), be
the prop and the teacher of this feeble poet, for a dagger
which has not received its angry temper from hard flint
stone is of no use for the serious matters of savage war.

Since a frail life has been given to us by the Lord, and, 10
alas! so often we run with body bent forward on the way of
wrongdoing, and we succumb to the spears of the hideous
enemy, may a constant reverence be offered to the merciful
Lord and may those who lack sustenance and shelter be led
often under our roof, in the manner of venerable Tobit. We 15
hasten to reject things that harm the body, and so why do
we preserve things that vex the soul, such as yellow gold?
Water overcomes burning coals; a secret act of charity over-
comes faults. If we worship the Lord of life and giver of

20 Rebus possessis spurcae sordes abigentur;
Augebuntur opes, ut prudentissimus illud
Testatur Salomon: "Quicunque fidelis honoras
Primiciis dominum frumenti, vini oleique,
Horrea nempe gravi tua conplebuntur acervo,
25 Millenosque prement vitum tua prela racemos,
Temetumque dabunt tibi multa toreumata lene."
    Cur adeo, miseri, tot dragmas totque talenta,
Tot conferre minas mundanaque colligere aera
Conamur, bis sex obliti discipulorum
30 Qui non terrenum dubitabant spernere censum
Ruderibusque canum mucoque equare tenaci?
Credula plebs quicquid preciosum contulit illis,
Ad plantas posuit reverentia dia piorum
Pupillis, viduis, peregrinis distribuendum.
35 Quisque deo assuescat dare, sit bene prodigus usu.
Seu bona seu mala sint, durant concepta per usum.
Quam flectis virgam ventis invicta fit arbor.
    Non modico fervore dei Laurentius ardens,
Primoris cupidi iecur insaciabile ludens,
40 Ferri in craticula crudeliter oppeciit quod
Tradidit indiguis crepitantis dona monetae
Que sibi dilectus moriens mandrita reliquit,
Sanctorum auditor non surdus mandatorum.
Que dominus mandans sese comitantibus inquit:
45 "Terrenis vestros, moneo, desistite cellis
Credere thesauros, ubi vestes murice tinctas
Arrepentum avide tinearum guttura rumpunt,
Degeneratque clamis Milesia vellere caro
Neta, sed et rutilans perit aurum erugine scabra,
50 Insuper et furvi ditem fures apotecam

wealth, foul uncleanness will be removed from our posses- 20
sions; our riches will be increased, as the wisest of men, Sol-
omon, attests: "Everyone of you who faithfully honors the
Lord with the firstfruits of grain and wine and oil, cer-
tainly your granaries will be filled with a heavy heap, and 25
your winepresses will crush thousands of clusters of grapes,
and many embossed cups will offer you mellow wine."

So why, wretched men, do we attempt to gather so many
coins, so many drachmas and talents, and to collect worldly
money, forgetful of the twelve disciples who did not hesitate
to spurn earthly wealth and to compare it to dog shit and 30
to sticky mucus? Whatever valuable thing the trusting peo-
ple brought to them, the divine reverence of the pious
placed it at their feet to be distributed to orphans, widows
and strangers. Whoever grows accustomed to give to God, 35
let him be suitably lavish in practice. Whether good or bad,
ideas endure through practice. The shoot that you bend be-
comes a tree unconquered by the winds.

Inflamed by great love of God, Lawrence, mocking the
insatiable passion of a greedy prefect, died in a cruel manner 40
on a gridiron because he handed over to those in need gifts
of rattling coins that a beloved cleric, a listener who was
not deaf to the sacred commands, left to him as he was dy-
ing. Enjoining these commands upon his companions, the
Lord said: "Cease, I admonish you, to entrust your treasures 45
to earthly storerooms, where the gullets of moths eagerly
creeping in rend your garments dyed with purple, and your
Milesian cloak woven from expensive fleece deteriorates,
but also your ruddy gold is destroyed by scaly rust, and swar-
thy thieves ravage your rich warehouse besides. Rather, I 50

Devastant; potius thesauros, consulo, vestros
Transferte in caelos, ubi vermis non manet ullus,
Tarmus, gurgulio, brucus ricinusque procul sunt."
    Hec scimus, sed non sapimus, quia non facimus, nam
55 Ille sapit vere qui quae scit agenda agit. Ergo
Larga manus grandi marsupia fenore plena
Pauperet. Abraham domino mactare volebat
Heredem serum, et nos non damus extera. Cur non?
Si terrena damus, celestia suscipiemus,
60 Nec nos inanes dimittet munera dantes
Inpensi sibi non dubius retributor honoris,
Cum prope vatidicae veniet promissa Sybillae.
Numquam conficiet victus penuria largum
Pauperibus, sed non ciniflonibus et parasitis.
65   Ultra quam satis est fatuus mihi nempe videtur
Parta labore sibi quisque ut patrimonia vastet.
Ganeo gallinam nunc et modo poscit orizam,
Et cui stipatur lepori hamio, caseus ovis,
Et renuens fieri satur escas mille ligurrit.
70 Nec minus instabiles frenesis colit ille rotatus,
Boletum ut gustans insanam, aconita, cicutam,
Qui vitae nummos cupidus preponit ut is qui
Ieiunum stomachum sustentat furfure sento,
Urticas, malvas, et holuscula cetera ruris
75 Decoquit in testa, cui pressam e fecibus usque
Spongia quinquennem vappam vel trulla ministret,
Panniculisque olim villano pollice textis
Membra tegit scabieque caput sordescere linquit,
Ut nec ei funebris equi sumpta osse medulla
80 Nec queat elleborum succurrere. Vincat harenas

exhort you, transfer your treasures to heaven, where no worm abides and where woodworm, weevil, locust, and tick are far removed."

We know these counsels, but we're not wise, since we don't act on them, for that man is truly wise who does what 55 he knows should be done. Thus, a generous hand impoverishes purses full of great interest. Abraham was willing to sacrifice the heir of his old age to the Lord, and we do not give up external things. Why not? If we give up earthly goods, we shall receive heavenly ones, and no doubt the rec- 60 ompenser of the honor paid to himself will not send us, who give gifts, away empty-handed, at the time when the promise of the prophesying Sibyl will come to pass. Scarcity of provisions will never make a man generous to the poor, [nor to] hairdressers and parasites.

Besides, anyone who would waste an inheritance that he 65 acquired for himself through work certainly seems excessively foolish to me. Now the glutton demands a hen, and now rice, and for him a fish is stuffed with hare and cheese with eggs, yet refusing to be sated, he licks up a thousand foods. Nor does that frenetic whirling foster any less unsta- 70 ble people, such as the greedy man who prefers money to life while tasting a [poisonous] mushroom, henbane, aconite, or hemlock, like the one who supports an empty stomach with rough bran, and cooks nettles, mallows, and other little vegetables of the field in an earthen pot, for whom 75 a sponge or a small ladle always serves five-year-old wine pressed from dregs, and who covers his limbs with little patches once woven by a villein's thumb, and allows his head to grow filthy with mange, so that neither marrow taken from the bone of a dead horse nor hellebore can help him. 80

Diviciis, "satis est" non umquam dicet avarus.
Quid quod cum in templo sacratas aspicit aras
Participumque dei suffragia poscere debet,
Curas eversa sibi sub tellure repostum

85 Iactat ad es, animae oblitus, dum proh dolor! eius
Spes, metus atque dolor rapit et petulantia mentem?
Hi sunt qui capiunt Loth despoliantque Gomorram.
Spiritus at noster, si a vero poscit amari
Melchisedech, fuget hos ter senis atque trecentis.

90   Inmoderata ligant viciosos vincla: tenetur
Hic luxu nimio, rictu ille cupidinis. Est qui
Lucris occultus miseram plantagine vitam
Ducat et omnigenis pascatur agrestibus herbis
Collectis, numerans emblemata fulta lapillis.

95 Et si forte obolus libram curtaverit absens,
Abiciens abacum "Ve" clamat terque quaterque;
Si quicquam superat, "Res sacratissima, salve,
Salve aurum, salve minio rubicundius, instar
Solis inaccessi, celesti clarius igne.

100 Nil te absente queo;" balbuttit "tu mihi vitam
Prestas," et labiis ridentibus oscula figit,
Figit et obtutus, o dira cupido, frequentes.

    Contra cui quondam millena fuere relicta
Iugera conpressis oculis in morte paternis,

105 Quique sibi centum vini manare trapetis
Vidit carradas et, regia copia, ter sex
Edes turritas habitabat et oppida celsa:
Nocturnis, cornu nil iam tribuente, rapinis
Vescitur. In cenum quale exercere cavillum

Let him surpass the sands with his riches, a greedy man will never say, "It's enough." What of the fact that when he looks at consecrated altars in church and ought to beg aid of God's helpers, he casts his cares toward money buried under the 85 overturned earth, forgetful of his soul, while, O the pain of it!, hope and fear, sorrow and wantonness ravage his mind? These are the ones who capture Lot and plunder Gomorrah. But our spirit, if it asks to be loved by the true Melchizedek, puts them to flight with 318 men.

Boundless chains fetter vicious men: this one is held by 90 excessive luxury, that one by the gaping mouth of desire. Here is one who, buried by wealth, leads a miserable life and is nourished by a plantain and every kind of wild herb gathered from the fields, while counting his sculpted reliefs inlaid with gems. And if by chance he's one penny in the red, 95 he throws aside his counting board and cries "Woe" three or four times; if there is any profit at all, "Hail most holy profit, hail gold, hail image of the unapproachable sun, redder than vermilion, brighter than heavenly fire, I can do 100 nothing without you," he stammers, "You give me life," and with smiling lips he kisses it and frequently fixes his gaze on it. O dread desire!

On the other hand, one who had a thousand acres left to him once his parents' eyes were pressed shut in death, and 105 who saw a hundred cartloads of wine flow from his presses and—a regal abundance!—who used to reside in eighteen turreted houses and lofty towns: now, when the horn [of Plenty] bestows nothing on him, he feeds on nocturnal

110 In pollente solet clarum prope dogma Boeti,
Fortuna vertente rotam quia multus honos et
Mobilis abscessit tantarum opulentia rerum.
Namque hic luxuriae percussus cuspide crassa
Sedulo pavones turdosque comedit et exlex
115 Pastillos faciens gracili sibi pollice pinsi
"Pascant agricolas" ait "hordeum, avena, siligo."
Iugiter in madidis vinaria tota popinis
Evacuare studens, veteri modo pretulit hornum
Vinum, trina modo laudavit dolia; sepe
120 Exsiccans perna fauces hillisque Lyeum
Vitis Amineae pateris ingentibus hausit
Evertitque cados donec iam Cecuba pleno
Redderet e baratro. Sic nil medium viciosis
Ignaris verbi Graecorum "Meaga." Quid
125 Ergo? Inter geminas angusto tramite valles
Pergamus caute; si nondum excelsa timemus,
Precipiti e clivo caput ad collis redeamus:
Rictibus illicitis, hoc est, cessemus hiare,
Divicias partas consumere ventre voraci,
130 Sed stipe non nimia mediocri et tegmine fultus
Absistat nebulo vel avarus dicier. Eia,
Quicquid opermentis, quicquid superest alimentis,
Hoc, repeto, modicis contenti demus egenis.
　　Ex hoc more, stilo veraci credite, bina
135 Commoda provenient, cor purum corporis atque
Grata valetudo. Sic gibbi dempta gravantis
Sarcina permisit per acum transire camelum,
Utpote Zacheum. Multi ob ieiunia pallent,

plunder. When Fortune turns her wheel toward the mud, 110
what a plaint is he wont to exercise against the one who
thrives, according to the famous teaching of Boethius, since
his great glory and the transitory opulence of such great
possessions has vanished. For indeed, this man pierced by
the thick spear of excess eagerly consumes peacocks and
thrushes and, exempt from rules, while causing little rolls 115
to be pounded out for him with a slender thumb, he says
"Let barley, oats, and winter wheat feed peasants." While
constantly striving to empty entire jugs of wine in sodden
eating-houses, recently he preferred this year's wine to the
old, then he praised three-year-old jars; often making his 120
throat dry with ham and sausages, he drank up the wine of
Aminea from huge bowls and turned bottles upside down
until at last he vomited Caecuban wine from his full maw.
Thus moderation means nothing to vicious men who are ig-
norant of the proverb of the Greeks: "Nothing to excess." 125
What then? Let us proceed cautiously on a narrow path
through twin valleys; if we do not yet fear the heights, let us
return from the steep slope to the top of the hill: that is, let
us stop gaping with our lawless mouths wide open, let us
stop devouring our acquired wealth in a voracious belly, but 130
let the man supported by a modest donation and in ordinary
clothes cease to be called a wastrel or a miser. Ah, whatever
is left of the clothes, whatever is left of the food, let us, con-
tent with a little, give this, I repeat, to those in need.

Trust the pen that conveys truth: from this custom will
come two good things, a pure heart and pleasing health 135
of body. So, when the burden of the hump weighing it
down has been removed, it permits a camel to pass through
a needle, as, for instance, Zacchaeus. Many men are pale

Ceu semper maratrum comedant potentve cuminum,
140 Sed male ieiunat, qui nil largitur egenti.
    Tercius Henricus Romane sceptriger arcis
"Frange tuum panem, deus hoc iubet, esurienti
Et nudos operi" mira est pietate secutus,
Intendens placare deum et precidere culpas
145 Tempore quo multis spoliavit civibus orbem
Inportuna fames et mille cadavera stravit.
Nonnullosque malis marcentibus ipse paterno,
Sintagma egregium, recreavit more pusillos.
Preterea innumeros nummis aluisse diurnis
150 Dicitur ille niger donec discesserit annus.
Felix qui nunc dat, quia posthac centuplum habebit.
Qui serit ille metet mature tempore messis.
    Nunc, deus, ut frugi carmen mihi suggere dignum
Patricii pia facta canam qui tempore eodem
155 Permultos pulso laeti precone refecit.
Inter quos macrum decrassavit Beradontem,
Qui languens Spire, gravis est ubi spiritus aure,
Viginti exsequiis, dictu miserabile, tandem est
Semianimis mixtus; lethargusque inpulit illum
160 Ignorare ubi sit, donec radiante diei
Lampade subducta monstravit cornua luna.
Tum circumspiciens "Ubi sum?" prorupit, at illi
Quidam suspirans e pectore reddidit ista:
"Suspice quam lata miseris recubamus in urna
165 Mixti funeribus; proiectus heri huc sum et ego exspes."
"Annon est tibi mens supera ad convexa redire?"

because of fasting, as if they always eat fennel or drink
cumin, but the man who bestows nothing on the needy fasts   140
improperly.

Henry III, ruler of the Roman citadel, with wondrous
compassion followed [the command to] "break your bread
for the hungry—God orders this—and cover the naked."
He intended to appease God and to take away faults at the
time when cruel famine robbed the world of many citizens   145
and stretched out a thousand corpses. And while men were
enfeebled from ills, he cared for some little ones in a fatherly
way—an excellent example! Moreover, he is said to have
supported countless folk with a daily allowance of money   150
until that somber year had passed away. Happy the man who
gives now, since he will have a hundredfold hereafter. He
who sows [now] will reap in the season of ripe harvest.

Now, God, suggest to me a worthy song, so that I may
sing of the pious deeds of the virtuous patrician who at that
same time refreshed many people after the herald of death   155
was banished. Among these he fattened Beradon, an emaci-
ated man who, lying feeble at Speyer, where the breath of
air is heavy, finally was mixed in, half-dead—deplorable to
say!—with twenty corpses; and his lethargy caused him not
to know where he was, until the moon showed her horns   160
when the shining lamp of day was removed. Then looking
around, he burst out with "Where am I?" But a certain man,
heaving a sigh from his chest, answered him in these words:
"See how we are lying intermingled with pitiable corpses in
a spacious burial urn; I was thrown down here yesterday, and   165
I am without hope." "Isn't it your intention to return to the
world above?"

"Non, quia dira fames, quae tam seva inminet orbi,
Nec me preteriet." "Tumulus non est mihi tanti
Ut iam sponte velim licet egram amittere vitam.
170 Si mala nunc fero, cum volet haec deus auferet a me,
Et quondam graviora tuli." Dumque ista vicissim
Reddunt, aurora premissa sol rutilantes
Producens radios nocturnas depulit umbras.
Hic Beradon clamat "Vivo!" ingeminatque per echo
175 "Vivo, nec infesta ceu cetera condita pubes
Morte cubans gravor." Hinc stupefacti pretereuntes.
Accurrere alacres et adhuc spirare videntes
E fossa adnexo fune eripuere misellum.
Huic predictus herus multisque stipendia fertur
180 Suppeditasse aliis. Factum hoc omnes imitari
Christicolas (hoc enim vite deducit ad aulam)
Hortor. Nam capiet, veluti porrigo, tenaces
Inferus, at domini celestis curia largos,
Quosque docere potest memorans de divite Lucas.
185   Sepius emendant incautum dampna aliena,
Flammarumque minae vicino ardente timentur.
Ergo curemus ne nos involvat avaros
Vortex Tartareus, sed luxuriam fugientes
Mammoneamque aciem faciat pausare per evum
190 Altithronus rector, cui regnum et gloria perpes.
De dandi virtute parum videor monuisse;
Sufficiant tamen hec prudentibus atque modestis.

"No, since the dreadful famine that so cruelly menaces the world will not pass me by." "A cairn is not worth so much to me that I'm now willing to lose my life, though it be a feeble one, of my own accord. If I endure evils now, God will 170 take these away from me when he wills, and I have borne worse before." And while they exchanged those words with one another, the sun, leading forth its reddish rays as the dawn went on ahead, drove away the shadows of night. This Beradon cries out, "I'm alive!" and an echo repeats it, "I'm 175 alive, and I'm not weighed down by savage death like the other young men lying piled up here." Men passing by were astonished by this. They ran to him quickly and, seeing him still breathing, they tied a rope to the wretched man and rescued him from the ditch. The aforementioned lord is said to have given contributions to this man and many others. I 180 urge all Christians to imitate this action (for this leads us to the audience chamber of life). Indeed, hell, like the mange, will take hold of grasping people, but the celestial court of the Lord will receive generous men, and those whom Luke can teach when he tells about the rich man.

Very often another's losses reform an incautious man, and 185 threats of fire are feared when a neighbor's place is burning. Therefore, let us take care that the vortex of Tartarus not carry us off in our avarice, but as we flee from excess and the battle line of Mammon, may the ruler throned on high grant us rest forever. To him belong dominion and everlast- 190 ing glory. I seem to have advised very little about the virtue of giving; however, let these words suffice for wise and modest men.

2

De eo, quod valde
resistendum sit libidini

Cede pudicitiae, iam cede, profana libido;
Prepes abi, pete triste chaos! Mergaris abysso.
195 Ambrosiam pollere ducem sine; ad horrida vade
Tartara et evanesce velut ventosa favilla,
Neu studeas populo gratam te adhibere fideli,
Feda lues, nec enim domino fide sociasti
Non modica Sodomas opera tua vota sequentes.
200   Haec pensans omnis sit pectore castus et ore.
Turpia non referat qui turpibus abstinet actis,
Ne puer aut simplex qui talia nescit ephebus
Verbis corruptus mollescat et avia temptet.
Scedula morsa cani docet illum rodere pelles.
205 Atque hinc doctrina caros deus imbuit ista:
"Suadeo, principio: lumbos precingite vestros,"
Ac si sic dicat: cum in vos obscena libido
Dimicat et sevis cremat ignibus ilia, docti
Parcite continuis escis et potibus; atqui
210 Crapula et ebrietas lascivi est fomes amoris:
Ex crebra ingluvie veniunt amor, ocia, risus.
Ocia mortificant animam; studium educat illam,
Atque bono studio damnosa vacatio tantum
Quantum a boglosso Lethea papavera distant.

2

Concerning the Fact That Lust
Must Be Strongly Resisted

Yield to modesty, yield now, impious lust; depart swiftly and seek the gloomy underworld! May you be plunged into the 195 abyss. Allow our immortal lady-leader to prevail; go to horrid Tartarus and vanish like ashes in the wind, and do not strive to appear pleasing to people of faith, foul plague, for you have not united to the Lord in faith the people of Sodom who follow your wishes with no little effort.

While pondering these words, let every man be chaste in 200 his heart and in speech. Let one who refrains from shameful deeds not recount shameful stories, lest a boy or a simple youth who doesn't know such things, corrupted by such talk, might become unmanly and attempt acts not attempted before. A strip [of leather] bitten by a dog teaches it to gnaw hides. And hence God instructs his dear ones 205 with this doctrine: "I exhort you first of all: gird your loins," as if he might speak thus: when obscene lust struggles against you and burns your private parts with fierce flames, be wise and abstain from continuous food and drink; certainly inebriation and drunkenness are the tinder of lascivi- 210 ous passion: from frequent gluttony come passion, idleness, and laughter. Idleness kills the soul; exertion nourishes it, and destructive leisure differs from good endeavors as much as the poppies of Lethe differ from oxtongue.

215   Qua labor est iugis, venarum flamma residit.
       Cerdo suat, scribat scriba, agros rusticus aptet,
       Clericus insudet libris nec siquid in illis
       Reppererit quod non promte occurrat sibi cesset.
       Non semper talus quod lusor postulat edit;
220   Sepe optata absunt, cum non optantur, habentur.
       Psalmi eciam prosunt; prece turpis deficit ardor
       Ut stipule ardenti seu stuppa iniecta camino,
       Aut ut in ignitis plumbum grave liquitur ollis.
       Quod sequitur post hoc, "Ardentes ferte lucernas,"
225   Gregorius sapiens sic digerit esse lucernas
       Flammigeras perhibens factorum exempla bonorum.
       Os igitur regat et referat bona mente pudicus,
       Nam bona agens et prava loquens sic acta tuentes
       Detinet, ut laborinthus, inextricabilis error.
230   Qui viridem et mundum se servat eo redit unde
       Venerat ut ramus curvatus moxque remissus.
           Mundicia domino magis acceptabile nil est.
       Hac illi Ioseph placuit celebrisque Susanna;
       Hac vindex iustus Phinees Iuditque severa.
235   Ergo diabolicis nolite locum dare factis,
       Credentes, nam sepe facit peccare facultas.
       Respuit incestos, quem virgo Maria profudit
       Non fantasmaticum, velud affirmat Manicheus,
       Nam vagit, sugit, crescit de virgine natus.
240   Quid mirabilius? Que plus ignota leguntur?
       Nullus apud veteres genitus de virgine fertur,
       Non Plato barbatus, non bello crudus Achilles,

Where there is continual toil, the fire in the blood sub- 215
sides. Let the cobbler stitch, the copyist copy, the peasant
prepare the fields, the cleric sweat over his books and not
give up if he has found something in them that does not
come to him readily. The dice does not always produce what
the player wants; often we lack things we want, but when 220
they're not wanted, we have them. The Psalms are also bene-
ficial; through prayer, shameful passion disappears like straw
or flax thrown into a fiery furnace, or just as heavy lead melts
in glowing-red pots. What follows after this, "Bring burning
lamps," the wise Gregory, calling them flame-bearing lamps, 225
so interpreted them to be examples of good deeds. There-
fore, let the man chaste in mind govern his tongue, and let
him recount good deeds, for by doing good deeds and talk-
ing about bad ones, just like a labyrinth, an inextricable
maze, he holds back those observing his actions. One who 230
keeps himself fresh and clean returns to the place whence
he came like a branch that has been bent and released right
away.

Nothing is more acceptable to the Lord than cleanliness.
Through this, Joseph and the renowned Susanna pleased
him; through this, Phineas, the just avenger, and stern Ju-
dith [pleased him]. So, believers, do not afford a place to di- 235
abolical deeds, for often an opportunity causes us to commit
sins. He rejected lewd men, the one whom the Virgin Mary
brought forth—not a phantasm, as a Manichean affirms, for,
born of a virgin, he cried, he sucked, he grew.

What is more wondrous? What stranger things do we 240
read? No one among the ancients is said to have been born
of a virgin, not bearded Plato, not Achilles cruel in war,

Non niveus Pallas prestanti corpore, quamquam
Anteveniret heros famosi nominis omnes;
245 Nec Caesar, quamvis opulento germine bombix
Declararet eum, nec quisquam ridiculorum
Quos pice, thure, mola coluit gens bruta deorum.
　　O Musae fragiles, o fallax nenia vatum
Qui tantum coitus transformatasque figuras
250 Finxerunt hominum! Nugas! Quid fabula Terei
Oenomaique valet, quid Horestis, quid Poliphemi?
Sic et merdosos sub merdoso Iove mille
Constituere deos illique dedere tridentem.
Si deus ille fuit, cur, Iuno, pelicibus te
255 Tot lesit dum thyrsigeras oppressit amicas,
Latonam, Ledam, Danen et Agenore natam,
Et Semelen Ioque vagam? Sed quid referam omnes?
Non decuit peccare deum, violare sororem,
Dedecus et scelus est et vi corrumpere multas.
260 Iupiter hoc egit. Deus haut fuit ergo vocandus,
Cum quem nos colimus, qui fons est metaque rerum,
Nullis infectus viciis insons habeatur.
Virginis ex utero ceu sponsus de thalamo ille
Prodiit, inque rubo versans non ussit eundem.
265 Nullus eum poterit vitanda patrasse probare,
Socratico quamquam cunctos discindere cornu
Noverit astantes, et Aristotiles fuit alter.
Nunc age, Nasoni, nunc Gallo, nunc Iuvenali
Et Parce parcant et Gratia sit pia. Verum
270 Alchimus, Arator, Sedulius atque Iuvencus

not snow-white Pallas with his superior body, although this hero of the famous name surpassed all others; not Caesar, 245 although fine silk declared him to be of wealthy stock, not any of the ridiculous gods whom the brutish gentiles worshipped with pitch, incense, and grain.

O frail muses, O false song of the seers who simply invented the unions and the transformed shapes of men! Non- 250 sense! What good is the story of Tereus and Oenomaus? What good is the story of Orestes? Or of Polyphemus? So also they created a thousand shitty gods under shitty Jove and gave to him a trident. If he was a god, why, Juno, did he betray you with so many mistresses when he bore down on 255 his thyrsus-bearing lovers, Latona, Leda, Danae, the daughter of Agenor, Semele, and wandering Io? But why should I repeat them all? It was not fitting for a god to sin, to violate a sister, and it is a disgrace and a crime to seduce many women by force. Jupiter did this. Thus, he scarcely ought to 260 have been called a god, since the one whom we worship, who is the origin and the end of things, is known to be innocent, not corrupted by any vices. He came forth from the Virgin's womb like a bridegroom from the bedchamber, and abiding in a bush, he did not burn it. No one could prove 265 that he performed deeds to be shunned, although he knew how to divide all those standing by with the horn of Socrates, and he was another Aristotle. Come now, let the Fates *(Parcae)* spare *(parcant)* Ovid, Gallus, Juvenal, and may Grace be kind to them. Certainly Alcimus, Arator, Sedulius, and 270

Non bene tornatis apponunt regia vasis
Fercula. Miror eos; non audeo vituperare.
   Nunc ad rem redeo: subvertit crapula castos.
Quid Daniel celebs captivus tresque pusilli
275 Quos, que confusas testatur nomine linguas,
Rex urbis tenuit? Cum se nimis esse dolerent,
Iconomum regis sociis facundior istis
Alloquitur Daniel: "Cum pane legumina nobis
Des; non plus petimus." Cui princeps eunuchorum:
280 "Magna rogas, et quae nequeunt fieri, quia rex, si
Vos plus equevis tenuesve macrosve videbit,
Hoc caput infensus faciet mucrone recidi."
Tuncque ad Malasser, namque is spado prefuit ipsis:
"Pastu vulgari denis nos pasce diebus,
285 Cumque tuis servis facito; tunc ut fore cernes"
Dixit. At ille pii Danielis verba benignus
Auribus acceptans votis assensit, et illi
Fulsere ante alios escis genialibus altos
Pingues.
   Nunc tu mi inquis: "Omitte supersticionem hanc!
290 Sit vulgo milium, cucumis, faba, caulis inunctus,
Buccellae lagani, sed triticeam cava pastam
Sartago dominis stridat nectarque suave
Pendulus attritis destillet culleus herbis."
   Scis quid ad haec reddo? Centum sibi musta propinent,
295 Fercula mille vorent: animam cum corpore perdunt.
Quod factor coniunxit homo non separet. Esto!

Juvencus serve regal courses in vessels not well fashioned. I marvel at these men; I don't dare to find fault with them.

Now I return to the point: drunkenness ruins chaste men. What about Daniel, the unmarried captive, and the three small boys whom the king held, the king of the city which 275 attests by its name that tongues were confounded? When they grieved to have eaten to excess, Daniel, more eloquent than those companions, addressed the king's steward: "Give us beans with our bread; we do not require more." The chief 280 of the eunuchs said to him: "You ask much, and what cannot be done, because if the king sees that you are thinner and leaner than your equals in age, he will be enraged and cause this head to be cut off with a sword." Then to Melzar, for this eunuch had charge of them, Daniel said: "Feed us with ordinary food for ten days, and do this with your servants; 285 then you'll see how it will be." Then that kind man, hearing the words of the devout Daniel, assented to his wishes, and those plump boys shone more than the others who were nourished by festive foods.

Now you say to me: "Give up this superstition! For the 290 common folk let there be millet, cucumber, beans, cabbage dressed with oil, and morsels of cake, but for lords let a hollow frying pan sizzle with wheat dough and let the wine bag hanging down distill sweet nectar from crushed herbs."

Do you know what I reply to these words? Let them drink a hundred new wines for themselves, let them devour a 295 thousand courses: they are destroying the soul with the body. Let man not separate what the Maker has joined to-

Verum prostibulum vetat alteriusque maritam.
Nonne pudicicia domino fautrice placentes
Monachus et mulier? Sarracenum pharetrato
300 Agmine correpti torvos vicere leones
Quod fieri absentis rivalis noluit ille.
Namque ubi spelei subiere foramen opacum,
Lactantem catulos distentis lacte papillis
Lambentemque uda lingua invenere leenam.
305 Occulti duplici cum diriguere pavore
Ne versans homines trux bestia faucibus amplis
Deglutiret eos interficerentve sequentes.
Verum qui vatem defendit ab ore leonum
Somnia solventem, misitque cibum esurienti,
310 His quoque providit, veniens nam torva repente
Belua dirupit profugos sine more cientem.
Dein dominum pepulit mordax lea moxque recurrens
Ad nidum pullis villosis unguibus abtis
Rupe ruit ceca desolavitque cavernam,
315 Dans tuta spacium castis exire fenestra.
    Precipue Christi nos edocet esse pudicos
Mater virgo, eadem quam presignavit Aaron
Virga sacerdotis, que torrida cortice sicco
Et vegetante carens uligine protulit ex se
320 Res miranda, nuces. Christum sine semine virgo
Sic genuit, qui hominem atque deum cruce conciliavit,
Ut corium et nucleum coadunat concava testa.

gether. So be it! Certainly he forbids a prostitute and the wife of another. With modesty as their protectress, were the monk and the woman not pleasing to their master? Seized 300 by a troop of Saracens wearing quivers, they overcame fierce lions because the monk was unwilling to become the rival of her absent lover. Indeed, when they entered the dark opening of the cave, they found a lioness with teats swollen by milk suckling her whelps and licking them with her moist tongue. Hidden, they became rigid with a twofold fear lest 305 the ferocious beast, turning her gaze upon men, might swallow them with her great jaws, or those in pursuit might kill them. Certainly, the one who defended from the mouth of lions the prophet who explained dreams, and sent food to the hungry prophet, also provided for them, for coming sud- 310 denly, the fierce beast dashed to pieces without restraint the one calling the fugitives. Then the snarling lioness attacked their master and, soon returning to her home, she rushed from the dark cavern seizing her young in her furry claws and abandoned the cave, giving the chaste ones a space to 315 leave through a secure opening.

The Mother of Christ especially teaches us to be pure, this same virgin whom Aaron presignified with a priest's rod, which of itself, parched, with dry bark and lacking life-giving moisture, produced almonds—a wondrous thing! So, 320 without seed, the Virgin gave birth to Christ, who, by the cross, reconciled man and God, just as a hollow shell unites the covering and the kernel.

3

De eo, quod Deus humiles diligat
et superbos contempnat

Eminus alta videt dominantum summus usias,
Quod parvum atque humile est prope respicit; ipse rogatus
325 Quondam a discipulis caeli quis maior in aula
Esset, respondit: "Sese qui mente quadrimum
Exibet, ille etenim non laude levatur inani."
Parvis acclinis si quando irascitur, uno
Ignoscit puncto; sic parvi sunt imitandi,
330 Non quod eis pepon est cuppa, et quod glarea sal est,
Quodque lutum pinsunt equitantque in fuste saligno.
Eximia est virtus popularem spernere laudem.
   Hinc est quod dominus mulcendo nos monet esse
Mites corde humiles, nostris spondens animabus
335 Tristibus amotis se gaudia leta daturum.
Quod si blanda dei nostris secludere verba
Auribus audemus, iam non mulcendo minatur:
"Vergit et ima petit qui se autumat esse supremum."
Scissa dei populo vada submersere superbos;
340 Milicia Iosephi madefacta est Iamnia caesa.
   Eheu, cur, homo, te sustollis inaniter atque
Ut vesica tumens cito quae displosa fatiscit?
Non te titillet reverentia vana vocatus

3

Concerning the Fact That God Loves the Humble and Despises the Proud

The highest of the rulers of all that is views lofty things from afar, but what is small and lowly, he regards up close; once asked by his disciples who would be greater in the court of 325 heaven, he replied: "The one who shows himself to be four years old at heart, certainly he is not lifted up by empty praise." If ever one well disposed to little ones is angry, he forgives them in an instant; so should little ones be imitated, not because to them a melon is a cup and snot their season- 330 ing, nor because they play patty cake with mud and ride on willow-wood clubs. [But because] to scorn popular praise is an outstanding virtue.

Thus it is that the Lord, addressing us kindly, advises us to be meek and humble of heart, promising that he will give blessed joys to our souls, with sorrows taken away. But if we 335 dare to shut out the soothing words of God from our ears, then, not lightening our burdens, he threatens: "The man who asserts that he is highest sinks and falls to the bottom." The sea that was divided for God's people submerged the proud; after the army of Joseph was slaughtered, Jamnia was 340 drowned.

Alas, why, O mankind, do you raise yourself up vainly and like a swollen balloon that bursts and quickly gapes open? Do not let a false sense of dignity titillate you when you are

Quisquis es ad taedas, ne, si tu in parte locaris
345 Iniussus prima, meliore superveniente
Amoveare rubens ineasque novissima merens.
Vivite, mortales, contriti corde nec este
Ore columbae et mente lupi, ceu plurima pars est!
Quales sunt qui, cum pupilla demere tardant
350 Tignum de propria, festucam fratris abhorrent,
Pendentemque retro clitellam appendere nolunt.
Omnibus est viciis fastus violentior, ergo
Qui fugat illum a se pollebit stemate primo.
Quanto maiorem pugilem pugil alto in Olympo
355 Cursu vel disco seu cestu sive palestra
Vicerit, ut dignum est, tanto maiora sequentur
Premia. Qui vere contritus vivit amicus
Est domini, at pravis tantum est onus atque superbis,
Quantum asino modius gravis, asper vitricus orbis.
360   Ut servanda caro sale non condita putrescit,
Sic et virtutes putere solent nisi custos
Ista frequenter eas exasperet, aut vigor artus
Deficit humanos cum solis Cancer anhelat
Igne, et pestiferas ruber adfert Sirius idus,
365 Horrisonaque replent algosas voce paludes
Ranarum strepitus, et strident dulce cicadae,
Lucifugaeque volant acclini vespere blattae,
Ni siccam exhaustus situla grandive cucullo
Fons puteusve gulam corroboret: haut secus omnes
370 Virtutes pereunt arentes igne tumoris,
Ni vero de fonte fluens contricio crebra
Assit et humorem siccis ferat. Hac pietate

invited to a wedding, whoever you are, lest, if you are seated in the first place unbidden, you be removed, red with shame, 345 when a better man arrives, and you sadly go to the very last place. O mortals, live contrite of heart and do not live with the face of a dove and the mind of a wolf, as most people do! Such are those who, while they are slow to remove the beam from their own eye, shudder at the mote in a brother's [eye], 350 and they are unwilling to weigh the pack hanging down behind [them]. Pride is more aggressive than all the vices, and so the man who drives it away from himself will win the first garland. The greater the athlete whom a champion defeats on lofty Olympus in running or with the discus or boxer's 355 glove or in wrestling, so much greater are the rewards that follow, as is fitting. The man who lives truly contrite is a friend of the Lord, but for the wicked and the proud, the burden is as great as a heavy bushel for an ass, a harsh stepfather for orphans.

Just as meat that is not seasoned and preserved with salt 360 becomes rotten, so also virtues are wont to rot unless this preserver frequently provokes them, or [as] liveliness abandons human limbs when the Crab gasps with the heat of the sun, and the reddish Dog Star brings forth its pestilential days, and the noisy din of frogs fills the weedy swamps 365 with horrid croaking, and cicadas sweetly creak, and lightshunning bugs are flying in the fading sunset, unless a spring or well water drawn in a bucket or a large cup refreshes the dry gullet: even so do all virtues perish, parched by the fire 370 of pride, unless frequent contrition flowing from the true fountain is present and brings moisture to them when they

Iesus apud Gabaon elementis imperitavit;
Hac Ruth freta Booz nubsit Moabitis, et hec res
375   Cognatum belle Susis erexit Edisse.
　　　Hanc inferniculae plus omnibus esse molestam
Virtutum gemmis quis clarent corda bonorum,
Qui dubitat, sacro quod vidi in codice pendat
"Vita patrum" dicto. Quidam venerabilis abbas
380   Nomine Macharius, meritis dignissimus, omnes
Rite suos docuit cilium deponere torvum,
Pectore se reputans humili minimo esse minorem,
Addit ut in bello dux vires militibus cum
Iunctus signifero densas perfringere turmas
385   Ante alios fervet, clipeo thoraceque tutus
Cominus hos framea necat, amento eminus illos.
Nominat hos, illos hortatur ut acria pugnent,
Eniochos imitans feriendo trucesque Suevos.
Hoc animata phalanx facto fit agillima pugnae,
390   Aclidas atque sparos crispans sevosque dolones.
At si deiectum formidantemque pericla
Aspexere ducem comites, et Martia virtus
Lenta manet, cessant dubii vertantur an obstent.
Sicque fit ut capti mutilentur, collaque bogae
395   Primatum stringant nisi censum sive vades dent.
　　　Non secus hac virtute suos precesserat omnes
Doctor Macharius, quo sic devocius eius
Exemplo fierent obnoxia pectora fratrum.
Angelus huic teter, quem rector Apollion Orci
400   Miserat, occurrens falcem gestavit acutam.
Vibrato minitans fatum crudele lacerto
Ac ringendo loquens: "O si te conficere, abba,

are dry. Through this piety Joshua commanded the elements at Gibeon; relying on this [piety], Ruth the Moabite married Boaz, and this raised up the kinsman of lovely Esther 375 at Susa.

Let one who doubts that this is irksome to the denizen of hell, more than all the gems of virtues through which shine the hearts of good people, consider what I have seen in a holy book called *The Life of the Fathers.* A certain venerable abbot named Macarius, a man most deserving of rewards, 380 duly taught all his followers to give up their fierce arrogance, since in his humble heart he considered himself lower than the lowest man, as in war a general adds to the strength of his soldiers when, allied with the standard-bearer, before others he is burning to break through the dense battle lines 385 and, protected by his shield and breastplate, he kills these with his sword in close combat, those at a distance with his sling. He calls these men by name, encourages those to fight fiercely, imitating the Heniochi and savage Swabians in slaying. When he does this, the infantry becomes spirited and most eager for battle, brandishing javelins and small spears 390 and cruel pikes. But if his comrades have seen their leader downcast and terrified of danger, and if his martial spirit remains sluggish, they stop, uncertain whether to turn back or take a stand, and so it happens that, captured, they are maimed, and chains bind the necks of their officers unless 395 they offer gifts or sureties.

In like manner Macarius the teacher surpassed all his followers in this virtue, so that the frail hearts of his brothers might become more devout through his example. A hideous angel whom Apollyon, ruler of the lower regions, had 400 sent rushed up to him wielding a sharp sickle. He shook his arm, threatened cruel death and, snarling, he said: "O Fa-

Audeat excelso lapsorum sydere quisquam,
Contra quos bellum est credentibus, hic tibi pronum
405 Certo dividerem tactu caput. Unica res est
Qua,—loquar an sileam?—cives precedis Avernos."
    Cui sanctus comi subridens reddidit ore:
"Ergo te adiuro per cui in presepe iacenti
Mistica dona deo reges tribuere Sabei,
410 Ut mihi rem lingua falsum vitante reveles."
Ille refert: "Ter in ebdomada non uteris esca,
Ast ego ieiunus per secula cuncta manebo
Et mansi et maneo. Media expergiscere nocte,
Semper ego vigilo. Sic cum sim maior in his te,
415 Tu maior nobis humili sub mente videris.
Nec nego nec valeo." Nullus falsis inimicum
Laudibus extollit. Quid apertius hac sine quam quod
Omnes virtutes virtute ruunt quasi murus
Si fundamento caret, aut domus absque columna?

4

De statu animae et
excellentia carnis

420 Quisque deo natus non peccat. Quomodo natus?
Non sicut quidam stulti credunt de anima, quod
Sit natura dei vel portio, nos deus ut sic

ther, if any of those who have fallen from the stars on high, against whom believers wage war, should dare to kill you, I would now split your bent head with a sure blow. There is 405
one thing in which—should I speak or be silent?—you surpass the denizens of hell."

Smiling at him with an affable smile, the saint replied: "Therefore, I adjure you through the one to whom the kings of Sheba offered mystical gifts to God as he lay in a manger, that you reveal to me this matter with a tongue that avoids 410
falsehood." He answers: "You do not take food three times in a week, but for all ages I shall remain and have remained and do remain fasting. You get up in the middle of the night, but I am always awake. So, although I am greater in these than you, you seem greater than us due to your humble 415
mind. I do not deny it, nor can I." No one extols his enemy with false praises. What is clearer than the fact that without this virtue, all virtues tumble down like a wall if it lacks a foundation, or a house without a supporting pillar?

4

On the State of the Soul and the Excellence of the Flesh

Whoever is born of God does not sin. How is he born? Not 420
as certain fools believe about the soul, that it is God's nature or a portion of God, so that God might thus be said to beget

Gignere dicatur. Scelus est hoc credere, nam cum
Eternus deus et mutabilitate carens sit,
425 Pars nequit esse dei quae delinquendo vacillat,
Nec valet esse deus quae seve obnoxia penae est.
De qua sic Augustinus doctor catus inquit:
"Non anima ex anima generatur, sed deus illam
Infundit carni formatae, sic microcosmum
430 Constituens, sed sive creet tunc sive crearit,
Solum nosse reor factorem." Credo quod ipsa
Carni pura datur; data morti subiacet Adae,
Nec regnum domini nisi fonte renata videbit.
Scemate corporeo requie penisve fruetur.
435 A domino per naturam non nascitur ullus,
Sed quisquis vero perfectus pollet amore,
Patre deo satus est; is non peccat, quia servat
Mandatum maius mandatis omnibus, hoc est:
"Dilige corde deum, tamquam te dilige fratrem."
440 Omnes in Christo fratres sumus. Unde tonantem
Patrem appellamus nostrum communiter omnes.
Hinc nos multa loqui deceat, nisi quod preciosae
Enarrans animae sententia longa salutem
Paucis accepta est. Pro cura corporis omnis
445 Delectat species medicandi discere mille,
Ut tolles ebulus fuget, utque agrimonia morbum
Tres collecta dies et decantata caducum,
Pentafilon dissenteriam, centauria febrem.
Heu, rari de anima plus quam de corpore curant!
450 Ut placeant forma terrenis luxuriosi,
Membra vaporiferis cogunt albescere termis;
Comere non cessant crines non ora lavare.

us. To believe this is wicked, for since God is eternal and lacking mutability, nothing can be a part of God that wavers by doing wrong, nor is that able to be God which is sub- 425 ject to harsh punishment. Concerning this, the wise teacher Augustine spoke as follows: "A soul is not produced from a soul, but God pours it into flesh that has been formed, thus creating a microcosm, but as to whether he created 430 [the soul] then or had already created it, I think that only the Maker [himself] knows." I believe that this soul is given to the flesh in a pure state; once given, it is subject to the death of Adam, and it will not see the Lord's kingdom un- less reborn through water. In its corporeal form it reaps the fruits of repose or punishments. No one is born of the Lord 435 through nature, but whoever is strong, perfect in true love, is begotten by God the Father; he does not sin, since he keeps the commandment greater than all commandments, that is: "Love God with your [whole] heart, and love your brother as yourself."

We are all brothers in Christ. Thus we all commonly call 440 the Thunderer our father. About this it might be fitting for us to say many things, except that a long opinion explaining the salvation of the precious soul is welcome to few. For the care of the body everyone is pleased to learn a thousand forms of healing, how danewort dispels goiters, and agri- 445 mony gathered over three days and then charmed drives away the falling sickness, cinquefoil gets rid of dysentery, and centaury expels a fever. Alas! Few men care about the soul more than the body. So that extravagant people may be 450 pleasing to mortals through their beauty, they force their limbs to become white in steam baths; they don't cease to comb their hair nor to wash their faces. So that they may

Ut sese regi commendent cuncta regenti,
Fratris amore animam decorare fere piget omnes.
455   At tu, qui domino gratum te reddere mavis,
Reice livorem, fidum qui scindit amorem.
Nil satius, nil, esse puta quam velle propinqui
Velle sequi, tamen ut non laudes si male quid vult.
Qui si sit talis quod possis corripere illum,
460 Corripe et ut cesset perverse vivere suade,
Peccantemque tui memor interdum fer amice,
Non quo nequiciae concordans sis, sed ut ille
Ex virtute tuae conpungatur pietatis.
Nemo malus subito damnandus et abiciendus;
465 Dilatum lolium docet hoc dilataque ficus.
Si fratrem fervere vides bonitatis amore,
Cum superis domino catigetis sedulus ymni!
    Quanta sit et qualis dilectio, Paule, notas, cum:
"Si linguis loquar angelicis, vero sine amore,
470 Tinnio ut aes" inquis "vel sicut cimbala clango.
Si mihi veridicum cedant presagia vatum,
At cordi suavis flagrantia desit amoris,
Nil sum. Preterea si cunctas quas habeo res,
Inpensasque meas in pulmentaria et escas
475 Pauperibus prodam sine amore nichil mihi prodest.
Non inflatur amor; non ambit nec sua querit.
Omnia sustinet, omnia sperat et omnia credit."
    Quid sit amor, pulchre declarat virgo Iohannes,
In cena Christi qui triste cubando gravavit
480 Pectus: "Amor deus est, et qui manet hoc in amore
In domino manet, et dominus dignatur in illo
Dum non vult ab amore pio cessare manere."

commend themselves to an all-powerful king, it disgusts almost everyone to adorn the soul with brotherly love.

But you, who prefer to make yourselves pleasing to the 455 Lord, cast away envy, which tears faithful love apart. Consider nothing better—nothing—than to be willing to follow the will of your neighbor, yet not so that you praise him if he desires anything wicked. If one is such that you might be able to reprove him, reprove him and encourage him to stop 460 living badly, and for the time being, mindful of yourself, bear with the sinner in an amiable way not so that you may be in concord with wickedness, but so that he may feel remorse on account of the excellence of your piety. No evil man should be suddenly condemned and cast aside; the cockle 465 that was preserved teaches this, and the fig that was saved. If you see your brother burning with the love of virtue, be zealous; with the catechists on high, sing praises to the Lord!

Paul, you indicate how great love is, and what kind, when you say: "If I speak with the tongues of angels, but without love, I sound like brass, or I clang like a cymbal. If the pre- 470 dictions of the truth-telling prophets yield to me, but the sweet ardor of love is absent from my heart, I am nothing. Beyond this, if I should give all that I possess, and all my expenditures on relishes and food to the poor, without love it 475 profits me nothing. Love is not puffed up; it is not ambitious and seeks not its own. Love bears all things, hopes all things, believes all things."

What love is, that virgin John who burdened the sorrowful breast of Christ by reclining there at the [Last] Supper declares beautifully: "God is love, and he who abides in this 480 love abides in the Lord, and the Lord deigns to abide in him while he does not wish to desist from pious love."

Nunc age, virtutem caelumque ascendere tempta!
Ut volitare nequit cauteris saucius ictu
485 Ales, ita invidiae quem dira sagitta retardat
Emulus ad caeli pertingere non valet aulam,
Et licet expresse trinum fateatur et unum.
Quisquis amore nitet, virtutes nundinat omnes
Collectasque tenet, virtutum nuncius ille est.
490 Edituus levi cum tintinnabula ferro
Pulsat et accendit candelam, tum bene sanum
Vulgus adest humerisque gerit suspensa sinistris
Pallia, summisso venerans altaria vultu.
Haut dubiique manent celebrandae munia missae,
495 Quos premissa cavi vox invitaverat aeris.
Pantherae ad vocem maculosae confluit omnis
Bestia, tortus item sub tofis se draco condit,
Cum tamen ingentes barros necet et cocodrillum.
Tempore cum verno cornus vel quelibet arbos
500 Producit fructum reparatis frondibus, estas
Pulverulenta gelu terras linquente propinquat,
In pacis signum caelo deus indidit Irim:
Sic et amiciciae cantum cum cor modulatur
Et viridi frondet claroque resplendet amore,
505 Omnigenis illud Christus virtutibus implet.
Quare nemo agitet fratrem zelo nisi iusto,
Quo Moyses aurum venerantes, quo Baalites
Tehbsites, Danielque vafer Beli famulantes.
Virtutem hanc semper qui vultis habere, dicatum
510 Christo basilicum persepe petatis asylum,
Et lacrimis abolete notas. Fuit utile regi
Pro vita tinxisse genas, deus annuet et nunc
Suppliciis vestris, modo sit conpunctio vera.

Come now, try virtue and climbing to heaven! Just as a
bird wounded by the blow of the arrow cannot fly, so also a   485
jealous man whom the dread arrow of envy hinders is not
able to reach the court of heaven, even if he clearly confesses
the trinity and unity [of God]. Whoever shines with love,
whoever procures all the virtues and keeps those he has ac-
quired, that man is the herald of virtues.

When the sacristan strikes the bells with a smooth iron   490
and lights the candle, then the respectable crowd ap-
proaches and wears cloaks suspended from their left shoul-
ders as with heads bowed they do homage to the altars.
Those whom the sound sent forth from the hollow bronze
has summoned await the office of the mass to be celebrated   495
without hesitating. Every beast crowds together at the cry
of the spotted panther, and likewise the coiled serpent con-
ceals itself under the rocks, although it kills mighty ele-
phants and the crocodile. In springtime, when the cornel
cherry or any tree at all produces fruit after its foliage is re-   500
vived, and when frost forsakes the land and the dusty sum-
mer is nigh, as a sign of peace God places Iris [the rainbow]
in the sky: so also, when the heart sings a song of friendship
and puts forth green leaves and shines with bright love,   505
Christ fills it with every kind of virtue.

Therefore, let no one reprove his brother except with the
righteous zeal, with which Moses [reproved] those worship-
ing gold, the Thisbite [Elijah] the prophets of Baal, and sly
Daniel the servants of Bel. You who wish to keep this vir-
tue always should very often seek a basilica consecrated to   510
Christ as a refuge, and wash away your marks of infamy with
tears. It was useful for a king to bathe his cheeks [with tears]
for his life, and now God will approve your supplications, as

Qui pius armilla malam perfodit hiulcam
515 Leviathan, ut qui se faucibus illius indunt
Peccando culpas deflendo evadere possint.
    Ergo relaxemus cunctis peccantibus in nos,
Si volumus, nobis deus ut peccata remittat.
Tunc eius nutu nostro bene pactio quadrat.
520 Sic fecit rex qui de inimicorum nece flevit;
Ardentem deus hunc, fratres sociumque popellum
Multimodis compsit virtutibus. Ipse et in alta
Unanimes habitare domo dat. Regula amoris
Exigit hoc: alii ne faxis quod tibi non vis,
525 Quodque cupis tibimet, fratri nichilominus optes.
    Novi quid referas. "Mihimet sum proximus" inquis.
Non decet Esopi figmenta salesve Terenti
Scripturis miscere sacris. Qui recte amat illi,
Vilescit topici cumulata pecunia regni;
530 Nil amat in terra nisi semper adire sacellum,
Apte phosforeae quod ad instar ducitur urbis.
Illa velut glaucis inimico sole coruscat,
Non mutando diem, sed continuando perennem,
Sic hec continuis aperitur mansio licnis,
535 Utque animas gremio leni fovet illa piorum,
Sic hec ossa tenet populo veneranda labanti.
Sumitur hic corpus celesti in sede tonantis,
Utque ibi diversis astant animalia formis
Quatuor aeternum laudantia carmine regem,
540 Sic in sacratis pinguntur murice muris.

long as there is true remorse. One who is pious pierces the gaping jaw of Leviathan with a hook, so that those who place themselves in his throat by sinning are able to escape by bewailing their faults. 515

Therefore, let us forgive all who sin against us, if we want God to remit our sins. Then his covenant rightly squares with our will. That's what the king who wept over the death of his enemies did; God adorned this ardent one, his brothers, and kindred populace with manifold virtues. And he allows those of one mind to dwell in a house on high. The rule of love demands this: that you not do unto another what you do not want [done to] yourself, and what you wish for yourself, you wish no less for your brother. 520 525

I know what you might reply. You say, "I am neighbor to myself." It's not fitting to mingle the fictions of Aesop or the witty sayings of Terence with sacred scripture. To one who loves rightly, the heaped-up money of this local realm is worthless; he loves nothing on earth, except always to approach the sanctuary, which is suitably introduced as an example of the shining city. Just as that city gleams in the sun that is hostile to those with bad eyes, not changing its day, but continuing the day forever, so does this dwelling lie open with its everlasting lamps, and just as that city sustains the souls of the faithful in its gentle bosom, so this one holds bones to be venerated by a people liable to err. Here the body is taken up in the heavenly seat of God, and just as four living creatures with diverse forms stand there praising the eternal King with their song, so are they painted in purple on these consecrated walls. 530 535 540

Sed quoniam nostro subscribere pauca libello
De formis horum presumpsimus, hec quoque ad huius
Ecclesiae exemplar typica signare figura
Quid valeant aperire libet. Genitricibus orti
545 Baptismum subeunt homines ut membra novelli
Sint hominis. Vituli tunc possunt iure vocari,
Cum de blandiciis viciorum pectora lenta
Virtutum stimulis agitant. Cervice leones
Sunt rigida quociens inferni tela tiranni
550 Tempnunt. In verum nitentia lumina solem
Cum figunt aquilae. Sic oratoria nostra
Haec docili depicta tenent animalia penna.
Ista igitur voto lugubri quisque frequentet
Qui gaudere cupit subtractis sordibus illic,
555 Et cum psalmista prostratus iugiter oret:
"A domino quiddam petii quod sepe requiram,
Ut me habitatorem capiat domus eius." Ad illam
Semita iusticiae ducit, non semita terrae.
    Errat quisque putans currendo posse beari;
560 Multi cursantes non vitam sed loca mutant.
Non Romam vidisse, sed hic bene vivere laus est.
Hic, homo, quere deum; deus est et regnat ubique.
Quem si tu reperire cupis, contempne caduca,
Exue te mundo cursantem ad gaudia, ne te
565 Mundus prepediat. Sic olim Christus amicos
Ammonuit saccos et peras spernere quando
Ingrederentur iter. Properantem namque retardat
Pondus, et ad teretes descendens instita talos
Intiba sulcantem retinet plerumque ligonem,
570 Nec prompte currit nisi qua sinit alveus unda.

But since we have ventured to write down a few words about the forms of these in our little book, I am pleased to explain also with a typological figure what they can signify according to the model of this church. Men born of mothers undergo baptism so that they may be members of the new man. Then they are able rightly to be called calves, when with goads of virtues they drive their sluggish hearts away from the flattery of vice. They are lions with unbowed necks as often as they scorn the weapons of the infernal tyrant. They are eagles when they direct their glistening eyes toward the true sun. Thus our churches have these living creatures portrayed with instructive pen. And so, whoever visits them with plaintive vow, wishing to rejoice there with his sins taken away, let him also prostrate himself and, along with the psalmist, continually pray: "I have asked for something valuable from the Lord which I shall seek often, that his house may accept me as a dweller therein." The path of justice leads to it, not an earthly path.

Whoever thinks he can be blessed by running is mistaken; many who run here and there do not change their life, but location. It is not to have seen Rome that is praiseworthy, but to live well here. O man, seek God here; God exists and reigns everywhere. If you want to find him, scorn transitory things, and free yourself from the world lest the world impede you as you run toward joys. So did Christ once admonish his friends to spurn wallets and bags when they were going on a journey. For indeed, a burden hinders one who is hurrying, likewise a flounce hanging down to smooth ankles. Endive often impedes the hoe as it cuts a furrow, and water does not run readily except where the riverbed allows.

545

550

555

560

565

570

5

De Eufronio docente, quod omnia in caritate condita sint et in ea consistant omnia

Parvus ego vidi, certa si mente recordor,
Eufronium; de quo memorabant tunc quod in eius
Pectore verus amor consisteret, illecebrosa
Omnia respueret, solitus sic dicere: "Fratres,
575 Scismaticos fugite et vinctos anathemate, sic ne
Vel dicatis: 'Ave'; fidei sociis date foedus.
Federe nil melius; consistit federe mundus."
    Haec cum discipulis iteraret sedulus, unus
Ex illis ait: "Hoc nobis, pater optime, fedus
580 Exprime quo mundus concordat iunctus!" Et ille:
"Hoc fedus deus est, sine quo factum nichil. Ipse
Cuncta in principio, Genesi testante, creavit,
Degenerem sine luce polum, sine germine terras,
Stagnaque legitimis nondum currentia ripis.
585 Tunc inmortales invisibilesque catervas
Spirituum fieri iussit, sed qualiter illos
Condiderit non est hominum comprendere; solus
Id factor novit. Credendum est denique factos.
Qua ratione? Deum preter sunt omnia facta;
590 Omnia sunt facta, factor non factus habetur.

5

On the Teaching of Euphronius That All Things Are Founded on Love and All Depend on It

As a small boy I saw Euphronius, if I recall rightly; men at that time used to say of him that true love resided in his heart, that he spurned all enticements, being accustomed to speak in this way: "Brothers, flee from schismatics and those 575 bound by excommunication, so that you do not even say 'Hail'; grant your bond of friendship to companions in the faith. Nothing is better than this compact; the world depends on this compact."

When the zealous man was going over these [doctrines] with his disciples, one of them said: "Good father, explain to us this compact by which the world is joined and brought 580 into harmony!" And he said: "This compact is God, without whom nothing was made. As Genesis declares, in the beginning he created all things, the heavens alien without light, the lands without sprouts, and the waters not yet running within their rightful banks. Then he commanded the im- 585 mortal, invisible band of spirits to be created, but how he fashioned them is not for men to comprehend; the Creator alone knows this. And so it must be believed that they were created. For what reason? All things were created, except God; all were created, but the Creator is not held to be cre- 590

Hos autem fecit, quo se per secula cuncta
Laudarent, digni divinum cernere vultum.
Qui tales potuere tamen peccare, superbus
Donec siderea fratrum delator ab aula
595 Concidit. Ex eius modo spirituum agmina lapsu
Confirmata mali nequeunt committere quicquam,
Nam custodit eos pietas livore remoto.
    "'Fiat lux' inquit deus, et lux ilico facta est.
Secernensque novo tenebras ex lumine nocti
600 Iussit abesse diem. Iam tunc inimica vicissim
Pugnarunt elementa modis discordibus, usque
Ipse sator placida iunxit contraria pace.
Ignem namque citum summam contraxit in arcem.
Hunc gravidumque solum mediator continet aer,
605 Ne vel terra cadat violento pondere mersa
Aut levitas puri sursum nimis evolet ignis.
Altos deinde lacus et flumina limite certo
Deducens pelagus concurrere iussit in unum—
Oceanum dicunt—totum qui circuit orbem.
610   "Tempore eo tellus sine gramine nuda manebat,
Ignorans gratos, ut nunc solet, edere fructus,
Donec eam lignis auctor mandavit et herbis
Vestiri variis, et quod mandaverat actum est.
Nec mora, procedunt porrectae in nubila pinus;
615 Stare novas subito videas in montibus alnos,
Buxos et patulis ulmos consurgere ramis,
Stare eciam mirtos, platanos, cedros, terebintos.
Tum primum cerasi rubuerunt germine fulvo,
Sentaque castaneae didicerunt poma feraces
620 Gignere, tum flavo canescere mala colore

ated. Moreover, he made them so that, worthy to look upon the divine countenance, they might praise him through all the ages. Yet despite their nature they nonetheless could sin, until the proud accuser of his brothers fell from the heavenly hall. Now made resolute after his fall, the multi- 595 tude of spirits cannot commit any evil, for their piety protects them, with envy removed.

"God said: 'Let there be light,' and instantly light was created. And separating the darkness from the new light, he commanded day to be apart from night. Already at that time 600 the hostile elements were contending with one another in discordant ways, until the Creator himself united those contradictory things in tranquil peace. In fact, he confined swift fire to the topmost height. Air, the mediator, holds this and the heavy land together, lest either the earth fall, plunged 605 down by its destructive weight, or the lightness of pure fire fly upward too much. Then, leading the deep lakes and streams within a definite boundary, he commanded the seas to rush together into one which surrounds the whole world —men call it ocean.

"At that time the earth remained bare, without grass, and 610 did not know how to put forth pleasing fruits, as it is now wont to do, until the Creator ordered it to be covered with trees and various plants, and what he ordered was done. Without delay, pine trees sprang forth and stretched to the clouds; suddenly you might see new alders standing on the 615 mountains, boxwoods and elms, with their wide branches, rise up and also myrtles, plane trees, cedars, and terebinths standing. Cherry trees then first grew red with their ruddy buds, and fertile chestnuts learned to produce their thorny fruits, and then apples began to glow with a golden hue, and 620

Cepere et nigra bace procedere lauro,
Et prodire suis glandes et amigdala ramis;
Tum pirus et prunus, tum mespila fructificavit.
Balsama tum et mirrae sudarunt robore guttae,
625 Thus, aloe resina, simul tymiamata cuncta,
Que produnt proceres irritamenta gulosos.
    "Dein caeli faciem vultu spectare sereno
Dignatus pater. Ut nullum discrimen haberent
Noxque diesque chao vidit permixta molesto.
630 Tum septem statuit cursu distante planetas.
E quibus est lampas cunctis insignior ardens
Tytana appellant, post hunc est maxima Luna.
Que duo dissimili lucis donavit honore,
Ut presente diem capiant terrestria Phebo,
635 Lunaque tranquillae splendescat tempore noctis.
Hinc menses, horas numeramus tempora et annos.
    "Mox et solifugis pinxit deus aera stellis,
Astraque constituit nautis in signa marinis.
Post hec squamigeros pisces squamisque carentes
640 Gurgitibus vastis innasci iussit, et alto
Grandia distribuit cetae scopulosaque monstra.
Ipse etiam levibus sator omne volatile pennis
Armavit quibus aerias modo verberat auras
Et quasi remigio vehementibus utitur alis.
645 Dein cum reptilibus iumenta ferasque creavit
Verbo. Velle fuit verbum, feliciter acta
Constant aeternae pacis conpage ligata.
Que pax est dominus, qui continet omnia palmo.
    "Qui simul inspexit mundum, 'Que fecimus' inquit
650 'Sunt bona. Nunc hominem restat plasmare sagacem
Qui simili nobis concordet imagine, quique

berries began to come forth on the black laurel, and acorns
and almonds to appear on their respective branches; then
the pear and plum bore fruit, then the medlar trees. Then
balsam and drops of myrrh oozed from the wood, together   625
with frankincense, resin of aloe and all spices, the entice-
ments that make nobles gluttonous.

"Then the Father deigned to look upon the face of the
sky with a serene countenance. He saw that night and day
were not different and were mingled together in irksome
chaos. Then he established seven planets with different or-   630
bits. Among these there is a lamp that blazes more brilliantly
than the rest. Men call it the sun, and after this the greatest
is the moon. He gave these two a dissimilar quality of light,
so that when Phoebus is in sight, things on earth have day-
light, and the moon shines at the time of tranquil night.   635
From this we reckon the months, hours, seasons and years.

"Next God adorned the sky with stars that flee the sun,
and he set out constellations as signs to sailors at sea. After
these he commanded that scaly fish and those without scales   640
be born in the vast waters, and in the deep he apportioned
great whales and monsters as big as crags. The Creator also
equipped every fowl with light feathers with which it now
beats the airy breezes and uses its vigorous wings like oars.
Then by a word he created cattle, along with reptiles and   645
wild beasts. His wish was his word, and the things happily
brought forth remain fixed in a bond of eternal peace. This
peace is the Lord, who holds all things in his palm.

"As soon as he looked upon the world, he said: 'The things
that we have made are good. Now it remains [for us] to form   650
a perceptive man to be in harmony with us, with a simi-
lar image, to rule over every created thing which we shall

Quam dabimus presit facture scilicet omni,
Quod mare alit, quod terra parit, quod in aere vivit.
Nos colat et nostri devotus obediat oris
655 Sermoni neque spiritui se credat iniquo,
Nec sapere insistat quam nos concedimus ultra.
Subdita cuncta ipsi, nobis sit subditus ipse.'
    "Sic fatus sacris limum tractare caducum
Non dedignatur manibus, terramque recentem
660 Prepollens opifex humanos format in artus.
Utque foco mollita fabri sub pollice cera
Quaslibet in formas vafra transvertitur arte,
Sic domini digitis se lenta argilla coaptat
Artificisque manum sequitur promptissima summi.
665 Haec ubi coniunctis ut nunc per singula membris
Constitit, aeterno spiramen ab ore recepit
Quod Greci psichen, animam dixere Latini.
Nec mora, plasma novum medio spiramine vivum
Surgit et in caelum sublimi suspicit ore,
670 Cetera cum prono terrena animalia collo
Despectent, quorum moritur cum corpore flatus.
    "Quare, homo, luminibus cordisque et corporis alta
Inspice, quae bona scis exerce, incognita disce!
Discere que nescis a quovis non pudeat te.
675 Plurima scire iuvat; sapiens non exulat usquam.
Scire bonum et facere satagentibus urbs patet, in qua
Nulla diem aeternum caligo interpolat, in qua
Sol athomis radiat non deficientibus; hic sol
Sol est iusticiae, pariles cui dicere laudes
680 Non cessant nitidae Cherubin Seraphinque coronae.
Illuc nemo valet nisi amore favente venire."

give him, namely, what the sea sustains, what the earth produces, what lives in the air. Let him worship us and faithfully obey the words of our mouth and not entrust himself to an 655
evil spirit, nor set out to know more than we have granted. Let all things be subject to him, [and] let him be subject to us.'

"Having spoken thus, the all-powerful Creator did not disdain to take lowly mud into his sacred hands, and he 660
shaped the fresh earth into human limbs. And just as wax softened in an oven is turned under the craftsman's thumb into all shapes by his artful skill, so did the pliant clay adapt itself to the Lord's fingers and most readily complied with the hand of the Supreme Maker. When he fashioned these, 665
with the limbs joined as now through their separate parts, he took from his eternal mouth a breath, which the Greeks call *psyche,* and the Romans call *anima.* Without delay, a new creature, alive with breath in its chest, arises and looks toward the heavens with face uplifted, while the rest of the liv- 670
ing creatures of earth, whose spirit dies with the body, look down with their necks bent forward.

"Therefore, mankind, with the eyes of your heart and of your body, look on high, practice what you know to be good, learn the unknown! Let it not shame you to learn from anyone what you do not know. To know many things is pleasing; 675
a wise man is never an exile. To those who do their best to know and to do good, the city lies open, in which no darkness spoils the eternal day, in which a sun with unfailing particles shines; this sun is the sun of justice, to whom a radiant crowd of cherubim and seraphim do not cease to sing fitting 680
praises. No one can come there unless love favors him."

6

De incontinentia sacerdotum

"Vera salus amor est; amor est perfectio vitae.
Et quis amor? Non femineus, sed celitus atque
In cunctos propter dominum diffusus amicos.
685   Et tamen uxorem quam lex tibi mancipat et dos
Non adamare veto. Laudabilis est amor ille,
Namque ut haberet homo sibi par quod amaret uti se,
Omniparens primum iussit dormire supinum,
Et tollens unam de costis illius Evam
690   Condidit ex ipsa. Fidos idcirco parentes
Linquet homo et grate se uxori iunget, eruntque
Una in carne duo dulcique fruentur amore.
      "Sed quod adulterii dampnosa sorde volutet
Se quisquam aut scortis inserviat, utile non est.
695   Nam bonus et sapiens vir Paulus, ut hoc prohiberet,
Unicuique suam concessit habere." "Quid ergo?
Monachus et tractans sanctorum sancta sacerdos
Assumentne sibi cum libertate maritas?"
      "Nequaquam. Cur hoc, ausculta! Rem tibi pandam.
700   Cum Galathas civesque Ephesi civesque Corinthi
Compluresque alios cepisset subdere Christo
Paulus, eos blandis primum dictis sapienter
Erudiit, validum teneris apponere panem
Devitans, ut eo cicius transferret eorum

6

On the Lack of Restraint of Priests

"Love is true salvation; love is the perfection of life. And which love? Not love of a woman, but love from heaven, and love extended to all friends because of the Lord. And yet, I 685 do not forbid you to love deeply the wife whom the law and a dowry subject to you. This love is praiseworthy, for in order that man might have an equal to love as himself, the Father of all commanded the first man to lie down to sleep, and taking one of his ribs, he created Eve from it. For that 690 reason a man will leave his devoted parents and will unite himself to his comely wife, and they will be two in one flesh, and will enjoy sweet love.

"But it is not helpful for anyone to wallow in the destructive filth of adultery, or attach himself to harlots. For in or- 695 der to prevent this, Paul, a good and wise man, allowed each one to have a wife of his own." "What, then? May the monk and the priest who has charge of the holy of holies take wives for themselves with freedom from restraint?"

"By no means. Listen to why this is! I'll explain the matter to you. When Paul began to make the Galatians and Ephe- 700 sians and citizens of Corinth and very many others subject to Christ, he wisely instructed them first with gentle words and avoided serving solid bread to children, so that in this

147

705 Pectora de cultu fanorum, sepe etenim fit
Dum rudis in veteri coalescit stipite ramus,
Aura vel tenui motus leviter cadit. Illud
Ecclesiam sancti qui plantavere novellam
Tractantes, quia perfectus fit nemo repente,
710 In convertendo gentes simulacra colentes
Saxea preceptis primo sunt mollibus usi.
Nam quis in idolio solitus potuque ciboque
Distendi atque ubivis inhonesta cubilia inire
Acria curaret doctorum attendere verba,
715 Si vellent penitus genialia culta vetare?

   "Tunc etiam sancti doctores signa stupenda
Fecere: ut taceam de claudo et Dorcade, sanant
Egros verba Petri. Quis nunc etiam prece curat
Languentem quemquam? Cur non fiunt modo signa?
720 An non sunt ulli virtutum stemate nostro
Tempore pollentes? Sane sunt, sed quia radix
Iam viget aecclesiae multos vegetata per annos,
Non opus est signis aut verbis suavibus. Ipse
Credentum populus viciorum fortia tela
725 Perpetitur, tamen obsistit nec subiacet illis:
Ferre annosa abies pluvios non abnuit austros.
Ergo lacte fuit tenerorum more riganda
Aecclesia infantum; quo coepit tempore nasci
Et blandis monitis ceu molli pulte cibanda.
730 "Sed postquam cepit validorum more vigere
Tyronum, solido pascenda cibo fuit, hoc est,
Preceptis gravibus subdenda. Et ob hoc venerandi
Rome pontifices, alio quos nomine vulgus

way he might more swiftly turn their hearts away from wor-   705
ship in their pagan temples, since often it happens [that]
while a young twig is growing on an old branch and is shaken
slightly by even a little breeze, it falls off. Considering this,
since no one suddenly becomes perfect, those saints who
propagated the newly founded church first used mild pre-   710
cepts in converting the peoples who worshiped images of
stone. For what man accustomed to be filled with drink and
food in his idol-temple and to go into shameful beds any-
where, would care to consider the stern words of teachers, if   715
they wanted to forbid marriage beds entirely?

"At that time also the holy teachers performed wondrous
signs: the words of Peter cured the sick, not to mention the
lame man and Dorcas. Who now, even by prayers, cures any-
one who is ill? Why are there no signs now? Or why are there   720
none held in high esteem for their garland of virtues in our
time? Certainly there are, but since the root of the church,
invigorated over many years, is now flourishing, there is no
need for signs or sweet words. This multitude of believers
braves the powerful weapons of the vices, yet it resists them   725
and is not subject to them: the aged fir tree does not refuse
to endure the rainy south winds. And so, like tender infants,
the church had to be nourished with milk during the time
when it had begun to grow and it had to be fed with sooth-
ing admonitions, as if with soft porridge.

"But after it began to thrive like strong new recruits, it   730
had to be fed on solid food, that is, it had to be subjected
to stern precepts. And on this account, the venerable pon-
tiffs in Rome, whom the common folk call by another name,

Appellat papas, interdixere maritas
735 Presbiteris ut qui cupiunt contingere sancti
Sacra dei mundos se corde et corpore servent,
Levitis etiam, quoniam funguntur et ipsi
Divinis sacris appellanturque ministri.

"Monachus a pompis mundanis sponte recessit.
740 Obiurgare illum non multum pertinet ad me
Nec cupio. Tamen hoc constanter dico, quod ille est
Monachus infelix qui non vult scire quid hoc sit:
Monachus et sancte vivendo monachus esse.
Velat eum vestis pullo fuscata colore,
745 Ut despectibilis mundo videatur inopsque;
Esto, sed interius si non vult candidus esse,
Extera nigredo nil confert, credite nobis.
At vos, presbiteri, pastores atque magistri
Aecclesiae, ex animis conubia pellite vestris!
750 Econtra inprudens dicit mihi: 'Qua ratione
Gaudia coniugii mihi subtrahis? Unde Iohannes
Editus est, Christum typico qui tinxit in amne?'

"Hoc ego sic solvo: veteris quis somnia legis
Comparet huic certae? Quis veris artubus umbram?
755 Quisve cimiterii metuat lemures quasi vera
Corpora? Prisca fuit lex huius legis imago,
Ut pictus vivi et currentis bubalus. Olim
Quassari iussit dentem pro dente vetus lex,
Sed dicit nova lex: 'In dextram mandibulam te
760 Si quis cedat, ei paciens prebeto aliam tu.'

"Composite mala vestra satis defenditis acta!
Turpe est quod proprium violas, onocrotale, nidum.

popes, forbade priests to have wives so that those who wish 735
to touch the sacraments of God as holy men might keep
themselves pure in mind and body; they forbade deacons
too [to have wives], since they perform divine rites and are
called ministers.

"The monk willingly withdrew from worldly pomp. To 740
reprove him does not concern me much, nor do I wish to.
Yet this I say firmly, that he is a miserable monk who does
not want to know what it means to be a monk and to be a
monk by living a holy life. A garment darkened by a mourn-
ful color clothes him, so that to the world he might seem 745
lowly and poor; so be it, but if he does not want to be white
on the inside, the outward blackness confers nothing, be-
lieve me. But you, priests, pastors, and teachers of the
church, banish marriage from your minds! On the other
hand, an ignorant man says to me: 'For what reason do you 750
take the joys of wedlock from me? Whence was John begot-
ten, who baptized Christ in the figurative river?'

"I explain this as follows: who compares the visions of the
old law to this sure one? Who compares a shadow to real
limbs? Who is afraid of ghosts in the cemetery as if they 755
were real bodies? The ancient law was the image of this law,
like a painted antelope is the image of a living, running one.
Formerly the old law commanded tooth [be broken] for
tooth, but the new law says: 'If anyone strikes you on the 760
right cheek, suffer it, and offer him the other.'

"You defend your evil deeds skillfully enough! It is shame-
ful, pelican, that you violate your own nest. You are wise in

Ad defendendum sapientes estis iniquum,
Ad rectum stulti, quapropter sic domini vas
765 'Prudentes,' inquit, 'sunt ut faciant mala, stulti
Ut faciant bona.' Ob hoc carnalem spernite luxum,
Namque deo nequeunt qui sunt in carne placere.
    "Ah miser, ad mensam domini qui putidus ire
Non horres sanctumque eius contingere corpus
770 Pollutis manibus! Capsas de thuris acerra
Quid suffire iuvat, putens cum tu cinicus sis?
Quid lavisse manus inmundo pectore prodest?
Quis mutare canem vel aqua vel pectine possit?
Anne tua qua te circumdas sanctificari
775 Veste putas? Tiriis inserto vestibus auro
Simia veletur, non simia desinit esse.
Quodsi patratas subduceret infula culpas
Et reliquae induviae divinis cultibus aptae,
Semper ego vellem vestitu incedere tali.
780 Non hac, crede mihi, tolluntur veste nec unda
Pensilis incurva quam continet urceus ansa,
Sed pocius lacrimis de corde fluentibus imo.
Constanter repeto testemque deum mihi sumo:
Presbitero nulli recte conceditur uxor.
785   "Ergo sacerdotes, muliebrem spernite cultum,
Et nec adulterio nec fornice perdite vosmet.
Nam quis adulterium sanus non exsecret, unde
Maxima gentiles scripserunt dampna poetae?
Si non turbasset Lacedemona Xanticus hospes
790 Absentique Helenam non surripuisset Atridae,
Quid Cous scriptor, quid magnus Homerus et exlex
Ennius, aut certe quem de se Mantua natum

defending what is unjust, fools in defending what is right, for which reason the vessel of the Lord spoke thus: 'They 765 are wise so that they may do evil, fools so that they may do good.' For this reason, avoid carnal excess, for indeed, those who are in the flesh cannot please God.

"Ah wretched man, who is not afraid to proceed while be-fouled to the Lord's altar and to touch his sacred body with impure hands! What good is it to perfume reliquaries with 770 a censer of incense, when you are a stinking Cynic? What benefit to have washed your hands, when your heart is un-clean? Who can change a dog with water or a comb? Do you think that you are made holy by the garment with which you 775 wrap yourself? Let an ape be clothed in purple garments with gold sewn in—it doesn't cease to be an ape. But if a chasuble and the other vestments suited to divine worship could take away past sins, I would wish always to walk in such vesture. Not by this garment are they taken away, be- 780 lieve me, nor by water which a hanging pitcher with a curved handle contains, but rather by tears flowing from the depths of the heart. I repeat constantly and take God as my wit-ness: to no priest is a wife rightly permitted.

"Therefore, priests, avoid devotion to women, and do not 785 destroy yourselves in adultery or brothels. For what sane man does not curse adultery, [the source] from which pagan poets wrote about the greatest losses? If the Trojan guest had not thrown Sparta into disorder, and had not stolen 790 Helen away from the absent Menelaus, what would the writer from Cos, what would mighty Homer and fearless Ennius, or surely he whom Mantua boasted was born of her,

Iactat, scripsissent? Si non hoc materia esset,
Unde tot egregios possent diducere versus?
795 Illis ingenium subtile deus dedit et cor
Scribendi quodcumque placeret eis; alioquin
Nequicquam excirent fictas Helicone Camenas.
Edere digna hederis nostri causa deus illis
Cessit, ut ex scriptis nos proficeremus eorum.
800   "Cunctos ergo decet mecharum spernere amorem,
Illos precipue qui sunt speculum laicorum,
Ut dum sinceram ducunt sine crimine vitam,
Intrepida possint subiectos carpere voce.
Nam turpe est ipsum quod culpa ligat monitorem,
805 Quod verrucosum verrucis plenus abhorret,
Utpote quod domini cupientem sumere corpus:
Cum laicum sese multis macerare diebus
Precipias dulcique absistere coniugis usu,
Tu matutinas Nictagis negligis; udus
810 Et fumans surgis post turpia facta tepenti
Coniugis e gremio sacramque inmundus ad aram
Accedis. Turpe est; nec solum turpe putes, sed
Plus quam turpe. Deus pro certo talia facta
Odit, et ipse deus, Paulo testante fideli,
815 Ecclesiae capud est. Quid mirum quod caput odit
Hoc detestari si cetera membra videntur?
Non bene conveniunt deus et dampnosa libido;
Non bene concordant Belial culturaque Christi.
Linquat sacra dei qui vult uxorius esse;
820 Respuat uxorem qui sacris se dicat almis.
Quem quid conveniat servare per omnia, dicam."

have written? If this had not been their subject, from what would they have been able to compose so many excellent verses? To them God gave a subtle nature and a heart for 795 writing whatever pleased them; otherwise, in vain would they have summoned made-up Muses from Helicon. God allowed them to produce songs worthy of ivy garlands for our sake, so that we might profit from their writings.

"Thus, it is fitting that all men avoid the love of adulter- 800 esses, especially those men who are a mirror for laymen, so that while they lead a pure life without sin, they can criticize those subject to them with undaunted speech. For it is shameful that guilt holds fast the admonisher himself, that a 805 man full of warts shudders at one with warts, seeing that he is one wishing to take up the Lord's body: while you direct a layman to torment himself for many days and to abstain from pleasant intercourse with his wife, you neglect your morning vigils, night worker; you arise damp and reeking af- 810 ter shameful acts from the warm bosom of your wife and, unclean, you approach the sacred altar. It is shameful; not only do you stink shamefully, but more than shamefully. God certainly hates such deeds, and, as the faithful Paul declares, God himself is the head of the church. What wonder if the 815 other members seem to detest what the head hates? God and pernicious lust do not go well together; Belial and the worship of Christ do not harmonize well. Let him who wants to be uxorious give up the sacred rites of God; let him 820 who dedicates himself to the nourishing sacraments refuse a wife. What is proper for him to observe in every respect, I shall [now] tell."

155

7

De eo, quid sit sacerdotibus
servandum quidve vitandum

"Non a coniugii prohibetur federe tantum
Presbiter: ingluviem devitet et ebrietatem;
Non sit linguosus nec scurrae more iocetur;
825 Nec male ditescat sextante lucrando deuncem;
Alea non sit ei neque fallax thessara curae.
In libris studeat morum. Sapientia lux est,
Sed sapiens sine moribus est puteus sine fune.
Undique se purum custodiat, undique tutum.
830 Hinc est quod quendam deus erudiens ait: 'Heus tu
Clama, ne cesses; exalta ut bucina vocem!'
Hoc ideo dixit: quia sepe docere volentem
Elinguem proprii sceleris mens conscia reddit,
Sed qui se a viciis novit procul esse remotum
835 Clangens ut lituus viciosos carpit aperte.
   "Doctores igitur sine fuco vivere debent
Simpliciter caste, populumque docere frequenter
Et placide, quoniam non est didascalus aptus
Castigare suos qui mansuetudine nescit.
840 Indomiti clunes et collum cautus agaso
Prurit equi blandis attactibus, atque ita porro
Pacatam strigili cervicem defricat, et tunc
It sonipes qua chamus agit stimulatque magister.
Sic doctor populi, qui corda ferocia nutrit,
845 Rite catechizet parochos virga baculoque:

7

Concerning What Should Be Observed or Avoided by Priests

"A priest should not only be prevented from the bond of marriage: let him avoid gluttony and drunkenness; let him not be a babbler nor jest like a buffoon; let him not grow rich wickedly by gaining eleven percent on a trifling amount; let him not care for gambling nor deceptive dice. Let him study books of good morals. Wisdom is light, but a wise man without morals is a well without a rope. Let a priest keep himself pure in every way, safe everywhere. Thus it is that God, instructing a certain one, says: 'Hark! Cry out and do not cease; lift up your voice like a trumpet!' He said this for this reason: because often the mind conscious of its own sin renders one who wishes to teach speechless, but one who knows that he is far removed from vices openly criticizes vicious men like a sounding clarion.

"Therefore, teachers ought to live plainly, purely, without deceit, and they ought to teach the populace frequently and mildly, since he is not a suitable instructor who does not know how to correct his students with gentleness. A cautious groom scratches the haunches and nape of an untamed horse with soothing strokes, and thus he next rubs down its subdued neck with a strigil, and then the steed goes where the halter leads and the master spurs it on. So the teacher of people, who nourishes savage hearts, should rightly instruct

825

830

835

840

845

Visitet infirmos et defunctis veniam oret;
Edicat placide ne quis persolvere Christo
Addubitet decimas, qui pinguibus indita glebis
Semina centuplicans gravidas emittit aristas.

850 "Sed si qui decimas tardant offerre negantque,
Iustis pastor eos monitis convincat et aptis,
Sic dicens: 'Homo, quid dubitas dare debita parva?
Parva deus poscit, qui posset poscere magna.
Namque creavit humum quem vomere scindis adunco.

855 Ars ab eo conponendi processit aratri;
Illa quibus constat—buris, dentalia, themo
Stiva, rote—ex eius fiunt tibi condita lignis;
Ille boves tibi dat; pluviam zephirosque tepentes
Mittit ut educant tua semina credita sulcis.

860 Et cum cuncta dei sint, solum ferre laborem
Te sulcando patet, pro quo decimam tibi partem
Sumere debebas et cetera linquere Christo.
Ipse autem clemens largusque novem tibi liquit
Partes ut decimam promtus des; non modo fructus

865 Dico soli, sed quicquid habes decimare iuberis.'
"Hec et quaeque bonus placido sermone loquatur
Doctor, et erudiat quod novit quemque decere;
Natos ammoneat parere parentibus, atque
Servos ut dominis studeant servire fideles;

870 Uxores doceat subiectas esse maritis,
Mites atque pios uxoribus esse maritos,
Cunctaque quae sanctae sint dicat idonea vitae.
Pravorum e manibus rapiat conamine summo
Quemque bonum, ut Raab, quae lini fascibus abdens

his parishioners in religion with a rod and staff: let him visit
the sick and pray for forgiveness for the dead; let him calmly
decree that no one who brings forth heavy beards of grain,
multiplying a hundred times the seeds planted in fertile soil,
should hesitate to pay tithes to Christ.

"But if there are those who delay and refuse to pay tithes, 850
let the pastor win them over with just and fitting admoni-
tions, speaking thus: 'O man, why do you hesitate to give the
little owed? God, who could demand great things, demands
little. Indeed, he created the earth that you cleave with a
curved plowshare. The skill of devising a plow proceeded 855
from him; those parts of which it is composed—the plow
beam, share beam, pole, handle, wheels—were made for you
from his trees; he gives you oxen; he sends the rain and warm
west winds so that your seeds entrusted to the furrows might
produce. And since all things belong to God, it is clear that 860
you bear the toil of plowing alone, for which reason you
ought to take a tenth part for yourself and leave the rest for
Christ. However, a merciful and generous Christ left nine
parts for you so that you might be ready to give a tenth; I
speak not only of the fruits of the earth, but you are com- 865
manded to tithe whatever you have.'

"Let the good teacher say these and all things with placid
speech, and let him teach what he knows is suitable for each
person; let him admonish children to obey their parents,
and servants to strive to serve their masters faithfully; let 870
him teach wives to be subject to their husbands, and hus-
bands to be gentle and kind to their wives, and let him talk
about all things that are suited to a holy life. With utmost
effort let him snatch every good man from the hands of the
wicked, as Rahab did, who, by hiding spies under bundles of

875 Legatos meruit celebrari laude perenni.
Nullum odii causa disturbet iniquus, itemque
Nullum defendat prava pietate rebellem,
Sed quodcunque docet vel agit discretio firmet.
   "Haec facere ignorans qui stultorum esse magister
880 Possit, non video, praesertim cum pateat quod
In foveam ambo ruunt si cecus eat duce ceco.
Hac in re quidam culpandi pontifices sunt,
Qui plerumque rudes sublimant et viciosos
Ordinibus stulte vitantes quaerere num sit
885 Servus quem sacrant aut liber, sobrius aut non;
Et quos transactae testes patet edere vitae
Dum mercede manus nolunt subducere ab omni.
Nam, si credendum est, quosdam quia clam manus uncta est,
Suscipiunt; a nonnullis indebita poscunt
890 Obsequia, et plures humanae laudis amore
Sanctificant. Karisma tuum, quod venditur ullo,
Spiritus alme, modo singultu defleo cordis,
Et merito, quia vendentum turbas et ementum
Exemplo legitur deus exagitasse flagello.
895 Nunc quoque in ordinibus poscentes munera sacris
Indigni Christo vivunt et munera dantes.
   "Cur rarus nunc est sapiens? Quia blanda videntur
Ocia proque libris sectatur fenora quisque,
Tractat non secum: tu tantum collige quod des.
900 Munera stultus amat, sapientem munera mulcent;
Iunge sales prose, venias sine munere, nil est.
Quodsi pro nichilo reputaret episcopus omnis
Munera inutilium et dignis preberet honores,
Non adeo multas Satanae temptatio mentes
905 Carperet, et mundum non tantus volveret error.
Sed nunc quod non dat probitas, nummus tribuit. Nunc

flax, deserved to be honored with perennial praise. Let him 875
trouble no one unjustly on account of hatred, and likewise
let him protect no rebel out of perverse piety, but let dis-
cernment fortify whatever he teaches or does.

"I don't see how one ignorant of how to do these things
can be a teacher of foolish men, especially since it is clear 880
that both fall into the ditch if a blind man walks with a blind
guide. In this matter, certain bishops must be blamed, who
very often elevate ignorant and vicious men to [holy] orders,
foolishly avoiding to ask whether the one whom they conse- 885
crate is slave or free, a sober man or not; and what witnesses
of his past life he is prepared to produce when they are un-
willing to keep their hands away from every bribe. Indeed,
if you can believe it, they accept certain ones because their
palm was secretly greased; from some they demand obedi- 890
ence that is not owed, and they ordain many for love of hu-
man praise. Your sacred gift, gracious spirit, which is sold
to anyone, I now weep over with sobbing in my heart, and
justly, since we read that as an example God drove out with
a whip the crowds of those selling and buying. Now also, 895
those in holy orders who demand bribes and who give bribes
live as men unworthy of Christ.

"Why is a wise man rare now? Because leisure seems
agreeable and everyone pursues compound interest instead
of books, for he does not say to himself: 'Just collect as much
as you give!' A fool loves bribes, and bribes soften up a wise 900
man; join wit to your words, but if you come without a bribe,
it's nothing. But if every bishop would consider the bribes
of useless men as nothing and would proffer honors to wor-
thy men, Satan's temptation would not pluck so many minds,
and so great an error would not roll the world along. But 905
now, what honesty does not bestow, money imparts. Now a

Dona ferens probus est; intrat, qui nil habet exit.
At tamen esse bonos aliquando videmus inemptos:
'Nil dedit, ite, mihi! Bene me potavit. Eamus!'
910   "O nummi, nummi, per vos emitur scelus omne;
Vestra presbiteri faciunt ope fasque nefasque!
Nec pensare volunt quantum deus extulit illos
Quando ad discipulos: 'Sanctum,' inquit, 'sumite flatum,
Ut quorum vultis sordes abolere patratas
915 Possitis, quorum vultis retinere queatis.'
Discipulis equidem dixit deus hoc, in eorum
Presbiteri vice sunt. Ergo cur non imitantur
Mores et vitam quorum sibi iura potenter
Asscribunt? Illi spreverunt coniugia atque
920 Carnis delicias. Hoc presbiteri modo nostri
Non faciunt. Idcirco quidem velut unda lavacri
In caenum iniusti descendunt inque profundum,
Et tamen emundant animas et ad ethera mittunt.
Sed precessorum si vellent esse sequaces,
925 Plures eveherent ad regna perennia. Namque
Exemplo melius quem verbo quisque docetur.
    "Ergo femineum, doctores, spernite amorem
Volventes animo vestri sublime cacumen
Iuris. Quae maior valet esse potentia quam quod
930 Solvitis evinctas culparum compede mentes?
Vos quoque fabellas contemnite prorsus aniles,
Parcite vana loqui, nolite lascescere quemquam
Verbis aut risu. Cur, si malo esse lecator,
Presbiter appeller? Vel cur quis religiosum
935 Me dicat, scurram quem conspicit esse loquacem?
Preterea argutas penitus vitate tabernas,
Si sapitis, neque vos cornuto credite Bacho.
Quis sane mentis denudat crimina vobis,

man 'bearing gifts' is honest; he goes in, while one who has nothing goes out. But yet, sometimes we see that good men are not bought: 'He gave me nothing. Get out! He gave me plenty to drink. Let's go!'

"O money, money, all wickedness is bought through you; 910 with your help, priests do right and wrong! They are unwilling to consider how much God exalted them when he said to his disciples: 'Receive the Holy Spirit, so that whose past stains you wish to efface, you can, and whose [sins] you wish 915 to retain, you may be able.' Indeed, God said this to his disciples, and priests are in their place. Therefore, why do they not imitate the morals and way of life of those whose rights they strongly claim for themselves? Those men spurned marriage and pleasures of the flesh. Our priests now don't 920 do this. For this reason also these unjust priests flow like bathwater into the mud and into the depths, and yet they cleanse souls and send them to heaven. But if they were willing to be followers of their predecessors, they would lead 925 forth more people to everlasting realms. For truly, everyone is taught better by example than by words.

"Therefore, teachers, spurn the love of women, while turning over in your mind the lofty pinnacle of your authority. What power could be greater than the fact that you set 930 free minds that are bound by shackles of sin? Also, utterly condemn old wives' tales, cease to speak of vain things, and do not abuse anyone with words or laughter. Why should I be called a priest if I prefer to be a lecher? Or why would anyone call me pious, when he sees that I am a babbling buf- 935 foon? Moreover, entirely avoid noisy taverns if you're wise, and don't entrust yourselves to horned Bacchus. What man of sound mind confesses his sins to you, whom he often sees

Vinosos quos sepe videt? Pocius fugit illud,
940 Pensans quod vino stimulati cuncta resignant.
    "Regibus et dominis servite, etsi reprobi sunt,
Sunt etenim vobis a summo rege statuti,
Ut reprimant nocuos, et honorent ac tueantur
Mites. Sepe bonis nequam rex imperat, ut Saul,
945 Sub quo sancti homines Samuhel Davidque fuere.
Sepe bonos legemque malus tutatur, ut idem
Iudeos rabie defendit ab Allophilorum.
Denique, quae regum sunt reddite regibus, et quae
Sunt domini domino. Regis reddatur ymago
950 Regi, sed domino domini reddatur imago.
Iusticia atque fides sunt restituenda tonanti.
Regibus inpendi debent reverentia amorque,
Nullus namque deo nisi permittente potens est.
Reges ergo boni venerandi et sunt imitandi,
955 Perversi non sunt imitandi, sed venerandi;
Talia principibus, vos ipsos reddite Christo.
    "Si quid subdiacon vel acolitus aut eciam ille
Cui nondum tribuit benedictio sancta coronam
(Et tamen inbutus libris Christoque dicatus),
960 Turpe gerunt, vetita non est a parte trahendum
Exemplar vitae. Decet ut sitis memores quod
Maioris semper gravius delicta notantur.
Omnibus este modis cauti; quodcumque docetis
Quodque agitis, causa perfecti fiat amoris.
965 Hic amor est non presbiteris dumtaxat habendus,
Sed cuncti vero debent in amore fideles
Vivere; verus amor non novit rodere quemquam."

EXPLICIT LIBER TERTIUS.

drunk with wine? Rather, he shuns that, considering that 940
men urged on by wine reveal everything.

"Serve kings and lords, even if they are reprobates, for
they have been appointed for you by the supreme King to
repress harmful men, and to honor and protect mild men.
Often a bad king rules good people, like Saul, under whom 945
there were the holy men, Samuel and David. Often an evil
king defends good men and the law, as the same [Saul] pro-
tected the Jews from the fury of the Philistines. Finally, ren-
der to kings what belongs to kings, and to the Lord what
belongs to the Lord. Let the image of the king be rendered
to the king, but let the image of the Lord be rendered to 950
the Lord. Justice and trust should be returned to the Thun-
derer. Respect and love ought to be paid to kings, for no one
is powerful unless God permits it. Therefore, good kings
should be paid homage and imitated, wicked kings should 955
not be imitated, but should be paid homage; render such
things to princes, [but] give yourselves to Christ.

"If a subdeacon or acolyte or even that one to whom a
holy blessing has not yet imparted tonsure, (and yet he has
been introduced to books and is devoted to Christ), does
something shameful, an example of life should not be drawn 960
from what is forbidden. You ought to remember that the
sins of an elder are always censured more severely. Be cau-
tious in every way; whatever you teach and what you do, let
it be for the sake of perfect love. This love must not belong 965
only to priests, but all the faithful ought to live in true love;
true love does not know how to slander anyone."

HERE THE THIRD BOOK ENDS.

I

De eo, quod fides sine operibus mortua sit

Huc usque Eufronius. Docto parete magistro,
Quisquis ubique, viri! Non parvus federis almi
Sit cultus vobis quod epistola sacra Iohannis
Undique commendat fratresque hortatur amare.
5   Sed dives multas cui reddit tribula gloces,
Cui spretis cumeris tenet area multa medimna
Atque choros, batis ad mensam vina feruntur,
Si fratri durus sua viscera claudit egenti,
Ille procul dubio longe est ab amore tonantis.
10   Regis apostatici famulos famulosque tonantis
Fraternus discernit amor. Quo plenius illud
Noscas: quisque suam signet Christi cruce frontem,
Ymnum quisque canat crocitantis dulcia galli,
Postque preces "amen" subiungat et "alleluia,"
15   Si fratrem rodit, quod agit nichil est. Idiota
Maximus est! Contra qui fratrem diligit, illum
Insanum cuncti licet appellentque cucullum,
Grammaticis et rhetoricis sapientior ille est.

166

I

Concerning the Fact That Faith Without Works Is Dead

Thus far [says] Euphronius. Obey the learned master, men, whoever and wherever you are! May you religiously observe the kind compact that the holy epistle of John commends everywhere and encourages brothers to love. But a rich man whose threshing sled yields much grain, whose threshing floor holds many bushels and measures, scorning his bins, whose wines are brought to the table in gallons, if, unfeeling, he shuts his heart to a brother in need, without doubt he is far from the love of the Thunderer. Brotherly love distinguishes between servants of the apostate king and servants of the Thunderer. So that you may come to know this more fully: whoever marks his forehead with the cross of Christ, whoever sings the hymn of the cock crowing sweet melodies, and who adds "Amen" and "Alleluia" after his prayers, if he slanders a brother, what he does is nothing. He is an exceedingly ignorant man! On the other hand, one who loves a brother, even if all men call him insane and a fool, is wiser than the grammarians and rhetoricians.

Omnes insudent libris quantumlibet, omnes
20 Tortarum invigilent enigmatibus rationum,
Illud et illud ament addiscere, vir bonus atque
Vir metuens dominum sapientes prevenit omnes.
Namque timor domini fons est et oricho sophiae.
Ergo timoratis famulemur celipotenti
25 Cordibus, et quoniam brevis istius est mora vitae,
Gaudia miremur moderatius ista caduca,
Optantes nobis patriae infinita supernae
Gaudia, que nullus gustu, grafio, ratione,
Quanta et qualia sunt exponere sufficit; hinc est
30 Quod quidam sapiens inquit: "Non audiit auris
Nec contemplata est acies nec cordis in imo
Percensere valet quisquam, quae conditor ipse
Sese credenti seseque paravit amanti."
Et quis amat dominum? Qui iungit opus fidei, nam
35 Cassa iacet virtus equitis si non habet arma,
Nil valet ingenium studioso si caret usu,
Nec nisi iuncta valent opera atque fides: sine flatu
Non est viva caro, nec viva fides sine factis.
Quid prodest solis dominum verbis profiteri?
40 Quid iuvat inferno contradixisse tiranno
Ipsius et pompis si vis ad omissa reverti?
Sus ad sentinam redit, ad vomitum canis; horum
Non pudet acta sequi? Multo prudentior est te
Infans; urticas ignemque timet semel ustus.
45 Quid dicam? Satius certe et venialius esset
Non cepisse viam veri quam linquere ceptam.
Perdere parta magis turpe est quam nulla parasse.
Ah pudet atque piget procerum de perdicione
Dicere multiplici! Quidam post illita fronti

Let all men sweat over books as much as they want, let all 20
stay awake over the riddles of contorted reckonings, let all
love to learn this and that, [but] a good man, a man who
fears the Lord, surpasses all wise men. Indeed, fear of the
Lord is the source and beginning of wisdom. Therefore, let
us serve the Ruler of Heaven with hearts full of awe, and, 25
since the time of this life is short, let us marvel at these tran-
sitory joys with more moderation, choosing for ourselves
the unending joys of the homeland above, whose greatness
and nature no one can sufficiently explain by foretaste, pen
or calculation; thus it is that a certain wise man said: "Ear 30
has not heard nor has the eye observed nor can anyone
reckon in the depths of his heart what the Creator has pre-
pared for the one who believes in him and loves him."

And who loves the Lord? The man who joins works to
faith, for a knight's prowess is useless if he has no weapons, 35
genius has no power if it lacks learned uses, and neither do
works and faith have power unless they are conjoined: with-
out a soul, flesh is not alive, nor is faith alive without deeds.
What good is it to profess belief in the Lord with words
alone? What benefit to have opposed the infernal tyrant and 40
his pomp if you're willing to revert to what you have re-
nounced? A sow returns to her sewer, a dog to its vomit; are
you not ashamed to follow their actions? An infant is much
wiser than you; once burned, it fears stinging nettles and
fire.

What shall I say? It would surely be better and more par- 45
donable not to have undertaken the way of truth than to
abandon it once undertaken. It is more shameful to lose
possessions than to have acquired none. Ah, it shames me
and grieves me to talk about the manifold perdition of our

50 Signa olei liquidum picta de pixide nardum
Sumentes flavos detecto vertice crines
Ungunt et mitras imponunt desuper albas.
Quorundam auriculas salpistae fistula mulcet
Non attendentum quod versiculus sonat iste:
55 "Non placant dominum blandae tibicinis odae,"
Non delectatur Saliorum carmine molli.
 Est aliud quod avet nimirum: ut semper agamus
Que iubet, et semper vigilemus corde nec umquam
Nos peccatorum sopor opprimat atque retardet.
60 Ignoramus enim quo tempore vel quibus horis
Iudex adveniat, num quando crepuscula lucem
Obscurant aut in mediae caligine noctis
Aut galli cantu vel summo mane velut fur.
Magna et amara dies domini subito veniet; tunc
65 Premia quisque suo capiet condigna labori.
 Nemo perfectus, nemo omni parte beatus,
Nullus vivit homo cunctis virtutibus esse
Qui valeat nitidus, non omnis in omnibus aptus.
Tellus illa piris, hec aptior est oleastris;
70 Illic fertilis spicas ager edit opimas,
Hic melius plenis vivescit vinea botris.
Sic homines variis clarent virtutibus: hic est
Sobrius, ille humilis, hic mitis et ille pudicus.
Inque sui patris conplura habitacula Christus
75 Retulit esse domo studia ob diversa piorum.
 Novi nec rennuo verum nec multa nec una
Sanctificat virtus hominem si non erit illi
Verus amor, per quem virtutes nos decet omnes
Cogere paulatim scalamque acquirere ad astra.
80 Paulatim ex multis pontem producere lignis

nobles! Certain ones, after the sign [of the cross] has been   50
smeared with oil on their brow, take clear nard from a
painted box and, with their head uncovered, grease their
golden locks and place white turbans over them. A player's
reed pipe delights the ears of certain ones who pay no heed
to what this little verse means: "The soothing songs of a   55
trumpeter do not please the Lord," nor is he charmed by the
tender song of the Salii.

There is something else that he wishes: (no surprise) that
we always do what he commands, and that we always be
watchful in our hearts, that the stupor of sinners never over-   60
whelm us and keep us back. For we know not in what season
or what hour the judge may come, whether when dusk dark-
ens the daylight, or in the gloom of midnight, or at cock-
crow, or at earliest dawn like a thief. The mighty, bitter day
of the Lord will come suddenly; then each one will receive   65
rewards worthy of his toil.

No one is perfect, no one is blessed in all respects, no
man is alive who can shine in all virtues, not every man can
be good in all things. That ground is suited to pears, this one
is more suited to wild olives; there a fertile field produces   70
copious grain, here a vineyard with abundant grapes thrives
better. In the same way men are illustrious for different vir-
tues: this one is temperate, that one humble, this one gentle,
and that one chaste. Christ told how in his father's house
there are many dwellings on account of the diverse endeav-   75
ors of the blessed.

I know and do not deny that certainly neither many vir-
tues, nor a single virtue makes a man holy if true love is not
in him, through which it is fitting for us to gather together
all the virtues little by little, and to secure a staircase to the
stars. A workman knows how to build a bridge little by little   80

Scit faber et multis turrim conponere saxis.
Hinc est quod domini spectans archana Iohannes
Diversis aulam gemmis constare supremam
Narrat, et ex illis bis sex specialiter effert.
85   Quarum, si potero, paucis misteria pandam,
Insuper et referam quo queque colore notetur.

2

De XII lapidibus
et misteriis eorum

Iaspis gramineo pollet viridique colore,
Significans firme fidei virtute virentes.
Celesti solio similis saphirus memoratur;
90   Iste figurat eos, qui Pauli dogma sequentes
Dicunt: "In caelis est conversatio nostra."
Ast hebes accensae calcedon more lucernae
Lucet et argutis mire sculptoribus obstat.
Designat sanctos feritas quos nulla malorum
95   Edomat, ardentes operum fervore bonorum,
Lucentes vitae cum dant exempla beatae.
Ardet non lucens qui secreto bene vivit;
Lucet non ardens bona qui loquitur male vivens.
Sed fari bene cum vivas male pessima res est.
100   Prestantem Scithicis in finibus esse smaragdum,

from many planks, and how to construct a tower from many stones. Thus it is that John, considering the Lord's mysteries, tells how the hall of heaven is composed of different gems, and of these he praises twelve in particular. If I can, 85 I'll explain their secrets in a few words, and besides, I'll tell which color marks each one.

2

On the Twelve Precious Stones and Their Secrets

The jasper is valued for its grassy, green color, signifying those who thrive in the virtue of steadfast faith. The sapphire is said to be like the throne of heaven; it represents 90 those who, following the teaching of Paul, declare: "Our citizenship is in heaven." But dull chalcedony shines like a lighted lamp and resists skillful stonecutters in a wondrous way. It denotes the saints whom no savagery of evil men van- 95 quishes, saints inflamed by the ardor of good works, shining when they give examples of a blessed life. One who lives rightly in private burns while not shining; one living wickedly, who talks about goodness, shines, but does not burn. But to speak morally when you live wickedly is the worst thing.

They say that the emerald is outstanding in the land of 100

Atque ibi grifes eam memorant servare feroces.
Hic lapis est viridis; circumfert aera sudum
Qua iacet, astantes sese speculantur in illo.
Ille fide virides prefert; huic additur aer,
105 Ut quisquis caeli dominum credendo fatetur
Alta poli secum sincero corde volutet.
    Sardonicen pingit species diversa colorum.
Hic lapis est rubeus, niveus, niger. Indicat illos
Denigrat quos mens humilis, mens casta dealbat,
110 Et qui non dubitant mortem pro fratre subire.
Sardius est rubrae similis terrae. Notat illos
Qui, cum sint hominum preclari laudibus, ipsi
Tamquam vas figuli se tractant esse caducos.
Crisolitus proprio splendet pulcherrimus auro
115 Scintillas emittit; et hic monstrat sapientes
Verbi scintillas in fratrum corda vomentes.
    Pallens atque virens valet hos signare berillus
Qui bonitate virent, humili sed pectore pallent.
Albens atque rubens viridisque topazius in se
120 Dicitur omnimodos lapidum cohibere colores.
Signat eos cunctis qui se virtutibus aptant.
Crisoprassum viridis commendat et aurea forma.
Quos lapis iste refert, nisi qui credunt sapienter?
Iacinctus lymphae radio solis decoratae
125 Persimilis designat eos qui in fluctibus istis
Solem iusticiae gestant in pectore semper.
Quam ponit prudens ametistum in fine Iohannes
Purpuream, roseam violaeque colore nitentem.
Sanctos pretendit fidei quos purpura vestit,
130 Qui mundo viles studio redolent pietatis,

174

the Scythians, and recount that ferocious griffins guard it there. This stone is green; it exudes clear air around where it lies, and those standing near see themselves in it. This stone represents those who are green in their faith; to this air is added in order that whoever acknowledges the Lord of 105 Heaven by believing [in him] may reflect on the heights of the firmament with a pure heart.

Colors of different kinds embellish the sardonyx. This stone is red, snow-white, and black. It indicates those whom a humble mind renders obscure, a chaste mind whitens, and those who do not hesitate to suffer death for a brother. The 110 sardius is similar to red earth. It signifies those who, although they are renowned because of men's praises, consider themselves frail, just like a potter's vessel. The chrysolite is resplendent, gorgeous with its own gold and sends 115 forth sparks; this stone too indicates wise men who pour sparks of the Word into their brothers' hearts.

The beryl, at once green and pale, can signify these men who flourish in goodness, but who are pale because of a humble heart. The white, red, and green topaz is said to contain all sorts of colors of precious stones in itself. It signifies 120 those who apply themselves to all the virtues. A green and golden appearance graces the chrysoprase. Whom does this stone refer to, except those who believe wisely? The jacinth, very similar to water adorned by a ray of the sun, represents 125 those who, amidst these waves [of the stormy world] always carry the sun of justice in their heart. At the end,—how prudent!—John places the amethyst, purple, rosy, and bright with the color of a violet. It stands for saints whom the purple garment of faith clothes, those who, though worthless in 130 the eyes of the world, are redolent in the zeal of their piety,

Martirium subeunt pro Christo sive propinquo.
Talibus ex gemmis norunt in corde bonorum
Edificare fides et amor durabile templum,
Non quale artifices terreni marmore glauco
135 Cementoque struunt; illud resolubile iure est
Quod manus edificat fragilis, sed quod deus ipse
Alpha vocatus et w fabricat, non corruit umquam.
    Attestante Iohanne deus dilectio vera est,
Et scitis quoniam absque deo durabile nil est.
140 Ergo si quid amor conponit cordis in antro,
Componit deus. Hic etiam firmissima petra est.
Supra quam quisquis sapiens fundaverit urbem
Virtutum, poterit securam ducere vitam.
Illam non aries validus, non hostica possunt
145 Spicula subruere, et ventis moti maris estus
Non subvertet eam; Boree quoque tuta resistit.
    Qui Christo dignum sincero pectore templum
Edificare cupit, sordes eliminet omnes
Et quae conantur pessundare scandala mentem,
150 Spiritus auxilium poscens a numine vero
Funditus evellat. Nisi corruptum ante pietur
Vas, inamarescit quod dulce infunditur. Hoc est:
Ni de corde prius viciorum prorsus agatur
Foetor, virtutes si quas inmittis, acescunt.
155 Hoc sanctus David manifesta voce notavit
Cum primo sibi cor mundari, deinde petivit
Ut sibi spiramen faciendi recta daretur.
    Sed mihi forte aliquis dicit: "Mala respuo, nulli
Quod noceat facio, nec latro sum nec adulter,
160 A cunctis absisto malis quantum fragilis me
Carnis permittit levitas. Quid plus mihi agendum est?"

and who suffer martyrdom for Christ or their neighbor. Out of such gems faith and love know how to build a lasting temple in the hearts of good people, not such as earthly masons construct with gray marble and mortar; what a perishable 135 hand builds is justly able to be dissolved, but what God himself makes, who is called alpha and omega, never falls down.

God is true love, as John attests, and you know that nothing apart from God is lasting. And so, if love puts anything 140 in the depths of the heart, God puts it there. Here also is the firmest rock. If any wise man establishes a city of virtues on this rock, he will be able to lead a secure life. A strong battering ram cannot demolish it, nor can enemy arrows, 145 and the surge of the sea stirred by winds will not destroy it; it also safely withstands the North Wind.

The man, pure in heart, who longs to build a temple worthy of Christ, let him get rid of all uncleanness and, begging the aid of the spirit from the true deity, let him utterly eradi- 150 cate the temptations that endeavor to conquer his mind. Unless a stained vessel is cleansed beforehand, a sweet liquid which is poured into it becomes bitter. This is the point: unless the stench of vices is utterly driven from the heart first, if you admit any virtues into the heart, they turn sour. Holy David indicated this with a clear voice when first he 155 asked that his heart be cleansed, then he asked that the spirit of doing what is right be granted to him.

But perhaps someone says to me: "I spurn wicked deeds, I do nothing harmful to anyone, I am neither a thief nor an adulterer, I refrain from all evil as much as the frail fickle- 160 ness of the flesh allows me. What more must I do?" It is not

Non satis est vitasse malum, latam viciorum
Dimisisse viam, nisi agas bona; nec satis est quod
Mitis es ut servus penae formidine tantum,
165   Ni bene ceu liber vivas bonitatis amore.

3

De eo, quod mundus sit contempnendus

Angusta est summam quae semita ducit ad arcem;
Quisquis eo tendis, fallacem despice mundum.
In cute dulcorem monstrat, latet intus amarum,
Ut iuvenes quorum digitos teres anulus ornat,
170   Qui crispos per colla pilos vernantia iactant
Et subtalares pictos ligulis et acutos
Luteolis decorant spreto perone pedestri,
Dicentes secum: "Quid pulchra nocet dare verba?"
Dum spondent bene, dum per famina ficta puellas
175   Inducunt stolidas, decerpto flore recedunt.
Utque solet blesis flenti nutricula parvo
Blandiri verbis, ita sese mundus amanti
Blanditur pro iusticia, ne lugeat istic.
Sed tu qui patriam curas attingere veram,
180   *Respue opes falsas, fuge caeca negocia mundi,*
Et cessa hunc atque hunc precurrere, ne cruciet te

enough to have avoided evil, to have abandoned the wide
way of vices, unless you do good; it is not enough that you
are meek like a slave out of fear of punishment alone, unless,   165
like a free man, you lead a moral life out of love of goodness.

3

On the Fact That the World
Should Be Scorned

Narrow is the path that leads to the highest citadel; you who
travel on it, shun this deceptive world. It shows sweetness
on the surface, [but] bitterness lurks within, like young men
whose smooth fingers a little ring adorns, who toss their   170
curly locks over their young necks and embellish their or-
nate pointed shoes with yellow laces after their plain boots
have been discarded, while saying to themselves: "What's
the harm in speaking pretty words?" While they are making
solemn promises, while they bring home dull-witted girls   175
using lying speeches, once their virginity has been taken,
they retreat. And as a nurse is accustomed to soothe a weep-
ing child with lisping words, so—instead of providing jus-
tice—the world soothes one who loves it, lest he mourn
there. But you who care to reach the true homeland, reject   180
false riches, flee the blind business of the world, and cease
to run about here and there, so that it does not torment you

Quod quis in hoc mundo sit fortunatior, et quod
Ubera vicini sint uberiora peculi.
   Nunc divina sacro subsunt humanaque nummo,
185 Sed pro toto animam quid prodest perdere mundo?
Capadocum regio tibi serviat et Garamantum,
Insuper Assiriae gens, et quae potat Hidaspen,
Denique si quicquid sub caeli nascitur axe,
Te tremat, ire tamen quo Iulius ivit oportet.
190 Exiguo mundi monarchos clauditur antro,
Cui Sporinna fuit necis et Calpurnia vates.
Herodesque abiit, quem virtus summa cecidit
Caesareae rapta pocientem coniuge fratris.
Respue opes falsas, fuge ceca negocia mundi!
195   Navus et egregius non es nisi lumina mille
Te spectent dicantque homines: "Hic omine dextro
Prodiit ad lucem; quem vestit musio tensus
Tergore castoreo, consuta nitedula bysso,
Renones crisii." Sic sic cenodoxia multos
200 Cecat. Nempe gulis vestitus dives et ostro
Quid nisi homo est vitam cui muscula vel brevis occat,
Qui ceu flos ferulae transit niveumque ligustrum?
Respue opes falsas, fuge ceca negocia mundi!
    Si cupis ingenuus dici, sis glutto neposque,
205 Ut saturo et crudo cum calo "Mandite!" dicat,
Reddas: "Non queo. Da tamen huc! Offa allicit offam.
Sed primum, quaeso, refer unde culina vaporet."
"Cum muria pisces, allec vel habebitis assum
Aut si plus placeat, caro, condimenta anatesque."
210 "Rustice nequaquam dominorum nutibus apte,

because someone in this world is more fortunate, and because the udders of your neighbor's cattle are fuller.

Now divine and human affairs are valued less than accursed money, but what does it profit to lose your soul for   185
the whole world? Let the lands of the Cappadocians and Garamantes serve you, and the people of Assyria besides, and those who drink the Hydaspes, and finally, if anything is born under the wheel of the heavens, let it tremble at you, yet you all the same must go where Julius has gone. The ruler   190
of the world, for whom Spurinna and Calpurnia were prophets of death, is enclosed in a small sepulcher. And Herod has passed away, whom the highest power cut down while he was master of Caesarea, after he ravished his brother's wife. Reject false riches, flee the blind business of the world!

You are not industrious and illustrious unless a thousand   195
eyes look at you and men say: "This fellow has come forth into the world with good luck; he wears tight wild-sheepskin with a beaver-fur back, dormouse stitched with fine chiffon, and grayish reindeer skin." Thus, thus, does vainglory blind many men. Of course, what is a rich man clothed in crim-   200
son and purple except a man whose life even a little fly destroys, a man who passes away like a fennel blossom and a snowy privet? Reject false riches, flee the blind business of the world!

If you wish to be called noble, be a glutton and a spendthrift, so that when a servant says "Eat!" to you, stuffed and   205
feeling heartburn, you might reply: "I can't. Yet, hand it over anyway! A lump attracts a lump. But first, I ask, tell me what smells [good] in the kitchen." "You'll have fish with brine, herring, or a roast or, if it might please you more, flesh, seasonings, and ducks." "Simpleton not at all suited to the com-   210

Aufer! An ignoras quod pendo domestica flocci?
Navita vel sutor seu mercennarius, et qui
Triturat far et molit, inmundusque subulcus
Hec comedant. Foveat me sorbiciuncula lenis,
215   Privatique cibi quos flagitat alvus herilis.
Esseda, plaustra, trahe quae gestant atque carine;
Sunt mea! Trade libens mihi rara cibaria, trade!"
    "Eia age, dumtaxat mihi dicite quid cupiatis,
Ursi aut iricii gustum, pavonis, oloris
220   Est mihi, doque." "'Valet' raro bene fecit. Haberem."
Si pavo placet et distinctis picus in alis,
Cur picam renuis? Si garrulitate cibaris,
Psitacus et pullis vestita monedula plumis
Te pascant! Alvum cur, inprobe, rumpere queris?
225   Euge! lavare satur dapibusque dapes coacerva
Non pensans venter quod dissolvetur et esca.
"Num modica Ganges cavus augeri indiget unda,
Aut Vosegus parvo ditari pondere ligni?
Ergo quid faciam? Mihi si rubigo tenaci
230   Obducit nummos, 'Ve vappe' dicitur 'illi!
Tantalus in medio sitit amne nec accipit inde.'
Porro si partis fruor, ut procus omnia vasto.
Seu bene agat seu non, infelix undique peccat."
    Si nescis quorsum nummus valet, accipe quorsum:
235   Debita naturae nummus solatia reddat.
Nec nimium serves discretus, nec nimium des.
In medio limes tutissimus est gradienti.
In cunctis modus est; nimium reprehenditur omne.
Quesitis igitur debes mediocriter uti,
240   Ut quod contento paucis superest, inopum sit.

mands of lords, take it away! Or don't you know that I care
not a straw for native foods? Let a sailor or shoemaker or
hired hand eat these, and one who threshes and grinds grain,
and a filthy swineherd. Let a small, mild sip warm me, and
special foods that a master's stomach demands. Bring forth   215
what wagons, carts, and ships carry; they are mine! Cheer-
fully deliver rare victuals to me! Bring them on!"

   "Come now, simply tell me what you desire and I'll give
it. I have an appetizer of bear or hedgehog, of peacock or
swan." "'It's healthy' rarely has done well. I'll have some." If   220
you like peacock and woodpecker with spotted wings, why
do you refuse magpie? If you're fed by chattering, let a par-
rot and a jackdaw covered with dark feathers nourish you!
Rascal, why do you seek to burst your belly? Oh, good! Full   225
of food, bathe and heap up feast upon feast, not considering
that the belly is worn out even by food. "Does the deep Gan-
ges need to be augmented with a little water, or the Vosges
to be enriched with a small load of wood? And so, what shall
I do? If rust overspreads the coins I hold fast, people say   230
'Woe to that good-for-nothing! Tantalus is thirsty in the
middle of a stream and doesn't drink from it.' But if I enjoy
what I've acquired, I'm wasting it all like a suitor. Whether
he acts rightly or not, an unfortunate man offends every-
where."

   If you don't know what money is good for, learn what for:
money bestows the comforts owed to nature. Be discerning.   235
Don't keep too much, don't give too much. A path in the
middle is safest for one who is walking. In all things there
is a limit; every excess is criticized. Thus, you ought to use
what you've gained in moderation, so that what is left over   240
for the man who is content with few possessions may belong
to the poor.

Sperne balatronum laudes scurrasque dicaces
Abice! Mens recti sibi conscia gloria vera est.
Scurrae cum coram tibi sesquipedale sonoro
Dant nomen plausu, post munera capta cachinnum
245 Tollunt absentes: "Evax! se furcifer ille
Auctumat esse probum palponum laude probatus!"
Insipiens aliis plus credit quam sibi de se.
    Evigilans tandem sodes ordire modestam
Vitam. "Ni fallor, mihi vis auferre leporem
250 Mundanum penitus." Vere, quia tempore parvo
Nobiscum durant liquidi oblectamina mundi.
Albin bellorum, studii tedebit Athenas,
Francigenasque mares lentis girare pigebit
Spadices loris operamque citis dare glaucis,
255 Seque neoptolemi resipiscent dedere ludis,
Gymnasium et peltas et cetera talia ponent.
Omnia presentis cessabunt ludicra vitae;
Quae quisquis probat esse dei convincitur hostis.
Nemo potest dominis pariter servire duobus.
260 Spreta magis tribus est infesti curia regis
Infantis postquam visere crepundia summi;
Haut secus ecclesiam qui veri principis aulam
Iam visit, mundi spem respuat atque timorem.
    Felix paupertas, quae nec metuis neque speras!
265 Namque scrobes Stigie capient terrena inhiantes.
Uxor Loth sal facta monet ne respiciamus.
Quocirca qui vis ad veram tendere Segor,
Respue opes falsas, fuge ceca negocia mundi
Illuc festinans ubi vere diviciae atque

Spurn the praises of buffoons and get rid of pert jesters! A mind that knows what is right for itself is a true glory. When jesters bestow a name a foot-and-a-half long on you in your presence, with resounding applause, then elsewhere, after they've received gifts, they arouse a guffaw: "Hurrah! That rogue thinks he's honorable because he was commended by the praise of flatterers!" The foolish man believes more about himself from others than from himself.

Finally, while being vigilant, please undertake a modest way of life. "Unless I'm mistaken, you want to take worldly charm away from me completely." Indeed, because the delights of this fluid world remain with us for a short time. The Elbe will be weary of wars, the Athenians of studies, the French will be loath to wheel about their brown stallions with slack reins and to bestow care on swift gray ones, and young squires will repent of devoting themselves to games, and they will put aside [military] training and shields and other such things. All the trifles of this present life will cease; whoever approves of these is shown to be an enemy of God. No one can equally serve two masters. The court of the hostile king was avoided by the Three Wise Men after they saw the rattle of the infant most high; just so, the man who has now seen a church, the hall of the true Prince, let him spurn the hope and fear of the world.

Blessed are you, poverty, that neither fears nor hopes! For indeed, the ditches of hell will receive those who gape at earthly goods. Lot's wife, turned to salt, warns us not to look back. For this reason, you who wish to proceed to the true Zoar, reject false riches, flee the blind business of the world while hurrying to that place where true riches and true joys

270 Gaudia vera manent, dolor est ubi nullus, ubi nec
Papilio solem nec tegula dimovet ymbrem,
Nemo gelu quatitur, nemo torretur ab estu,
Pacis ubi vere locus est vitaeque perennis.
Ne dicas, "Cras incipiam bene vivere," sed nunc
275 Incipe; ne tardes. Facilis sequitur via ceptum.
Accelera, dum tempus habes. Inopina repente
Mors venit et iuncto locupletem paupere tollit,
Quique hodie vivit si vivat cras quoque nescit.
Sed mortis variae quicumque color rapiet te,
280 Si te preripiet iustum, securus abibis.
Ergo, age, festinus mundanos effuge casses;
Respue opes falsas, fuge ceca negotia mundi
Dum te dira sinit mors. Ne fugere incipias tunc
Quando fuge non est locus. Inde suis deus inquit
285 Asseclis: "Curae vobis sit ne fuga vestra
Tempore in hiberno fiat vel sabbato," in ista
Non multum licet die. Nive cum tegit Alpes
Tristis hiemps, iter aggressis via commoda non est.
Sic post hanc vitam nulli se corrigere, hostem
290 Infernum effugere tempus. Qui presbitero nunc
Crimina quae gessit profiteri negligit, et qui
Nunc ex corde suos non vult deflere reatus:
Post obitum supplex veniam poscet, nec habebit.
Occidit Euridice postquam respexit et Orpheus,
295 In cassum flevit. "Nugaris, agagula"; longus
Inquit Yperephanes, "quid tot proverbia ructas?
Nil quod perdat habens latronem non timet, et nil
Prorsus ais. Dives semper manet anxius, et tu

abide, where there is no pain, where no tent hides the sun   270
and no roof keeps away the rain, where no one trembles be-
cause of ice, no one is parched from the heat, where there is
a place of true peace and everlasting life.

Lest you might say, "Tomorrow I'll begin to live rightly," I   275
say begin now; don't delay. An easy path follows this begin-
ning. Make haste, while you have time. Unexpected death
comes suddenly and carries off the rich man along with the
pauper, and one who is alive today doesn't know if he'll be
alive tomorrow too. But whatever the color of the motley
death that will snatch you away, you will depart untroubled   280
if it falls upon you as a just man. Therefore, come, flee in
haste from worldly snares; reject false riches, flee the blind
business of the world as long as cruel death permits you.
Don't begin to flee at a time when there is no opportunity
for flight. Thus God said to his followers: "Take care that   285
your flight not be in the winter season or on the Sabbath,"
[for] on that day not much is allowed. When harsh winter
covers the Alps with snow, the way is not easy for those hav-
ing undertaken a journey.

Thus, after this life no one has time to reform himself, to   290
escape the infernal enemy. One who now neglects to confess
the sins he has committed to a priest, and who now is un-
willing sincerely to deplore his guilt: he will beg pardon as
a suppliant after death, and he will not get it. After Or-
pheus looked back, Eurydice died, and he wept in vain. Tall   295
Hiperefanes says, "You're talking nonsense, you babbler;
why are you belching out so many proverbs? One who has
nothing to lose doesn't fear a robber, and you are certainly

Pauper es invitus. Nosti quid Oratius inquit?
300 Virtus et nobilitas sine re plus carice sordet."
Respue opes falsas, fuge ceca negotia mundi!
"Quid tantum garris, homo mensurae tripedalis?
Raro breves humiles vidi rufosque fideles."
Accipe quod reddo: longos miror sapientes,
305 Albos audaces; non iure calumnior a te.
Tu scis quod sapiens Zebedei filius inter
Cetera dicit: "Amans mundana deum fugat a se."
"Vin semper vivam bene nec prevaricer unquam
Eterni mandata dei?" Quis semper iniquam
310 Obpugnare potest aciem, nisi quem iuvat ille?
Quo retrahente manus Amalehc leo sevit ut Afer?
Nemo. Sed idcirco debemus tendere nisu
Omnes unanimi caelestis ad atria vitae.
"At minime scimus quis perventurus eo sit."
315 Solus namque deus novit quos destinet illuc.
Ergo qui bonus est illustratusque videtur
Virtutum radiis non ampulletur in illis.
Viventis recte laus est in fine canenda.
Nauta licet placidis committat carbasa ventis,
320 Non prius est tutus quam corripit anchora portum.
Adde quod Hesperias cum Titan vergit in undas,
Dignam laude diem demum quae claruit aiunt.
Et qui finetenus non servit premia perdit.
Stultus cepta probat bona; prudens ultima spectat.
325 Hec ego vos doceo, docuit me summa sophia,
Scilicet omnipotens. Haec exercete, fideles.

saying nothing. A rich man remains always anxious, and you
are a reluctant pauper. Do you know what Horace said? Vir-   300
tue and nobility without property are more worthless than
sedge." Reject false riches, flee the blind business of the
world! "Why do you chatter so much, you three-foot dwarf?
I've rarely seen humble short men or trustworthy redheads."

Hear what I reply: I'm astonished that tall men are wise,
[or that] pale men are bold; I'm accused unjustly by you.   305
You know what the wise son of Zebediah said among other
things. "One who loves worldly things drives God away from
himself." "Do you want me to live rightly always and never
to violate the commands of God Everlasting?" Who can al-
ways resist an unequal battle line, except one whom he   310
helps? No one. When he withdrew his hand, Amalek raged
like an African lion. But for that reason we ought all to
march with single-minded effort toward the halls of celes-
tial life. "But we do not know who is going to reach there."
In fact, God alone knows whom he might destine for that   315
place.

Therefore, let the man who is good and who seems il-
luminated by rays of virtue not be puffed up in those mat-
ters. Praise of one who lives rightly should be sung at the
end [of his life]. Although a sailor entrusts his sails to calm
winds, he is not safe before his anchor takes hold in port.   320
Add the fact that when the sun inclines toward the western
seas, men say at last that the day that was bright was worthy
of praise. And the man who does not persevere to the end
loses his rewards. A fool approves good beginnings; a wise
man looks to the end. These things that I teach you, the   325
highest wisdom, namely the Almighty, has taught me. Prac-
tice them, O men of faith!

4

De eo, quod non possit regnum caelorum acquiri sine patientia

Codicibus sacris ad nostrum tendere docma
Illita quem lateat? Quoniam si iugiter illis
Pupula pascatur, quam novimus esse lucernam
330 Corporis, et spectet divina volumina crebro,
Ferre probra et forti certare docemur agone.
Lectus Iob fimus est, Stephanus lapidum ymbre necatur,
Mauricius gladio, Vincentius igne catastae.
Ergo, viri, quibus est demissum nomen ab illo,
335 Prodiit irradians hirto qui e corpore Christus,
Ut sol cum rapido ventorum turbine mixtae
Fulmina producunt nubes, tonitrusque fragosi
Mortales terrent pavidos tempestaque grando,
Effulget subita discissa nube nitela,
340 Condigno signate gradu vestigia Christi.
      Qui, quos arguta seduxit mango loquela
Furvus ab Egipto deducere reddere sponte
Dignatus, scribis voluit simul et Phariseis
Vendi per Scarioth, facibus sudibusque prehendi,
345 Dignanterque pati feralis flagra Pilati,
Atque cruci figi, velud hoc predixit Esayas:
"Crimina nostra gerens stauros oblatus in ara
Sponte sua est." Rursusque alibi scriptum reperitur:

4

On the Fact That the Kingdom of Heaven Cannot Be Acquired without Suffering

From whom is it concealed that what has been written in sacred texts pertains to our teaching? Because if the eye feasts on those continually, the eye which we know to be the light of the body, and it repeatedly looks at the divine books, we are taught to bear reproaches and to fight in a brave struggle. Job's bed was dung, Stephen was killed by a shower of stones, Maurice by a sword, Vincent by fire on a scaffold. Therefore, men, you who derived your name from him, Christ, the one who came forth from a hairy body shining like the sun when clouds mixed together by the swift whirl of winds produce lightning, and roaring thunder and stormy hail terrify fearful mortals, then a sudden brightness shines forth as the clouds separate, follow with worthy step the traces of Christ.

Christ, having deigned to lead out of Egypt and to restore freely those whom a swarthy slave dealer seduced with sly speech, was willing to be sold by Judas to both scribes and Pharisees, to be seized with torches and stakes, to suffer with complaisance the scourges of savage Pilate, and to be fastened to a cross, just as Isaiah foretold: "Bearing our sins, he was sacrificed of his own will on the altar of the cross." And again

330

335

340

345

"Aspicient ad me quem confixere nefandi."
350 Quisquis avet recto post illum calle venire,
Se neget atque crucem patiendo baiolet in se.
"Si recte arboribus cannas potes equiperare
Maceriam muro, mortalem conice Christo."
   Haec, fateor, nequeo paradigmata solvere firme.
355 Sed tamen et pauper differt a divite, nam cum
Horridus autumno cedente coagulat algor
Terras, et glacie constringit Aquarius amnes,
Pellibus incedit vulpinis dives, at isti
Mastrugam prebet detonsus forfice vervex,
360 Et sic ad flores ambo servantur apricos.
Muscose quercus imitantur fronde miricae
Sidereas humili, celsas viburna cupressos,
Labruscae vites foliis, pomaria dumi.
   Loricae confidit eques scuto atque galero,
365 At nos alma fides tegat et tolerantia fortis.
Forcior est patiens robusto milite qui se
Promovet evertens et propugnacula et urbes.
Qui nimium fragiles probra momentanea ferre
Horretis, quid tunc, cum scintillante vorabit
370 Sulphure vos cui non salamandria prevalet ignis?
Aut qui nunc pugnis inpacta vivere bucca
Pulsataque alapis facie diffidis, atroci
Agmine vallatus miror quo corpore possis
Ignitos clatros, ignita repagula ferre?
375   Discipuli humanis innarunt fluctibus, et quos
Vipera non lesit, seps, anphivena, parias,
Scorpius et scitalis, prester, natrix et ophites,
Sibilus et cencris, dipsas, iaculi atque lacertae
Mordebant homines, sed eos patientia eorum

elsewhere we find it written: "Impious men will look upon me whom they have pierced." Whoever longs to come after 350 him on the right path, let him deny himself and, by suffering within, carry his cross. "If you can rightly compare reeds to trees, a garden enclosure to a city wall, [then] compare a mortal man to Christ."

I cannot truly explain these examples, I confess. But yet, 355 a pauper differs from a rich man; for when shivering cold grips the land as autumn departs, and Aquarius freezes the rivers with ice, a rich man goes out in fox pelts, but for this pauper a wether shorn with shears offers a pelt, and thus 360 both are saved for flowers in the sunshine. In their lowly foliage, mossy tamarisks imitate lofty oaks, osier shrubs imitate tall cypresses, wild vines [imitate] vineyard vines with their leaves, brambles [imitate] orchards.

A knight puts his trust in a cuirass, shield, and helmet, 365 but kind faith and firm endurance protect us. One who suffers is stronger than a hardy soldier who pushes onward overthrowing both ramparts and cities. You who are too frail, who shudder to bear momentary reproaches, what then, when fire over which the salamander does not prevail 370 will devour you with glowing sulfur? Or you who now despair to live because your cheek has been hit by fists and your face struck by blows, with what body, I wonder, will you be able to endure glowing grates and fiery bars when you've been surrounded by a dreadful troop [in hell]?

The disciples swam amidst human streams, and men bit 375 those whom the viper did not hurt, or the *seps*, the *amphisbaena*, the *parias*, the scorpion and the *scytale*, the *prester*, the *natrix* and *ophites*, the hissing *cencris*, *dipsas*, *jaculi* and lizards,

380 Coniunxit superis. Hinc est quod fluctibus olim
Archa levata Noe, quia, dum tumidi probra mundi
Subsannant quatiuntque bonos, ad sidera tollunt.
Virtus quoque cadit, quam non pacientia fulcit.
Erumpnas igitur pro Christi perfer amore
385 Has, qui sanctorum fieri iubarisque supremi
Affectas consors. Oportunum tibi nunc est
Tempus quaerendi celestia. Si modo non vis
Vincier adversis, age nunc ne te tenebrarum
Accipiant sedes, ubi nulla licentia sonti
390 Evenit incluso. Non illic filia matri,
Non frater fratri valet esse sororve sorori
Auxilio. Quid avus, patruus vel avunculus illic
Cognatis, avia aut amita aut matertera prosunt?
Non de Tartareo dampnatam gurgite levir
395 Germani sociam, nec salvus amasius olim
Caram diripiet; nurui non proderit illic
Fida socrus, socerumque gener non eruet igni
Addictum Stigio. Pravis et pectore rectis
Eximium discrimen erit, Petro atque Neroni,
400 Herodi et tinctis insonti sanguine cunis.
    Sed mihi dicit homo Sicula ferventior Ethna
Stultus: "Amo tacitos et garrula abominor ora.
Vin, sodes, ut non qui cornicatur inepte
Vapulet, et quaevis liceat blaterare procaci?
405 Paucis est gratus diffundere cuncta paratus.
Flet Iesus si non ulciscatur puer, et quid
Maiores faciant? Infesti sunt mihi scurrae;
Moroso risor, taciturno garrulus obstat,

but their suffering united them to the saints above. Thus it 380
is that long ago Noah's ark was lifted up by waves, since,
while the reproaches of this haughty world deride and ha-
rass good men, they raise them up to the stars. Virtue also
falls, if patience does not support it. Therefore, bear these
tribulations for love of Christ, you who are striving to be- 385
come a colleague of the saints and a sharer of the supreme
splendor. Now is the opportune time for you to seek heav-
enly things. If you don't want to be bound by adversaries
now, act now so that the realm of darkness not receive you,
where there is no freedom for the guilty man confined there. 390
In that place a daughter cannot be a help to her mother, nor
brother to brother or sister to sister. What good are a grand-
father, or fraternal or maternal uncles to relatives in that
place, or a grandmother, or fraternal or maternal aunts? A
brother-in-law will not snatch his brother's doomed spouse
away from the infernal whirlpool, nor will a saved lover 395
snatch away his loved one ever; in that place a faithful
mother-in-law will not benefit her daughter-in-law, and a
son-in-law will not rescue his father-in-law sentenced to the
fire of hell. There will be a distinct difference between the
wicked and the right of heart, between Peter and Nero, be- 400
tween Herod and cradles stained with innocent blood.

But a foolish man hotter than Sicilian Etna says to me:
"I love silent men and abhor chattering mouths. Please! Do
you want one who caws absurdly like a crow not to be
flogged, and one who is impudent to be allowed to babble 405
whatever he wishes? Pleasing is the man prepared to pour
everything out in a few words. An injured boy weeps if he's
not avenged, but what should adults do? Buffoons are hos-
tile to me; a mocker opposes a peevish man, a babbler op-

Scurra leccatori se iungit, honestus honesto,
410 Parvum parvus amat. Sic quisque parem sibi querit."
    "Sed mihi dic per eum qui rura polumque gubernat:
Quid tibi falsa nocet detractio, probrave iusto?
Hoc patere. Hoc sanctos examinat ut focus aurum."
"Dic, queso, collumne iubes ferientibus aptem
415 Inmotum, mirerque manus? Quis inire salutem
Optans, scalpello ventrem rimante secandus,
Lentus membra manet nisi firma fidicula frenet
Brachia cum pedibus? Da cardiaco piponellam,
Nauseat. Ictericus cretam, raphanum peducosus
420 Invitus bibit, os apoplexicus a basilisca
Contrahit." Insulsi qui ignominiam esse putatis
Grandem si stultus vobis infert mala quisquam,
Ni vindicta assit subitanea, et hunc mage torvis
Quam linx aut Biciae, quae hominem, si credere fas est,
425 Intuitu perimunt, oculis lustrare soletis.
    Seminecem, iuvenis, tu te inter balnea fingis:
Mutus es, ut sumpta fertur canis esse rubeta,
Surdus es, ut Marsis se prebet cantibus aspis,
Cecus es, ut non plus videas quam cecula lucem,
430 Ut querula tenuis recreata novacula cote
Pubere te vultu prolixa segrege barba
Reddat, et incedas nitidus per iuncea menta.
Seria ridiculo quid obest sermone notare?
Sic fac nocticulam simules gravitate soporem,
435 Ut tua vir rabidus sarcire piacula quivis

poses a silent one, a buffoon attaches himself to a lecher, an honorable man to an honorable man, a little one loves a 410 little one. Thus, everyone seeks his equal."

"But tell me for the sake of him who rules lands and sky: why does false detraction injure you, or reproaches injure a just man? Suffer this. This tests saints as fire tests gold." "Tell me, I pray, are you ordering that I make my neck motionless 415 for those striking it and that I admire their hands? What man wishing to enter into good health, who must be cut by a scalpel probing his belly, remains immovable in his limbs unless a strong cord restrain his arms and feet? Give burnet to someone with heartburn, he'll vomit. A jaundiced man doesn't want to drink chalk, one with lice doesn't want rad- 420 ish, an apoplectic draws his mouth away from basil." Silly are you who think that it's a great disgrace if some fool insults you, unless there is sudden vengeance, and you're wont to cast on him eyes wilder than [those of] a lynx or Scythian witches which, if we can believe it, kill a man by their glance 425 [alone].

Young man, you make yourself half-dead in the baths: you're dumb, just as a dog is said to be after it's eaten a toad, you're deaf, just as an asp offers itself to Marsian snake charmers' songs, you're blind, so that you see light no more than a blind lizard, in order that a thin razor restored by a 430 whining whetstone may give you back a youthful countenance without your long beard and so that you may go forth shining through beards resembling rushes. What stops [us] from censuring serious matters with amusing satire? Thus, make yourself feign night-loving sleep by your sluggishness, so that any madman may be able to mend your faults with 435

Ictibus aut sanna queat, ornerisque iuventa
Virtutum placida summoto crine notarum.
    Qui paulum lesus fumantem imitare Vesevum,
Nec te metiri vis materiam cariosam,
440 Quando pro Christo ferres tormenta vel ignes?
Deficeres presente malo quem raptus ad alta
Exul signavit sexcentis undecies sex.
Hic pia sanctorum collegia mortificabit;
Multos prodigiis, multos feritate domabit.
445 Tunc sacer Helyas, tunc vivax occidet Enoch.
O quot precones habet ille malus modo. Quorum
Probra et acroma frequens fer, et es martyr sine ferro!
    Pauper cui nulla est possessio, parva suppellex,
Imbricibus trabibusque humeros oneratus et illis
450 Que naves portare solent, a littore migras
Propellisve ratem remis tensoque rudente,
Scandis ad antemnam residesque in margine prorae,
Non tibi sollicitus quod sis casurus in ima,
Et nec bruma tuum sedat nec cauma laborem
455 Vivere quo possis, et tecum sic ais: "Adam
Stultus honore nitens non intellexit; ob hoc nunc
Vivit per magnos humana propago labores."
Murilego dormitanti cecoque tacenti
Raro quid offertur: suda, ne limina noctu
460 Suffodiens oculos perdas aut in cruce vitam.
    An dubitas ergo mundi mala lubrica ferre
Ne sis perpetuo cariturus lumine? Si te
Vexat anhela tysis, cacexica sive catarrus,
Absinti, gamandreae tibi bethoniceaeve

blows or a sneer, and you may be adorned with the quiet youth of virtues when the hair of your sins has been removed.

Offended a little, do you want to imitate smoking Vesuvius, and do you not want to consider yourself corrupted matter, seeing that you might endure torments or fire for 440 Christ? You will be disheartened at the presence of the wicked one whom the exile transported on high signified by 666. He will destroy the devout company of saints; he will overcome many by signs, many by savagery. Then holy Eli- 445 jah, then long-lived Enoch will fall. O, how many heralds does that wicked one now have! Endure their reproaches and frequent buffoonery, and you are a martyr without the sword!

A poor man who has no property, little furniture, whose shoulders are loaded with tiles and beams and those things that ships are wont to convey, you move away from shore 450 or propel the boat with oars and a taut rope, you climb up on the mast and sit on the edge of the prow, unconcerned for your safety, lest you fall to the bottom, and neither does winter nor heat allay the toil by which you need to live, and 455 thus you say to yourself: "Stupid Adam shining in honor did not understand; because of him the human race now lives through great hardships." Rarely is anything offered to a sleeping cat or a blind man who remains silent: work hard, lest while undermining doors at night you lose your eyes or 460 your life on a cross.

Or do you hesitate, therefore, to endure the world's shifting evils lest you be cut off from perpetual light? If a gasping cough, consumption, or catarrh distresses you, you swallow the juice of wormwood, germander, or betony; if gout

465 Hauritur sucus; si gutta nocet tibi, queris
Numquid flebothomi, numquid cauteria prosint.
Ergo magis pro anima tolerare decebit amara
Scilicet irrisus non fastidire vel ictus,
Nam nisi tristicia lucratur gaudia nemo,
470 Nec nisi legitime certantem laurea cinget.

EXPLICIT LIBER QUARTUS.

hurts you, you ask whether lancets and cautery are benefi- 465
cial. Therefore, it will be more fitting to endure bitter words
for your soul, that is to say, not to flinch from derision or
blows, for no one gains joys except through sorrow, nor does
laurel crown anyone who does not participate legitimately 470
in the competition.

HERE THE FOURTH BOOK ENDS.

Oratio ad Sanctam Trinitatem
et fides de resurrectione
carnis

O sator, o soboles, o sancte spiritus, une
Subsistens sine fine deus, quem nostra mathesis
Separe non scindit ductu (luit Arrius illud),
Da, precor, ut superae, compos sit Amarcius aulae
5 Apprendens fidei litus celeste saburra.
Cesar et Emathiae strages et fama Catonis
Lucanum celebrem faciunt; laudatur Opheltem
Stacius evolvens devotaque prelia Dirces,
Et Marii referens virtutem astumque Iugurthae.
10 Te, deus, et calamus meus et mea lingua resultat.
     Sed titubo. Qua voce canam, qua mente sacrem te?
Quippe angina notis fauces corrumpit obesas
Squalida virosis priscae et rubiginis urit
Pectus condicio. Contra tibi caelicolarum
15 Concentu puro gaudent iubilare catervae,
Ter proclamantes ob trina vocabula "Sanctus."
Attamen hoc figmen tua quod manus effigiavit,
Respice me clemens, ysopoque asperge tuique—
Magna peto!—civem da vel minimum fore regni.
20 Credo quod ut reduci meus ecclesiaeque redemptor
Carne resurrexit vere palpatus edensque,
Sic ego de terra redidivo corpore surgam
Inque mea, qua carne modo tegor, ante tribunal
Christi stabo meis de factis discutiendus.

A Prayer to the Holy Trinity and [a Profession of] Faith Concerning the Resurrection of the Flesh

O Father, O Son, O Holy Spirit, subsisting without end one and the same God, whom our reckoning does not divide by a separate line (Arrius paid the penalty for that!), grant, I pray, that Amarcius, reaching the celestial shore by the ballast of his faith, might be a sharer in the court above. Caesar 5 and the slaughter at Pharsalia and Cato's glory make Lucan famous; Statius is praised for unfolding [the story of] Opheltes and the accursed strife at Thebes, and [Sallust is praised] for reporting Marius's virtue and Jugurtha's cunning. God, let my pen and my tongue resound [with] you. 10

But I totter. With what voice shall I sing, with what mind shall I worship you? Indeed, a foul infection corrupts throats swollen with stinking spots, and ancient rustiness corrodes my chest. On the other hand, to you, the company of heaven dwellers is glad to shout joyfully in pure harmony, crying out 15 "Holy" three times on account of the three names [of God]. But yet, merciful God, look upon me, this image which your hand fashioned, and sprinkle me with hyssop, and—I seek great things!—grant that I might be a citizen, even the least, of your kingdom. I believe that just as my redeemer, and the 20 church's, arose with renewed flesh, truly touched and truly eating, so shall I rise from the earth with a restored body and in my flesh, with which I am now covered, I shall stand before the judgment seat of Christ to be examined about my deeds.

25   Credo quod extremis, tuba quando novissima clanget,
       Prodibunt e sarcofagis hominum ossa; quod amnes,
       Quod rapuere ferae, quodque ussit flamma, redibit,
       Preter cum Christo qui surrexisse leguntur.
       Credo quod vitae fuerint quicumque perennis
30   Participes nulla cum debilitate redibunt;
       Quorum grex ut sol nitidus comitabitur agnum
       Gaudens, et reprobos aeternus puniet ignis.
       Tunc non me Stigiam circumversare Caribdim
       Permittas neque predonem sorbere minacem,
35   Sed pietate tua meritis prestante sacrisque,
       Qua Ionam vasti rapuisti piscis ab alvo,
       Leviathan patulis rape me de faucibus atque
       Sedibus inde tuis ubi digna tibi sine fine
       Carmina vocalis iustorum concio pangit.

EXPLICIT LIBER AMARCII.

I believe that at the end, when the last trumpet will 25
sound, the bones of men will go forth from their tombs;
what rivers, what wild beasts have snatched away, what fire
has burned, will return, besides those who, we read, have
risen with Christ. I believe that all who were sharers of ever-
lasting life will return with no infirmity; this flock, rejoicing, 30
shining like the sun, will accompany the Lamb, and eternal
fire will punish the reprobates. Then may you grant that Sty-
gian Charybdis not swirl about me and that the menacing
pirate not swallow me up, but with your pity and sacred 35
kindness preserving me, by which you snatched Jonah from
the belly of the great fish, snatch me from the gaping jaws of
Leviathan and thence to your dwelling place where the so-
norous assembly of the just sing worthy songs to you with-
out end.

HERE ENDS THE BOOK OF AMARCIUS.

EUPOLEMIUS

Contra Messyam violenti prelia Caci
Detestanda cano, dudum quem fortibus armis
In dominum pugnasse suum nimiumque potenter
Instruxisse ferunt acies Iebusea per arva,
5   Que circa Solimam sita sunt.
                     Non hic mihi Clio,
Non mihi Calliape, sed summa vocanda sophya est.
Omnipotens, qui cuncta regis, quem credere vita,
Quem coluisse salus, quem solum credimus unum,
Credimus et trinum, cui "Sanctus" ter repetitum
10 Celicus ordo canit: vires mihi suggere, laudem
Ut possim cantare tuam, nam te duce bellum
Hoc gestum est victusque dolet te presule Cacus.
    Iam pater Antropus sevo sub principe captus
Cum genitis a se planxit sua fata duobus.
15 Maior erat natu Iudas, sed iunior Ethnis
Nomen habens. Illis animus distabat et etas,
Namque minor Cacum vesanus amavit et eius
Iussa sequens studuit nescire, quis Agatus esset.
    Hoc etenim suasore miser simulacra vereri
20 Et Zoroastree fallacia murmura secte
Atque deis didicit campos implere lacusque.

HERE BEGINS THE BOOK OF *EUPOLEMIUS.*

I sing of cursed battles of violent Cacus against Messiah. People tell that Cacus fought with stout arms for a long time against his lord and that all too arrogantly he drew up battle lines among the fields of Jebus, which are located around Je- 5 rusalem.

In this matter I must call upon, not Clio or Calliope, but the highest wisdom. All-powerful, who rule everything, to believe in whom is life, to have worshipped whom is salvation, whom we believe to be only one and yet threefold, to whom the heavenly host sings "Holy" three times repeated: 10 grant me the strength to sing your praise, for under your leadership this war was waged and under your charge vanquished Cacus grieves.

At this point father Antropus, held captive under a cruel prince, lamented, together with his two sons, his destiny. 15 The elder by birth was Judas, whereas the younger had the name Ethnis. They differed in character as well as in age, for the younger one was madly in love with Cacus and, following his orders, strove to forget who Agatus was.

Indeed, at the persuasion of this one—Cacus—, the wretch learned to worship idols and the deceptive mutter- 20 ings of Zoroaster's cult, and to fill the fields and lakes with

At senior Cedarei non sponte tiranni
Sub ditione fuit dominumque suum, licet absens
Captivusque, tamen devota mente colebat.
25   Hec secum volvens pius Agatus inquid ad unum,
Cui nomen Moyses—namque hic et fortis et audax
Miles erat nullique viro, quid Hebrea sonaret
Pagina, plus notum—"Mihi conversacio Iude
Sancta placet doleoque nimis, quod tam bona iusti
30 Vita viri Caco nimium dominante gravatur.
Vade, age: Caldaicam velox urbem pete, namque
In Babilone manet, totamque ex ordine tristi
Pandito mesticie causam, quod mereat ipse,
Quod sub Amartigenis tanta feritate prematur.
35 Non me culpandum sciat, immo suum genitorem
Abstractum verbis Bethelis ab urbe dolosis.
Attamen Anphicopam legatos Polipatremque
Fortes atque bonos misi, mea nuncia Caco
Dicturos, ut eum dimitteret. Hoc quia frustra
40 Temptatum video, volo bella movere meosque
Solvere captivos. Haec illi verba referto
Solatura gravem cordis, mihi crede, dolorem."
    Iussa facit Moyses. Quam clara Semiramis urbem
Coctilium cinxisse datur compage petrarum
45 Ingressus dictis Iudam compellat amicis.
Ille ubi cognovit, quo germine natus et a quo
Missus erat, gaudens excepit et in sua tecta
Inducens iuvenem "Mihi gracior hospes adesse
Nullus posset," ait, "causa missoris et eius,
50 Quem tantum video fultum virtutibus ad me
Legatum venisse. Cibos aptate, ministri,
Restantemque diem totum ducamus ovantes."

gods. But the elder was not of his own free will under the
domination of the Kedarite tyrant and, although absent and
captive, nevertheless worshipped his lord with a reverent
mind.

Turning over in his mind these matters, pious Agatus said   25
to one whose name was Moses—for he was both a valiant
and bold soldier, and to no man was better known what the
Hebrew scriptures expressed—"Judas's holy way of living
pleases me and I grieve exceedingly that the good life of so
righteous a man is made burdensome by the excessive domi-   30
nation of Cacus. Come along, go: swiftly seek out the Chal-
dean city, for he remains in Babylon, and relate to the sad
man in due course the whole reason for the sorrow, that he
deserves to be oppressed by the great ferocity of Amarti-
genes. Let him know that I am not to blame—on the con-   35
trary, that his father was taken away from the city of Bethel
by deceitful words. But nevertheless I sent Anphicopas and
Polipater, valiant and good men, as envoys to relate my mes-
sage to Cacus—that he should release Judas. Because I see
that this effort was made in vain, I wish to wage war and free   40
my captive people. Report these words to him to assuage
the grief—believe me, deep—of his heart."

Moses carried out the orders. After entering the city
which famous Semiramis is said to have ringed with a struc-
ture of baked bricks, he addressed Judas with friendly words.   45
When Judas came to know the stock of which Moses had
been born and by whom he had been sent, he received him
with joy and, leading the young man into his house, said,
"No guest could be more welcome to me here, on account of
his sender and himself, whom I see has come to me as a great   50
envoy, upheld by virtues. Prepare the food, servants, and let
us spend all that remains of the day in celebrating." Since

Sexta fuit siquidem Moysi veniente diei
Hora, ideo dixit, "totum ducamus ovantes."
55   Hospite cum grato postquam consederat hospes
Alternisque diem leti duxere loquelis,
Tandem suspirans imo de pectore Iudas
"Felices," inquid, "quos capcio non tenet et qui
Gratanter dominis possunt servire soluti!
60 En ego, quod nequeo lacrimans nisi dicere, culpa
Nescio qua teneor longo iam tempore captus
Meque premit, qui non deberet."

                      Ad hec bonus hospes
"Ni te sermonis longi graviumque laborum,
Quos tibi quosque tuis possem memorare, pigeret,
65 Quo modo sis captus, quod te non nosse fateris,
Vel cur tuque, tuus frater sub principe Caco
Sitis et a vobis descendens certa propago,
Dissererem," dixit.

              Tum Iudas, "Tolle 'pigeret.'
Immo pergratum mihi ages opus."

                     Incipit ille,
70 "Urbs est dicta Iebus per multos cognita fines,
Quam veteres dixere Salem, quo nomine bino
Iuncto appellat eam mutato gramate vulgus.
Hanc Solimam plerumque solent efferre Latini
Gramatici.

         "Colit ut coluit rex Agatus illam.
75 Ipse trucem Cacum, feritas est cuius ubique
Haut ignota, duces comitesque suos super omnes
Extulit usque adeo, ut dictus tum Phosphorus esset.
Sed retinere diu nescit male cautus honorem
Prosperitasque necat fatuum. Nam protinus ille

noon was the hour of the day when Moses came, for that reason he said, "Let us spend all the day in celebrating."

After the host had sat down with his welcome guest and they had passed the day happily in exchanging words, at length Judas, sighing from the bottom of his heart, said, "Fortunate are those who are not held captive and who can without constraint serve their lords willingly! Look, I—and this I cannot say except in tears—have been a captive already for a long time, held for I know not what sin, and he who ought not to do so oppresses me."

In reply the good guest said, "Unless you would be bothered by a long speech and the grievous toils, which I could recall to you and your people, I would discuss how you were made a captive, which you profess that you do not know, and why you, your brother, and your legitimate progeny are under Prince Cacus."

Then Judas said, "Let's have none of that 'You would be bothered.' Quite the contrary, you will be doing me a great pleasure."

That one, Moses, began: "The city called Jebus, which the ancients named Salem, is well known in many regions. The common crowd designates it by joining both names, with one letter changed. Generally Latin grammarians have the habit of styling it Solima.

"King Agatus cherishes it now as he did before. He elevated savage Cacus, whose wildness is known everywhere, so far above all his dukes and counts that he was then called Phosphorus. But an incautious man cannot hold onto an office for long, and prosperity is fatal to a fool. For at once that

80　Infelix contra dominum tumet atque velut par
　　Imperium regis sibi vendicat: unde potestas
　　Regia primatem merito permota superbum
　　Deiecit solio atque dato privavit honore
　　Miliciamque ducis tumefacti compulit una
85　Cedere. Dux pulsus Cedar secedit et inde
　　Tendit in Egiptum; dat ei cognomen uterque
　　Sepe locus, quia sepe manet proscriptus utrimque.
　　　　"Tunc exsanguem Aphilum Superifanemque superbum
　　Adscivit socios, quibus auxiliantibus omne
90　Patraret scelus inque sua persistere posset
　　Nequicia et regem crebris offendere bellis.
　　Apolidem postquam summoverat, Agatus unum
　　Dilectum Bethele sibi nutrivit alumnum
　　Indolis eximie, qui te post edidit exul
95　In Caldeorum terra. Desiderat illi
　　Rex, si proficiat, solium, quod Cacus habebat,
　　Et regni conferre locum. Pro ceca, quid hec est,
　　Invidia, alterius quod semper honore liquescis?
　　Impiger ut Cacus cognovit talia, secum
100　Infremuit sociosque suos crudelis atroces
　　Consuluit, nec enim poterat sufferre malignus,
　　Ut sibi subtracto melior frueretur honore.
　　　　"Dumque sub ancipiti volvebat pectore curas,
　　'Quid dubitas?' Aphilus, 'Quid,' ait, 'fortissime ductor,
105　Ambigis? Attempta bellis, in qua manet, urbem,
　　Ille vir! Et quid, si tibi Marte favente potenter
　　Victor eris? Res in dubio est. Quid agas, nisi temptes?
　　Sive dolo mavis certare, dolos ineamus;

wretch swelled up against his lord and, as though an equal, he claimed for himself the king's dominion. For this reason, rightly provoked, the royal authority cast down the haughty nobleman from the throne, stripped him of the office that had been granted, and forced the knights of the overweening duke to yield at the same time. After being ousted, the duke went off to Kedar and headed from there into Egypt. He is often nicknamed after one or the other of the two places, since often, outlawed, he stayed in one or the other of them.

"Then he took upon his staff as allies bloodless Aphilus and haughty Superifanes, with whose aid he committed crimes of every sort, and was able to persevere in his wickedness and to vex the king with frequent wars. After he had expelled Apolides, Agatus reared in Bethel a foster child of excellent disposition who was beloved to him and who afterward as an exile in the land of the Chaldeans begot you. The king desired to confer upon him, if he should succeed, the throne and the site of the kingdom that Cacus used to hold. Alas, blind envy, why is it that you always waste away when another receives an office? As soon as ever-active Cacus learned of such developments, he roared out his angry thoughts and in his savagery consulted his frightful allies, for out of malice he could not bear to see anyone better enjoy the office that had been wrested from him.

"And as he was pondering these concerns with a wavering heart, Aphilus said, 'Why do you hesitate? Why, most valiant leader, do you hesitate? Put to the test in war the city in which that man stays! And what if you are victorious, with Mars favoring you strongly? The outcome is in doubt. What should you do, if not put it to the test? Or if you prefer to fight using deceit, let us undertake deceits; certainly it mat-

Nempe mea nil distat, utrum bellando dolisve
110 Vincam, dum vincam. Sed quid moror? Incipe, vinces!
Dic, age: quis, cui sit virtus et tanta proborum
Copia quanta tibi sociorum, dedecus illud,
Tu quod habes, tollerare velit? Validusne magis tu,
Multo nobilior, multo sollercior? Illi,
115 Qui te possesso iam subplantavit honore,
Postponendus eras, te cum bonus Agatus egit?
Turba puerilis quod ubi statuit sibi regem,
Eligit hunc regemque vocat regemque salutat,
Huic caput inclinat, sed eum mox abicit atque,
120 Quem tunc vult, alium depulso subrogat. Et quid
Hic aliud factum est? Non illic causa nec hic est.
Quare, si mecum sentis et sunt tibi cure
Que loquor, invades hominem vitaque carebit;
Aut si tam bonus es, quod non ego, tollere vitam
125 Ut nolis iuveni, capiatur et in peregrinas
Ducatur partes vita cariturus amena,
Ut subtractus honor tibi non racione sed ira
Nec tibi nec sit ei.'
          "Sic postquam dixit, atrocem
Frendentemque tamen tantum stimulavit in iram,
130 Quantum nota movent Eleum sibila glaucum
Vel quales Epiros alit, qui carcere nondum
Recluso crebris feriunt hinnitibus auras,
Et piger est vectes tollens properanter agaso.
   "Tunc erat inter eos, quo non astucior alter
135 Invidieque capax magis; illi nomen Ofites.
Quem, quia versutum plenumque dolis videt, acer
Cacus, ut Antropum temptet subvertere, mittens

ters nothing to me, whether I win through war or deceits, so 110
long as I win. But why do I delay? Begin—you will conquer!
Come on, tell: what person, who had the courage and great
supply of able allies that you have, would care to endure the
dishonor that you have suffered? Are you not stronger, much
nobler, much cleverer? Did you have to be held in lower es- 115
teem than the one who displaced you from the office you
already possessed, when good Agatus drove you out? Now
when a childish throng sets up a king for itself, they choose
him, call him king, hail him as king, and bow their heads to
him, but soon they reject him and, once he has been driven
off, substitute another whom they then want. And what else 120
happened in this case? There is no justification in either that
case or this one. For this reason, if you agree with me and if
what I say concerns you, you will attack this man and he will
lose his life. Otherwise, if you are so good (as I am not!) that
you do not wish to take the life of a young man, let him be 125
made a captive and led into foreign lands to lose his lovely
life, so that the office wrested from you not in reason but in
anger may belong neither to you nor to him.'

"After speaking in such a fashion, he spurred Cacus—
though he was already cruel and teeth-gnashing—so greatly
into anger as the familiar hissings provoke a blue-grey horse 130
at Olympia or horses of the sort reared at Epirus; before
the barrier has even been opened, these horses make the air
reverberate with whinny after whinny, and the groom who
hastily shoots back the bars seems sluggish to them.

"In those days there was among them one unexcelled in
craft and capacity for envy; his name was Ofites. Fierce 135
Cacus, because he saw that Ofites was wily and deceitful,
sent him to try to overthrow Antropus. He said, 'Go, good

'I, bone,' ait, 'iuvenemque, dolis quia fallere nosti,
Falle dolis! Neque enim poterit, velut arbitror, ulla
140 Simplex arte capi cicius quam fraude, benignus
Dum credit verbis nec in herba cogitat anguem.
Vade igitur! Si te fortuna remiserit ad me
Propositi nostri victorem, munera certe
Multa tibi tribuam nec erit mihi gracior ullus.'
145   "Hec postquam ducibus placuere, dolosus Ophites
Antropo parat insidias et, ne sua nullas
Fraus habeat vires, forte in Bethele morantem
Antifrononta petit.
                    "Quo blandis fallere verbis
Non vixit magis aptus homo, sermone suavis
150 Et facie gratus; voluit seducere si quem,
Arrisit. Quem rex Solimanus semper habebat
Suspectum iuvenemque suum Bethele manentem
Obtestatus erat, ne crederet illius umquam
Consiliis, iam possessum si nollet honorem
155 Maioremque dein, si sic perstaret, habendum
Perdere et eternum damnandus inire laborem.
     "Hoc ergo assumpto sibi complice fraudis Ofites.
Pergit ad Antropi pulcre vernancia tecta.
Illic ortus erat viridissimus omnigenisque
160 Consitus arboribus gignentibus, ut memoratur,
Diversi generis fructus variique saporis.
Illic fons etiam scatet, ex quo quatuor amnes
Emanare ferunt. In eodem nascitur horto
Tus et mirra fluit preciosaque balsama stillant,
165 Multaque preterea sunt oblectancia visus
Illic humanos.

man, and trick the young man with your deceits, because you know how to trick with deceits! For, as I judge, the 140 simple-hearted cannot be caught more swiftly by any device than by fraud, seeing that a kindly man trusts words and does not consider the snake in the grass. Head along, then! If fortune sends you back to me as victor in our project, I will certainly bestow many gifts upon you, and no one will be more pleasing in my sight.'

"Once these words met with the approval of the dukes, 145 deceitful Ofites laid an ambush for Antropus and, so that his fraud would have effect, he sought out Antifronon who as chance had it was staying in Bethel.

"No person better equipped than he at deceiving with winning words ever existed, urbane in speech and attrac- 150 tive in appearance; if he wished to lead someone astray, he flashed a smile. The king of Jerusalem always held him suspect and adjured his young man who stayed in Bethel never to trust the counsels of that Antifronon, unless he wished to lose the office he already possessed and the greater one he 155 would have later, if he persevered in the same way, and to be condemned to undergo everlasting toil.

"Therefore, after taking this Antifronon as his accomplice in fraud, Ofites heads toward the beautifully verdant dwelling of Antropus. In that place there was a garden, very 160 green and planted with all manner of trees, which, as is related, produced fruits of different types and varying tastes. In that place also a fountain wells up, from which people report that four rivers flow forth. In the same garden frankincense grows, myrrh flows, and the precious gum of the balsam tree drips; and, in addition, many other things enticing 165 to human eyes are found in that place.

              "Ibi tunc de more sedentem
Inveniunt iuvenem, quem sic affatur Ofites,
'Ingenio pollens etatis et integritate,
Regie vir, quam grata tibi, quam florida sedes,
170 Ut decet ingenuum! Nec, ut invideam, hec tibi dico,
Sed magis admiror, cur te Solimanus, ut aiunt,
Iusserit indigenis Luze bene credere cunctis
Excepto virtute suos qui comminus adstans
Impiger Antifronon cives supereminet omnes.'
175   "Ille refert, 'Vere mihi rex—nam cur ego verum
Hoc presente negem?—remonens precepit, ut omnes
Diligerem, quos hec vicinos urbs habet, unum
178 Hunc devitarem; cito traderer huius iniquis
181 Artibus, aiebat.'
               "Subicit male fidus Ofites,
179 'Hunc devitares, quia te cito traderet, inquis,
180 Artibus iste suis. Non est ita! Sed quoniam rex
182 Cognovit quam sit sollers paciensque laborum,
184 Vitandum tibi censet eum; cui si socieris,
185 Ne sibi te faciat similem, timet, hercule, et ipsi
Par fieres magnisque diis—et si mihi prudens
Credis, eris! Sed enim vult hac in sede quietum
Et mundo ignotum miseram te ducere vitam.
Hoc autem duce, si modo te subieceris illi
190 Egregio fortique viro, per tocius orbis
Climata notus eris.'
                 "Sic postquam fatus, amicum
Attollens iuvenis vultum 'Mihi cerneris,' inquit,
'Providus et tibi quis monstrarit nescio nostrum,
Sicut habet se, nosse statum. Res ipsa movet me

"There then they find the young man, sitting in his usual way, and Ofites addresses him in this way: 'O kingly man, powerful in intellect and in the soundness of your youth, how pleasant, how flourishing a site you have, as befits a 170 freeborn man! And I do not say these things to you out of envy, but rather I wonder why the Jerusalemite, as they say, ordered you to trust completely all the natives of Luza, apart from energetic Antifronon, standing right here, who outstrips all his fellow citizens in virtue.'

"That Antropus replies, 'In truth—for why should I deny 175 the truth even though Antifronon is present?—the king warned me a second time and commanded me to love all the neighbors this city holds, but to shun this one man. I would be betrayed swiftly by his wicked wiles, he said.'

"Untrustworthy Ofites interposes, 'You say you should shun him, because he would betray you swiftly by his wiles. 180 It is not so! But since the king knows how clever and tolerant of hard work Antifronon is, he judges that you ought to avoid him. If you should ally yourself with him, King Agatus 185 fears that Antifronon would make you like him, by Hercules, and that you would become equal to Agatus himself and the great gods—and if you wisely believe me, you will be! But in fact he wishes you to live out a wretched life in this place, peaceable and unknown to the world. Under this duke, however, if only you subject yourself to that outstand- 190 ing and brave man, you will be known throughout the regions of the whole world.'

"After he had spoken in this manner, the young Antropus raised his face with a friendly look and said, 'I detect that you have foresight, and that someone or other has made you acquainted with our situation, such as it is. The very state of

195 Consilio parere tuo. Quis enim male credat
     Iuranti?' (Iurabat enim.)
                              "Tunc ambo rogabant
     Infaustum iuvenem fallacis tecta tiranni
     Visere. Vix limen spondentis amica sed hostis
     Contigerat, tectus subito circumvolat hostis:
200 Torvus Amartigenis, satus Antifrononte ducisque
     Intimus Apolide, iuvenem rapit atque revinctis
     Post tergum manibus comitante abducit Ofite.
     Sic pastor vincto pretentis cassibus agno
     Irritare lupum noctu solet; ille bidentis
205 Crebris illectus balatibus advolat et spe
     Prede captus hiat, sed eum plaga precipitem mox
     Innectit nexumque tenet, dum rusticus acer
     Advenit et frustra temptantem evadere telo
     Traicit et stupidum perfosso preripit agnum.
210   "Cacus ut optatum consistere comminus hostem
     Vidit 'Io, comites! Quante nos nostraque cure
     Sint superis,' inquid, 'probat huius captio. Quo non
     Capto mererem, sed rex videor mihi capto.
     Quam bene disposuit rex Agatus, ut miser hic me
215 Deiceret solio! Dis inmortalibus esset
     Dedecus eternum meritoque fatisceret orbis,
     Hibrida, polluto si tu fruerere ducatu,
     Qui Caco permissus erat, ceu siquis honeste
     Abstrahat armillam sponse scrofeque lutosas
220 Ad nares transferre velit.' Sic fatur et illum

affairs prompts me to obey your counsel—for who would do   195
wrong to trust a person who takes an oath?' (For Ofites was
swearing.)

   "Then both asked the unfortunate young man to visit the
dwelling of the treacherous tyrant. Scarcely had he set foot
upon the threshold of the one who promised friendly acts,
but who was an enemy, when suddenly a concealed enemy
swoops out to surround him: grim Amartigenes, born of An-   200
tifronon and an intimate of Duke Apolides, seizes the young
man and, accompanied by Ofites, leads him off with his
hands tied behind his back. In the same way a shepherd is
accustomed to rouse a wolf at night with a lamb tied up in a
snare that has been laid out; that wolf, enticed by the re-
peated bleatings of the sheep, flies to the attack and, caught   205
by hope of booty, opens wide its jaws, but the snare ties it up
immediately as it rushes forward and holds it fast, until the
keen peasant arrives, runs it through with the pike as it tries
in vain to escape, and, after he has pierced it, snatches the
stunned lamb from it in time.

   "As Cacus saw his eagerly awaited enemy come to a halt   210
nearby, he said, 'Hurrah, comrades! The capture of this man
confirms how much we and our affairs are of concern to the
gods. Had he not been captured, I would mourn, but now
that he has been captured, I seem to myself to be a king.
How well King Agatus arranged it, that this wretch should   215
cast me down from my throne! It would be an everlasting
dishonor to the immortal gods and the world would rightly
grow weary, mongrel, if you were to enjoy the defiled leader-
ship that had been granted to Cacus, just as if someone
should tear a bracelet from a respectable wife and should in-
tend to shift it to the mud-smeared nostrils of a sow.' So he   220

Tradit Amartigeni religatum colla catenis,
Ut semper sit servus ei, nisi liberet illum
Agatus, et dat ei regnum Babilonis; eodem
Transtulit ille virum.
                          "Solimane ceptriger urbis
225 Comperiens tantis deceptum fraudibus esse
Dilectum iuvenem dolet et simul infremit ira.
Multaque prequestus, quod non sibi caverit et quod
Non exhorruerit contra sua iussa doloso
Credere, Plirisophum, quo non industrior alter
230 Inpigriorque fuit, quam vir seductus habebat,
Custodire iubet sedem; versatilis illi
Ensis erat sternens obstancia fulminis instar.
   "At miser Antropus sub iniquo principe tentus,
Ut tandem gemitus et tristia verba quierunt,
235 Uxorem iunxit sibi, que, clarissime Iuda,
Te peperit fratremque tuum. Multum fit adultis
Mens dispar vobis et discordatis ut olim
Infelicis Ade geniti de semine fratres.
Et si forte tuas nondum pervenit ad aures
240 Historia hec, dicam, quia et est dicenda iuvatque
Aures bella pias. Hic solus non genitus vir
Germanos—hec prima fuit generatio—binos
Edidit. Alter erat pastor gregis, alter arator;
Nomen aratori Cain, Abel opilioni.
245 Hi cum diverso ferrent libamina nutu,
Abel dona deus contempto fratre recepit.
Ille, velut fieri solet, ex melioris honore
Lividus eque sua merens sine fine repulsa
Insontem, nisi si summo placuisse reatus

speaks and surrenders that one, bound with chains about his neck, to Amartigenes, to be his slave forever, unless Agatus should set him free. He gives the realm of Babylon to Amartigenes; he shifted Antropus to the same place.

"The scepter-holding ruler of the city Jerusalem, Agatus, 225 learning that the beloved young man had been tricked by such great deceits, grieves and at the same time growls with anger. Complaining beforehand with many words that Antropus did not watch out for himself and that he did not feel terrified to trust (against the bidding of Agatus) in the deceitful one, Agatus orders Plirisophus, than whom no one 230 else was more diligent or energetic, to guard the place that the man who had been led astray had occupied; he had a whirling two-edged sword, capable of cutting down everything that came in its path, like a thunderbolt.

"But wretched Antropus, held under the iniquitous prince, when at length his groans and sad words subsided, 235 wedded a wife who bore you, most renowned Judas, and your brother. Fully grown, the two of you come to have much dissimilar dispositions and you differ just as did once upon a time the brothers born from the seed of unfortunate Adam. And if by chance this story has not yet reached your ears, I will relate it, because it too must be related and be- 240 cause a pretty tale benefits pious ears. He, the only unborn man, begot two brothers: this was the first generation. One was a herder of a flock, the other a plowman; the plowman was named Cain, the shepherd Abel. When these two 245 brought offerings with different intentions, God accepted the gifts of Abel and scorned his brother. The latter, as is accustomed to happen, was jealous at the honor of his better and sorrowed without limit over his rebuff. He slew an innocent man, unless to have pleased God can be called a

250 Dicitur, interimit; non secius aspera tigris
Mortificat vitulum trepidumve rapax lupus agnum
Instigante fame. Vox ilico sanguinis Abel
It celo dominumque, suos qui vindicat omnes,
Postulat ultorem.
        "Cur, o manus impia, frustra
255 In sanctos sevis extinguere lumina mundi
Affectans? Certe plumbatis adde catastas,
Non tamen a domini, quos ipse gubernat, amore
Secernes umquam. Non pensas, inprobe tortor,
Qui sunt quos perimis? Nasci facit ista beatos
260 Mors reprobosque mori.
           "Sed nunc ad omissa revertor.
Vos duo sicut adhuc sub Caco mente fuistis
Principe diversa, tu nolens, ille libenter.
Namque puer sevi mores laudare tiranni
Cepit et, offendunt summum quecumque tonantem,
265 Hoc didicit monitore libens: homicidia amare
Et Sodomitarum ritu gaudere sinistro
Celumque et terras et flumina credere plena
Numinibus. Pro quo scelerum studio vehementer
Carus erat Caco, tu spernens illa molestus.
270   "Agatus interea vestri sermone parentis
Blando delusi casum miseratus ad istas
Polipatrem terras sibi coniuncto magis acri
Anphicopa solaturos te dirigit, atqui
Insignes virtute viros, tamen hic magis asper
275 Consiliis fuerat rigidoque minacior ore,
Usque adeo celebs, ut precidenda pudicus
Diceret incestum prepucia.

crime; in the same way a harsh tiger puts to death a calf, or a 250
predatory wolf a fearful lamb, when hunger goads. Immedi-
ately the voice of Abel's blood goes to heaven and calls upon
the lord, who takes vengeance for all his people, as avenger.

"O impious hand, why do you rage in vain against saints, 255
striving to snuff the lights of the world? I have no doubts:
add hot grills to lead-tipped whips, but you will still never
sunder from the love of the lord those whom he governs. Do
you not consider, wicked torturer, who they are whom you
annihilate? This death causes the blessed to be born and the
wicked to die.

"But now I return to the events I have left out. The two 260
of you, just as you still are, were of different minds about be-
ing under Prince Cacus: you were unwilling, he was willing.
For example, the boy began to praise the ways of the savage
tyrant and under this instructor learned willingly everything
that vexes the highest thunderer: to love acts of murder, to 265
rejoice in the perverse practice of Sodomites, and to believe
the sky, land, and rivers are filled with divine spirits. Because
of this zeal for villainies he was exceedingly dear to Cacus,
whereas you in spurning them were odious.

"In the meantime Agatus took pity on the plight of your 270
father, who had been duped by smooth talking, and he dis-
patched Polipater, with very keen Anphicopas allied to him,
to these lands to console you. Certainly these men were dis-
tinguished by their virtue, but nevertheless Anphicopas was
harsher in his counsels and more menacing in his stern de- 275
meanor, chaste to the point where the modest man declared
foreskins an unchastity, to be cut off.

"Rex dedit illis
Mandatum, quod Amartigeni scelerumque magistro
Deferrent Caco. Tu quem dixi magis acrem,
280 Alter enim populis haut ignotus fuit istis,
Accipis hospicio (satis esse memor potes, hec non
Multum res vetus est) dictisque per omnia pares
Hospitis Anphicope. Tuus hunc nec cernere curat
Elluo germanus fedaque libidine fervens
285 Gaudet eis pocius sociis, quibus omnia cordi
Turpia; semper enim similis similem sibi querit
Dissimilemque fugit. Ceu siquis vivere sancte
Incestum moneat scurram scortoque pudicam
Commendet vitam, non plus sibi conferat, ac si
290 In spinis querat ficus, in vepribus uvas:
Sic et monstrantem, quid honestum quid minus, Ethnis
Flagiciis tectus cunctis linguaque manuque
Impiger Anphicopam sprevit conviciaque ultro
Addidit, 'Unde venit nobis novus iste magister,
295 Tam serus studii, quem tunc venisse decebat,
Cum primum exivit verbosus agagula predo?
Nempe trucidator vitatur iure petrinos
Assuetus, si fama canit rata, sanguine cultros
Humano temerare, docens ignota, cruentus
300 Et mordax iuvenum censor. Quam raro fideles
Sunt rufi'—nam rufus erat—'quam raro benigni!
Qui sapit, hunc fugiat: vafer est et fraus alit ipsum,
Iste die tota rixatur de nuce quassa.
Denique quantum vult rapidus fluit.'
"Ipseque crudus
305 Antiphrononciades ambos despexit et illum
Precipue tamen irrisit, quem scilicet ante

"The king gave them a directive to convey to Amarti-genes and to Cacus, the master of misdeeds. You, Judas, re-ceived hospitably the one whom I called very keen, for the other one was hardly unfamiliar to these peoples (you can remember well enough, this event is not so very remote) and you obeyed in all respects the commands of your guest, Anphicopas. Your brother, the squanderer, did not care to see him and, burning with foul lust, instead took pleasure in his comrades, in whose hearts all turpitudes are found; for like always seeks like and flees unlike. Just as, if some-one should admonish an unchaste man-about-town to lead a saintly life and should commend a modest life to a harlot, it would not do him any more good than if he should seek figs among thorns or grapes among the briar bushes, so too Eth-nis, covered with scandals of every sort, in word and deed actively spurned Anphicopas as he pointed out what was de-cent and what was less so. And Ethnis added insults to boot: 'From where did this new master come to us, such a late learner? He should have come then, when the wordy, pimp-ing bandit first came forth. Certainly the butcher is rightly avoided, the one who is accustomed to pollute stone knives with human blood, if rumor tells rightly; who teaches igno-ble acts; and who is bloodthirsty and a biting critic of young men. How seldom redheads are trustworthy'—for Anphico-pas was a redhead—'how seldom kind! A wise man would flee him: he is crafty, and deceit nurtures him. He quarrels the whole day long over a hollow nut. In short, he produces as fast a flow of words as he wants.'

"And the cruel son of Antifronon, Amartigenes himself, despised both of them and yet particularly mocked that one, Polipater, whom of course he had known previously. Hav-

Norat, Polipatrem. Quem non clementer adortus
'Tune, senex,' ait, 'hunc nimis audax in mea duxti
Regna meis libertatem conscissere servis?
310 O hominem miserum, stolidum sine mente, ducatum
Ut cuiquam prodesse suum putet? An, quia venit
Te duce tutus erit, duce nutanti, duce ceco?
Quos ego iam dudum teneo longumque tenebo
Debentes servire michi Cacoque, putastis
315 Tuque comesque tuus tam caute abducere? Laudem
Tunc sane vobis nimiam pareretis, at ingens—
De damno taceo—michi dedecus. Haut ita tute
Eveniet, si vi sunt nobis eripiendi.
Vis ea tristis erit multo de sanguine pugna.
320 Vester nos contra bellum princeps geret, ut si
Currendo celeres griphas celeresque volando
Cristiger atemtet gallus vel sedula tortum
In giros mordere velit formica draconem.
Vos igitur ne vana duos spes erigat. Ante
325 Partus Danubium bibet et Germanus Hidaspen,
Ante colet silvas delphinus stagnaque dente
Transverso metuendus aper, quam, quod petitis vos,
Fiat, ut hos linquam gratos mihi non tamen eque.
Et si adeo tentos vester regnator amavit
330 Sub dicione mea, cur, ut vos mitteret ad me,
Distulit usque modo, ceu tu garris, probus atque
Obtimus? Hinc vero pietas inmensa probatur?
Captivis cupiens succurrere distulit hic, ut
Si male vellet eis, cruciandi tempus haberet
335 Prolixum dominans? Cui quo non eriperentur,

ing accosted him rudely, he said, 'Old man, have you all too
boldly led this man into my realm to decree freedom for my
servants? O wretched man, foolish without sense, to think   310
that his leadership could help anyone! Or will he be safe be-
cause he came with you as leader, a tottering leader, a blind
leader? Did you and your companion think that you could
lead away with so little risk those whom I have been hold-
ing now for a long time and whom I will still hold for a long
time, because they must serve me and Cacus? Then clearly   315
you would occasion very great praise for yourselves, but
enormous dishonor for me—not to mention the loss. It will
hardly turn out so safely, if they have to be wrenched from
us by force. That force will entail a gloomy fight with much
bloodshed. Your prince will wage war against us, as if a   320
crested cock should attack swift-running and swift-flying
griffins, or as if an industrious ant should wish to gnaw at a
snake twisted into coils. Therefore, let not vain hope cause
the two of you to take heart. The Parthian will drink of the 325
Danube and the German of the Jhelum, the dolphin will in-
habit the woods and the boar, to be feared for its slanted
tusk, the ponds before what you are seeking should hap-
pen—that I should desert these men who are pleasing, al-
though not equally, to me. And if your ruler loved those held
under my authority so much, why did he delay sending you   330
to me until now? Is he as upright and good as you keep jab-
bering that he is? By this behavior indeed is an immeasur-
able piety confirmed? Although desiring to relieve the cap-
tives, he delayed, so that the one who held them in his
control would have an extended time to torture them if he
wished them ill? So that they should not be snatched away   335

Segniter affectans agiles belloque probatos,
Deformem tremulumque senem rufumque fidelem,
Vir bonus et prudens direxit. Nempe iocosum
Et risu dignum tales ad regia missos
340 Iussa ferenda viros mihi, quem vaga fama per omnes
Iam fecit celebrem terras, Cacoque potenti.
Nec tamen admiror, stolidos quod misit ineptus,
Nec michi, quos habeo, retinendi marcida spes est.'
     "Dixerat. Ast egra iam dudum mente volutat
345 Verba ducis secumque fremens similisque dolenti
Vir venerandus ait, 'Nequaquam cecus et amens
Iure tibi videor, cum non sit cecus et amens,
Qui videt atque sapit. Quod membra vacillo, facit, que
Omne quod est ortum labefactat, decolor etas.
350 Non tamen ignoro penitus, quid strennua virtus
Inter bella queat, somno neque semper inerti
Parebam. Reges me parvula viderat Hoba,
Ut tu sat nosti, leva sita parte Damasci
Bis binos, totidem quos regibus amplius uno
355 Inclita comprensis hilararat palma, et eorum
Agmina paulo plus uno medioque maniplo
Sternere, ceu veteres nimbis nivibusque solutis
Termodon ripas superans rapidusque Cinapes
Precipitare solet quercus; predamque revexi
360 Hostibus afflictis et totam letificavi
Pentapolim. Tamen hoc quid confert, cum tibi viles
Degeneresque adeo videamur? At o utinam me
Solum carpsisses, non hunc quoque!'

from this one, the good and foresighted man looked only halfheartedly for able and seasoned warriors, and dispatched a misshapen and doddering old man and his trusty redhead. It is certainly humorous and laughable that such men were sent to relay royal commands to me, whom wandering fame 340 has already made widely known throughout all lands, and to powerful Cacus. But nonetheless I do not marvel that he foolishly sent dullards, and my hope is not fading of retaining control of the people whom I hold.'

"He had spoken. In contrast, the venerable man, muttering to himself and like a person in pain, for a long time pon- 345 dered with troubled mind the words of the duke and said, 'Not at all rightly do I seem blind and demented to you, since a person who sees and understands cannot be blind and demented. A degenerate age, which causes everything that has been born to fall apart, makes me totter in my limbs. Nonetheless I am not altogether unaware of what ac- 350 tive manliness can achieve in the midst of war, and I did not always succumb to idle sleep. As you know well enough, little Hobah, situated on the left hand of Damascus, saw me with a little more than one and a half companies lay low four kings, whom a distinguished victory had made joyous when 355 they captured their same number of kings plus one, and their armies, just as the river Thermodon as it overtops its banks and the swift Cynapses regularly send old oaks hurtling when rains and snows have been released; and I brought back booty once the enemy had been shattered, and I 360 brought joy to all Pentapolis. Nevertheless, what does this matter, since we seem to you so base and unworthy? But O I wish that you would carp at me alone, not him as well!'

"Non tulit ultra
Sevus Hiperefanes—nam tunc ibi forte manebat
365 Commentor scelerum—sed acerba concitus ira
Sic ait, 'Huncne tibi tot reddere verba loquacem
Barbatum et rapidi torrentis more fluentem?
Quem nos—sed captum prestat servare suisque
Iungere cognatis; quem tu si linquere velles,
370 Linquere non sinerem. Rex Agatus et satus ipso
Hunc hominem vehementer amant; quem quando movere
Cepimus, inceptum peragamus fortiter. Atqui
Semper eis infensus eram semperque nocivus;
Ledere consiliis illos, si ledere possem
375 Consiliis, studui. Nostro secessit ab illis
Apolides suasu. Varius quoque sensit Ophites,
Quam fidus sibi fautor eram, cum fallere missus
Incautum tandem me persuasore fefellit
Antropum. Nunc hos retinendos censeo, namque
380 Coniuncti generis non debent condicione
Secerni; sequitur proles persepe parentes.
Non dubium, tentis quin multum gaudeat istis
Cacus, legatos quamquam ius ledere non sit.
Nil agit, esse pius si vult, qui degit in aula.'
385 "His instigatus monitis Babilonius heros
Legatos tenet, insolitum, captos. Ibi paucos
Evolvens annos senior maturus obivit.
Tum vero Ramathus factis Cacique ducisque
Illius infremuit. Nec iam legacio regi
390 Ut primum tranquilla placet, ducibusque profanis
Qui bellum indicam pro captis teque tuoque
Fratre bonisque viris huc missis, e quibus alter

"Savage Hiperefanes did not tolerate it any longer—for by chance the inventor of crimes was present there at that time—but aroused by bitter anger he said as follows, 'Are we 365 to think that this one, talkative, bearded, and flowing like a swift-rushing stream, utters so many words in reply to you? Whom we—but it is better to keep him captive and to unite him with his relatives; if you should wish to leave him, I would not allow it. King Agatus and the one born of him 370 love this man with a passion. Since we have already begun to disturb Agatus, let us carry through bravely what has been begun. And yet I was always hostile and always injurious to them; if I could damage them by plotting, I desired to cause damage by plotting. At my persuasion Apolides parted ways 375 with them. Many-faced Ofites also recognized how trusty a supporter of his I was, when he was sent to deceive unsuspecting Antropus and, at length, deceived him through my persuasion. Now I recommend that they should be detained, for blood relatives ought not to be kept separate in 380 legal status; very often children follow parents. Doubtless Cacus would rejoice greatly in having these men detained, although it is not right to harm envoys. If a man wishes to be virtuous, he accomplishes nothing by passing time in a court.'

"Prompted by these warnings the Babylonian hero holds 385 the envoys captive—not customary conduct! The elder, spending a few years there, passed away at a ripe old age. Then indeed Ramathus—Agatus—roared in rage at the deeds of Cacus and his duke. The idea of a peaceful deputa- 390 tion does not now commend itself to the king as it did at the beginning, and he directs me, chosen from a large number, here to proclaim war against the impious dukes on behalf of the captives—you, your brother, and the good men

Vivit adhuc misere, veteranus decidit alter,
Huc me ex non paucis selectum dirigit. Ergo
395 Curas mitte; malis finem faciet deus istis
Ocius ac speras, maioraque gaudia magnas
Vincent erumnas. Divinum respice Ioseph,
Ut post invidiam fratrum, post carceris umbras,
Quas insons subiit, Phariis regnavit in horis.
400 Hoc laudis vatum iocundus transtulit error
Munus ad Ipolitum revocatum Peonis arte.
      "Pensa etiam duros sub iniquo rege labores
Dilecti summo populi, Memphitica pro quo
Plagas terra decem passa est, tandemque malignum
405 Regem dimissos, quos ignis in aere duxit
Nocte, die nubes, fatalibus in mare rubrum
Sectatum cuneis canit haut spernenda vetustas.
Nempe dei cetus crudi post dira tiranni
Tempora postque sacram celis rorantibus escam
410 Et latices de rupe datos, quos fingitur Hammon
Sirtibus in Libicis fudisse, deo duce terram
Querens melliffluam per multa pericula, tandem
Promissa letus potitur tellure colonus."
      Nondum hec ex toto Moyses depromserat omni
415 Ascultante domo, cum miles honestus et armis
Inclitus Eleimon, quo consultore potiri
Consuevit Ramathus solito ventura referre
Set non cassa fide, plenum feritate cohortes
Ducentem bis quinque Nomum prope nunciat esse.

sent here, of whom one, Anphicopas, still lives wretchedly,
whereas the other older one has died. Therefore put aside 395
your cares; God will put an end to these ills more swiftly
than you hope, and greater joys will overcome great hard-
ships. Reflect upon divine Joseph, how after the envy of his
brothers and the darkness of prison, which he underwent
though innocent, he ruled over the lands of Pharoah. An 400
amusing blunder by poets transferred this tribute of praise
to Hippolytus, who was brought back by the craft of Paean
Apollo.

"Consider also the hard labors, under an unjust king, of
the people beloved to the supreme one, Agatus; on account
of him the land of Memphis suffered ten plagues, and finally 405
the wicked king pursued into the Red Sea with his doomed
troops the people who had been released and whom a fire in
the air guided by night and a cloud by day; so sings an an-
cient tradition that must not be scorned. To be sure, the as-
sembly of God, after the dreadful times of the bloodthirsty
tyrant, after the sacred food from the dewy heavens and the
springs of running water produced from a rocky cliff, which 410
Ammon is alleged to have poured forth in the sands of
Libya, seeking the land of honey through many dangers,
with God as guide, at long last happily takes possession of
the promised land as settlers."

Moses had not yet delivered this whole speech, as the en-
tire household listened, when Eleimon, a soldier who was 415
honorable and renowned in arms, whom Ramathus was ac-
customed to use as an advisor because he habitually related
in good faith things to come, announces that Nomus, filled
with wildness, is nearby, leading ten cohorts.

420 Ilicet arreptis heros letissimus armis
Cornipedem scandit Moyses dapibusque videre
Dilectum spretis festinat et, hospite frustra
Pugnantem revocante, virum dum cernat et ipse
Secum armatus eat, ruit efferus. Haut aliter quam
425 In nemore Albano sevum cum murmurat ursa,
Subiecta quamvis preda tum forte Molosus
Vellicat audaci retro si dente frementem,
Cessat subpositum versare canemque protervum
Rictu Vulturno vehementior involat acri;
430 Sic celer assumpto Moyses Eleimone frenis
Tendit laxatis.
               Sed postquam lumine claro
Cernere erat celso socias in monte phalanges,
"Acceleremus," ait dux laudatissimus iste,
"Annuat ille modo, cui parent omnia; certus
435 Advenit ereptor sub iniquo principe captis.
Sed tamen admiror, cur non huc ipse veniret
Messias, ut eos Caci bellando cruentis
Eriperet manibus vel saltem, quem sibi fidum
Cognoscit mage fratre suo, qui me bene quique
440 Legatos hilari suscepit mente priores."
Illi suspirans imo de pectore mitis
Reddidit Eleimon, "Si sunt rata, que mihi dudum
Agatus exposuit—que non rata non fore credo,
Nescit enim nisi vera loqui—durabit eorum
445 Captio, ter denis dum mundus et octo pruinis
Horreat. Hec Iudas, ut nunc est, tarda putabit
Tempora, germano gaudente quidem modo. Verum
Illo preteritam culpabit tempore vitam,

238

At once the hero, Moses, most gladly grabs his weapons 420
and mounts his stallion. Spurning the banquet, he hastens
to see his beloved and, as his host in vain calls him back, he
rushes off wildly to set eyes on Nomus fighting and to go out
armed with him. Just as when a she-bear rumbles savagely in 425
an Alban grove, if, even though she casts down her booty, a
Molossian hound then still happens to snap at her from be-
hind with a bold tooth as she growls, she ceases to worry at
what she has put down and she flies with open mouth at the
violent dog more forcefully than a piercing Volturnian wind;
in the same way swift Moses, having picked up Eleimon, 430
heads off with loosened reins.

But after it was possible with a sharp eye to discern the
allied troops on the lofty mountain, this most praiseworthy
leader said, "Let us hasten. May he now nod his assent,
to whom all things are obedient; a sure liberator comes to 435
those held under the unjust prince. But nevertheless I won-
der why Messiah himself would not come here to liberate
them from the bloody hands of Cacus by engaging in battle
or at least to liberate the one whom he knows is more faith-
ful to him than his brother, the one who received me well 440
and who received the earlier envoys with a joyful dispo-
sition."

Meek Eleimon, sighing from the bottom of his heart, re-
plied to him, "If the facts that Agatus expounded to me a
while ago are established—and I do not believe that they
will not be established, for he is unable to say anything un-
true—their captivity will last until the world is stiff with the 445
cold of thirty-eight winters. Judas, as he is now, will think
this period of time slow, whereas his brother will rejoice, at
least now. But he will find fault with his bygone life during

Cum rex rege satus presens geret aspera bella.
450 Hic post dimidium iam dicti temporis orbi
Pacifer adveniet; reliquos exegimus annos.
Hoc autem sibi cur placeat, tibi non queo causam
Reddere; quod vero dixisti, cur sibi fidum
Vel Iudam non eriperet, te non latet esse
455 Ignarum, Iude qualis sit vita futura.
Nam predico tibi (si que predicere novi,
Que non cassa putes): quando horrida prelia presens
Moverit Agatides, pre cunctis sentiet hostem,
Quem modo pre cunctis sibi iactas esse fidelem;
460 Quique Iovis gipsum ceu verum numen adorat
Atque manu factis petit Ethnis opem simulacris,
Rectum sectari summumque timere tonantem
Incipiet totusque deo famulabitur orbis."
    Talia dum memorat vates doctissimus ultra
465 Quam satis est, celerem dulci sermone retardat
Et gratas sensim compellit adire cohortes.
Interea sevus per dura, per ardua Cacus
Discurrens oportuno iam tempore postquam
Milite collecto latis Babilonis in arvis
470 Constitit et iamiam bellandi tempus adesse
Comperit. Inflatum sic est affatus Aplestem—
Mos erat huius opes amplas terraque marique
Quesitis dapibus consumere et eius in alvo
Sepe timallus aprum, rombus capream, lupus ursum
475 Litibus occultis pressabat—"Dura procaces
(Ut magnum!) nobis Iebusei bella minantur,
Sed confido tamen, quia nos Victoria tristes
Haut faciet. Dic ergo meo mea nuncia Iude:

that period, when a king born of a king, bodily present, will
wage harsh wars. After half of the aforesaid time this peace-   450
maker will arrive in the world; we have completed the re-
maining years. However, I cannot report to you the reason
why this should be agreeable to him; but because you asked
why he did not snatch away even Judas, who is faithful to
him, it is no secret that you do not know what sort of life   455
Judas will lead. For I foretell to you (if I can foretell anything
that you would not think groundless): when the son of Aga-
tus in person wages frightful battles, above all others he will
perceive as an enemy the one who you now boast is faithful
to him above all others. And Ethnis, who adores a plaster   460
figure of Jove as if it were a true god and who seeks aid from
handmade images, will begin to follow what is right and to
fear the lofty thunderer, Agatus, and the whole world will
serve God."

    As the most learned prophet recalls such events at all too   465
great length, he slows down with sweet speech swift Moses
and constrains the welcome cohorts to move up little by
little. Meanwhile, since the time is now advantageous, sav-
age Cacus runs about over rough ground and uphill, gathers
his soldiers, takes a stand on the broad fields of Babylon,   470
and learns that the time for fighting is nearly at hand. In the
following words he addresses bloated Aplestes—it was the
habit of this man to exhaust abundant resources in ban-
quet foods sought out on land and sea, and in hidden strife
within his belly grayling jostled against boar, turbot against
roebuck, wolf against bear—"The impudent Jerusalemites   475
threaten us with hard wars (how great a matter!), but I trust
nevertheless that Victory will hardly make us sad. There-
fore, relate my message to my Judas:

'Care, memento, licent quot quantaque nunc tibi quamque
480　Acceptus semper nobis huc usque fuisti,
　　Nec solvi cupias; numquam magis esse solutus,
　　Quam nunc es, poteris, cum, que tibi cumque voluptas
　　Suadet, liber agas. Hinc, numina testor, ademptus
　　Verus eris servus. Quam servicium premit acre,
485　Est mala libertas. Quapropter, si sapis, omnem
　　Ponens mesticiam canta; cantans epulare
　　Cornigeroque satur muscho dispone cohortes!
　　Sit tuus exemplo frater tibi, voce fideli
　　Me dominum vocat ipse suum preceptaque nostra
490　Mente gerit laeta nec numine fidit in uno
　　Ipse deos faciens sibi; gaudet et utitur omni
　　Blandicia, ut regem, non servum dicere possis.
　　Securus quisquis que vult agit omnia, rex est.
　　Hos fratris ritus imitare tueque magister
495　Esto voluptati gratissimus et mea mecum
　　Regna tene mecumque stude communia regna
　　Defensare libens! Sevorum copia grandis
　　Armorum et probitas invicta labore virorum
　　Spem palme magnam mihi dant et numina nostre
500　Cuncta favent parti.'"
　　　　　　　　　Sic ore locutus Aplesti
　　Conflatum fulvo, quem Iude deferat, auro
　　Dat vitulum. Inde Iovem taurum finxisse poetas
　　Autumo, quando bovem simulavit, Agenore natam
　　Ut violaret amans, pars orbis tercia cuius
505　Nomen habet.
　　　　　　　　Fert ille datum sub pectore curas
　　Versanti dubias, bellum culpetne probetne

242

'Dear one, remember how many things, and what great things, are now possible for you and how you have always been, down to the present, agreeable to us. Do not wish to be released; you can never have greater release than you do now, since you can do freely whatever pleasure persuades you. I call to witness the gods that when taken away from here, you will truly be a slave. A freedom that harsh servitude oppresses is bad. For this reason, if you are wise, put aside all sadness and sing; while singing, banquet and, when sated with a horned calf, marshal your troops! Let your brother be a model for you; with a trusty voice he calls me his lord and carries out my bidding with a happy disposition. Making gods for himself, he does not trust in one divinity; he rejoices and enjoys all sorts of delights, so that you could call him a king, not a slave. Whoever does everything he wishes without anxiety is a king. Imitate these practices of your brother, be a most welcome master to your pleasure, rule my kingdom with me, and endeavor with me willingly to defend our shared kingdom! A large supply of savage arms and the excellence of men unconquered by toil give great hope of victory to me, and all the gods favor our party.'"

Having spoken thus from his mouth, he gives Aplestes a calf forged of tawny gold to carry down to Judas. For this reason, I suppose, the poets imagined Jupiter as a bull, when he took on bovine form so that as a lover he might ravish the daughter of Agenor, whose name is borne by a third of the world.

That Judas takes the gift with a heart pondering critical worries, whether he should blame or approve the war

Pro sese ceptum. Tandem sentencia Caci
Edomuit malesuada virum mentemque reducit
A primo rectore suo. Iam penitet acri
510 Anphicope hospicium scripturarumque perito
Concessisse larem Moysi; iam nomen abhorret
Regis eoque sati diuturnaque servicia illi
Sub Caco dominante placent et, prorsus ab illo
Mutatus qui nuper erat, fit turpis ut Ethnis
515 Ganeo, rixator, mechus cultorque deorum
Cunctaque lascive probat oblectamina carnis.
Ergo vir egregius modo factus apostata, Caci
Precepta aggressus totum deducit edendo
Atque bibendo diem ventremque ingurgitat album.
520 Utque magis placeat uentri famulando cruentis
Principibus, Moysi, bene quem susceperat ante,
Derogat atque Nomo: "Dominos quid detinet illos?
Vulgus iners, puto, preludunt pugnareque primum
Discunt. Et discant; ego cunctis prefero certe
525 Huius bella modi: canitur, potatur, amatur."
    Sic dicens pateram tollit plenamque Lieo
Inpiger evertit totamque domum stimulat se
Sic faciendo sequi; vacuant ingentia vasa
Convive tenuesque ciphos; resalutat Aplestes.
530 Post ubi multa dies iterumque iterumque repostis
Absumpta est dapibus, iubet omnes surgere Cacus
Parvos atque senes et festo carmine muscho
Psallere cornigero. Surgunt letaque corona
Circueunt variasque sonat petulancia voces,
535 Sicut leta strepit prope mixtum melle Coapsin
Grus inter cignos vacuove ciconia rostro,
Aut ubi preceptor multos cantare scolares

undertaken on his behalf. At last the view of Cacus, which gave evil counsel, overcame the man and led his mind away from his first ruler. Now he rues having granted hospitality to keen Anphicopas and his home to Moses learned in the scriptures; now he recoils from the name of the king, Agatus, and of his son, Messiah. Eternal servitude beneath Lord Cacus pleases him and, thoroughly transformed from the person he was recently, he became base like Ethnis, a debauchee, brawler, adulterer, and worshipper of false gods. He approves all enticements of the lustful flesh. Accordingly, an outstanding man now become an apostate, having undertaken the commands of Cacus, he spends the whole day in eating and drinking, and he stuffs his stomach until it turns pale. And so that he may please the bloodthirsty princes more while attending to his stomach, he speaks derogatorily of Moses, whom he had received well before, and Nomus: "What is keeping those lords? The untrained mob! I think they are rehearsing and learning for the first time to fight. And let them learn; for my part, I certainly prefer to all others wars of this sort: singing, drinking, lovemaking."

Speaking in such a way, he raises a libation dish full of wine, energetically turns it upside down empty, and incites the whole household to follow him in so doing. The banqueters empty giant vessels and slender drinking glasses; Aplestes replies to their toasts. Afterward, when many a day has been spent in banquets laid out again and again, Cacus orders all, young and old, to rise and to sing in festive song to the horned calf. They rise and go round in a happy circle, and their wantonness produces varied sounds, just as the happy crane among swans or the stork with empty beak screeches near the Choaspes, the water of which is mixed with honey, or when an instructor coaches many pupils to

Erudit, ingenii prope vim discriminat omnes,
Hi faciles, illi longas longo ordine neumas
540 Discunt et varium strepitum dat dissona turba.
    Iamque propinquabant Solimani forcia regis
Agmina et in planos serie descendere longa
Montis prerupti superato vertice campos
Ceperunt. Ibi dum disiectas tramite turmas
545 Angusto Moyses de more recolligit et dum
Premonet, ut certo procedant ordine iuncti,
Advolat Ektrifon, qui nunciat Apolidarum
Signiferum Iudam coniuratumque malignis
Hostibus et veri cultum liquisse tonantis
550 Et Frigios muscho modulos cecinisse fabrili.
Denique narrat eum velle inpugnare verendum
Agaton et niti, quo longo tempore torvi
Servus Amartigenis patriisque procul sit ab oris,
Preterea multos ex illa parte coactos
555 Esse duces Caci socios et nominat illos:
Antifrononciaden altoremque eius Aplestem
Et Fuscum fortemque Aphilum fortemque Diglossam.
Sevus Iperfanes iuvat hos censorque litandi
Politeon pecoris—populos hic subdidit omnes
560 Preter Pragmanos, primum quos cernit in ortu
Oppositum Geminis sol cum fugat Arcitenentem
Dexteriora tenens—tenuique Crisargirus ore
Et nimium Pirtalmus atrox. Fert omnibus Ethnis
Et Iudas malefidus opem, magnosque paratus
565 Hostibus esse refert omnesque ad bella feroces.
    His stupet auditis Moyses et nobile quassans
Tristi fronte caput clara sic voce profatur,

sing, he divides them all according to the strength of their
talent: these learn the easy notes, those long notes in a long
series, and the inharmonious throng produces a varied din. 540

And now the stout forces of the king of Jerusalem are ap-
proaching and, having surmounted the peak of the precipi-
tous mountain, they began to descend in a long column onto
the level fields. There, as Moses in the usual way pulls to-
gether the troops scattered by the narrow footpath and as 545
he cautions them to advance marshaled in a set order, Ektri-
fon flies up and announces that Judas, the standard-bearer
of the Apolides and the sworn ally of the wicked enemies,
has both abandoned the worship of the true thunderer and 550
sung Phrygian measures to the man-made calf. Finally he re-
counts that Judas wishes to besiege revered Agatus and that
he is endeavoring to be for a long time the slave of harsh
Amartigenes and far from the borders of his homeland.
What is more, he tells that many dukes of Cacus have been 555
assembled from that party, and he names those allies: the
son of Antifronon, Amartigenes; his foster father, Aplestes;
Fuscus; valiant Aphilus; and valiant Diglossa. Savage Hiper-
efanes aids them, as does Politeon, the judge of sacrifi-
cial animals—he subdued all peoples except the Brahmins, 560
whom the sun perceives first in rising when, heading south-
ward, it puts to flight Sagittarius opposite Gemini—and
Crisargirus of the pinched face and overly harsh Pirtalmus.
Ethnis and untrustworthy Judas bring aid to all of them, and 565
Ektrifon reports that the enemies have great equipment
and that all are keen for battle.

Upon hearing these reports, Moses is astounded and,
shaking his noble head with a sad brow, he declares as fol-

"Vera mihi, Eleymon, de Iuda vaticinatum
Te fateor, nati Ramatho quod maximus hostis
570 Fiat adhuc. Hoc nunc impletum dicere possis,
Ni duo prepediant, quod in eius parte stat Ethnis
Et nondum Agatites committit prelia presens.
Sed quia tot tantique viri crudelia nobis
Bella parant, nos tam paucos confligere non est
575 In multos fortes cautum, quia stultus habetur,
Non audax, temere quisquis pugnam facit, est hoc,
Qui non consulte bellat. Nec ego hec loquor, ut qui
Cetum formidem; cui causa istuc veniendi
Pugna fuit, claramque mihi sic querere famam.
580 Non ego magna minor de me; res ipsa probabit,
Quod valeam."
                        Simul hec dicens bellare paratum
Atque renitentem multumque diuque etiamque
Iratum remanere Nomum vix cogit et ipse
Inpiger assumpto pugnaci Eleimone nec non
585 Levita cunctis somnoque meroque gravatis
Et belli prorsus securis hostica noctu
Castra petens primum preacuta cuspide segnem
Plagat Ieream, Iude vigilem; iugulisque
Innumeris enses funesta cede cruentant
590 Tres nullo prohibente viri calcantque peremptos
Bisque decem tribus adiectis tentoria cesis
Hostibus evacuant. Non segnius ac lupus acer
Irrumpens noctu caulas, quas non bene pastor
Muniit incautus, ringit solitamque cruentis
595 Dentibus exercet rabiem laceratque ferina
Mansuetum feritate gregem nec cogitat ulli
Parcere, sed totum necat insaciatus ovile;

lows in a loud voice: "Eleymon, I admit that you prophesied
truly to me about Judas, that he would become the greatest
enemy so far of Messiah, the son of Ramathus. You could 570
say that this had now been fulfilled, were there not two ob-
stacles, namely, that Ethnis remains in Cacus's party and
that the son of Agatus is not yet present to wage war. But
because so many and such great men ready cruel wars against
us, it is not wise for so few of us to join battle against so
many valiant men, because whoever enters battle rashly is 575
held to be foolish and not brave—that is, whoever who does
not war prudently. I do not say these things because I would
fear the encounter; for me the reason for coming here was
to fight and thus to acquire high renown for myself. I do not 580
just threaten great things about myself; the outcome itself
will confirm what I am worth."

At the same time as he says these things, he can scarcely
compel angry Nomus to stay, who has been ready to fight,
struggling, and very angry for a long time and still now. In
his zeal, he himself takes along combative Eleimon and Le-
vite. While all are weighed down by sleep and wine and are 585
utterly free from concern about war, he seeks out the enemy
camp by night and first wounds with a sharp-pointed spear
slothful Iereas, Judas's sentry. With no one to stop them, the 590
three men bloody their swords on countless throats in a
deathly slaughter, trample those they have slain, and clear
out twenty-three tents after cutting down their enemies.
No more slowly than a fierce wolf as it bursts by night into
sheepfolds that a careless shepherd did not protect well,
snarls, indulges its characteristic rage with bloody teeth, 595
tears apart the meek flock with bestial wildness, and does
not think to spare any of them, but unsated slaughters the

Sic bellator atrox Moyses eiusque sequaces
Sopitos cedendo fremunt.
                    Sed et ipse scelestis
600 Iudas quod ducibus consensit, vulnere multo
Afflictus viteque sue diffisus utrasque
Ad celum tendit palmas oratque salutem.
Illum seminecem suadente Eleymone liquit
Magnanimus Moyses. Sed cum iam tanta iaceret
605 Cesorum strages et vastus ubique tumultus
In castris fieret, prostratis pluribus hostes
Diffugiunt ipsique duces formidine ceca
Dispersi properant evadere, non aliter quam
Remigio molli veniente per aera milvo
610 Galline pulli horrescunt sparsique volatu
Qualicumque domum penna trepidante requirunt.
Sic eciam, cum rex Sirie Samarica vastis
Agminibus circumsedisset menia, quadam
Nocte deus belli strepitu perterruit hostes
615 Inque fuga celeri fecit sperare salutem
Monstrifera cedente fame.
                      Tunc hoste fugato
Victor seductum dictis castigat amaris
Solaturque simul, "Ne desperes, bone Iuda"—
Desperarat enim—"properatam posse salutem
620 Adventare tibi; nescit peccantibus in se
Restituisse vicem Ramathus, quem sepe videmus
Adversos refovere sibi. Modo peniteat te
A recta cessisse via partemque profani
Laudavisse ducis, liceat mihi vera referre.
625 Non, quod te decuit, fecisti, quem stabilem nos
Et firme mentis rebamus. At amodo tantum
Horrescas patrare nefas. Age, clara potentis

whole sheep pen; so do the terrifying warrior Moses and his followers growl as they cut down the sleepers.

But Judas himself, accursed because he conspired with the dukes, is injured by many wounds and doubts that he will live; he stretches out both hands to heaven and prays for salvation. Through the persuasion of Eleimon, noble-spirited Moses left him half-dead. But since so great a massacre of slain men already lies about and an immense uproar arises everywhere in the camp, the enemies, with many laid low, flee in different directions and even the leaders, scattered by blind terror, hasten to escape, no differently from when, as a bird of prey comes through the air on its supple wings, a hen's chicks shudder and, spread about in whatever sort of flight they can manage, try to find home with trembling wings. So, likewise, when the king of Syria had besieged with immense forces the walls of Samaria, on a certain night God with the clatter of battle terrified the enemy and made them hope for safety in swift flight as the portent-producing famine came to an end.

Then, once the enemy has been put to flight, the conqueror, Moses, at one and the same time chides the wayward man with bitter words and consoles him: "Do not lose hope, good Judas"—for he had despaired—"that salvation can come to you in a hurry; Ramathus, or Agatus, who as we often see takes back into his bosom those who have opposed him, is unwilling to take revenge upon those who sin against him. Just repent of having gone away from the right path and of having praised the party of the impious duke, if I may relate what is true. You did not do as befitted you, you whom we thought to be steady and of resolute mind. But from now on, may you shudder to commit so great a crime. Come on,

Castra Nomi repetas, cui non infortibus armis,
Cum voluit, licuit misero tibi ferre salutem.
630 Nam quod tunc nobis animi, mea cura, fuisse
Credis, ut Atrifon celeri tua facta relatu
Detexit? Turbare meam dolor iraque mentem
Ceperunt pariter, fremui belloque ferocem
A bello prohibere Nomum conamine summo
635 Nisus eram, sed vix illud tamen inpetravi;
Nunc tamen adducam committere plurima pro te
Prelia dispositum."
                    Dixit. Tunc inclitus ista
Subdidit Eleimon, "Moysen tibi certa locutum
Vera scias. Horrenda Nomo duce flendaque multis
640 Matribus his fient in campis prelia. Post hunc
Ingenio consurget Oron ventura canendi
Prepollens belloque ferus. Post forcia facta
Illius eximie laudis pius Agatus, ut te
Eripiat, mittet Messiam. Tunc Iebusei
645 Iudee in campis asperrima bella videbunt."
     Hec ubi depromsit noti pietate per orbem
Lingua viri prudens ac non ignara futuri,
Iudas dimissus vultum similisque pudenti,
Quippe pudenda videns se commisisse, spopondit
650 Vlterius se non facturum talia, multa
Inficians fedisque probris et voce paterna
Inproperata sibi.
                    Quo gaudens Omino, regis
Consiliator, ait, "Video, mihi quod placet, istum

seek out again the famed camp of powerful Nomus, to
whom it was possible, when he wished, to bring salvation to
you in your wretchedness by means of his stout weapons. 630
For what frame of mind do you believe we had then, you
who are my care, when in a swift account Atrifon revealed
your deeds? Grief and anger began to disturb my mind
equally, I roared and strove with the utmost effort to hold
back from war Nomus, who is fierce in war, but nonetheless 635
I scarcely obtained that result; nevertheless I will now bring
him over to our side while he is disposed to wage many bat-
tles on your behalf."

He spoke. Then renowned Eleimon added these words:
"You should know that Moses has spoken indisputable
truths to you. While Nomus is leader, terrible battles, to be
lamented by many mothers, will take place on these fields. 640
After him will rise Oron, wild in war and superior in the tal-
ent of prophesying events to come. After the valiant deeds
of Oron, dutiful Agatus, worthy of uncommon praise, will
send Messiah to snatch you away. Then the Jebusites will see 645
the harshest of wars on the fields of Judaea."

When the foresighted and prophetic tongue of the man
who was known throughout the world for his piety had ut-
tered these words, Judas, downcast in his face and looking
like a man ashamed, as was no doubt to be expected because
he saw that he had perpetrated shameful acts, pledged that 650
he would not do such things any more; he disowned respon-
sibility for many deeds for which he had been blamed, in
both coarse reproaches and a fatherly voice.

Omino, the counselor of the king, rejoiced in this and
said, "I see that he regrets the offence, which pleases me.

Penitet admissi. Veniat Nomus et premat acri
655 Congressu solitis innitens viribus hostes,
Qui nostros homines affligunt seque tenere
Iure fatentur eos, acres et cede piorum
Numquam et supplicio saciati, sanguine numquam.
Utque hiat Hircanis in saltibus horrida tigris,
660 Que semel armenti pollutas sanguine fauces
Semper habet cupidas hausti sine fine cruoris,
Sic tibi, Cace ferox, insontes ledere numquam
Sufficit; inmerita captorum pascere pena.
    "Nec tamen hac feritate diu letabere, si me
665 Vite auctor, deus, incolumem servaverit. Omnis,
Qui tumide petit alta, cadet. Voluere Gigantes
Una mente poli pulsare cacumina quondam
Sideria turri, sed virtus summa superbos
Confundens lathomos, quod nomen huic dedit urbi,
670 Ceptum linquere opus per dissona compulit ora.
Inde poesis habet vero diversa sequentes
Terrigenas validos Ossam et Pelion altum
Coniecisse super maiorem ambobus Olimpum
Pellendis fera bella deis inferre volentes;
675 Nec mora, Flegreis divum convenit in arvis
Agmen et inmanes trifido Saturnius hostes
Fulmine disiectos ardentibus indidit Ethne
Speluncis.
        "Ad te redeo, qui plurima uastans
Regna Giganteis bachare ferocior ausis,

Let Nomus come and, relying on his usual strengths, oppress in a fierce encounter the enemies who bring ruin upon 655 our people and who declare that they have the right to hold them; they are savage in slaughtering the pious and are never sated by either torture or blood. And as the dreadful tiger in the Hyrcanian groves opens wide its mouth and, having 660 once defiled its maw with the blood of cattle, will always desire to guzzle gore endlessly, so you, fierce Cacus, are never satisfied with harming the innocent; you grow fat upon the undeserved punishment of captives.

"Yet you will not take joy in this ferocity for long, if God, 665 the creator of life, keeps me safe and sound. Everyone who proudly seeks the heights will fall. Once upon a time the Giants were unanimous in wanting to strike the peaks of heaven with a starry tower, but the highest virtue confounded the haughty stonemasons and constrained them through their discordant utterances to abandon the project they had undertaken; this gave the city its name. In conse- 670 quence, poetry, diverging from the truth, holds that mighty earth dwellers threw together Ossa and lofty Pelion atop Olympus (which is greater than both of them), because they wished to inflict wild war upon the gods and expel them. 675 Without delay, the forces of the gods assembled in the Phlegraean fields, and Jupiter, born of Saturn, having scattered the tremendous enemies with his three-pronged thunderbolt, thrust them into the burning caves of Mount Etna.

"I return now to you, Cacus, son of perdition, who lay waste to many realms and run riot more fiercely than the

680 Apolide. Tantum ne te tua prospera tollant,
   Inprobe! Non semper mollis cadit arbore sorba.
   Atqui tempus erit, quo tu de clade bonorum
   Nunc gaudens doleas exempta clade bonorum."
   Sic ait atque Nomum Moyse comitante revisit.

EXPLICIT LIBER PRIMUS.

Giants in their audacity. Do not let your successes exalt you 680
so much, miscreant! The sorb apple does not always fall
softly from the tree. What is more, the time will come when
you who rejoice now over the slaughter of good men will
grieve once the slaughter of good men has been redeemed."
Thus he spoke and, accompanied by Moses, returned to
Nomus.

HERE ENDS THE FIRST BOOK.

Iam nitidum referente iubar Titane fugantur
Sidera et humenti noctis caligine pulsa
Clara dies aperit clausum mortalibus orbem,
Cum subito volucris funesta per atria rumor
5 Spargitur Apolide Solimani regis adesse
Prevalidas acies et tristia bella minantes.
    Protinus armatas frendens ad signa cohortes
Cogit et audaci committere prelia dextra
Hortatur parte promittens maxima palme
10 Premia, seque viros acres bellique scientes
Agricolas contra pugnaturos docet, et quos
Cultus inornatus, facies nigra, pallor in ore
Luridus ignavos probet, utque suis animatis
Mens assurgat, eos collaudat et increpat hostes.
15 Preterea meminisse suos monet esse tuenda
Multa sibi (patriam, uxores natosque domosque),
Utque voluptatem solitam retinere (voluptas
Res illis gratissima erat) valeant et amoris
Oblectamentis carni predulcibus uti.
20   Iamque videbantur validi propiare manipli
Principis invicti clipeique et cetera multo
Sole repercusso nituerunt arma decore
Belligerumque levi nubes consurgit equorum

Already the stars are put to flight as Titan brings back his
bright radiance and, after the moist obscurity of the night
has been dispelled, the shining day opens up to mortals the
world that has been concealed, when suddenly a winged ru-
mor is spread about through the deathly halls of Apolides —   5
of Cacus — that the doughty battle lines of the king of Jeru-
salem are nearby and threatening dire wars.

Gnashing his teeth, he at once gathers the armed cohorts
under the standards and encourages them to engage in bat-
tle with bold right hand, promising them the greatest re-
wards from the victory gained. He informs them that they,
brave and well-versed in war, are going to combat farmers   10
shown to be ignoble by their unadorned attire, their dark
looks, and the sallow pallor of their faces. To heighten the
courage in his spirited men, he praises them and upbraids
the enemy. In addition, he advises them to remember that   15
they must protect many things (native land, wives, children,
and homes) and that they must prevail to keep their accus-
tomed joy (joy was the most pleasing thing to them) and to
enjoy the delights of love, which are exceedingly sweet to
the flesh.

And already the strong companies of the unconquered   20
prince are seen approaching. The shields and other arms
shine with much beauty from the reflected sun, and a cloud
rises up from the light dust stirred by the hooves of the war-

Pulvere commoto pedibus. Babilonius heros
25 Acri mente tumens nec curat in urbe manere
Hostiles cuneos, sed in equis milite lecto
Fortunam temptare suam magis eligit arvis.
Omnibus ergo ruit portis armata iuventus.
Ac veluti siciens algentem corniger undam
30 Cervus anhelanti cursu festinat adire,
Haut secus infausti bellum dira agmina Caci
Exoptant animique tument.
                                    Iam clangit utrimque
Bucina et infestis concurritur undique signis.
Concursu crispata crepant hastilia primo
35 Missaque tela volant; dein sevos comminus enses
Stringentes certant et, dum certatur utrimque,
Fit strages cumulata virum. Moysi inpigra regem
Interimit manus Amonosim, Nomus acer Acastum,
Sother Linglaum; gladio violentus Acastus,
40 Linglaus iaculo cadit, alta rector in unda,
Quem Moyses trepide fugientem perculit hasta
Atque cavis inmersit aquis, tumidumque tiranni
Aurigam cesi dominoque favere parantem
Demisit Stratona neci.
                                    Ferit ense cruento
45 Euzelus Datan in nullo dissimilem illi,
Legibus adversum quem terra obsurbuit; unde
Infernos penetrasse domos finxere poete
Anfioraon, amans munus quem prodidit uxor.
Nec magis Euzelo pius aut servancior equi
50 Ullus erat nec degit adhuc;
                                    dumque acria miscet
Prelia, multorum post funera facta cruenta

horses. The Babylonian hero, Cacus, inflamed by his fierce 25
disposition, does not bother to await the enemy formations
in the city, but opts instead to test his luck on the level fields
with carefully chosen soldiers. Therefore armed youths rush
from all the gates. Just as a horned stag when thirsty hastens 30
at a breathless run to approach cool water, so the dreadful
troops of accursed Cacus hope for war and their spirits are
inflamed.

Now on each side the trumpet blares and everywhere
battle is joined against enemy standards. Spear shafts bran-
dished in the first encounter clatter, and spears that have 35
been shot fly; then, drawing their savage swords at close
quarters, they fight and, as both sides fight, the slaughter of
men mounts. The ever-active hand of Moses takes the life
of King Amonosis, keen Nomus the life of Acastus, Sother
the life of Linglaus; violent Acastus falls dead by the sword, 40
Linglaus by the dart. The ruler falls in the deep waves; Mo-
ses felled him with a spear as he fled in fright and immersed
him in deep waters, and sent off to destruction Straton, the
haughty charioteer of the slain tyrant, as he prepared to
back up his lord.

With a bloody sword Euzelus strikes Dathan, who dif- 45
fered in no way from that man whom the earth swallowed
up, contrary to its laws. For this reason poets alleged that
Amphiaraus, whom his wife betrayed for the love of a
gift, entered into underworld abodes. There was then and
lives now no one more dutiful or observant of fairness than
Euzelus.

And as he joined in keen battles, Moses, after causing the 50
deaths of many, drove forth combative Aplestes at bloody

Cuspide pugnacem Moyses proturbat Aplestem.
Nec minus ille gravi ferientem repulit hasta
Et circumspiciens saxum grave corripit inque
55 Adversum misit collatis viribus hostem.
Quod vir prevalidus parma cedente recepit,
Vixque stetit titubante gradu. Nil ille moratus
Ictum iterat vulnusque librat, sed precipit illum
Belliger ense minax et forti sauciat ictu
60 Munitos thorace humeros, et forsitan Orco
Misisset Iesum, si non truculentus adesset
Antifrononciades. Iuvenilibus ille lacertis
Inflixit Moysi letale per intima ventris
Vulnus et ancipiti transegit viscera telo.
65   Ille tamen moriens insignem sustulit orbem
Donavitque Nomo celatum mira relatu,
Quot deus ex nichilo fecisset cuncta diebus.
Sol ibi fulgebat, currebant flumina, terras
Ingens occeanus cinxit, triplicemque quaternis
70 Cernere erat liquide discretum partibus orbem
Factaque priscorum magna argumenta virorum;
Inter que cunctis animantibus in cataclismo
Deletis, nisi que Noe collegerat; arca
Tollebatur aqua coopertis montibus, unde
75 Deucalionei processit fabula nimbi.
    Labitur egregius Moyses, haut illius inpar,
De Pelusiacis bis sex qui previus arvis
Per deserta tribus spacioso tempore duxit
Ignotumque deo meruit tumulante sepulcrum.
80 Succedit Moysi, quem fecit gloria belli

sword point. No less did that Aplestes repel Moses as Moses struck him with a weighty spear and, looking round, he seized a heavy stone and hurled it with all his might against 55 the enemy opposite. His shield giving way, the exceptionally strong man took the force of the stone and scarcely remained standing on his tottering feet. That Aplestes, not delaying at all, repeated the blow and was poised to achieve a wound, but the warrior forestalled him by threatening with his sword and wounded his shoulders, although pro- 60 tected by a cuirass, with a stout blow. There is a chance that he would have injured him and sent him to hell, had not the ferocious son of Antifronon — Amartigenes — been near. With the strength of youthful arms he inflicted a mortal wound in the inmost parts of Moses's stomach and pierced his vital organs with a two-edged spear.

Although dying, he nevertheless held up his noteworthy 65 shield and gave it, embossed with things wondrous to report, to Nomus — namely, in how many days God created all things from nothing. There the sun shone, rivers ran, the huge ocean ringed the land, and it was possible to perceive clearly the threefold disk, divided into four parts, and the 70 great events enacted by early men. Among these themes was that all creatures were destroyed in a cataclysm, except those that Noah had assembled; as the mountains were covered with water, the ark was raised up. From this event grew 75 up the tale of Deucalion's storm.

Down slipped outstanding Moses, in every way the match of that man who, leading the way from the fields of Pelusium, guided the twelve tribes over a protracted time through the wilderness and who earned an unknown tomb when God buried him. As successor to Moses came noble- 80

Regibus et populis celebrem per climata mundi,
Magnanimus Sother. Illi clipeus fuit omnem
Virtutem Iosue depictus et horrida bella:
Ut tumida occubuit Iericho, cum sola meretrix
85 Non cecidisse suas, quia sic voluit deus, edes
Letabatur. Ibi Gabaon populosa suaque
Eternum famosa fide: mirabile dictu,
Sole morante dies extenditur—esse putares
Veros quos pinxit radios manus—unde Micenis
90 Fingitur aversus cenam fugisse Thieste
Aut quod eam noctem geminavit Iupiter, in qua
Alcide pressit genitricem.
                              Strennuus isto
Munitus Sother scuto metit inpiger omnes
Oppositos. Ceu sevus aper, cum colligit iram,
95 Fulmineo rapidos invadit dente Molosos,
Non homines non tela timet, sed in ipsa paventis
Spumanti rictu venabula nititur hostis,
Sic in confertas Sother ruit efferus alas
Et stravit ferro reges regumque catervas.
100 Effudit validumque Iabin validumque Iaphian,
Dux erat iste Lachis, dux ille potens fuit Asor;
His adiungit Hiram famosum et milite multo
Pollentem Seon, ampli quem gloria regni
Fecit et ubertas inmensa tumescere rerum.
105   Isque ubi Sotherea letum capiencia dextra
Corpora tanta ducum rivosque cruoris ab uno
Fusi inpune viro videt "Optime ductor, an omnes
Claram perdemus hodie cum corpore famam?
Tergane semiviris, fuimus quibus ante timori,"
110 Exclamat, "dabimus Iebuseis? Rustica nostras

spirited Sother, whom the glory of war made famous among kings and peoples throughout all regions of the world. He had a shield depicting all the bravery and the frightful wars of Joshua: as when proud Jericho fell down while a single harlot rejoiced that her household did not perish, because 85 God so willed. There was populous Gibeon, famed everlastingly for its faith: wondrous to tell, the day is lengthened as the sun lingered. (You would think the hand-painted rays were real.) On the basis of this event it is alleged that the 90 sun turned backward from Mycenae and fled the banquet of Thyestes, or that Jupiter doubled that night, on which he had intercourse with Hercules' mother.

Vigorous Sother, protected by this shield, actively mowed down all who opposed him. Just as when a wild boar musters its anger, attacks the swift Molossian hounds with its flash- 95 ing tusk, and fears neither men nor spears, but strains with frothing maw toward the very hunting spears of the fear-stricken enemy, so Sother rushed wildly against the assembled squadrons and laid low with his sword kings and squadrons of kings. He struck to the ground strong Jabin and 100 strong Japhia; the former was the powerful duke of Hazor, the latter the duke of Lachish. To them he adds Horam of great fame and mighty Sihon of many soldiers, whom the glory of a large realm and limitless abundance of property caused to swell with pride.

When he sees so many bodies of leaders meeting their 105 death at Sother's right hand and streams of gore spilt by one man without retribution, Sihon cries out, "Best leader, will all of us lose today our good reputations as well as our lives? Shall we flee from these Jebusite half-men, in whom we induced fear in the past? Swarms of peasants besiege our bat- 110

Inpugnant acies examina; prospice, numquem
Inter eos videas ortum de sanguine equestri.
Hic evaginant gladios, quibus esset aratrum
Conveniens regere et longos sulcando ligones.
115 Apta gerunt colaphis a summo vertice rasi
Colla, breves etiam non tecto poplite vestes,
Ut Satiros saltare putes; pro Iupiter, hi nos
Ut stipulas nullo detenti vulnere calcant
Sub pedibus? Si sic ageremur cede virorum,
120 Damnum esset levius ferremque eger minus, at nunc
Indignor stupeoque simul."
                         Dum talia iactat,
Vulnificum Sother vibrans hastile per ora
"Ut stupeas, faciamus," ait, "Quandoque nocere
Rustica tela queunt equiti." Pariterque loquacis
125 Impedit ora ducis iaculo per guttura misso.
   Tum vero exarsit nec voci ireve pepercit
Sevus Amartigenis volucrique simillimus Austro
Sothera bellantem fatali cuspide turbans
"Ecquid," ait, "Sother, nondum de sanguine nostro
130 Hausisti satis? An te inpune, miserrime, reris
Tot stravisse duces et tanta cadavera telis
Obtrivisse tuis? Moysi te fama ferebat,
Ut memini (nec erat vanum, quod fama ferebat
Et quod Amartigenes meminit ferus), esse sodalem
135 Eius, quem nuper pallentibus addidit umbris
Ista manus. Nimium, qui te moriendo preivit,
Prosequeris lente, sed ni fractis mihi desim
Viribus, horribilem moriendo sequeris ad Orcum
Premissum socium."

tle lines; look whether or not you see one man among them who comes of knightly blood. Now they, who would fittingly guide the plow and long hoes in making furrows, unsheathe swords. Shorn from the very top (of their heads down), they 115 have necks designed for receiving blows and also short garments that leave their hams uncovered, so that you would think satyrs were frolicking; by Jove, this kind of people, checked by no wound, treads us down like stubble beneath their feet? If we were thus driven back by a slaughter caused by real men, the injury would be more trifling and I would 120 not take it so hard, but now I am at once disdainful and astounded."

While he made such boasts, Sother, brandishing in his face a spear capable of inflicting wounds, said, "Let us commit deeds to astound you. Sometimes the spears of peasants can harm a knight." Simultaneously he stopped the mouth of the talkative leader with a dart shot through his throat. 125

Then indeed savage Amartigenes blazes up and refrains from neither words nor anger. Very much like the fleet south wind he stirs up Sother who is warring with a deadly spear point and says, "So, Sother, have you not drunk enough of our blood yet? Or do you think, most miserable wretch, that 130 you could without retribution lay low so many dukes and destroy with your missiles such mighty corpses? As I recall, a rumor held (and what rumor held and what wild Amartigenes recalls is not idle) that you were a comrade of Moses, 135 whom this hand of mine recently added to the pale shades. You follow all too slowly the one who preceded you in dying but unless my might has been broken and I fail myself, in dying you will follow to terrifying hell the ally who was sent in advance of you."

Sic fatur et appetit hasta
140 Pugnantem ac valido nequicquam corpore contra
Nitentem. Tamen haut cito vincitur, utpote qui non
Segniter infensum mucrone repelleret hostem
Ancipiti. Pugnant et uterque viriliter, ille
Fulmineo ense minax, hic nodosa acrior hasta.
145 Conflixere mora, tanta est industria, longa,
Ut cum fidentem robusto corpore taurum
Aggreditur forti leo pectore; pugnat uterque,
Acriter, hic cauda metuendus, cornibus ille;
Hic ferit, ille petit nec cessant, donec abire
150 Alterutrum sua deficiens fiducia cogit.
Sed dum prevalidis invicti viribus ambo
Certavere duces sudore fluente per artus
Sotheris, ah nimium nimiumque sibi Iebuseus
Confidens hastam truncare parabat adacto
155 Funeream ferro, sed caucior ille retracta
Cuspide frustratum fugiente per ilia pilo
Enecat.
        Exultant Caldei, ad sidera clamor
Tollitur et multa victorem laude coronant
"Antifrononciades sacrata cuspide leto
160 Bina dedit nostre nimium facientia parti
Corpora," psallentes.
                Sed pergite, gratia qua vos
Eterni ducat regis, gaudeteque semper,
Felices anime; licet heu patris acta luatis,
Sed tamen ad tempus. Dum fertilis in mare curret
165 Eufrates et dum per tempora quatuor anni
Solaris stabili volventur secula ciclo,

So he speaks and with his spear attacks Sother, who fights 140
and, with his mighty body, struggles against him to no avail.
Nevertheless he is not overcome swiftly, inasmuch as he
briskly rebuffed the aggressive enemy with a two-edged
sword. Each of them fights manfully, the latter threatening
with his lightning-like sword, the former quite brave with
his knotty spear. They struggled over a long period of time, 145
their application being as great as when a brave-hearted lion
assails a bull that trusts in its sturdy body; each one fights
keenly, the first to be feared for its tail and the second for its
horns; the former strikes, the latter makes an assault, and
they do not retreat until waning confidence compels both 150
of them to retire. But as both dukes unconquered in their
mighty strength competed, as sweat poured over the limbs
of Sother, the Jerusalemite—alas, all too, all too trusting
in himself—made ready to lop off the lethal spear with a
plunge of the sword, but that one, Amartigenes, quite cau- 155
tiously drew back the spear point and killed off his thwarted
opponent as the spear slipped into his groin.

The Chaldeans exult, a shout of triumph is raised heav-
enward, and they crown the conqueror with much praise,
singing, "The son of Antifronon, Amartigenes, has put to
death with consecrated spear point two bodies that had 160
been accomplishing all too much against our side."

But proceed where the grace of the everlasting king leads
you and rejoice forever, blessed souls; possibly you may en-
dure expiation for the deeds of your father (alas!), but never-
theless you will do so only for a time. So long as the fruitful
Euphrates runs into the sea and so long as the centuries pass
in a fixed circuit through the four seasons of the solar year, 165

Nomina perpetuum durabunt vestra per evum
Et vos magnificis cum scriptis fama loquetur.
    Postquam milicie Ramathi cecidere columne,
170 Famosi virtute viri, Babilonia pubes
Auspice successu solito magis aspera sevit.
Acer Politeon et crudelissimus armis
Antifrononte satus cumque illis turgidus Ethnis
Sternunt Iudaicas funesta cede phalanges
175 Disiunguntque globos legionum, iamque parabant
Agatide temptare fugam.
                  Tunc nobilis heros,
Cui Crito nomen erat, Moysi de semine cretus,
Prosiliens "Que vos agitat dementia? Quonam
Exanimes ruitis? Densa inter milia," clamat,
180 "Non pudet ignava circum formidine, pelli?
His monstris non me Panocius—inspice torvum
Politeona!—magis Sciticus terreret, ut illi
Tota mole graves cooperti corporis aures
Diffundunt, aut quos Getulia fertur habere
185 Vicinos, agiles pedibus qui corpus obumbrant
Scinopodes totum, aut oculatus Lemnia pectus.
Illorum similes hos possis dicere, si non
Bissina fuscorum decoraret membra lacerna
Et ferrugineo vestis variata colore
190 Lutea. State, viri, vulgo nec cedat inermi
Bellis apta manus ferroque accincta iuventus!
State nec indecorem vobis concedite palmam
Hostibus et tantum ne formidetis eorum
Defectum virtute gregem! Plus strennuus unus
195 Confert quam resides in sollicitudine mille;
Adiuvat audaces Fortuna, gravatur inertes.

your names will endure forevermore and fame will speak of you in splendid writings.

After the pillars of Ramathus's knighthood, men renowned for their virtue, fell, the Babylonian youths rage more harshly than usual with the promise of success. Violent Politeon and Amartigenes, the one born of Antifronon, most savage in his weapons, and with them swollen Ethnis strike down the Judaic phalanxes in murderous slaughter and break asunder the closely packed throngs of legions, and already the soldiers of Agatus were making ready to attempt flight.

Then the noble hero, born of Moses's seed, whose name was Crito, leaps out and shouts, "What madness moves you? Where are you rushing mindlessly? Does it not cause shame to be routed in close-packed thousands on account of base fear? Look at harsh Politeon: a Scythian Panotian would not frighten me more than these monsters, when they, heavy with the whole mass of their covered bodies, spread out their ears; nor would those whom Gaetulia is reported to have as neighbors, the swift Sciopods, who shade their entire body with their feet; nor would a Lemnia, who has eyes in his chest. You could say that these were like those, if a linen mantle and a yellow garment variegated with a dark purplish color did not embellish their swarthy limbs. Stand fast, men, and do not allow a band well-suited to wars and young men girded with swords to yield before an unarmed rabble. Stand fast and do not hand over to enemies a victory that is shameful to you; and do not fear the great, cowardly herd of them! One vigorous person contributes more than a thousand who are paralyzed in anxiety. Fortune helps the

170

175

180

185

190

195

Quid moror? Este viri! Si me ductore paratis
Conspirare, nigros exheredabimus istos
Ethiopum populos."
                    Dixit, Partoque fugaci
200 Ocior alipedem calcaribus urget adactis
Disiectosque fugat Caldeos acer et unctum
Politeona ferit, valido qui saucius ictu
Egreditur pugna. Cernentes talia (quidni?
Plus movet exemplum quam suasio multa paventes),
205 Acrius Agatide pugnant. Ferit ense Sirorum
Gothoniel satrapam, cui prolatu grave nomen
Barbara lingua dedit. Fuit atro Gothonieli
Doxius auxilio tanta inter milia pugnans
Solus utraque manu ceu dextra; paupere quamvis
210 Velatus sua membra sago, tamen aspera movit
Prelia.
          Quem contra Nabateis finibus ortus
Prosiliens Egon tumido sic ore profatur,
"Quo, miserande, ruis, cui non est lancea, non est
Vulnificus mucro? Que tanta socordia mentem
215 Cepit, ut ad pugnam peregrino rasile lignum
Apcius afferres?" Fustem videt hostis et hostem
Ense carere putat, qui non caret ense, dolonem,
Quod donavit ei nomen dolus, ipse repostum
In baculo gestans. Atque addit, "Pallida monstrat
220 Te medicum facies, aut hec exotica pixis
Efficit aut certe quoniam sugendo minutor
Elicis egroti (dictu quoque turpe) cruorem
Sicut hirudo tenax."

bold, oppresses the idle. Why do I pause? Be men! If you are ready to join together for battle with me as your leader, we will disinherit these black peoples of the Ethiopians!"

He spoke, and faster than a fleeing Parthian he pressed   200
on his swift-footed steed by applying the spurs, bravely put to flight the scattered Chaldeans, and struck anointed Politeon, who was wounded by the stout blow and left the fight. Seeing such events, the sons of Agatus fought more keenly   205
(and why not, since example moves the fearful more than prolonged persuasion?). Othniel struck with his sword the satrap of the Syrians, to whom an uncouth language gave a name ponderous to pronounce. Doxius, fighting alone among so many thousands and using each hand as if it were his right, provided aid to dark Othniel. Although Doxius's limbs were covered with a poor woolen cloak, nevertheless   210
he waged harsh battle.

Against him Egon, born in the lands of Nabataea, springs forth and proclaims as follows with boastful mouth, "Where, wretch, do you rush, who have no lance and no wounding sword point? What great foolishness has seized your mind,   215
that you should bring to a fight a polished piece of wood better suited to a pilgrim?" He sees the staff of his foe and thinks that his foe has no sword, although he does have one: he carries stored away in a staff a sword-stick *(dolo),* a name that deceit *(dolus)* gave to it. He adds, "Your wan face shows   220
you to be a doctor; either this foreign medicine box causes you to be one, or to be sure you are one because by sucking as a blood-letter you extract the gore of a sick person (it is vile even to speak of this) like a clinging leech."

Tunc pectore Doxius acri

Subridens "Premit aut ornat sua quemque facultas.

225 Cui non est sonipes, aiunt, pede pergat oportet,

Et nos adtulimus baculum, quia defuit ensis.

Sed quia sum medicus, nimio tibi sanguine pullas

Flebothemo venas temptabo ferire minutor,"

Fatur et hostili capulo tenus abdit in alvo

230 Ancipitem sicam crassosque eviscerat artus;

Stridit aqualiculus, stridunt prepinguia sica

Viscera versata ferventi sanguine contra,

Ut lacus inmerso stricta cum forpice ferro

Ignito fervere solet, quantove per artum

235 Ebullit spina stridore lageus adempta.

    Et dum per medias rumpens Crito fortiter alas

Dimicat atque ducum tristi dat corpora leto,

Torvus Amartigenes, fortunatissimus armis,

Incursans alacrem sic eminus inquit ad hostem,

240 "En, tuus in bello, Crito—depone arma!—magister.

Quo tegeris, nostrum—non nostrum iure, sed ista

Affirmat sic esse manus—scutum cito redde!

Redde cito, miser!"

              Ille refert, "Tua dextra fatetur

Hoc scutum esse tuum, non sic mea dextra; fatetur

245 Munimen dignum me defensore, sub hoc me

Oppetere aut alios satius prosternere quam sic

Ut pecus hostili iugulandum dedere dextre

Robustasque manus ad vincula feda plicare.

Ast ubi me vita hec defecerit, hoc sibi Iudas

250 Pignus amicicie semper, volo, servet."

                    At ille,

"Et Iudas meus est: bene laudo—sed hoc male laudo,

Then keen-hearted Doxius smiles: "Each person's re-
sources either weigh him down or else embellish him. Peo- 225
ple say that he who has no horse should proceed on foot.
And in fact we brought a walking stick, because there was
no sword. But because I am a doctor, I will endeavor as a
blood-letter to cut open with a lancet your veins, which are
dark colored with an excess of blood." He speaks and then
he buries a two-headed dagger to the hilt in the belly of his
foe and disembowels his stout body. The potbelly hisses, the 230
overly fat bowels hiss as blood seethes out in response when
the dagger has been twisted, just as a lake is accustomed to
seethe after a red-hot sword, held in tightly pressed tongs, is
immersed or with the same hiss as when wine spouts out 235
through a narrow opening after the tap has been pulled.

And as Crito bursts bravely through the middle of the
flanks, darts out, and puts the bodies of dukes to dire death,
grim Amartigenes, most fortunate in arms, charges and
speaks thus from afar to his brisk foe, "Here is your master 240
in war! Put down your weapons, Crito! Quickly surrender
our shield by which you are protected—not ours by right,
but because this hand of mine affirms it to be so. Surrender
it quickly, wretch!"

That one, Crito, replies, "Your right hand claims that this
shield is yours, but my right hand does not; it claims it is a 245
defense worthy of me as protector, that beneath it I should
die or slay others rather than surrender like a sheep to have
my throat cut by an enemy's right hand or to submit my
powerful hands to foul bonds. But when this life has failed
me, I wish that Judas may forever keep this token of friend- 250
ship for himself."

Whereupon that one said, "Judas too is mine: that is ex-

Tot nostros socios quod manibus addere nigris
Ausus es. Illorum tu vulnera vulnere pendes
Inferiasque tuo sument de sanguine, ut ultis
255 Errandum non sit longis ambagibus umbris,
Sed certas habitent sedes." Nec plura locutus
Tendit in adversum stricto mucrone, sed ille
Iam licet incassum Borea avertente sagittam
Miserat.
        Unde fremens ductor Babilonius, "At tu
260 Cercius accipies, mea quod tibi dextera donat,"
Inquit, et invicto caput hostis contudit ense
Infringens levem cono cedente galerum
Ac subicit frendens, "Adamantem corpore duro
Obstructum tueare licet rituve Acheloi
265 Mutere aut simules variantem Prothea vultus,
Non sic effugies. Scelerum dabis, impie, penas."
His dictis ictum fortem dedit atque trilicem
Loricam penetrans humeros a pectore vellit.
Protinus extincto radiantem corpore parmam
270 Diripit et celeri percurrit non sine laude
Picturam visu.
        Celebrem celaverat illic
Artificis Geodeona manus vellusque videres
Et mirabiliter terris arentibus udum
Et mirabiliter terra madida undique siccum.
275 Quin et Samsonis dura inter brachia nutat
Exspirare leo compulsus frugiferique
Vulpibus inmissis ardent cum vitibus agri.
Allophilum tum mille viros prosternit aselli
Mandibula claususque ruit—res mira relatu—

cellent—but not excellent is that you dared to add so many
of our allies to the dark spirits of the dead. You will pay
for their wounds with a wound, and they will consume sacri-
ficial offerings from your blood, so that the shades when
avenged will not need to wander in long meanderings, but   255
instead will occupy fixed abodes." Speaking no more, he
made his way with drawn sword toward his opponent, who
had already let fly an arrow, albeit in vain, because the north
wind diverted it.

Roaring at this the Babylonian leader said, "But you will   260
receive with more certainty what my right hand gives you!"
And with his unconquered sword he pounded to pieces his
enemy's head, breaking the smooth helmet as the pointed
peak gave way, and gnashing his teeth added, "Although you
protect a steely spirit encased in a hard body, change in the   265
manner of Achelous, or imitate Proteus as he alters his ap-
pearance, in so doing you will not escape. You will pay the
penalties for your crimes, impious man." Having spoken
these words, he delivered a stout blow and, piercing his
shoulders, tore the triple-threaded corselet from his chest.
At once he ripped the shining shield from the lifeless body   270
and with a quick glance ran over the praiseworthy picture.

There the hand of an artisan had engraved famous
Gideon, and you could see the fleece, both miraculously wet
when the earth was parched and miraculously dry when all
around the earth was moist. What is more, the lion, con-   275
strained to die, sags in the hard arms of Samson, and the
fruitful fields, together with the vines, burn after the foxes
have been sent in. Then, with the jawbone of an ass he lays
low a thousand Philistines, and although shut up he rushes
out and—an event marvelous to relate—carries the gates of

280 Fertque humeris Gaze portas. Post inclita facta
Dalila perdit eum.
                Virtutem transtulit istam
Error ad Alciden Millesius: eius, ut aiunt,
Pervigil occubuit clava draco rexque tricorpor
Occidit inque sua iactura dicior Idra.
285 Terruit umbrarum regem Arpiasque fugavit,
Antheum Libicos populantem perculit agros
Et Cacum Tuscos. Post forcia gesta cremavit
Deianira virum. Clipeus defertur Iude,
Tradidit ille Nomo.
                Postquam belli Crito nodus
290 Opeciit nec iam rabiem potuere cruenti
Ferre ducis, Ramathi retro cessere cohortes:
Ut contra cursum rapidi cum ducitur amnis
Puppis et adversa veniencia flamina parte,
Tum si forte rudens vento fluctuque carina
295 Tardata nimium distentus rumpitur, et vi
Flaminis et fluvii vasto ratis inpete pulsa
Remige nequicquam clamante, "Tenete!" recurrit.
   Instant Apolide cedentibus, asperat acres
Bellantum mentes successus; tergaque cedunt
300 Palantum et dictis mordacibus hostica pungunt
Pectora: "Deiecti, segnes, timidi fugitivi:
Sic nos iam dudum, sic vos pugnare decebat.
Vobis gesta prius probat exitus: esse deorum
Aspernatores et ficte non dubitastis
305 Vivere. Non semper bonitas simulata latebit.
Expectate, viri! Vellemus pauca locuti

Gaza on his shoulders. After these famed deeds Delilah de- 280
stroys him.

By mistake Milesian tales credited this manliness to Her-
cules. According to them, it was by his club that the ever-
watchful dragon perished and the three-bodied king died,
as did the Hydra, which grew more powerful in its loss of a
head. He daunted the king of the underworld and put the 285
Harpies to flight; he struck down Antaeus who was laying
waste to the Libyan fields and Cacus to the Italian. After
these bold actions Deianira burned her husband. The shield
is passed down to Judas, who handed it to Nomus.

After Crito, the war's knot, met death, and the cohorts 290
of Ramathus could not now endure the frenzy of the gory
duke, they fell back. It is just as when a ship is steered against
the current of a swift stream and against gales coming from
the opposite direction: if by chance a hawser bursts when
stretched too tight by the wind as the keel is slowed down
by waves, then the vessel is stricken by both the force of the 295
gale and the awesome onset of the current, and it slips back,
even though the oarsmen shout out in vain, "Hold firm!"

The followers of Cacus press upon them as they fall back,
success makes the keen minds of warriors grow harsh; they
smite the backs of stragglers and pierce the hearts of their 300
enemies with biting words: "Abject, slothful, fearful run-
aways: it was right some while ago for us to fight in this way,
it was right for you to fight in this way. The outcome con-
firms what you did previously: you did not hesitate to scorn
the gods and to live falsely. Feigned goodness will not al- 305
ways lie hidden. Wait, men! We have spoken few words; we
would like to say more to you. Did you hear? Stand still a

Plura loqui vobis. Audistis? State parumper!"
Talibus irrident fugientes, quoque caterve
Pollebant ductore, Nomum pluresque potentes
310 Plectendos capiunt aut bogis colla terendos.
    Iamque hilares turme superatis hostibus urbem
Ingenti repetunt strepitu palmaque superbi
Psallant atque litant divis omnesque per aras
Tura adolent geniumque vocant Bachumque frequentant
315 Deducuntque epulando diem.
                          Sol pronus in altum
Vergebat, non totus adhuc sed parte videndus
Exigua, quantum nova seu prope mense peracto
Luna nitoris habet, cum tanta e strage virorum
Nobilis Eleimon—vatem tutante supremo—
320 Adveniens Ramatho gemitu lacrimabile mixto
Nunciat acta ducum suadetque, ut mittat Orontem,
Qui pugnam reparet captosque reducere temptet.
Consilium regi placuit multaque probatum
Virtute, hostiles recidiva in bella catervas
325 Qui poscat pugne securas, mittit Orontem.
Ille bis octonas sic rege iubente cohortes
Armat et Eufraten ductor petit acer in armis.
    Ut subitus rumor Iebuseos esse propinquos
Nunciat, "En, iterum vulgus desiderat illud—
330 Namque equites non iure vocem, quos cultus et ipsa
Ruricolas monstrat facies—dare terga secundo,
Nec satis est unum confusis dedecus," inquit
Apolides, "Demus, quod avent, et nota capessant

little while!" With such words they mock the fugitives and they capture a good many powerful men and Nomus, under whose leadership the squadrons had prospered, either to be   310 beaten or to have their necks chafed by chains.

And now, having overcome their enemies, the joyful formations return to the city to the accompaniment of a mighty noise. Proud of their triumph, they sing, offer sacrifice to the gods, burn incense at all the altars, call upon their guardian spirit, drink repeated libations of wine, and pass the day   315 in feasting.

Sloping down into the sea was the sun, with not all of it still to be seen, but only a slight part, having as much brightness as the moon when new or when a lunar month has almost ended, when from so great a slaughter of men noble Eleimon—a prophet under the protection of the highest one—approaches and, in a moan mingled with tears, pro-   320 claims to Ramathus the deeds of the dukes and persuades him to send Oron to resume the fight and to try to bring home the captives. This counsel gains the king's approval and he sends Oron, praised for great manliness, to challenge to renewed wars the enemy squadrons while they are uncon-   325 cerned about battle. Because the king so orders, that one, Oron, arms sixteen cohorts and, as leader, keen in arms, makes for the Euphrates.

When a sudden rumor proclaims that the Jebusites are near, Apolides—Cacus—says, "Look, again that common rabble—for I could not rightly call knights those whose   330 clothing and very faces prove to be boors—yearns to turn tail a second time, and one dishonor is not enough for those who were already destroyed. Let us grant what they long for, and let the men take up their well-known weapons. Seize

Arma viri. Capite arma, viri! Vos denuo palma
335   Poscit parta semel; iam iam mente auguror, et quod
Auguror, illud erit, victores nos fore."
                                  Necdum
Finierat, mediis dictis intercipit Ethnis:
"Et mihi non minor est palme spes; at tamen ut mens
Sit magis ampla tuis, Parcarum, precipe, fila
340   Consulat Ermadolon perplexaque fata deorum.
Nullus eo melior misteria Manibus atris
Exprimere et sagas archana rogare volucres
Fatorum vel in Assiria pendere mathesi,
Visurus, quid Plias agat Trivieque molestus
345   Imbrifer Orion crinitaque stella cometes,
Aut tripodas Phebi aut trepidancia, si cupit, exta
Visere."
            Conclamant omnes et dura sororum
Licia divino rimari pectore mixtim
Vociferando iubent. Tantus petit alta tumultus,
350   Quantus, Caucaseas cum Chorus et orrifer Eurus
Certatim silvas quaciunt, dum robora curvant
Dumque levant, fragor esse solet. Iam sole propinquo
Astra diem fugiunt surgensque ex equore Titan
Celsum cernit Aton; tum, sicut gentis erat mos,
355   Flamen procedens redimitus timpora vittis
Primum vix moto breve quiddam ruminat ore,
Inde scrobes ternas faciens—tibi, Iupiter, unam,
Unam Neptuno, dis infernalibus unam—
Scalpit humum, ter ad alta oculos, ter versus ad ima
360   Inmissaque mola taurum necat; eruta cuius
Viscera condit humi fossisque inmurmurat atris

your weapons, men! Victory, having been awarded once,   335
calls you anew; already now in my mind I foretell, and what
I foretell will take place, that we will be victors."

He has not yet finished, when Ethnis interrupts him in
the middle of his words: "I also have no less a hope of vic-
tory; but nevertheless, so that the will of your men may be
greater, order Ermadolon to consult the threads of the Par-   340
cae and the intertwined fates of the gods. No one is better
able than he to extract from the dark spirits of the dead the
sense of mysteries; to seek from prophetic birds the secrets
of the fates; to rely upon Assyrian astrology; to see what can
be caused by one of the Pleiades, by Orion who brings rain   345
and is hateful to Diana, and by a long-haired star, a comet; or
to contemplate the tripods of Phoebus or, if he wishes, the
quivering entrails of a victim."

All raise a shout together and, crying out pell-mell, order
him to examine with his divine mind the harsh threads of
the sisters, the Fates. Just as great an uproar rises skyward as
the din there usually is when the northwest and the chilling   350
southeast wind compete in shaking the woods of the Cauca-
sus mountains, as they bow oaks and lift them back up. Now
that the sun is nearby, the stars flee the daylight and Titan,
rising from the surface of the water, perceives lofty Athos;
then, as was the custom of heathen people, a priest, com-   355
ing out with fillets bound around his temples, first mutters
something brief, his mouth barely moving, and then scrapes
the ground, making three channels—one for you, Jupiter;
one for Neptune; and one for the gods of the underworld—
and turning his eyes thrice aloft and thrice downward. After   360
sprinkling the sacrificial grain, he slays a bull; he wrenches
out its entrails, puts them on the ground, mutters at the

Et ringit cultroque secat sua membra cietque
Horridus effuso Phebeum sanguine numen.
    Exiliit visis interpres callidus extis
365 Letior exclamans, "Multum tibi, maxime Pean,
Omnigenisque deis debemus. Quippe secunde
Res michi monstrantur: pars hostica marcida torpet
Inproba, nostra micat. 'Io,' bis 'io' dicite, cuncti,
Magnificate deos! Mihi se Pasithea litanti
370 Ostendit letam; certa est victoria nobis."
    His dictis arrecti animi bellumque iuventus
Exoptant et, seve, tibi, Gradive, iuvencum
Prestantem mactant, vaccam tibi, torva virago,
Qualis es, anguina cum celas casside vultum
375 Et belli cupiens niveum tegis egide corpus.
    Iamque pii regis pubes armata videri
A longe poterat, directa domare tyrannos.
Unius verique dei firmissima cultrix,
Et magis ac vicina magis fulgentibus armis
380 Indubitata fuit, Getica cum sevior ursa
Alipedem Cacus rapit et "Mea tollite," dixit,
"Signa, viri, latisque alacres erumpite portis!"
Parent precepto leti cunctisque per urbem
Erumpunt portis, velud olim vividus amnis
385 Duris obstructus palis arcenteque clausus
Sepe ruit vehemens tumidoque repagula fluctu
Exuperans; quacumque patet locus, inpiger exit
Atque viam parat ipse sibi.

dark ditches, snarls, carves its limbs with a knife, and, look-
ing wild from the bloodshed, summons the divine power of
Phoebus Apollo.

After inspecting the inner organs, the skillful interpreter
leaps for joy, shouting out happily, "We owe much to you, 365
greatest Paean Apollo, and to the multifarious gods. For in-
deed the matter is shown to me to be favorable: the inferior
enemy party lies numb and enfeebled, whereas ours moves
rapidly. Say 'Hurrah,' all of you, twice 'Hurrah!' Glorify the
gods! As I made sacrifice, Pasithea showed herself joyously
to me; victory is assured us." 370

Their courage aroused by these words, the young men
long for war and offer a fine bullock to you, savage Mars, to
you a cow, grim virago, Minerva, as you are when you hide
your face within a helmet covered with images of snakes and 375
when, desiring war, you cover your snow-white body with
the aegis.

The armed youths of the pious king could already be seen
from afar, dispatched to vanquish tyrants. Most steadfast
devotees of the one and true God, they were free from
doubt as they drew nearer and nearer with their gleaming
weapons, when Cacus, more savage than a Thracian bear, 380
seized a fleet-footed horse and said, "Raise my standards,
men, and sally swiftly through the broad gates." They obey
the command joyously and sally through all the gates
throughout the city, just as sometimes a vigorous river 385
dammed by hard wooden piles and contained by a confining
levee rushes violently and surmounts the restraints with its
swollen flow; wherever a place lies open it goes out briskly
and makes a route ready for itself.

Crudele secundo
Bellum oritur tristique sono fera classica utrosque
390 Exacuunt. Sed non, quamvis exercitus esset
Amplior, hostiles in se tot funera partes,
Quot videre prius, nam plus virtutis habebat
Turma prior. Bello tamen haut cito victor in isto
Extitit Apolides, et utrimque miserrima cedes
395 Commissa est.
                    Vasti membris animisque Gethei
Corpore non animo parvus de sanguine mixto
Iesseius torta lapidem in cava timpora funda
Misit; qui lapsus tremefacto pectore lata
Ilice glandifera texit produccior arva.
400 Cum caderet, tellus tremuit magnamque ruinam
Corporis inmensi moles dedit, ut diuturno
Dilabens evo, que celum vertice pulsat,
Impete precipitis Circi petit infima turris.
Accurrit victor strictoque viriliter ense
405 Amputat obnixe lentissima colla precantis.
Nec mirum dextra tantum cecidisse gigantem
Iesseii; qui cum puer esset, tristibus ursis
Intulit atque lupis mortem domuitque leones.
Ad Larisseum stilus hoc gentilis Achillem
410 Transtulit; ipse etiam citaram citharedus habebat.
Qua Davit regis mentem sedavit atrocem,
Nec quisquam melior magnorum facta virorum
Inclita, cum voluit, fidibus replicare canoris.
Sed non tanta virum dura inter prelia virtus
415 Tutari potuit, quin fata subiret acerba.
Nam post inmensam stragem quam fecerat, illum

For a second time dreadful war arises and wild trumpets inflamed men of both groups with their grim sound. But although the army was larger, the enemy party did not see 390 so many corpses before them as they had seen earlier, for the earlier squadron had had more courage. Nevertheless Apolides — Cacus — did not emerge swiftly as victor in this battle, and most deplorable slaughter was perpetrated on both sides.

Jesse's son, small in body but not in spirit, of mixed an- 395 cestry, whirled a sling and shot a stone against the hollow temples of the Gittite, Goliath, who was awesome in both limbs and courage. After Goliath's heart was made to tremble with fear and he fell, he stretched out, longer than an acorn-producing holm oak, and covered broad fields. When 400 he fell, the earth trembled and the mass of his huge body caused great ruin, just as a tower, which strikes the heavens with its peak but which is collapsing from extreme age, topples down to the lowest point from the onset of a rushing northwest wind. The victor ran up and, with sword manfully drawn, resolutely severs Goliath's very tough neck as he 405 pleads for mercy. No wonder that so great a giant fell by the right hand of Jesse's son; when David was a boy, he inflicted death upon grim bears and wolves, and he subdued lions.

Pagan writings attributed this deed to Achilles of Larissa; he too was a cithara player and had a cithara. With it David 410 put to rest the savage mood of the king, and no one was better able, when he wished, to rehearse on tuneful strings famous deeds of great men.

But in the middle of harsh battles, not even such great courage could protect the man from suffering bitter fate. 415 For after the boundless slaughter he had caused, Amarti-

(Asperior dubium bello an felicior ense,
Quo multos alios fortesque bonosque peremit)
Antifrononte satus, Ionatham gladio ferus Ethnis,
420 Fuscus Irineum iaculo prostravit, Adonem
Cuspide sevus Oron, letoque dedisset Aplestem
Illius insignis nisi te de morte maneret
Gloria, Sarcodoma; tamen acri vulnere bello
Saucius egreditur.
                Temeratis sanguine pugnant
425 Ensibus et seva sevit pars utraque cede.
Cum solito gravius Caci certante caterva
Agatide triti cedunt. Cedentibus instant
Caldei, cernensque Aphilus crudelis Orontem
Inter condensas pugnantem fortiter alas
430 Multumque hostilis fundentem sanguinis, illum
Impiger incurrens nitido validum dedit ictum
Ense super galeam. Tinnitum reddidit illa:
Non maior, fagus cum ceditur alta bipenni,
Fit sonus, aut fortis concussa fronte iuvenci.
435   Nec mora Caldei properant Aphiloque straboni
Auxilium pugnando ferunt. Coit omnis in unum
Bellica turba, tamen diuturno fervidus ille
Hostes conflictu prohibet. Iam parma sagittis
Hirta stetit velud ericius, nec sustinet ultra
440 Vulneribus sevis afflictus fessa movere
Brachia. Conprendunt vinctum paucosque petentes;
Cetera diffugiunt dumosa per avia pubes.
   Ut captum Iudas (facinus!) conspexit Orontem,
"Numquid," ait, "sic vivet Oron, sic vivet acerbus

genes, the son of Antifronon (it is uncertain whether he was fiercer in war or more fortunate in the sword to have killed many other brave and good men) laid him low. Wild Ethnis laid low Jonathan with a sword; Fuscus, Irineus with a jave- 420 lin; savage Oron, Adon with a spear—and Oron would have put Aplestes to death, if the glory from the death of that distinguished man had not been destined for you, Sarcodo- mas; nevertheless he left the battle, injured by a critical wound.

They fight with swords defiled with blood, and each side 425 rages in savage slaughter. The worn-out sons of Agatus fall back as Cacus's band vies more intensely than usual. The Chaldeans press upon them as they fall back, and savage Aphilus, discerning Oron as he fights bravely amid the close-packed squadrons and spills much enemy blood, runs up to 430 him briskly and delivers with his glittering sword a stout blow upon his helmet. In response the helmet produces a ringing: no greater a sound is made when a tall beech tree is felled by an ax or is battered by the forehead of a strong bull-ock.

Without delay, the Chaldeans hasten and in fighting bring 435 aid to squint-eyed Aphilus. The entire warlike crowd comes together against one man, but he in his passion wards off his foes through incessant combat. His small shield already bristles with arrows like a hedgehog and, impaired by dire wounds, he cannot bear any longer to move his tired arms. 440 They capture him and the few still attacking and fetter him; the other youths scatter in flight through the thicketed by-ways.

As Judas (what an outrage!) caught sight of captive Oron, he said, "Is it really possible that Oron will thus live, that the

445 Bellator, nostri tantum qui sanguinis hausit?
Non hunc eripiet rex Agatus. Este pii vos,
Si placet; infandum fundet mea dextra cruorem."
Sic ait et rigido capti vitalia pilo
Perrupit, qui lapsus equo moriendo momordit
450 Terram obituque gravi vacuavit spiritus artus.
    Nondum discincti calor ossa reliquerat hostis,
Prorsus et extinctum Iudas deflevit Orontem.
Sed quid vana iuvat querimonia, cum mala plangens
Linquere, que plangit, non vult? Auget sibi culpam,
455 Qui fundit lacrimas, si non ex corde. Resumit,
Quod vomuit, canis et cenum siccus repetit sus:
Sic eciam Iudas, ubi per spacium breve letum
Oris divini deplorat, rursus ad acrem
Vertitur invidiam regemque favente Diglossa
460 Blasphemat tumido ore pium partemque in utramque
Lubricus incerto ceu flamine canna movetur.
    Caldei reduces bis capto ex hoste triumpho
Ut fecere Iovi Caco suadente deisque
Omnibus (ut mos est gentis) libamina, Iudam
465 Politeon stabili neutra cum parte manere
Indignans animo, presso clamore tumultu—
Namque tumultus erat populis plaudentibus hostes
Terga dedisse suos—"Iuda, quo nos," ait, "usque
Suspendes, parti dum queris utrique placere,
470 Mobilior foliis, que succi pondere cassa
Huc illuc volitant incerto flamine Libra
Educente tuos, Hiperione nate, iugales?

grim warrior who drained so much of our blood will thus   445
live? King Agatus will not rescue him. Be pious, you, if you
will; my right hand will shed unspeakable blood." So he
spoke and thrust with a stiff javelin through the vital organs
of the captive, who slipped from his horse and in dying bit   450
the dust; his spirit emptied his limbs in a painful death.

Not yet had warmth left the bones of the disarmed en-
emy, and immediately Judas mourned dead Oron. But what
good is idle lamentation, when a person does not wish to
abandon the evils that he bemoans? A person who sheds
tears increases his blame if the tears do not come from the   455
heart. The dog reeats its own vomit and the pig once dry re-
turns to the mud: so also Judas, after lamenting for a brief
spell the death of the divine mouth, Oron, reverts to keen
envy. With Diglossa providing support, he blasphemed with   460
haughty mouth against the pious king and, shifting like a
reed in a changing breeze, he was drawn toward both par-
ties.

As the Chaldeans returned in a triumph captured twice
from their foe and, at the urging of Cacus, made offerings to
Jupiter and all the gods (such is the custom of pagans), Polit-   465
eon took offense that Judas stayed in neither party with a
constant heart, and he said, once the uproar had been stilled
by his shout—for there was an uproar as the people clapped
their hands that their enemies had turned tail—"How long,
Judas, are you going to keep us in uncertainty, as you seek to
please both groups, you who are more easily swayed than   470
leaves, which have lost the weight of sap and flutter here and
there in a changing breeze when Libra leads forth your team
of horses, son of Hyperion? Cherish constantly that which

Dilige constanter, quod amas. Non cogimus ullum
Nequicia nobis laudem dare; cogimus autem
475 Virtutis studio, quia cui placet ipsa, placemus.
    "Atqui non melior bello fuit illa iuventus,
Que peciit sontes sub Adrasto principe Tebas,
Quamquam illic acer Tideus pugnaret et armis
Inclitus Hipomedon aspernatorque deorum
480 Procerus Capaneus; nec Achaia maior in armis
Laomedonteam coiit subvertere Troiam.
Nam quantum censes, si verum obtundere non vis,
Antifrononte satum, cui non Calidonius heros,
Non Aiax, non ipse, Frigum timor unus, Achilles
485 Anteferendus erit? Vario nec maior Vlixi
Quam tibi, Cace, dolus.
                    "Nec me inter nomina tanta
Celarim, trifidi qui subieci mihi regna
Orbis. Me noti precioso vellere Seres,
Bactria queque colit parvo gens corpore nidos,
490 Gathmus et infamis monstrosa gente Catippus
Pertimuit, qua Nissa ferax prolesque Philippi
Transiit Erculeas pugnaci milite metas,
Qua vastus Ganges bis quinis fontibus exit
Contra surgentem sua ducens hostia Phebum,
495 Queque bibunt Habanem, que te quoque, Gamula, gentes,
Quaque meat Torides, qua dives Icusia sedes
Carmannis. Domui Partos fugiendo timendos
Persasque et notas Asuero principe Susas.
Me timet Assirius, me qui vicinus Araxes
500 Gentibus Hircanis spaciosum permeat orbem
Sauromatesque celer domitorem vidit et acres

you love. We do not compel anyone to render praise to us
through wickedness; rather, we compel through a desire for
valor, because whoever likes valor, likes us.   475

"What is more, no better in war were those young men,
who under Prince Adrastus attacked guilty Thebes, even
though keen Tydeus was fighting there, and Hippomedon
renowned in arms and tall Capaneus, scorner of the gods;   480
nor did a greater Achaea rally in arms to overthrow Laome-
don's Troy. For, if you do not wish to stifle the truth, how
great do you consider the son of Antifronon, that is, Amar-
tigenes, above whom neither the Calydonian hero, nor Ajax,
nor even Achilles, the lone terror of the Phrygians, must be   485
ranked? Nor does wily Ulysses have greater craft than you,
Cacus.

"Among such great names I would not conceal myself,
who have made subject to myself the realms of the tripar-
tite world. The Chinese known for precious fleece took
fright at me, and so did the slight-bodied Bactrian people
who dwell in nests; Cadmus and Cathippus, notorious for   490
its monstrous race; the land where fertile Nyssa is and where
the offspring of Philip crossed the pillars of Hercules with
doughty soldiers, where the awesome Ganges goes forth
from ten wellheads and guides its waters opposite the rising
sun toward its mouths; the peoples who drink of the Hypa-   495
nis and who drink of you, too, Gamula; where the Theriodes
flows; and where wealthy Icosium is home to the Carma-
nians. I vanquished the Parthians who must be feared as
they flee; the Persians; and the people of Susa, well known
under Prince Ahasuerus. The Assyrian fears me; the river
Araxes, which is near the Hyrcanian peoples and passes   500
through the wide world, and the swift Sarmatian saw me as

Eniochi ac celeber Frixeo vellere Fasis
Queque duos inter nomen retraxit ab ipsis
Terra iacens fluvios et fama clara Damascus.
505 Me truculentus Hiber pernixque ad bella Gelonus
Cappadocesque timent et, quem piratica pascit
Preda, Cilix Galateque truces quosque Hermus et Hermum
Augens Meander sinuosa circuit unda
Et quas fama refert (si credimus omnia fame)
510 Invenisse notas, fruitur quibus Attica, gentes
Cathmee atque, quibus meat umbra sinistra, Sabei
Et Friges et genti Nabatee affinis Idume
Meotisque palus glaciali frigore semper
Stricta et Amazoniis tellus celeberrima bellis,
515 Et qua Ripheis manans de montibus alto
Gurgite divisum Tanais disterminat orbem,
Secretique dei cultor mihi cessit Apella.
Me metuit Meroe, tepido que conparat Austro
Hircanum Borean, umbreque ignara Siene.
520 Me Rodos atque Paphos, me norunt Ciclades omnes
Ismariusque Ebrus clarique Macedones armis
Affinesque tibi, late vulgata Chorinte,
Archades; et doctis sum non ignotus Athenis.
Formidatque meum Romana potencia nomen
525 Et tellus Athesi gelidoque rigata Caico
Et Dacus Moschis vicinus et acer Alanus
Pannoniusque ferox et corpore Noricus ingens
Gensque cenozephalis quondam vicina Sueva.
Te quoque concussi, cervicis Vandale dure,
530 Te, Dana signatis oculis, te, Frixo rebellis,
Quosque Mogon pagos et quos intersecat Albis,

vanquisher, and so did the brave Heniochi; the Phasis, famed
for the fleece of Phrixus; the land lying between two rivers
that took its name from them; and Damascus of well-known
repute. I am feared by the ferocious Hiberian; the Gelonian,   505
swift to war; the Cappadocians; the Cilician, who feeds
upon the booty of piracy; the grim Galatians; the people
whom the Hermus and its tributary, the Meander, surround
in a snaking flow; and the Cadmean peoples whom rumor
reports (if we put stock in everything rumor relates) to have   510
discovered the alphabet that the Greeks use; the Sabaeans,
for whom shadows fall to the left; the Phrygians; Idume,
contiguous with the people of Nabataea; the swamp of
Maeotis always bound by icy cold; the land most famed for
the wars of the Amazons; and where the Tanais, flowing   515
down from the Riphaean mountains in a deep torrent,
bounds the world that has been surveyed. Apella too, wor-
shipper of a hidden god, yielded to me. Meroe, which puts a
hot south wind in the same class with a Hyrcanian north
wind, feared me, as did Syene, which knows no shade. Rho-   520
des, Paphos, all the Cyclades, the Thracian Hebrus, the
Macedonians renowned in arms, and your neighbors, widely
heralded Corinth, the Arcadians, know me; and I am not
unknown in sage Athens. Even the power at Rome fears my
name, as well as the lands watered by the Adige and the fro-   525
zen Caicus; the Dacian, neighbor of the Moschi; the brave
Alan; the fierce Pannonian; the Norican, giant in body; and
the tribe of the Suebi, once neighbor of the Cynocephali. I
shattered you also, hard-necked Vandal; you, Dane with dis-   530
tinctive eyes; you, insurgent Frisian; and districts that the
Main and the Elbe cut through, and where the deep-

Quaque fluit Rhodani cavus augens stagna Lemannus.
Me Mosella merus nec palmite vilior Alsa
Cognoscit, me Belga suos girare caballos
535 Doctus et Alverni tumido sermone faceti
Allobrogesque fide dubii fidensque sagittis
Nervius et pugnax Rotomus mollesque Equitani
Et tibi vicini, iactans Verimande, Rutheni.
Vasconasque vagos domui claramque Tholosam
540 Et Betim Gadesque sitas sub sole cadente
Et cum Scottigenis disiunctos orbe Brittanos.
Cumque Siracusio funde Balearicus auctor
Me tremit et regio Tyria de gente profectis
Possessa et frugum non parca Canopica tellus
545 Priscaque Cirene Leptisque et regius Ippon,
Queque nigris colitur triplex provincia Mauris,
Marmarideque leves et cum Garamante Galaula
Et gens Ethiopum non ullo signa ferentis
Pressa poli spacio, nisi quod Bovis ungula metam
550 Excessit, flexo cum poblite procubuit Bos.
Denique nulla vacat mundi regio mihi, que non
Sit sceptris subiecta meis et serviat ultro.
     "En, rex iste tuus, modo quem laudas, modo damnas,
Bis victus bello, qua spe (iam credo) valebit
555 Amplius in nostros pugnam transmittere fines?"
     Tunc Cacus subicit, "Pugnam transmitteret ipse?
Bellum re vera non hic erit amplius ullum;
Si iuvat hoc et pascit eum, quod adhuc superetur,
In propria tellure sua superabitur. Illuc
560 Ibimus et forti metabimur agmine castra."

channeled Lake Geneva, a tributary of the Rhône's waters, courses. The pure Moselle and the Ill, no less estimable for its vine shoots, know me, as do the Belgian, adept at wheeling his horses; the Arvernians, clever in their bombastic 535 speech; the Allobroges, wavering in their loyalty; the Nervian, reliant upon arrows; the belligerent Rouennais; the soft Aquitanians; and the Ruthenians who are your neighbors, boastful Vermandois. I mastered the nomadic Vascones; renowned Toulouse; Baetis; Cadiz, located close to the set- 540 ting sun; and the Britons, sundered with the Irish from the world. Together with the Syracusan, the Balearic, creator of the sling, shudders at my sight, as do the region held by those who set out from the Tyrian nation; the Egyptian land, not stinting in fruits; ancient Cyrene; Leptis; Hippo Regius; 545 the tripartite province that is inhabited by black Moors; the swift Marmaridae; the Galaulian, together with the Garamantes; the Ethiopian people, not covered by any area of heaven that contains signs of the zodiac, were it not that the hoof of Taurus passed the boundary, when Taurus sank down 550 with a bent leg. In short, no district of the world is free from me, which has not been subjected to my dominion and does not serve of its own free will.

"Look, what hope is there that this king of yours, twice conquered in war (I don't doubt this), whom you praise in one breath and damn in the next, will avail in carrying the 555 fight any further into our territories?"

Then Cacus interjects, "He would carry the fight himself? To tell the truth, no additional war will take place here; if this pleases and gratifies him, that he should be overcome still further, he will be overcome in his own land. We will go 560 there and, with a strong army, we will lay out camps."

His motus Iudas sermonibus Agaton atque
Spernit eo natum penitus vitamque deorum
Pensat et exemplum vivendi sumit ab illis:
Iupiter in quamvis venerem docet ire licenter;
565　Euchius ut multum bibat atque canore iuvetur
Suadet Apollo lira; magicas Cillenius artes
Commendat, Cereremque sibi proponit edendo.

　　Sic degente viro, tempus simul atque statutum
Exegit solis metam, rex Agatus a se
570　Messiam genitum, sibi qui fuit unicus, ire
Precipit et sevos reparata in bella tyrannos
Poscere.

　　　　Tum vates, quo nullus amancior equi,
Inclitus Eleimon paucis presentibus orsus,
"Quid iuvat incassum tociens confligere summis
575　Viribus? Et multo pudet ac miseret simul atris
Milite consumpto bellis nos esse inimicis
Ludibrio? Numquam, nostre nisi dux aciei
Occidat in bello, validos superabimus hostes.
Ergo tibi natoque tuo (nisi si melius vos
580　Conicitis quicquam), presaga mente quod edo,
Si placet: Est Bethlem caste paupercula fame,
Parthenie, quam Taumoto cognomine dicunt,
Stirpis Davitice. Cuius (nec sit pudor) artus
Messias si veste suos obduxerit inque
585　Mortem sponte ruit, pro certo credite, parti
Illius haut modico continget honore triumphus.

　　"Ac ne, quod dedimus, te frangat, regia proles,
Consilium, Decius, perpende, quid egerit et quid
Regulus; ambo brevi nolentes parcere vite

Stirred by these words, Judas scorns Agatus and his son entirely, and he weighs the advantages of the life of the gods and takes from them a model for living: Jupiter teaches him to engage freely in any form whatsoever of sexual intercourse; Bacchus recommends drinking a great deal, Apollo 565 with the lyre to be delighted by song; the god born on Mount Cyllene commends magic arts; and Judas holds up Ceres as an example to himself in eating.

While the man is spending his life in this way, King Agatus (as soon as the established length of time reached the turning point of the sun) orders Messiah born of him, who 570 was his only son, to go and challenge the savage tyrants to renewed wars.

Then the prophet, renowned Eleimon, who loved justice more than anyone, began to say to the few people present, "What is the use of waging battle in vain so many times with utmost strength? And does it not at once cause much shame 575 and excite pity that, with our soldiers destroyed in direful wars, we are an object of ridicule to our enemies? We will never overcome our mighty foes unless the leader of our forces perishes in war. Therefore—if you and your son agree to what I make known with a prescient mind (unless you have a better idea!) —there is in Bethlehem a poor woman 580 from the stock of David, of chaste renown, Parthenie, whom they call by the nickname Taumoto. If Messiah covers his limbs with her clothing (and may there be no shame about it) and if he rushes to death of his own free will, believe for a 585 certainty that a triumph of no mean distinction will be granted to his side.

"But so that the advice we have given not distress you, son of a king, bear in mind what Decius and Regulus did;

299

590 Sponte sua, sic fama refert, pro clade suorum
Tollenda letum subiere. Quid ergo fideli
Tu de te censes, vane si gloria laudis
Paganos mortem non formidare subegit?
Te vero perpes post tristia fata manebit
595 Gloria; te locuples, te pauper ad ethera tollet."
   Desierat vates. Sentencia dia diserti
Principibus placuit, ducibusque ad bella vocatis
Messias sumpto muliebri tecmine sese
Vestit et umbonem membrana triplice tectum
600 Sumit et ad pugnam duodenis milibus exit.
   Nunc mihi, te queso, bone spiritus, Agatidarum
Nomina pande ducum, tua, sicut vis et ubi vis,
Munera qui tribuis!
                    Dux primus in arma trecentos
Pistena fert equites Abrahe de stirpe beata
605 Editus. Huic circum precioso compta smaragdo
Parma fuit. Stetit in medio delusa prophete
Turba sacerdotum, cum misso desuper igne;
Helie "Dominus deus est" plebs ante rebellis
Clamavit, sterilesque iacent annis tribus agri
610 Et medio populi pro nequicia. Hinc, puto, facta est
Urentis terram Phetontis fabula, currum
Cum regeret.
             Civisque tuus, Nine pessima quondam,
Eutropius brevis et rugosa fronte severus
Auxit Iudaicos sexcentis ensibus enses.
615 Itque potens Agapes Bethelius horrida in arma
Exacuens bis mille viros.

as the rumor goes, both had no desire to spare their own short lives and underwent death voluntarily to forestall the slaughter of their people. What, then, do you think about yourself, a true believer, if the glory of empty praise has compelled pagans not to fear death? In truth, everlasting glory will await you after bitter death; rich and poor alike will extol you to the skies!" 590

595

The prophet ceased speaking. The divinely inspired advice of the sage met with the approval of the princes, and after the dukes had been called to war, Messiah took upon him the covering of a woman, dressed himself, took up a shield covered with three layers of hide, and went out with twelve thousand to battle. 600

Now I ask you, good spirit, who bestow gifts as you wish and when you wish: reveal to me the names of the dukes on the side of Agatus!

The first duke into arms, Pistena, born of Abraham's blessed stock, brought three hundred knights. He had a small shield adorned in a circle round with expensive emerald. In the middle stood the throng of pagan priests deluded by the prophet when fire was sent down from above; the previously insurgent people cried out to Elijah, "The Lord is God," and the fields lie barren for three and a half years because of the people's wickedness. From this, I think, came about the myth of Phaëthon burning the earth when he was guiding the chariot. 605

610

Your citizen, O Nineveh once so wicked, Eutropius, short and austere with his wrinkled forehead, increased the Judaic swordsmen by six hundred swords. Powerful Agapes of Bethel went into dreadful war, rousing two thousand men to passion. 615

Hic pocula Iude
Bina tulit, laudabile opus. Nam sculptus in uno
In somnis cernit tangentes ethera scalas
Iacob cum domino luctans nervoque recedens
620 Debilis; idcirco nervos Iudeus abhorret.
Ex hoc Meonius finxisse poeta putatur
In volucres socios ducis esse deam ferientis
Mutatos. Alter pereuntes crater habebat
Hostes egregii Davit, quas ipse peremtos
625 Pictus ibi (insolitum) luxit. Tamen ista decora
Munera concilians regem sibi sustulit Ethnis
Post mortem ducis Agatide.
                                Sequitur comes illum
Multa laude nitens niveoque spadone superbus
Leuconous rigidusque Paton de germine sacro
630 Iob veniens, multo fuscatus sole suasque
Munitus suras ocreis veluti rosa rubris.
Tu quoque, Behttanicis in menibus orte, superbis
Risus, ceruleo vectus burdone, sequester
Amplum subsidium claris, Tapine, tulisti
635 Regibus. Insequitur collecto milite fortis
Sarcodomas, tuus, o Daniel venerande, propinquus.
    Omnes hi Solimam ter mille ad bella feroces
Adduxere viros et per quot volvitur annus
Tritus sole dies, crescit cum Februus una.
640   Sed postquam belli, qua Cace manes, reparandi
Rumor Achemenias index vagus attigit oras,
Continuo magni magno coiere paratu
Sub Caco rectore duces et grande putantes
Expectare domi violentos dedecus hostes
645 Iudeam bacis olee palmisque opulentam

He won two of Judas's goblets, praiseworthy workmanship. Upon one was sculpted Jacob as in his sleep he perceives a ladder touching heaven, wrestles with the Lord, and withdraws, weakened in his sinew; on this account the   620
Jew abominates sinews. On this basis the Maeonian poet, Homer, is thought to have imagined that the companions of the leader who wounded the goddess were changed into birds. The other vessel depicted the enemies of outstanding David as they died; as pictured there, he himself grieved   625
over them after they had died (a strange sight). Yet Ethnis, reconciling the king to himself, picked up these handsome gifts after the death of the duke, the son of Agatus.

Following him was Count Leuconous, resplendent with much praise and proud of his snow-white gelding, and stern Paton, a descendant from the sacred seed of Job, darkened   630
by much sun and protected about his calves by greaves ruddy like a rose. You also, Tapinus, who were born within the walls of Bethany, an object of laughter to the proud, conveyed on a dark-colored mule, as mediator brought great aid to famed kings. Brave Sarcodomas, your relative, O revered Daniel,   635
followed with knights rallied.

All of these brought to war in Jerusalem three thousand fierce men, plus the number of days through which passes the annual cycle, traversed by the sun, when February is increased by one day.

But after the rumor—a wandering informant—of the renewed war reached the boundaries of Persia, where you,   640
Cacus, were staying, at once with great trappings the great dukes assembled under the guidance of Cacus. Thinking it a major dishonor to await destructive enemies at home, they   645
attacked Judaea, which abounds in the fruits of the olives

Agminibus peciere suis vectique quadrigis
Et, plus quam satis est, pompa venere superba.
Urbs est Iudee Iordane bifonte propinquo
Condita semiferis olim sedes Chananeis;

650 Nomen ei Ihericho, quam nubilus Eurus ab ortu
Aspicit, Asphaltus calido vicinus ab axe est.
Hunc pugne legere locum bellumque profanus
Contra cognatum Caco duce movit Iudas.

    Roscidus ascendens terris infudit Eous

655 Lumen et obscuro gelidas sublatus Olimpo
Sol dempsit tenebras, cum parte in utraque iuventus
Elatis cupide properant confligere signis
Horrisonisque tubis acuunt in prelia mentes.

    Principium belli, Messie signifer acris

660 Ethnidis ense cadit; qui, sic voluit deus, arma
Mox Cedarei fugiens ducis ad Solimanum
Regem legatos mittit Cacumque odiosum
Asserit esse sibi; grates agit Agatus illi
Placatusque viro.

                    Mactatum sanguine crassum

665 Politeona tua prosternis, Pistena, dextra;
Leuconous Fuscum, Cresterius acer Aelptin
Fudit. Iperfanes Tapinum territat hasta
Rostratosque pedes curvans pellesque gulatas
Et manicas amplas ostentans "Rustice," dixit,

670 "Cede loco nec te pannosus ad arma potentum
Misce! Quid facit hic gestande burdo farine
Apcior? Hercle, lutum peronibus his potes altum
Trudere! Vah, tantum molitori me esse locutum
Penitet."

and in palms, with their troops. Riding in chariots, they came with more than sufficient proud ostentation. There is a city of Judaea, once the abode of half-wild Canaanites, established near the two-fonted Jordan; its name is Jericho. 650 The cloudy east wind gazes upon it from the east; the lake of Asphalt is close on the warm side. They selected this place for the fight and, under Duke Cacus, impious Judas waged war against his kinsman, Messiah.

The dewy morning star as it rose shed light upon the earth, and the sun, raised up, dispelled the chill shades from 655 the dark heavens, when on each side young men with upraised standards hastened eagerly to contend with spears and with frightful-sounding trumpets they whetted their courage for battles.

The prelude of war, the standard-bearer of keen Messiah, falls by the sword of Ethnis. Just as God so willed, Ethnis 660 soon flees the weapons of the Kedarite duke, sends envoys to the king of Jerusalem, and alleges that Cacus has become disagreeable to him; Agatus thanks that man and is reconciled with him.

Pistena, with your right hand you lay low Politeon, slain 665 sacrificially, coated with blood. Leuconous slays Fuscus; brave Chresterius, Aelptes. Hiperefanes strikes terror into Tapinus with a spear and, wearing shoes with curved points and showing off a coat with a fur collar and puffed sleeves, he said, "Peasant, make way and do not meddle, clad in rags, 670 in the warfare of the powerful! What is this mule, better suited for carrying meal, doing here? By Hercules, you can trample deep mud with those clodhoppers! Ugh, I regret even having spoken to a miller."

"Accipio," dixit Tapinus equoque
675 Transverso tumide salientis cuspide timpus
Perfodiens sella suspensum decutit alta.

Argutumque Agapes Heretum mucrone corusco
Prostravit fortemque Aphilum fortemque Diglossam,
Pirtalmumque ferunt dextra cecidisse Patontis.
680 Tu quoque qui tociens vitaras vulnus, Apleste,
Letiferum, moriens te Sarcodomas dedit Orco.

Ante omnes, Caci fiducia tota, cruentus
Sevit Amartigenes; cui dux Solimanus avaram
Cedis et heroum pollutam sanguine dextram
685 Amputat atque femur. Saliit manus, ut sude forti
Aut iacto saxo divise cauda colubre
Inproba sepe micat; torpet manus inpigra, multis
Fatalis ducibus. Sub equinam pristinus alvum
Victor procubuit vultumque supinus atrocem
690 Frendet adhuc; tunc Cacus eum sociique levabant
Pulvere squalentem mestique in castra ferebant
Seminecem clipeo.

Nec adhuc voluere tyranni
Cedere; iam tepido manabant arva cruore
Atque in sulphureum clarumque bitumine stagnum
695 Iordanis regum volvendo cadavera duxit.

Dum sic pugnatur, Messiam conspicit acer
Cacus et adversum cupiens occidere strictum
Vibravit gladium capitique infligere vulnus
Mortiferum voluit, sed parma providus ille
700 Invicta calibe et ferro fortem ictum.
Dissiliens partes mucro Caceius in tres

"I accept that," says Tapinus and, when the horse was 675
turned sideways, with his spear point he bores through the
temple of the proudly capering man and strikes him down as
he dangles from the high saddle.

With a flashing sword Agapes slew shrewd Heretus, bold
Aphilus, and bold Diglossa, and they report that Pirtalmus
fell by the right hand of Paton. You also, Aplestes, who so 680
many times avoided a deadly wound—Sarcodomas, while
dying, sent you to hell.

Before all others raged bloody Amartigenes, in whom re-
sided the complete confidence of Cacus; the Jerusalemite
duke lopped off his thigh and right hand, which was greedy
for carnage and defiled with the blood of heroes. The hand 685
twitched, just as the unrelenting tail of a serpent that has
been cut in two by a stout stake or a well-hurled stone quiv-
ers often; now the ever-moving hand, deadly to many dukes,
lay motionless. The erstwhile victor sank down under the
horse's belly and, lying with his grim face upward, he still 690
gnashed his teeth; then Cacus and his comrades lifted him,
crusted with dirt, and sadly carried him half-dead on a shield
into camp.

But the tyrants still did not wish to yield; already the
fields were dripping with warm gore and the Jordan, as it
rolled along the corpses of kings, took them to the sulfurous 695
morass renowned for its bitumen.

While the battle thus rages, fierce Cacus catches sight of
Messiah. Wishing to strike down his opponent, he bran-
dishes his drawn sword and wants to deal a fatal blow to the
head, but that one, Messiah, foresighted with his small
shield, sustains the force of the strong blow with uncon- 700
quered steel and iron. Cacus's sword shatters into three

Frustratum ceco fecit trepidare pavore;
Quid faciat, nescit dubius, fugiatne uel obstet.
   Interea cernens Iudam "Vir strennue," dixit,
705 "Huc ades et gladio, qui me exarmaverat, hostem
Sterne truci uel pelle manu!"
                         Nihil ille moratus
Efferus incursat iuvenem, quem talibus heros
Premonet, "O demens nimiumque oblite propinqui
Sanguinis atque pie fidei, mala cepta relinque!
710 Messias ego sum; veni te solvere bellis.
Aspicis ora, manus."
                  Cui Iudas ore minaci,
"Nescio, tu qui sis; pugnans volo discere, qui sis.
'Agatides sum,' inquis, mentiris; non tibi certe
Agatus est genitor. Credi potes indice vultu
715 Filius esse fabri, fabrique es filius. Istam,
Quisquis es, esse tibi lucem experiere supremam."
   Sic ait et regem crispata fortiter hasta
Proturbare parat; quem nolens ledere cede
Delirumque fugit Messias; ille nepotem
720 (O scelus!) insequitur fugientem. Ne suus in se
Peccet cognatus, rex vult, nec vult tamen ille
A detestando vecors resipiscere cepto.
Iam fugiens trepido Solime prope menia cursu
Venerat; hic secum vatis pia dicta recensens
725 Constitit et sevis nolens arcere furentem
Armis inmotus stabat.
               Ferus advolat ille
Et rigida miti dat cuspide vulnera quinque:

parts and makes him tremble, thwarted, in blind fear; he does not know what to do, undecided whether to flee or resist.

In the meantime he perceived Judas and said, "Vigorous 705 man, come here and slay with your grim sword or drive off with your hand the enemy who has disarmed me!"

Without any delay that one, Judas, attacked the young man wildly; the hero cautioned him with such words: "O madman, all too forgetful of blood ties and pious faith, abandon these wicked undertakings! I am Messiah; I have come 710 to free you from wars. You see my face and hands."

Judas responded to him with a threatening face, "I do not know who you are; I wish to learn through fighting who you are. 'I am the son of Agatus,' you say, but you lie; Agatus is surely not your father. By the look of your face, you could be 715 taken for the son of a carpenter—and you are the son of a carpenter! Whoever you are, you will realize that this day is your last."

So he spoke and, shaking his spear boldly, he made ready to drive away the king. Not wishing to harm him with bloodshed, Messiah fled the lunatic; but that one pursued his flee- 720 ing relative (what a crime!). The king wished that his kinsman not sin against him; and yet that one, in his insanity, did not wish to come back to his senses and desist from the execrable undertaking. Now fleeing in a fearful course he had come close to the walls of Jerusalem; here, reflecting in his mind upon the pious words of the prophet, he stopped and 725 stood unmoved, not wishing to repulse the man raging with savage weapons.

That one, Judas, flew wildly to the attack and dealt his gentle opponent five wounds with an unyielding spear: an

Simplex, cum geritur sacram mactandus ad aram
Pro populi noxa, non est taciturnior agnus.
730 Ille labat, dumque ille labat, terrore caterva
Apolide subito (dictu mirabile) languens
Fugit et infames verterunt terga tiranni.
Tunc primum Cacum Messie nobilis iram
Expavisse ferunt, quod ei congressus inermis
735 Abscessit—nec in hoc habuit satis.
                                    Inpiger illi
Intulit Eutropius plagam trepidumque fugavit,
Et parta est leto Messie palma salubri;
Moxque catenatis licuit remeare solutis
Nexibus in terram felici nomine Sion.
740 Leta magis non illa fuit generacio, quam rex
Cirus restituit post mesta decem et tria lustra,
Cum muta in canis pendebant organa ramis.
     Tempus erat, cum Vergiliis repetentibus ortum
Sole flagrans Aries equaverat astra diei,
745 Quando duci Iudas vitam truculentus ademit.
     Illius adveniens planctu iam livida mater
Et flavas disiecta comas his ethera pulsat,
"O celi sacra stirps, o proles unica, tene
Sic decuit pugnare tuis, ut te dare morti
750 Non formidares et tanta subire pericla?
Inspice me: tua sum genitrix! Heu, cur mihi non das
Responsum? Cur non 'Dolor hic mihi, mater, et hic est'
Te referente gemens doleo solorque dolentem?
Me miseram! Quid agam? Quid dicam? Quid queror? Iste
755 Inpius occidit, quodsi quid cordis haberet
Humani (certe fera uel plus quam fera) non hoc

innocent lamb is no more silent when it is taken to a sacred altar to be sacrificed for the people's sin. He tottered and, as he tottered, the troops of Apolides, weakening suddenly with extreme fear (a marvel to relate) fled, and the notorious tyrants turned tail. They report that then for the first time Cacus grew frightened at the wrath of noble Messiah, because after joining battle with him he retreated unarmed —and he was not content in this. 730 735

Zealous Eutropius inflicted upon him a wound and put him to flight in fear, and the palm of victory went to Messiah for his redemptive death; and soon the enchained were released from bonds and were permitted to return to the land with the blessed name of Zion. No happier was that generation, which King Cyrus restored after sixty-five sad years, when they hung silent instruments on pale white boughs. 740

It was the time when, as the Pleiades went back eastward, Aries, burning with the sun, made the nighttime stars equal in length to the day, when ferocious Judas deprived the duke of his life. 745

His mother, already now wan from lamentation, her blond hair disheveled, arrives and assails heaven with these words: "O sacred scion of heaven, O only child, did it befit you to fight in such a fashion for your people, that you did not dread to put yourself to death and to undergo such great dangers? Look at me: I am your mother. Alas, why do you not answer me? Why do you not report 'It hurts me here, mother, and here,' as I, moaning, feel pain and console you in your pain? Woe is me! What shall I do? What shall I say? Of what do I complain? This impious one slew you, but if he had any trace of a human heart (surely he is a wild beast or 750 755

Patrasset facinus. Non te durus Scitha, non te
Teutonus haut facilis vibrato parcere ferro
Confecit; consanguinea cecidisse manu te
760 Et plango et stupeo."
                 Set tu, mater pia, noli
Plangere, quem cernis defunctum, plangere noli!
Utilis hec mors est, vitam multis dabat hec mors.
Tollunt perfusos Iebusei sanguine sacro
Artus extincti iuvenis multumque gementes
765 Condunt regali corpus regale sepulcro.
Mirum, quod refero: iam tercia clarior omni
Sole dies oritur, cum Messiam redivivum
Veraces homines se vidisse in Galilea
Asseruere. Pius gaudens pater acciit illum
770 Inque trono meritum fecit regnare paterno.
     Hec longe sunt gesta prius, quam Tusca iuventus
Destrueret Solimam, que nunc habet Helia nomen;
Golgotheque locus muris inclusus habetur.
     Qui sensu mentem cupit exercere profundo,
775 Prelia rimetur, que scripsimus, arteque iugi
Prelia discuciens (quid enim non discitur usu?)
Inveniet fracto, bene que sapit, osse medullam.
     Summa sophia, tuus grates refero tibi scriptor;
Hoc opus incepi per te ceptumque peregi,
780 Ut sit lac teneris et fortis fortibus esca.

EXPLICIT LIBER *EUPOLEMII.*

even worse than a wild beast), he would not have committed this atrocity. It was not a hard Scythian who killed you, nor a Teuton, far from ready to spare once the sword has been brandished; I both mourn and am astounded that you fell at the hand of a blood relative."

But you, pious mother, do not mourn, do not mourn for the one whom you see lifeless! This death is useful, this death granted life to many. The Jerusalemites carry off the limbs of the dead youth, drenched with sacred blood. Groaning greatly, they bury the kingly body in a kingly tomb. What I have to report is a miracle: now a third day, brighter than all other sunrises, breaks, when reliable people maintained that they saw Messiah brought back to life in Galilee. Rejoicing, his pious father summoned him and made him rule, as he deserved, on the paternal throne. 760 765 770

These events took place long before the young men of Italy destroyed Jerusalem, which now has the name Aelia; and the site of Golgotha is contained, enclosed within its walls.

Let the person who wishes to train his mind in a deep understanding scrutinize the battles that we have recorded, and in examining the battles with constant skill (for what is not learned through practice?) he will find, once the bone has been broken, the marrow, which has a good taste. 775

Highest wisdom, as your writer I render thanks to you; through you I began this task and finished what was begun, that it might be milk to those tender of age and strong meat to those strong of age. 780

HERE ENDS THE BOOK OF *EUPOLEMIUS*.

Note on the Texts

The Latin text of Amarcius's *Sermones* printed here is adapted principally from the critical edition of Karl Manitius (MGH, 1969), who established his version from two manuscripts: Dresden A. 167a (13th century); Copenhagen, Konigl. Bibl. MS Fabr. 81 (13th century). He was also able to consult the *editio princeps* published in 1888 by his father, Max Manitius, as well as conjectures offered on the text in reviews by M. Petschenig, L. Traube, E. Voigt, and W. Wattenbach, and in an article by W. B. Sedgwick. Our text is the beneficiary of the combined efforts of these scholars. The alterations that we have made chiefly concern orthography, punctuation, and, of course, correction of (a few) misprints in Karl Manitius's edition. In addition, after careful consideration of sense and context, we have accepted a number of variant readings and conjectures; these are recorded in Notes to the Texts.

Eupolemius

The *Eupolemius* survived until the mid-twentieth century in two manuscripts. The Besançon manuscript, believed to have been written in the second half of the twelfth century, is still extant. The Dresden one, a copy of the Besançon manuscript thought to have been made in the early thirteenth century, perished in the Allied bombing of Dresden in the late days of World War Two. As a result, its text is available only as recorded in the edition by Max Manitius and in his subsequent publications on the poem.

The poem has been edited only twice, once each by a father and his son, Max and Karl Manitius, in 1891 and 1973, respectively. Neither publication elicited as much of a scholarly response as it deserved, but the first translation into a modern language and the set of textual notes that I published one hundred years after the first edition drew more attention to the *Eupolemius*. The present edition and translation rest on the work of the Manitiuses as well as on the first English translation but incorporate many changes. Some typographical errors have been corrected. The Latin has been repunctuated in many places, most often to clarify the relationship between it and the English as well as frequently to reduce the superabundance of commas; also for the last-mentioned reason, many parenthetical comments have been placed within parentheses rather than commas. Only when the differences reflect a substantially different understanding of the text have these changes been indicated in the notes to the text. On a higher plane, single letters, syllables, and words have been emended, and in one case lines have been rearranged (and one line athetized). For most of these modifications I have only myself to blame, but for others I am indebted to four German and Austrian scholars—Peter Jacobsen, Christine Ratkowitsch, Thomas Gärtner, and Kurt Smolak—who have offered suggestions for furthering the work of Karl Manitius, my own past scholarship, or both. Any changes from Manitius's text not credited to other scholars are my own.

The orthography has been left in its medieval form, which means that *f* appears in most cases where *ph* would be printed in a classicizing edition, *i* where *y*. Both *ae* and *oe* are expressed by *e*. The consonant *d* may be found where *t* would be expected *(velud)* and vice versa *(Dauit)*, *b* where *p* *(obtatus* and *poblite),* and *c* where *t* *(eciam)*. The letters *xs* are reduced to *x* *(exuperans)*, *ph* to *f*.

In the notes, lemmas, in roman type, precede colons, while other readings follow. Sigla and comments are in italics.

Notes to the Texts

SATIRES

Book 1

91	differre: referre
151	Sors: Mors
170	sorde: sorte
327	laete: laetae
346	viribusque: veribusque
397	gnarum: gnavum
401	igni: iugi
501	harae: are

Book 2

1	stirps: strips *(also at line 216)*
354	energima: energia
427	offertus: offertur
475	quos: quibus
510	vulgo levis: vulgilevis
518	decoros: decorus
563	certe: certae

Book 3

25	prement: premet
60	inanes: inmunes

119	trina: trima
344	tu: te
369	haut: aut
377	quis (= quibus): quis
434	fruetur: videtur
446	tolles: tollas
453	cuncta: cuncti
467	catigetis: catienis
836	fuco: fusco
884	stulte: stultae
889	non: enim
908	inemptos: ineptos

Book 4

70	fertilis: fertilius
77	illi: illic
92	Ast: Est
203	ceca: caeca
258	hostis: hostes
288	tristis: tristes
300	Virtus et: et *(omitted)*
359	forfice: forpice

EUPOLEMIUS

Abbreviations

Unless otherwise specified, readings reflect the consonance of *B* and *D* as printed in *M*.

Codices

B = Besançon, Bibliothèque Municipale, MS 536, fol. 1v–21r.
D = Dresden, Sächsische Landesbibliothek, MS Dc. 171a, fol. 17r–38v (destroyed).

Scholars

G = Thomas Gärtner. "Zu den dichterischen Quellen und zum Text der allegorischen Bibeldichtung des Eupolemius." *Deutsches Archiv für Erforschung des Mittelalters* 58 (2002): 549–62.

J = Peter Christian Jacobsen. Review of *M*. *Mittellateinisches Jahrbuch* 13 (1978): 304–7.

M = Karl Manitius, ed. *Eupolemius. Das Bibelgedicht*. Monumenta Germaniae Historica, Quellen zur Geistesgeschichte des Mittelalters 9. Weimar, 1973.

R = Christine Ratkowitsch. "Der Eupolemius—Ein Epos aus dem Jahre 1096?" *Filologia Mediolatina* 6/7 (1999–2000): 215–71.

Book 1

Incipit liber eupolemii *B*: Eupolemius *D (in a later hand)*

1   Messyam: christum *added superscript B*; violenti: diuitis *added superscript B*; Caci: diaboli *added superscript B*

12   Cacus: diabolus *added superscript B*

13   Antropus: homo *added superscript B*

15   Ethnis: Gentilis *added superscript B*

17   Cacum: malum *added superscript B*

18   Agatus: bonus deus *added superscript B*

19   simulacra *BM*: simuchra *D*

20   Zorastree: proprium nomen *added superscript B*

22   senior Cedarei *B*: senior tenebros cedarei *D*, tenebros<i> *added superscript B*

34   Amartigenis: originalis peccati *added superscript B*

35   immo suum: annosum *added superscript B*

36   Bethelis: domus Dei *(omitted by M) added superscript B*

37   Anphicopam: circumcisio *added superscript B*; Polipatremque: patrem multorum *(misread as* multipl<icem?> *M; compare gloss to 1.272) added superscript B*

40   Temptatum *DM*: Tepmtatum *B*

45   compellat *BM*: compellit *D*

50   tantum *BDM*: tantis *after correction by sixteenth-century hand B*

54   ovantes: gaudentes *added superscript B*

66   tuque tuus frater *BM*: tuque tuusque frater *D*

69   illi *before correction to* ille *B*

71   Salem: pacis *added superscript* (*misread as* uicis *M*)*,* ierusalem *added subscript B*

74   illam: sancti spiritus docet me que suis . . . (*ends illegibly*) *as a pen-test in top margin B*

77   Phosphorus: lucifer *added superscript B*

78   causus *before correction* to cautus *D*

88   Aphilum: sine amore *added superscript B*; Superifanemque: superifamemque *D*, Superbia *added superscript B*

92   Apolidem: perdicionis filium *added superscript B*

93   Dilectum *DM*: Delictum *B*

97   Pro ceca, quid hec est: pro . . . cca (*two letters erased*) quid hec est *B* (*not in D*)

104   Aphilus *M*: amphilus *BD*; si non amore inuidia *added superscript B*

105   urbem *BM*: urbe *D*

108   ineamus; : ineamus, *M*

113   quod *M*: quid *BD*

116   eras, te cum bonus Agatus egit?: eras? Tecum bonus Agatus egit. *M*, eras? Te cum bonus Agatus egit, *R*

124   non ego *BD*: non nego *M*

129   stimulavit *M*: simulauit *BD*

135   Ofites: serpentinus *added superscript B*

139   arbitror *DM*: arbitor *B*

140–41 quam fraude, benignus / dum *R*: quam fraude benignus, / dum *M*

145   Ophites: serpens *added superscript B*

146   nullas *BM*: nullus *D*

147   in Bethele: in paradiso *added superscript B*

148   Antifrononta: contraria sapiens *added superscript B*

150   voluit: ille *added superscript B*; Et facie gratus; voluit: Et facie gratus, voluit *M*

154   iam: *over erased* si *B*

157   Ofites: serpens *added superscript B*

159   ortus: paradisus *added superscript B*

161 Diversi: cuius rei *added superscript B*

162 quatuor amnes: Phison. Geon. Tygris. Eufrates. *added superscript B*

167 Ofites: serpens *added superscript B*

169 Regie vir: o *added superscript BD*; grata: s<cilicet> est *added superscript B*

170 ingenuum *BM*: ingenium *D*; invideam *BM*: inuidiam *D*

172 Luze: bethel *added superscript B*; credere cunctis: i<d est> sumere cibum *added superscript B*

174 Antifronon cives: ligno scientie boni et mali *added superscript B*

177–84 *BDM present the lines in this order, with 183 (here athetized)* Antifronon, et erat sollers paciensque laborum. *In B the scribe placed the mark* ∴ *in the margin to the left of verses 178 and 181 to indicate the need for rearrangement. M printed as 183 a gloss on 182, which the scribe added in the margin below 185.*

181 Ofites: serp<ens> *added superscript B*

185 sibi te: tibi se *BDM*

186 fieres magnisque: scientes bonum et malum *added superscript B*

187 Credis, eris: Credis eris *M*, Credideris *D*

194 movet *BD*: monet *M*

195–96 Consilio parere tuo. Quis enim male credat / Iuranti?' (Iurabat enim.): Consilio parere tuo'. Quis enim male credat / Iuranti? — iurabat enim. *M*

200 Amartigenis: peccati origo *added superscript B*

201 Apolide: filii perdicionis *added superscript B*

220 fatur *(compare 2.139)*: fatus *BDM*

224 ceptriger: agatus *added superscript B*

229 Plirisophum: plenitudo scientie *added superscript B*

233 Antropus: adam *added superscript B*

236 fit *M*: sit *BD*; adultis *BM*: adultus *D*

241 bella: bona *added superscript B*; Hic solus: antropus adam *added superscript B*

243 Edidit. Alter: Edidit, alter *M*; Edidit *DM*: Ededit *B*

244 opilioni *BM*: opinioni *D*

245 Hi: hic *BDM*; nutu: uoluntate *added superscript B*

248 repulsa: penitencia *added superscript B*

249 summo: s<cilicet> deo *added superscript B*; reatus: s<cilicet> esse
added superscript B

250 secius: i *erased D*; aliter *added superscript B*

254 Cur, o manus impia: exclamat auctor *added superscript B*

258 tortor *DM*: torton *B*

263 puer sevi: gentilitas ethnis *added superscript B*

266 *Line omitted by scribe, added in right margin with* signes de renvoi *to
signal its placement B*

272 Polipatrem terras: patrem multorum habram *added superscript B*;
acri: atri *before correction D*

273 Anphicopa: circumcisio *added superscript B*

279 Tu quem: Tu, quem *M*

288 Incestum *DM*: Inscestum *B*; scortoque: scurtoque *before correc-
tion D*

298 cultros *M*: cultos *BD*

299 temerare: polluere *added superscript B*

304 fluit: fluat *BDM*

305 Antiphrononciades *M*: Antiphoononciades *BD*

330 cur, ut vos *metri causa, in accord with transposition marks in B*: ut vos,
cur (cur *over erasure*) *BDM*

333 Captivis *BDM*: Captiuus *before correction B*

334 eis *M*: eius *BD*

340 viros: viris *BDM*

343 marcida: uana *added superscript B*

344 ast *G*: at *BDM*

350 strennua *M*: sternua *BD*

352 Reges: tu *added superscript B*

354 quos regibus: reg. dico *added superscript B*

355 palma, et eorum *M*: palma et *(added unclearly)* deorum *B*, palma
deorum *D*

356 paulo: .XVIII. *added superscript B*; uno: .CC. *added superscript B*;
medioque: .C. *added superscript B*; maniplo: cum *added super-
script B*

361 quid *M*: quod *BD*

363 carpsisses: uituperasses *added superscript B*

368   nos: non *before correction* B; prestat: melius *added superscript* B;
       suisque: permitamus discedere *added in right margin* B
370   Agatus et satus ipso: pater et iesus christus (*misread as* tunc *M*)
       filius dei *added superscript* B
373   nocivus; : nocivus *M*
376   Apolides: filius perdicionis *added superscript, and in the left margin*
       diabolus B; varius *M*: variis BD; quoque: quot *before correction* B;
       Ophites: serpens *added superscript* B
380   generis: genere BDM
381   persepe BM: presepe D
388   Ramathus: excelsus *added superscript* B
392   alter: circumcisio *added superscript* B
395   mitte: o iuda *added superscript* B
400   vatum G: votum BDM
402   Pensa etiam, : Pensa, etiam *M*
405   aere *M*: aera BD
407   vetustas: vestustas *M*; vetustis BD
414   depromserat DM: depromiserat B
415   Ascultante (*with n added above the line*) B, Auscultante D
416   Eleimon: misercors *added superscript* B
419   Nomum: legem in decem preceptis *added in left margin* B
420   Ilicet *M*: Ilicit B, Elicit D
428   canemque BM: canemve D
429   Vulturno BDM: uultulno *before correction* D; acri; : acri. *M*
433   Acceleremus: Acceleramus BDM
439   suo BM: fuo D; me bene: id est (*overlooked by* M) moysen *added*
       superscript B
445   denis: XL ann<i>s s<cilicet> *added superscript* B
447   quidem modo. Verum : quidem modo verum. *M*
449   geret R: gerit BDM
451   exegimus BDM: explebimus R
452   placeat *M*: placiat BD
464–65 doctissimus ultra/Quam satis est, celerem: doctissimus, ultra/
       Quam satis est celerem *M*
466   sensim: sensis BDM

471 inflatum *M*: inflatam *BD*; Aplestem: insaciabilis *added superscript B*

476 Ut: o quam *added superscript B*

479 Care: iuda *added superscript B*

483 Suadet *BD*: Suadat *M*

491 utitur *M*: ictitur *BD*

500 Sic *BD*: Si *M*

513 et, prorsus ab illo *G*: et prorsus, ab illo *M*

515 rixator *M*: rixatur *BD*

524 ego *M*: ergo *BD*

527 domum *M*: domumque *BD*

529 Convive *DM*: Conuie *B*

534 petulancia *M*: petulencia *B*, petulantia *D*

537 multos *BM*: multas *D*

540 turba: Descendebat moyses portans duas tabulas conscriptas X
     preceptis *added superscript B*

546 procedant: precedant *BDM*; iuncti *M*: uincti *BD*

547 Advolat Ektrifon: audiebatur inimica uox *added superscript B*

550 muscho: uitulo *added superscript B*

553 Servus *M*: Serus *BD*; sit *M*: fit *BD*

554 coactos *BDM*: congregatos *in right margin B*

557 Fuscum: libidinem *added superscript B*; Aphilum: inuidiam *added
     superscript B*; Diglossam: bilinguem *added superscript B*

559 Politeon *BM*: Politeim *D*; multorum deorum *added superscript B*

562 Crisargirus: auaricia *added superscript B*

563 Pirtalmus: igneis oculis id est ira *added superscript B*

570 Fiat adhuc. Hoc: Fiat adhuc, hoc *M*

577 consulte *M*: consulta *BD*

578 formidem *M*: formidinem *BD*

579 famam. : famam *M*

580 Non *BDM*: *perhaps* Nunc?

588 Ieream *M*: iera *D*; sacerdotem aaron *added superscript B*

594 cruentis *BDM*: Benedicans *added as a pen-test superscript B*

627 nefas. Age: nefas, age *M*; age: ego *BD*

630 nobis animi, mea: nobis, animi mea *M*; mea: o *added superscript B*

639 Nomo *M*: nemo *BD*

640 prelia. Post: prelia, post *M*

641   Oron: uidens *added superscript B*

644   Messiam. Tunc: Messiam, tunc *M*

651   fedisque *M* (*tentatively in apparatus*): fidisque *BD*

658   saciati, sanguine: saciati sanguine *M*

659   Hircanis *M*: hirtanis *BD*

669   lathomos *M*: lathomas *BD*; lapidum cesores *added superscript B*

675   Flegreis *M*: flegeis *BD*

677   ardentibus *BD*: ardentbus *M*

681   arbore *BDM*: arbori *before correction B*

Book 2

Explicit liber primus. Incipit secundus *in darker ink D*

2   caligine *DM*: caligene *B*

3   aperit *M*: aperiit *BD*

5   Spargitur *M*: Spargit *BD*

9   maxima *BM*: maxime *D*

11   pugnaturos *M*: pugnaturus *BD*

22   repercusso *DM*: reperso *B*

23   levi *BM*: leni *D*

34   hastilia *M*: hostilia *BD*

38   Amonosim: proprium nomen pharaonis *added superscript B*; Acastum: acaustum *D*; sine cast<itate> *added superscript B*

39   Sother: saluator *added superscript B*; Linglaum: lingens populus *added superscript B*

40   Linglaus *M*: Linguaus *BD*

44   Stratona: exercitum *added superscript B*

45   Euzelus: bonum odium *added superscript B*; Datan: proprium nomen *added superscript B*

47   finxere *M*: fingere *BD*

49   Nec: Nunc *BDM. Or* Non (*compare 2.85*)

50   Ullus *BD*: Nullus *Manitius*

56   parma: fiducia *added superscript B*

57   gradu. Nil: gradu, nil *M*

60   humeros *DM*: homeros *B*

65   orbem: clipeum *added superscript B*

327

66–68 relatu,/Quot deus ex nichilo fecisset cuncta diebus./Sol ibi *G*:
relatu./Quod deus ex nichilo fecisset cuncta, diebus/Sol ibi
BDM; relatu,/Quod deus ex nichilo fecisset cuncta diebus/sex
ibi *R*

68   flumina: fulmina *BDM*

76   egreaius *B*

77   previus: preuiis *BD*

79   sepulcrum: sepulcrhum *D*

85   Non: Nunc *BDM*

87–90 Eternum famosa fide: mirabile dictu,/Sole morante dies extend-
itur—esse putares/Veros quos pinxit radios manus—unde
Micenis/Fingitur aversus cenam fugisse Thieste. : Eternum fa-
mosa fide, mirabile dictu,/Sole morante dies extenditur, esse
putares/Veros quos pinxit radios manus; unde Micenis/Fingitur
aversus cenam fugisse Thieste *M*

90   aversus *M*: adversus *BD*; Thieste *M*: thiecte *BD*

93   metit *BDM*: mittit *before correction B*

111   prospice *DM*: propsice *B*

117   hi nos *BM*: binos *D*

118   nullo *M*: nollo *BD*

120   levius *DM*: levis *B*

123   ait, "Quandoque: ait 'quandoque *M*

124   equiti: equati *before correction D*; Pariterque *BJG*: pariter *DM*

125   Impedit *BDM*: impetit *in apparatus M*

126   ireve *D*: iręve *BM*

138   Orcum *DM*: oreum *B*

144   hasta. : hasta *BM*

145   longa, : longa. *BM*

155   Funeream *BM*: Funereani *D*

160   nostre *BM*: nostr (*second* o *erased*) *D*

161–68 psallentes. Sed . . . loquetur. : psallentes "sed . . . loquetur." *M*

169   columne *BM*: columnę *D*

172   crudelissimus *BM*: crudelissimiss *D*

173   Antifrononte *BM*: Attifrononte *D*

174   phalanges: populos *added superscript B*

176   Agatide: milites agate (*instead of* Agati) *added superscript B*

177   Crito: iudex *added superscript B*

180   formidine *DM*: formidene *B*

181   Panocius *M*: panoeius *BD*

182   Politeona: idolatria *added superscript B*

186   oculatus: oculum habens s<cilicet> *added superscript B*

187   Illorum *BDM*: illius *after correction B*

188   lacerna: vestis *added superscript B*

190   Lutea: vestis *added superscript B*

193   formidetis *M*: formideris *BD*

197   Quid *DM*: Quod *B*

199   Partoque: pardoque *BDM*

201   Caldeos *BM*: chaldeos *D*

205   Agatide *DM*: agadite *B*

206   Gothoniel: proprium nomen *added superscript B*; nomen: chusan-
        rathaim *in right margin B*

207   Gothonieli *M*: gothonieni *B*, gothohieli *before correction to* gothon-
        iel *D*

208   Doxius: Gloriosus *added superscript B*

209   dextra; : dextra, *M*

211   Quem *M*: que *BD*

212   Egon: rex probus *added superscript B*

213   ruis, *M*: ruis? *BD*

214   mucro? *M*: mucro *BD*

216–19 afferres?" . . . gestans. : afferres? . . . gestans." *(in apparatus) M*

217   ense, dolonem: ense; dolonem *M*

220   exotica: peregrina *added superscript B*

223   hirudo *M*: hirundo *with erasure of* n *B,* hirundo *D*

224   quemque *M*: queque *BD*

225   aiunt: s<cilicet> homines *added superscript B*; N *in the right mar-
        gin B*

226   adtulimus *BDM* d *corrected from* t *D*

227   pullas: s<cilicet> nigras *in the margin B*

228   minutor *DM*: minator *B*

229   capulo tenus: usque ad capulum *added superscript B,* lo tenus *over
        possible erasure, with three-letter gap following B*

230   crassosque *M*: crassusque *BD*

232 ferventi: feruenti *with* u *over erased* i *B*
236 Crito *BM*: cito *D*
238 Amartigenes *DM*: amortigenes *B*
244 dextra; fatetur *M*: dextra fatetur: *B*
246 Oppetere aut alios satius *DM*: e aut alios sacius *over erasure B*
255 Errandum *M*: erandum *BD*
261 caput *M*: cap' *B* , capud *D*; contudit DM: *with* d *over erased* s *B*
262 galerum: curuitas galee *added superscript B*
264 Acheloi *M*: achelca *BD*
265 Mutere *ZG*: Nutere *BD*
279 relatu *DM*: *second letter* a *erased at end B*
280 inclita *DM*: inclica *B*
281 Dalila *DM*: Dalica *corrected B*
283 Pervigil occubuit *DM*: Peruil occ cubuit *B*
284 Idra.: Idra, *M*
287 Tuscos *DM*: tuscoss *B*
293 veniencia *BM*: uenientia *D*
294 vento *DM*: *after* uento *erasure of a second* uento *B*
298 Instant *DM*: Istant *(with* stant *probably over an erasure) B*
301 timidi fugitivi: : timidi, fugitivi, *M*
304 dubitastis *BM*: *with* stis *over an erasure D*
309 ductore *M (in apparatus)*: doctore *BDM*
311 Iamque *M*: I *as initial B; space for three letters followed by* amque *D*
313 divis *M*: diuas *BD*
319 Eleimon *BM* : eleymon *D*
321 Orontem *DM*: orantem *B*
325 mittit *M*: mittat *BD*; Orontem *DM*: orantem *B*
326 octonas *M*: octanas *BD*
340 Ermadolon: pres<es> *or* <ul> falsitatis *added superscript B*; perplex-aque: obscura *added superscript B*
342 Exprimere: inquirere *added superscript B*
343 Assiria *M*: assiriam *BD*; mathesi: disciplina *in the margin B*
346 trepidancia *G*: tergencia *BDM*, turgencia ? *G*
354 Aton; tum, sicut gentis erat mos *M*: atonitum sicut erat gentis erat mos *D, (with gap of around six letters between* sicut *and* erat*) B*

356 quiddam *BDM*: *gap of approximately one letter between* quid *and* dam *B*

357 Iupiter *BDM*: iubiter *before correction D*

358 infernalibus unam *BDM*: *gap of roughly eight letters between the words B*

359 versus *BM*: uisus *D*

360 necat; eruta *BDM*: *gap of roughly five letters between the words B*

362 cultroque *M*: cultoque *BD*

363 Phebeum *BM*: phepeum *D*

365 Pean *BM*: paean *D*

367 michi *BM*: mihi *D*

368 micat: percutit *added superscript B*

369 Pasithea: diana *in right margin B*

372 Gradive: mars *added superscript B*

373 Prestantem: <p>ulcrum *in left margin B*; virago *BDM*: uirabo *before correction D*

377 directa: missa *added superscript B*; domare *DM*: domore *B*; tyrannos.: tyrannos *BM*, tirannos *D*

381 Alipedem: equum *added superscript B*

383 cunctisque: cunctasque *BDM*

384 portis: portas *BDM*

385 clausus *BM*: clusus *D*

387 quacumque *M*: quacum *BD*

390 quamvis *BDM*: uis *added superscript B*

392 Quot *M*: Quod *BD*

393 Prior. Bello: prior; bello *M*, prior bello; *B*

395 Gethei: Golie *added superscript B*

397 Iesseius: dauid *added superscript B*, Iesseus *D*

405 lentissima *M (Virgil,* Aeneid *11.829)*: dentissima *BD*, densissima *M (in apparatus)*

408 leones *M*: leonem *D*, leonem *before correction B*

410 Transtulit; ipse etiam citaram: Transtulit, ipse etiam (eciam *D*), citaram *M*

413 fidibus *BM*: fibidim *D*

417–18 (Asperior . . . peremit): Asperior . . . peremit, *M*

418 alios fortesque *M*: aliosque fortes *BD*

420 Fuscus: Libido *in left margin B*; Irineum: pacificum *added superscript BM*; Adonem *M*: adone *BD*; ado *in left margin,* s<cilicet> uoluptat *in right margin B*

421 Oron *DM*: oran *B*

422 nisi *BM*: ni *D*

423 Sarcodoma: carnem domans *added superscript,* Geta *in left margin B*

427 triti *BM*: tristi *D*

428 Aphilus *BM*: amphilus *D*; Orontem *DM*: orantem *B*

435 Caldei *BM*: chaldei *D*; Aphiloque *BM*: amphiloque *D*

436 pugnando *DM*: pugnagdo *B*

437 diuturno *M*: diuturna *BD*

441 Brachia. Conprendunt: Brachia, conprendunt *M*, Brachia conprehendunt *BD.* petentes;: petentes, *M*

443 Ut *M*: Vt *(with* V *perhaps over an erasure)*, Et *D*; Orontem *DM*: orantem *B*

444 vivet *BM*: uiuit *D*

451 discincti *M*: destincti *BD*

451–52 hostis,/Prorsus et: hostis/Prorsus, et *M*

452 et extinctum *DM*: et et tinctum *B*

453 iuvat *M*: iuuat *(with one letter erased between* u *and* u) *B*

459 Diglossa *BM*: diglossam *D*

461 Lubricus *M*: Lubicus *BD*

465 Politeon *M*: peliteon *BD*

469 Suspendes *BDM*: Suspendens *before correction B.* placere, : placere. *M,* placere? *B*

470 pondere *M*: pendere *BD*

471 flamine *M*: flamina *BD*

472 iugales? *M*: iugales *(no question mark) BD*

475 placet: t *over erasure D*

477 Tebas *BM*: thebas *D*

480 Capaneus *M*: capeneus *BD*; Achaia: Grecia *added superscript B*

481 Laomedonteam *M*: Laomodeamneam *B*, Laomedeam *D*

482 obtundere: ocultare *added superscript B*

486 nomina *BM*: omnia *D*

487 Celarim, trifidi *M*: celari terfidi *BD*

489   queque *DM*: quemque *B*; nidos *M*: nidas *BD*

491   qua *M*: quia *BD*; Philippi: alexander *added superscript B*

495   quoque *DM*: quote *B*

497   Partos *BM*: *after* par *two letters erased (correction of* d *to* t?) *D*

498   Susas *M*: fusas *BD*

503   Queque *M*: Quemque *BD*; ab ipsis *M*: ab ipsa *B (corrected from* ap
       ipsa) *D*

512   Idume *DM*: idiume *B*

515   montibus *M*: montilis *B*

521   Ismariusque *BM*: Hismariusque *D*

523   ignotus *BM*: ignotis *D*

526   Alanus *BM*: alamis *D*

528   Sueva: Suevis *BDM*

530   Dana *BDM*: Dane?

531   Mogon *BDM*: Mogus?; pagos *BM*: pagon *D*

532   Rhodani: Rheni *BM*, reni *D*

538   iactans *BM*: ianctans *D*

539   Vasconasque *BM*: Vuasconasque *D*

540   Betim *M*: Beti' *B*, Beturi *D (M. Manitius)*

543   gente *M*: iente *BD*

545   Leptisque *BM*: leptis et *D*

548   ferentis *BDM*: *after* fer *a* u *erased (*feruentis, *suggested by* Ethiops) *B*

550   poblite *BDM*: p *corrected from* b *B*

554   credo *M*: cedo *BD*

557   *This line is not in D*

558   hoc et pascit: *over erasure D*

564–65 licenter;/Euchius ut multum bibat atque : licenter,/Euchius, ut
       multum bibat, atque *M*

567   Commendat *BDM*: Commendet *before correction B*

573   Eleimon *BM*: eleymon *D*

581   Bethlem *DM*: behlem *B*

582   Parthenie *BM*: Partheme *D*; uirgo *added superscript B*

601   Agatidarum *BM*: agati clarum *D*

604   Pistena: fides *added superscript B*

612   Nine: niniue *added superscript B*

613   brevis et: bona conuersio *(as gloss on* Eutropius) *added superscript B*

614   sexcentis: sex opera misericordie *added superscript B*

615   Bethelius *M*: pethelius *BD*

618   tangentes *BM*: tangentia *D*

620   nervos *BDM*: neruus *before correction D*; Iudeus *BDM*: eus *over erasure D*

624   egregii *DM*: egreii *B*; peremtos *BM*: peremptos *D*

629   Leuconous: alba mens *added superscript B*; Paton: pacientia *added superscript B*

630   suasque: castitas *in right margin B*

632   Behttanicis *BM*: bethanicis *D*

633   burdone *M*: bardone *BD;* sequester: et equiscis *BDM,* et equinis *M (apparatus)*, esquippis *R*, et equestris *Ziolkowski* "Eupolemiana"

634   Amplum: Amplis *BDM*; Tapine: humilitas *added superscript B*

636   Sarcodomas: abstin<entia> *in right margin B*. o *with mark to indicate exclamation*; Daniel *BM*: danihel *D*

641   Rumor Achemenias *BM*: Rumor quam ac hemenias *(quam misplaced here from after* post *640) D*

642   coiere *BM*: coigere *D*

645   opulentam *M*: epulentam *BD*

650   Ihericho *BM*: iericho *D*

654   ascendens *BDM*: d *corrected from* s (ascensens) *D*

658   mentes. : mentes, *M*

665   Politeona *BM*: Poitheona *D*; Pistena: pasteria *BD*

666   Leuconous *M*: Lauconous *BD;* Cresterius: Crisargirus *DM*, crisargius *B*, Eutropius *R (tentatively)*; Aelptin: Aelphin *BDM*: Aelpton *M (in apparatus)*; sine spe *added superscript B*

672   Apcior *BM*: Abcior *D*

674   Accipio *DM*: acipio *B*

675   tumide *BM*: tumede *D*

678   Prostravit fortemque *R*: Prostravit, fortemque M; Diglossam, *R*: Diglossam *M*

679   Pirtalmumque *M*: Pittalmumque *BD*

684   Cedis et *M*: Cedisset *BD*

688   pristinus: protinus *BDM*

689   Victor *BD*: Victus *M (in apparatus)*

691   squalentem *M*: sualentem *BD*

694   stagnum *DM*: stangnum *B*

701   in tres *DM*: *perhaps* ultres *B*

703   obstet *M*: obstat *BD*

704   "Vir strennue," *R* 230: vir strennue *M*; rennue dixit *missing in D*

705   ades *BM*: adhes *D*

706   Nihil *BM*: nichil *after correction from* nilhil *D*

716   experiere *M*: experire *BD*

719   fugit *DM*: fuit *B*

720   suus *DM*: suis *B*

727   miti *BM*: nuti *D*

735   Abscessit; nec in hoc habuit satis: Inpiger illi *J 304*: Abscessit nec in hoc habuit satis. Inpiger illi *M*. Inpiger *DM*: inpigier *B*

739   Sion *BM*: syon *D*

740   generacio *BM*: generatio *D*

743   Vergiliis *M*: u'giliis *B;* Virgiliis *D*

757   Scitha *M*: cithia *B (second* i *erased) D*

759   cecidisse *BDM*: cedisse *with* ci *superscript B*

760   Set *BM*: sed *D*

762   dabat *BM*: dabit *D*

763   perfusos *M*: perfusus *BD*

773   Golgotheque *DM*: Godgotheque *B*

778   grates refero tibi *M*: grates tibi refero tibi *BD*

781   Explicit liber Eupolemii *(entire explicit in larger letters) BM*: *missing in D*

Notes to the Translations

Satires

Letter to Candidus Theophystius

22   Manzeribus. From a Hebrew word for "bastard," (cf. Deuteronomy 23:2) manzer (mamzer) was used by Sedulius (Carm. 5.256) and Venantius Fortunatus (Carm. 5.5.75).

Book 1

4   "Vigorous battle of the virtues" and vices surely alludes to Pruden-tius's *Psychomachia.*

11   Matthew 3:4.

14   Isaiah 3:16.

62   Matthew 24:51.

64   Ephesians 6:12.

78   St. Jerome, *Epistles* 22.32.3.

81   Joshua 7:1–21.

84   *Pauper christus* literally means "anointed pauper"; for "*Judaeus Apella,*" see Horace, *Satires* 1.5.100.

86   *Cristatus,* literally "wearing a plumed helmet," puns on *christus* above, while *excoriatus,* "stripped of skin," plays on the stock in-terpretation of Apella as "without a [fore]skin."

94   2 Maccabees 5:16.

122   Literally, "little wheels of silver."

154   An allusion to tonsure.

160   Psalms 118:176; Matthew 9:36.

161   John 10:12–13.

337

172   There is a major problem of syntactic coherence here, noted by Manitius. Michael Winterbottom has suggested a lacuna.

181   "You" refers to Lust.

186   John 14:10.

189   This list of heretics is found in Isidore, *Etymologiae* 8.5.12–64.

204   Romans 12:11.

205   Matthew 10:16.

209   Judges 16:6; 3 Kings 11:1.

229   Lucretius 4.1026–29.

253   Psalms 146:4.

254   Psalms 89:4.

259   Isaiah 14:12; Luke 10:18.

264   Genesis 2:7.

265   Genesis 3:6, 17–19.

269   Ecclesiasticus 50:15; Genesis 1:11.

282   Note that the following lines contain images of puffing up or swelling [with pride]. Raby used this passage on the *nouveau riche* to illustrate the often-obscure manner of Amarcius's poetry in *A History of Secular Latin Poetry in the Middle Ages,* vol. 1 (Oxford, 1997 repr.), 402.

292   Ecclesiastes 9:12.

313   Exodus 5:1–9.

317   Matthew 23:4.

325   John 12:12–14.

328   Genesis 8:11.

359   Ceres, goddess of grain; Lyaeus, god of wine.

385   I.e., Luxury.

418   Modus Liebinc, or "The Snow Child." No. 14 in *The Cambridge Songs,* edited and translated by Jan M. Ziolkowski (New York, 1994), 62–69 (text). For a discussion of the passage in Amarcius, see xliv–liii.

421   Numbers 10:7.

432   I.e., covers their eyes with a hood.

437   Genesis 3:1–6.

441   Genesis 49:10.

443   Deuteronomy 9:24–26.

Book 2

63 Genesis 3:1–6.
83 Luke 2:22–24.
86 Luke 2:25–28.
89 Luke 2:51.
91 Psalms 37:9.
92 Matthew 3:13.
94 Matthew 3:4.
97 Matthew 4:1.
103 John 8:59.
104 John 13:2.
107 Matthew 26:23.
111 Numbers 21:6; John 3:14.
118 4 Kings 4:31–34.
129 Amarcius again borrows mythical lore from Prudentius (esp. *Contra Orationem Symmachi* 1) to mock the Jews' disbelief in Christ.
145 Athos and Atlas are very high mountains, used here to suggest improbability, or impossibility.
152 Psalms 18:6–7.
156 Genesis 3:22–24.
160 Genesis 3:19.
169 Psalms 86:5.
183 Isaiah 53:1.
190 Isaiah 53:8–9.
193 Psalms 13:2–3.
195 Psalms 115:11.
203 Malachi 3:6.
204 Exodus 2:10, 6:20.
206 Deuteronomy 32:4.
212 Psalms 1:1.
221 John 1:14.
223 John 1:1.
224 Proverbs 8:22–30.
225 Psalms 109:3.
231 Proverbs 8:24.
235 Micah 5:2.
238 Daniel 3:19.
247 Daniel 3:91–93.

250 Daniel 2:34.

254 Psalms 117:22.

261 Zechariah 1.1.

264 Esther 13:2 (for "gentibus optatam pacem").

266 Zechariah 9:9–10.

278 Daniel 7:13–14.

280 Psalms 106:42.

284 I have tried to retain some of the alliteration and emphatic repetition of the Latin text here.

293 The sense of this obscure line seems to be that a flatterer is despicable, whether he wears shoes (rich) or not (poor).

295 Romans 1:32.

302 Ezekiel 3:18–19.

306 Leviticus 11:7; Deuteronomy 14:8.

307 Exodus 12:8; Numbers 9:11.

308 Baruch 4:15.

309 2 Corinthians 3:6.

310 Romans 7:25.

314 Exodus 12:7, 22.

317 Jeremiah 1:1.

322 Jeremiah 13:23.

323 2 Corinthians 11:23.

328 Jeremiah 8:7.

329 Isaiah 1.1.

334 Isaiah 1:2–3.

336 In reviewing the "sacrilegious cults" here (lines 337–64), Amarcius draws heavily on Virgil's *Aeneid* and Prudentius's *Contra Orationem Symmachi* 1, as well as other sources.

371 The following examples of Christ's miracles (lines 372–407) are all taken from the Gospels.

372 Mark 7:25.

373 Matthew 8:5–10.

374 Luke 13:11–13.

375 I.e., the woman is so bent over by her ailment that she cannot look upward.

376 John 5:2–3.

395 John 9:1, 6–7.

396 Matthew 11:5.

402 John 11:1, 17, 43–44.

417 Psalms 24:8.

418 Ecclesiastes 2:16.

420 Psalms 1:2.

424 Proverbs 11:27; Matthew 7:7.

426 Psalms 50:19.

430 Matthew 25:32, 41.

434 Matthew 25:12.

436 Proverbs 12:15.

457 Apocalypse 12:9.

479 Genesis 4:3–8.

494 I.e., silk.

497 Luke 15:11.

498 Luke 15:22, 29.

515 1 Corinthians 4:13.

517 1 Kings 2:8; Psalms 112:7.

519 Genesis 27:41.

520 The reference here is uncertain, but the circumstances accord well with Judges 7, where Gideon, son of Joash, dismissed many from his army at the spring *(fons)* of Harod. Adar may be a corruption of the Latin for Harod, Arad.

545 1 Maccabees 7:5–9.

546 Amarcius takes the examples of Alcimus, Nicanor, Judas, Menelaus, and Onias (below) from 1 and 2 Maccabees; "the Numidian" is Jugurtha. See Sallust, *Bellum Jugurthinum* 101.6, and Prudentius, *Contra Orationem Symmachi* 1.525.

548 2 Maccabees 4:23, 32–34.

550 Proverbs 24:9.

559 2 Kings 15:12–23.

572 Psalms 37:6.

581 2 Kings 12:13.

582 4 Kings 7:1–2, 17–20.

583 The bald prophet is Elisha (Eliseus). See 4 Kings 2:23.

587 Ezekiel 33:11; Psalms 33:15.

588 Acts 9:3–5.

589 Acts 17:18–23.

Book 3

151 Matthew 19:29.

152 Galatians 6:7–9.

154 I.e., Henry III, German king and Holy Roman Emperor, named above (line 141).

184 The story of the rich man (Dives) and Lazarus is found in Luke 16.

186 Amarcius's phrasing here draws upon Horace, *Epistles* 1.18.84.

190 1 Paralipomenon 29:11; Apocalypse 1:6.

196 Job 21:18.

206 Luke 12:35.

210 Luke 21:34.

214 The poppies of Lethe are soporific (cf. *Georgics* 4.545), while bugloss is a plant described by Pliny the Elder as similar to an ox's tongue.

221 In the *Vita Antonii* (39.3), the recitation of Psalms is described as beneficial for driving away demons.

222 Isaiah 5:24.

223 Jeremiah 6:29.

226 For *lucernae ardentes,* "burning lamps," see Luke 12:35; St. Gregory the Great's allegorization of them is found in the *Moralia in Job,* 28.12. *"What follows after this"* refers to *"sint lumbi vestri praecincti"* in Luke.

233 Genesis 39:7; Daniel 13.

234 Numbers 25:7–8; Judith 13:14.

235 Ephesians 4:27.

249 "transformatas figuras" alludes to Ovid's *Metamorphoses,* especially 1.1–2.

263 Psalms 18:6.

264 Exodus 3:2.

267 The horn *(cornu)* is a military metaphor for "courage." See Horace, *Odes* 3.21.18; Psalms 131:17.

276 I.e., Babylon (from Babel). See Daniel 1:1–16 for Amarcius's allusions here.

278 Daniel 1:12–16.

295 Matthew 10:28.

296 Matthew 19:6.

299 The story of St. Malchus ("the monk") is taken from St. Jerome's *Vita Malchi.*

308   Daniel 6:22.

309   Daniel 2:27; Psalms 145:7.

318   Numbers 17:8.

321   Ephesians 2:16.

323   Psalms 137:6.

327   Matthew 18:4.

335   Matthew 11:29.

338   Matthew 23:12.

340   These examples of punished pride are taken from Exodus 14 and 1
        Maccabees 5:55–61; 2 Maccabees 12:8–9.

343   Luke 14:8–9.

347   Psalms 50:19.

348   Matthew 7:15.

349   Matthew 7:3–5.

352   Ecclesiasticus 10:15.

370   Psalms 21:16

373   Joshua 10:13.

374   Ruth 4:13.

375   Esther 2:5, 7:3.

399   Apocalypse 9:11.

400   Apocalypse 14:14.

407   Matthew 2:1–11.

409   Psalms 71:10; Isaiah 60:6.

420   1 John 3:9, 5:18.

432   John 3:3–5.

439   Matthew 22:37–39.

459   Ecclesiasticus 19:12–14; Matthew 18:15.

465   Matthew 13:24–30; Luke 13:6–9.

476   1 Corinthians 13:1–7.

479   John 13:23–25.

482   1 John 4:16.

493   3 Kings 1:31.

498   In medieval bestiaries, the "spotted" panther is called a symbol of
        Christ, and the serpent *(draco)* symbolizes the devil.

499   Genesis 35:16 ("verno tempore").

502   Genesis 9:13–16.

507   Exodus 32.

508 3 Kings 18:40; Daniel 14:20–21.

512 The story of King Hezekiah, who "turned his face to the wall" and "wept with much weeping," is told in 4 Kings 20.

514 Job 40:20–21.

518 1 John 1:9.

520 King David. See 2 Kings 1:11–12.

524 Tobit 4:16.

525 Matthew 7:12.

531 Apocalypse 21:10.

539 Apocalypse 4:6–7.

545 1 Corinthians 6:15, 12:27.

555 Psalms 26:4.

560 Here Amarcius borrows from Horace, *Epistles* 1.11.27.

565 Luke 10:3–4.

576 2 John 10.

580 1 John 4:8.

582 Genesis 1:1–2.

594 Apocalypse 12:10.

598 Genesis 1:3–5

600 Genesis 1:6–10.

610 Genesis 2:5.

627 Genesis 1:14–18.

631 Daniel 10:6; Apocalypse 4:5.

639 Genesis 1:20–21.

645 Genesis 1:24.

648 Ephesians 2:14

649 Genesis 1:25–28.

679 Malachi 4:2.

682 Colossians 3:14.

684 Romans 5:5.

687 Genesis 2:18–24.

695 1 Corinthians 7:2.

702 1 Corinthians 3:1; Hebrews 5:12–14.

707 3 Kings 19:12.

712 1 Corinthians 8:7–10.

716 Acts 2:43, 5:12.

718 Acts 3:1–10, 9:36–41.

725 Leviticus 15:3.

758 Exodus 21:24; Leviticus 24:20; Deuteronomy 19:21.

759 Matthew 5:38–39.

762 According to medieval bestiaries, the pelican killed its own young but then restored them to life with its own blood.

764 Acts 9:15.

765 Romans 16:19; 1 Corinthians 3:18.

767 Romans 8:8.

791 K. Manitius identifies "the writer from Cos" as Philetas, an elegist cited by Ovid (*Ars Amatoria* 3.329).

814 Ephesians 5:23: *Christus caput est ecclesiae.*

818 2 Corinthians 6:15.

831 Isaiah 58:1.

845 Psalms 22:4; Galatians 6:6.

849 Matthew 13:8.

850 Exodus 22:29.

854 Deuteronomy 21:3.

868 Ephesians 6:1–8; Colossians 3:20–25.

870 Ephesians 5:22–25; Colossians 3:18–19.

871 1 Peter 3:1–7.

874 Joshua 2:1–6.

884 1 Timothy 3:2; Titus 1:6.

893 John 2:14–15.

915 John 20:22–23.

934 James 1:26.

944 1 Kings 10.

947 Psalms 55:1.

948 Matthew 22:21.

953 Proverbs 8:15; Romans 13:1.

Book 4

3 1 John 2–4.

9 1 John 3:17.

13 This line probably refers to the "Hymn for Cock-Crow" of Prudentius (*Cathemerinon* 1), or to the "*Hymnus ad Gallicinium*" (*Aeterne rerum Conditor*) of St. Ambrose.

14   Apocalypse 19:4.

22   Psalms 110:10.

23   Proverbs 18:4

25   Wisdom 15:9.

28   Peter Abelard began a famous hymn for Saturday vespers celebrating the joys of the celestial homeland with the words "*O quanta qualia sunt,*" echoing Amarcius's phrase here.

30   1 Corinthians 2:9, echoing Isaiah 64:4.

42   2 Peter 2:22; Proverbs 26:11.

45   2 Peter 2:21.

58   Matthew 24:42–44.

60   Matthew 24:36.

62   Mark 13:35.

64   Apocalypse 6:14–17.

65   1 Corinthians 3:8.

74   John 14:2.

84   Apocalypse 21:19–20; Prudentius, *Psychomachia* 851–67.

113   Psalms 2:9; Apocalypse 2:27.

126   Malachi 4:2.

138   1 John 4:8, 16.

141   Matthew 7:24.

155   Psalms 50:12.

162   Matthew 7:13.

166   Matthew 7:14.

185   Matthew 16:26.

191   In his *Life of the Deified Julius* (89), Suetonius reported that Spurinna the soothsayer and Calpurnia, Caesar's wife, voiced premonitions of his impending death.

192   Acts 12:23.

214   2 Kings 13:6–10.

227   These lines seem to reply to the question posed to the glutton in line 221.

240   Luke 11:41.

258   James 4:4.

259   Matthew 6:24.

260   Matthew 2:11–12.

266   Genesis 19:26.

267   Genesis 19:22–23.

270   Apocalypse 21:4.

285   Matthew 24:20.

286   Acts 1:12.

295   "Tall Hiperefanes" (from *hyperephanos,* "arrogant") appears as "savage Hiperefanes" in *Eupolemius* (e.g., 1.364, 1.558). The following lines (296–309) are an exchange between the haughty proponent of worldly wealth and Amarcius, advocate of *contemptus mundi.*

306   Matthew 4:21.

307   James 4:4.

311   Exodus 17:11–12.

329   Matthew 6:22.

331   2 Timothy 2:5.

332   Job 2:8; Acts 7:57–58.

335   With the phrase *irradians hirto e corpore,* Amarcius seems to allude to Christ's Resurrection, from a human body to divine glory.

340   1 Peter 2:21.

342   A reference to Pharaoh (?).

346   Romans 9:29.

347   John 1:29.

348   Isaiah 53:6.

349   Zechariah 12:10; John 19:37.

350   Matthew 16:24.

351   Luke 14:27.

366   Proverbs 16:32.

369   Medieval bestiaries, following Pliny the Elder (*Natural History* 10.188, 29.76), reported that the salamander was immune to fire and, in fact, put out fires.

371   Matthew 5:39.

375   Mark 16:18.

376   The catalog of serpents in lines 376–78 is borrowed from Lucan (9.712–23), except for *ophites,* which is used as a proper name in *Eupolemius* (e.g., 1.145 *et passim*).

380   Genesis 7:17.

400 Matthew 2:16.

413 Wisdom 3:6; Proverbs 17:3.

432 Lines 431–33 are difficult to read in the manuscript, according to K. Manitius. In a strained analogy, Amarcius points out that young men submit to barbers' razors "in the baths" in order to restore youthful looks when their beards are shaven. So also, they should endure men's blows and sneers in order to mend their faults when the "hair of their sins" *(crine notarum)* has been removed (lines 434–37).

441 Apocalypse 1:9.

442 The "exile transported on high" is St. John, author of the Apocalypse, in which "the beast" is signified by number 666 (13:18).

443 Apocalypse 13:7.

444 2 Thessalonians 2:9.

459 Manitius suggested that these lines might refer to burglary.

470 2 Timothy 2:5.

Prayer to the Holy Trinity

14 Isaiah 6:2.

20 Job 19–25.

21 Luke 24:39–41.

23 Romans 14:10.

25 1 Corinthians 15:52.

EUPOLEMIUS

Book 1

1 Cacus: glossed as "the devil" in *B* at this point, as "evil" at Book 1.17. Messiah: glossed as "Christ" in *B*.

4 The fields of Jebus: Jerusalem. Jebus is mentioned in Judges 10 with the explanation "Jebus, which by another name is called Jerusalem," and in 1 Paralipomenon 4 with the explanation "Jerusalem, which is Jebus, where the Jebusites were the inhabitants of the land." The name seems to have been a backformation from the name of the tribe.

5 Clio, one of the nine Muses: associated with history.

6 Calliope, another Muse: associated with epic poetry. The highest wisdom is God, which is mentioned again in the epilogue to the poem at 2.778 (as well as in Amarcius, *Satires* 1.195 and 4.325).

9 Isaiah 6:3: "And they [the seraphim] cried one to another, and said: Holy, holy, holy, the Lord God of hosts, all the earth is full of his glory."

13 Antropus: glossed as "Man" in *B*, Antropus corresponds to Adam.

15 Judas personifies Judaism. Ethnis: glossed as "Gentile" in *B*.

18 Agatus: glossed as Good God in *B*, Agatus is king of Jerusalem.

20 Zoroaster: Zoroastrianism, the ancient Persian religion founded in the sixth century BCE by Zoroaster (Zarathustra), was associated in the Middle Ages with polytheism. Its dualism held that man's afterlife depends on the good and evil in his life.

22 The Kedarites were a desert-dwelling tribe of nomadic herdsmen, often identified with Arabs. They are mentioned here because the element *Kedar* (name of a son of Ishmael in Genesis 25:13) was etymologized as "darkness or sadness" by Jerome (*Liber interpretationis hebraicorum nominum* Lag. 4.6–7, 48.13–14, 57.5) and others. Accordingly, the word is glossed "dark" in *B*. Thus "Kedarite tyrant" is equivalent to "the prince of darkness."

31–32 The Chaldean city is Babylon, as the poet himself explains.

34 Amartigenes, whose name means "birth of sin" in Greek, is a separate character who personifies the "Original Sin" (as his name is glossed in *B* at this line) or the "Origin of Sin" (in *B* at 1.200).

36 Bethel: the interpretation of the name, not provided here, appears in Genesis 28:17, "this is no other but the house of God."

37 The name Anphicopas is constructed out of Greek equivalents to the Latin roots of the word circumcision (as the glossator in *B* notes at 1.37 and 1.273). Thus it is a fabricated word: the actual Greek noun for circumcision is *peritome*. This character personifies the covenant of circumcision pronounced to Abraham in Genesis 17:10–14. Polipater indicates Abraham, the first of the Jewish patriarchs and the father of the faithful. The meaning of Abraham's name is explained in Genesis 17:5 (compare Isidore's *Etymologiae* 7.7.2): "Neither shall thy name be called any more

Abram, but thou shalt be called Abraham, because I have made thee a father of many nations." The glossator in *B* identifies Polipater as "Abram, father of many" at 1.272.

43 Semiramis: an Assyrian princess who became the stuff of many ancient legends. Two important sources for her building of brick walls around Babylon were Ovid, *Metamorphoses* 4.57–58, and Isidore, *Etymologiae* 15.1.4.

44 Literally, "baked stones."

50 Alternative translations include "this man upheld only by virtues." In *B* a sixteenth-century hand made the attractive emendation "this man upheld by such great virtues" (*tantum* to *tantis*).

53–54 The Latin specifies literally "the sixth hour": sext was the fourth of the seven canonical hours for prayer.

63 "a long speech and the grievous toils": an example of the rhetorical figure hendiadys, which could be translated less literally "a long speech about the grievous toils."

70–415 In this long speech Moses provides the background, based largely on the biblical books of Numbers and Deuteronomy, to the contentions that follow in the remainder of Book 1 and in all of Book 2.

70–74 The poet refers to the modification of Jebus-Salem to Jerusalem. Although he attributes his information to grammarians, his source was probably Isidore, *Etymologiae* 15.1.5: "The Jews assert that Shem, the son of Noah, whom they call Melchisedech, first founded in Syria the city Salem after the flood; the realm of the same Melchisedech was in the same city. Afterward the city was held by the Jebusites, from whom it took the name Jebus; and so when the two names Jebus and Salem were put together it was called Jerusalem (Hierusalem), which afterward by Solomon was called Hierosolyma—almost as if it were Hierosolomonia. This place is called Solyma corruptly by poets . . ."

74 "Colit ut coluit": the verb is here translated objectively as "to cherish," although when used subjectively of gods it most often meant "to dwell in a place, usually by virtue of being worshipped there" (*Oxford Latin Dictionary colo*[1] 2).

75–85 This passage describes allegorically the fall of Lucifer. This episode is not recounted systematically in the Bible, but in the Vulgate (Isaiah 14:12) the prophet Isaiah applies the epithet Lucifer to the king of Babylon, who boasted that he would ascend to the heavens and become the equal of God but who was later cast down to the deepest pit. Under the influence of a single verse in the New Testament (Luke 10:18), the name was assigned to Satan, in the context of the story that Satan—called Lucifer—was cast down from heaven for his pride.

77   The Greek elements *Phos-phorus* are the equivalent of the Latin *Luci-fer* (light-bringing).

78   In lines 78, 83, and elsewhere the Latin word *honor* suggests both the office that Cacus occupied and the honor associated with the office.

85   Kedar stands for "(the realm of) darkness" (hell).

88   Aphilus from the Greek "without love, loveless." Superifanes, who appears later as Hiperefanes: modeled on the Greek *huperefanes* ("overweening, arrogant").

92   Apolides is Cacus. The name Apolides is glossed as "son of perdition" in *B*. In John 17:12 and 2 Thessalonians 2:3 this phrase in Latin ("filius perditionis") translates the Greek. If a patronymic ending is added to the stem of the last word in the Greek phrase, the result would be Apolides. In the event that the glossator was wrong, then the name could be connected with the Greek *ápolis* (without a city, cityless).

94   The foster child is Antropus.

106–7 These lines could be translated in several ways: "And why, if you are victorious with Mars favoring you strongly, is the outcome in doubt?" or "And what if you are victorious, with Mars favoring you strongly? Is the outcome in doubt?"

115–16 The second half line, if construed as the start of a new sentence with the following simile, could be translated "Good Agatus did with you as a childish throng, when it sets up a king for itself: it chooses him . . ."

124–25 Or retain the reading *non ego* and translate: "Otherwise, if you are so good (as I am not!) . . ."

130   The Latin adjective refers to Elis, a Greek state in which Olympia was located.

131   Epirus, a district in northwest Greece (now Albania).

135 and elsewhere   The name Ophites is derived from the Greek word for "serpent" or "snake." Ophites represents the serpent in the story of the Fall (Genesis 3:1–15).

148   The name Antifronon is constructed on the basis of Greek elements meaning "opposed to wisdom or prudence."

162   The four rivers of paradise, as the gloss in *B* specifies, as named in Genesis 2:10–14 are Phison, Gehon, Tigris, and Euphrates.

170   "ut invideam": *Oxford Latin Dictionary ut* 28 f (introducing an unlikely motive ironically suggested by the speaker).

171   The Jerusalemite is Agatus: see 1.74.

172   Luza corresponds to Bethel, which in turn (as "house of God") stands for paradise. Genesis 28:19: "And he called the name of the city Bethel, which before was called Luza." The connection between the two names is discussed in Isidore, *Etymologiae* 15.1.22.

174   Antifronon surpasses his fellow citizens, as a gloss in *B* explicates, "through the tree of the knowledge of good and evil."

176   "even though he is present": Antifronon.

217   *Hibrida* is glossed "innulus" (in standard classical spelling and pronunciation, *hinnulus,* a hinny) in *B.* The word *hybrida* referred to a half-breed person or animal.

220   The epic convention of placing "sic fatus" and closely related phrases (compare 2.139) after speeches supports keeping the simile within quotation marks.

227   The relatively uncommon verb *praequeror* usually meant "to complain (or lament) beforehand" (thus this same line opening in Ovid, *Metamorphoses* 4.251). Alternatively, the prefix could be meant as an intensive.

229   The name Plirisophus is glossed (on the basis of its Greek elements) "fullness of knowledge" in *B.* The gloss draws attention to the cherubim, of whom Isidore observes (*Etymologiae* 7.5.22): "they are rendered from Hebrew into our language 'multitude of knowledge.'" According to Genesis 3:24, God "cast out Adam; and placed before the paradise of pleasure cherubims, and a flaming sword, turning every way, to keep the way of the tree of life."

233   *B* glosses Antropus as being Adam here and at 1.241.

235   The word "wife" is not glossed: the glossator may have hesitated
      between Eve and Lilith, who in rabbinical writings is reputed to
      have been Adam's first wife. If the woman is equivalent to Eve, it
      is remarkable that she enters the scene after Antropus, the first
      man, has been ejected from the garden.

236–54 Moses likens the dispositions of Ethnis and Judas to those of Cain
      and Abel. This is one of four instances in which the poet juxta-
      poses characters in his poem to ones in the Bible: compare 2.44–
      48, 2.76–79, and 2.740–47.

245   An alternative translation: "with God's will being different in each
      case."

248   "and sorrowed without limit over his defeat": the last word is
      glossed "Penitence" in *B*.

252–53 Compare Genesis 4:10: "And he said to him, 'What hast thou
      done? The voice of thy brother's blood crieth to me from the
      earth.'"

254–59 The start of this speech is glossed "The creator cries out." If the
      glossator is correct, then this whole speech should be attributed
      to the poet (or, less likely, God) rather than to Moses.

263   In *B* "the boy" is glossed "The gentiles: Ethnis."

281   Alternatively, "you receive in your home."

296   K. Manitius translates *agagula* as "a jabberer" on the strength of
      Sextus Amarcius 4.295, but he points out that in Odo of Cluny's
      Occupatio 2.148 the word means "pimp." The latter meaning fits
      the context here better; whereas "a jabberer" would simply re-
      peat the import of *verbosus*, "pimp" would add a third insult to
      the two of "wordy" and "bandit."

312   The same line ending ("duce ceco") occurs in Sextus Amarcius
      3.881, with clear reference to Matthew 15:14 and Luke 6:39.

324–27 These lines present a string of impossible situations (known in
      classical rhetoric as adynata or impossibilia) derived from Ro-
      man poetry. The Jhelum, referred to by its Latin name Hy-
      daspes, is a tributary of the river Indus and is far from where the
      Germans live. The Danube flows from Germany to the Black
      Sea, whereas the Parthians inhabited northeastern Iran.

340   If the reading *viris* of the manuscripts and Manitius is retained, translate as "that such creatures were sent . . . to real men, to me." In favor of emendation is the fact that *talis, -e* is used without specification only in reference to words—and compare 1.392 "viris huc missis."

344   "Dixerat; at . . ." In *B* "at" is corrected to *ac* with a superscript *c*. Either *at* or *ac* would construe: *at* would have contrastive force, whereas *ac* would have temporal force (*Oxford Latin Dictionary atque* 5c "and thereupon," used often after verbs of speaking).

349   "degenerate age": in Virgil (*Aeneid* 8.326) the Latin phrase describes the generation that followed the Golden Age.

352–61 Polipater relates the events that culminated in Abraham's rescue of his brother Lot at Hobah (Genesis 14:8–16: compare Prudentius, *Psychomachia* "Praefatio" 15–37). Four kings defeated five other kings, among them the kings of Sodom and Gomorrah. The four kings took captive Lot, who dwelled in Sodom. When Abraham learned of this, he took 318 servants, overcame the 4 kings, and recovered his brother.

352   The glossator in *B* apparently mistook the noun *reges* (kings) for the homographic verb form "you will rule," because he wrote *tu* (you) above it to identify the person of the verb.

354   The glossator identifies the antecedent of *quos* by writing "reg. dico" ("kings, I say") above it.

356   "a little more" is glossed with the Roman numeral XVIII, "one" with CC, and "a half" with C, for a total of 318.

357–61 This simile makes use of two Thracian rivers mentioned in Roman poetry, the Thermodon (Ovid and other poets) and Cynapses (Ovid, *Ex Ponto* 4.10.49). The adjective *veteres* (old) could modify either *ripas* (over its old banks) or *quercus* (old oaks).

361   As Isidore explains (*Etymologiae* 14.3.24), "Pentapolis is a region located on the boundary of Arabia and Palestine. It is so named from the five cities of impious men which were consumed by fire from heaven." Pentapolis (Genesis 14:2, 14:8) comprised the five cities whose kings were defeated by the four kings, who were defeated in turn by Abraham.

367   The mention of facial hair appears unexpectedly, but emendation

to a form of *barbarus, -a, -um* or of *balbus, -a, -um* is metrically impossible.

368   In *B* the marginal gloss can be construed as explaining to the reader the thought broken by the aposiopesis ("let us allow him to depart"). Possibly Hiperefanes had in mind at first instead to kill Polipater, but then reconsidered and decided to hold him captive.

376   Above Apolides in *B* is the gloss "the son of perdition," which in turn is glossed in the left margin "the devil."

380   The reading *genere* in both manuscripts would mark the only instance in the *Eupolemius* in which a short syllable is lengthened at the caesura and a rare occasion on which the poet rhymed the caesura with the line ending. If the reading is kept, translate "for men who are genealogically connected ought not to be kept separate in their situation."

388   Ramathus is a byname for Agatus. Among other things, Ramathus offers the poet a trisyllable with different scansion from Agatus. Ramathus is glossed "lofty" in *B,* in accordance with exegetical interpretations of the biblical place name Ramath (Jerome, *Liber interpretationis* Lag. 30.1–2).

393   "of whom one": the gloss in *B* identifies him as "circumcision" (which means Anphicopas).

395   "put aside your cares": the gloss in *B* names the addressee of this remark "O Judas."

397–99 Exhorting Judas to take heart, Moses presents a brief history of the biblical figure Joseph: see Genesis 37, 39, and 41. In it he emphasizes Joseph's rise to power under Pharaoh.

400–401 A comparison between Joseph and the figure of Greek myth Hippolytus. The same parallel is drawn in the *Eclogue of Theodulus* 125–32. The common element, not mentioned by the *Eupolemius* poet, is the chastity of both men in response to aggressive advances by married women. After spurning an attempt at seduction, Joseph was falsely accused of rape by the wife of his master, Potiphar, just as Hippolytus was by his stepmother, Phaedra.

401   Paean was a Greek god of healing who was identified with Apollo.

Among other authors, Virgil related that Hippolytus, after being slain as a result of a beast sent by the sea god at the request of his father, Theseus, after the false accusation of rape by Phaedra, was brought back to life by Asclepius (or Aesculapius). Asclepius was the son of Apollo and Coronis.

402–12 Moses recounts to Judas the escape of the Israelites from Egypt.

408–9 On the dew from heaven that fed the children of Israel, see Exodus 16:13–14 and Isaiah 45:8.

410 On the water that Moses caused to appear by striking his rod upon the rock of Horeb, see Exodus 17:6 and Numbers 20:11.

410–11 The parallels between Moses and Ammon do not appear in the *Eclogue of Theodulus*. After the Roman conquest of Egypt the Egyptian deity Amun was equated with the Roman god Jupiter. The oracle of Jupiter Ammon was situated at the Siwa oasis in Libya. Tradition held that when Bacchus was conquering Africa, his forces came close to perishing for lack of water. At this juncture a ram appeared and led them to the oasis.

419 A gloss in *B* equates Nomus with "the law in the ten commandments."

421–22 "Spurning the banquet" is glossed in B as "that is, through abstinence."

425 Near Alba Longa (probably not understood as Albania).

426 Dogs of the Molossian breed, renowned in antiquity, which originated in an area in the interior of Epirus.

429 Volturnus (Vulturnus) was a name for a southeast wind.

445 The text specifies that Israel will spend thirty-eight years of wandering in the wilderness, a number supported by Deuteronomy 2:14. The seeming contradiction of the gloss in *B* ("which is to say, 40 years") has its basis in Numbers 14.33–34.

471 Aplestes (from the Greek adjective *aplestos, -on*), glossed "insatiable" in *B,* represents Avarice.

472 If taken literally, the phrase "terraque marique" should be translated "by land and sea" and construed with "quesitis" (as if a legitimate past participle meaning "sought."

501–5 The poet draws a parallel between the golden calf of the Bible (Exodus 32:4–35, Deuteronomy 9:8–21, 3 Kings 12:28–32, Acts 7:41) and the bull into which Jupiter metamorphosed, in order to achieve the rape of Europa. The same parallel is made in the *Eclogue of Theodulus* 141–48.

516   Alternatively, *lascive* could be an adverb ("he approves lustfully all the enticements of the flesh").

519   The second half line is based upon Persius, *Satires* 3.98 "turgidus hic epulis atque albo uentre lauatur" ("Stuffed from banqueting and with a white belly he goes bathing"). The white belly may be the result of dropsy.

520   A translation that followed the Latin word order more logically would be "And to please even more his stomach as it does service to the bloodthirsty princes." But his denigration of Moses and Nomus is likelier to please Cacus than his own belly. Another option is to construe "bloodthirsty princes" in apposition to Moses and Nomus; but would the poet use that adjective to describe them?

533–34   "letaque corona/Circueunt": the noun and adjective could mean either "in a happy circle" or "with a festive garland," while the verb could be translated either transitively "they encircle" or intransitively "they go round."

535   The Choaspes was a river in Susiana renowned for its sweetness.

540–41   Between these verses is written the gloss "Moses went down, carrying two tablets on which were inscribed the ten commandments" (Exodus 32:15).

544–45   Alternatively, "Moses pulls together the troops, scattered in the usual way because of the narrow footpath."

547   The gloss in *B* explains "a hostile voice was heard." The Apolidae, meaning "sons of perdition," are the followers of Cacus.

550   Phrygian melodies were employed in celebrations of the goddess Cybele, also known as Magna Mater ("Great Mother").

557   Fuscus is glossed "lust" in *B,* Aphilus "envy," and Diglossa "two-tongued." Fuscus is odd man out in this list, since his looks to be the only non-Greek name.

559   Politeon is glossed "of many gods" in *B*.

560   The Brahmins were regarded by ancient ethnographers as a tribe or tribes in India.

561–62 The bow holder is sometimes Diana, the moon goddess, but here must be Sagittarius (the ninth sign), since he is masculine and opposite Gemini (the third sign) in the Zodiac.

562 In *B* a gloss over Crisargirus equates this character with "Greed," and a gloss to the right explains: "In Greek Crison means gold; Argiros, silver."

563 In *B* a gloss over Piritalmus explains "with fiery eyes, that is, Anger."

585 Levite poses a problem. Although Aaron is so identified in the Bible (Exodus 4:14), the character identified in the glosses as Aaron is Iereas (in 1.588) rather than Levita. The term could allude to the sons of Levi, who in Exodus 32:26–29 punish the offering of the golden calf.

588 Iereas (from some form of the Greek root *hiero-*, "sacred" or "priestly") is glossed "the priest Aaron" (or "the priest of Aaron") in *B*.

590–92 Compare Virgil, *Aeneid* 1.469–73.

591 The numbers could be construed with either "tents" ("twenty tents with three added") or "enemies" ("twenty slain enemies with three added"). In either event, the number probably alludes to the twenty-three thousand slain in Exodus 32:28.

599 The adjective *scelestis* (accursed) could describe either Judas or the dukes.

612–16 The king of Syria in question is Benadad, who besieged Samaria and caused a great famine (4 Kings 6:24–25). He and the Syrians were frightened into lifting the siege when the Lord made them hear the noise of a great army (4 Kings 7:6–7).

641 Oron, from the Greek verb *horao*, means "one who sees" or (as it is glossed in *B*) "seeing." The character may be seen as simultaneously personifying prophetic power and representing the prophets of the Hebrew Bible collectively.

643 The phrase "of uncommon praise" could describe either Oron or Agatus.

652 Omino's name, unglossed in *B*, plays fittingly on the word *omen*, since Omino prophesies.

666–78 The poet draws a parallel between the building of the tower of

Babel in the Bible (Genesis 11:3–9) and the gigantomachy in Greek myth (recounted in such Latin sources as Virgil, *Georgics* 1.278–83 and Ovid, *Metamorphoses* 1.151–62). The same parallel is found in the *Eclogue of Theodulus* 85–92.

669   Babel was interpreted etymologically as meaning "confusion."

671–78 The Giants in the war with the gods were said to have attempted to heap Ossa and Olympus on Pelion, or Pelion and Ossa on Olympus, in order to scale heaven. Ossa was a mountain in the north of Thessaly, connected with Pelion on the southeast and divided from Olympus on the northwest by the vale of Tempe. Phlegra was the site of the battle between the gods and Giants.

671   Or "poetry holds that thereafter the giants, following beliefs that departed from the truth . . ." This interpretation of the last three words gains weight from the last three of Horace, *Satires* 1.3, "laudet diversa sequentis" ("that he should praise those who follow other paths"); for the meaning of *diversa* (diverging), compare Horace, *Satires* 1.3.114.

672   Metrically this line is perhaps meant to recall Virgil, *Georgics* 1.281–83, in which an emphatic hiatus (as well as three elisions and many spondees) helps to convey the lumbering efforts of giants as they move huge masses. But whereas Virgil presents the mountains in the order Pelion-Ossa-Olympus (from the ground up), the *Eupolemius* poet follows the order first recorded in Homer (*Odyssey* 11.315–16), which was retained by Horace, *Odes* 3.4.52 (although without mention of Ossa); Propertius, 2.1.19–20; and others.

681   Alternatively, the adjective "soft" could not be meant adverbially but could instead signify the ripeness of the fruit.

Book 2

1–3   Elaborate descriptions of daybreak belong to the stock in trade of classical Latin poetry. Titan was often used to designate the sun, since the sun god was the son of the Titan, Hyperion.

38   Amonosis could derive from Amenophis, the name of an Egyptian king which is attested repeatedly in Jerome. *B* provides the gloss

"proper name of Pharoahs." Alternatively, Amonosis could be connected with the name of the Egyptian divinity (H)am(m)on. Then again, it could be a neologism meaning "without unity" (*a-* + *mon-* + *-osis*). On Acastus, *B* provides the gloss "without chastity."

39   *B* glosses Sother simply as "savior," without specifying that the savior in question is Joshua, protagonist of the biblical book named after him. On the etymology of Joshua as "lord savior," see Jerome, *Liber interpretationis,* p. 76.28, and Isidore, *Etymologiae* 7.6.51. *B* glosses as "the licking people," whence (if the gloss is correct) it appears that the name combines the Latin *lingo -ere* (to lick) and Greek *laós* (people). Jerome interpreted the name Amalek as meaning "licking people" (*Liber interpretationis* p. 61.2).

44   Straton is glossed "army" (the meaning of the word in Greek) in *B*.

45–48   In 2.45 and 2.76 the poet takes pains to emphasize that his characters, Dathan and Moses, are not identical with the corresponding biblical personages, whom he proceeds to compare with figures of classical mythology. The same parallel between the biblical Dathan (Numbers 16) and the Greek mythological Amphiaraus is drawn in the *Eclogue of Theodulus* 149–54.

45   In *B* Euzelus is glossed "good hate" and Dathan "proper noun." The second gloss is a concise means of signaling that the word is an actual name, in this case taken from the Bible.

46   "Contrary to its laws" could describe not only the earth but also Dathan, who opposed the laws of Moses and God.

46–48   Amphiaraus was one of the Seven against Thebes, who in Greek legend undertook an unsuccessful expedition to settle a dispute over rulership between the brothers Polynices and Eteocles. Amphiaraus and his companions were betrayed by his wife, out of her desire for a necklace (Hyginus, *Fabulae* 73). As Amphiaraus fled Periclymenus (one of the Theban defenders), he was swallowed up with his chariot by the earth.

51   Because the length of its final syllable is equivocal, "bloody" could modify not "sword point" but instead "deaths."

56   *B* glosses shield as "faith."

69–70   The "threefold disk" could refer to either the disk of the world or to the disk-shaped shield. For a triple-threaded (or three-ply) corselet, see 2.267–68. The four parts could be the sun, rivers, ocean, and land.

72–75   The *Eclogue of Theodulus* (69–76) likewise juxtaposed the flood associated with Noah and the Ark in the Bible (Genesis 6–7) to the deluge in Greco-Roman myth that involved Pyrrha and Deucalion. According to the myth, Jupiter, angered at the evils of the Bronze Age, caused a flood that destroyed all except Pyrrha (daughter of Epimetheus) and Deucalion (a son of Prometheus), who survived in an ark built by Deucalion. The two repeopled the world by casting behind them stones, which became men and women.

77   Pelusium, a city of Egypt at the mouth of the Nile, here by synecdoche Egypt as a whole.

80–82   Moses is succeeded by Sother.

82–89   Sother's Greek name was interpreted etymologically correctly in *B* as "savior" at 2.39, which makes him equivalent to Joshua, whose name has the same meaning. Here the identification between the two is intensified, since Sother carries a shield on which Joshua's feats are pictured (compare the depiction on Aeneas's shield of his descendants' feats (*Aeneid* 8.617–731)—but with the major distinction that whereas in the Roman epic future achievements are depicted, in the medieval one past events are shown.

84–86   On Jericho, see Joshua 6:20–25.

86–92   The same parallel between the lengthening of the days in Joshua and the Amphitryon myth appears in the *Eclogue of Theodulus* 165–72.

86   On Gibeon, see Joshua 10:2.

88   On the lengthening of the day, see Joshua 10:12–14.

90   In Greek myth Thyestes seduced Aerope, the wife of his brother Atreus. Later Thyestes sent Plisthenes, son of Atreus, to kill Atreus, but instead Atreus killed Plisthenes. For revenge Atreus first feigned forgiveness and then fed the two children of Thyestes to his brother at a banquet.

91–92   In Greek mythology Zeus assumed the likeness of Amphitryon in order to spend a night, which he prolonged for his pleasure, with Amphitryon's wife, Alcmena. From this union was born Hercules, who was often designated by the patronymic Alcides; Amphitryon was son of Alcaeus.

100–101　On Jabin, king of Hazor, see Joshua 11; on Japhia, king of Lachish, Joshua 10.

102　Horam was king of Gezer (Joshua 10:33).

103　Sihon was king of the Amorites, mentioned (among other passages) at Joshua 9:10.

122　Alternatively, "shooting the spear through his mouth."

148　The poet seems to have confused the lion and the manticore. Whereas there is no tradition that the lion was dangerous for its tail (although the *Physiologus* mentions that the lion could sweep away its tracks with its tail), the manticore was believed to have a tail armed with projectiles. Although the etymology of the manticore (man-killer) may refer to the lion, the *Eupolemius* poet would not have known this fact.

161–68　K. Manitius takes these lines not as an authorial digression but rather as a continuation of the victory song of the Chaldeans.

177　Crito (from the Greek *krites,* "judge"), glossed in *B* as "judge," represents the judges of the Old Testament collectively.

181–84　Isidore, *Etymologiae* 11.3.19: "People report that the Panotians are in Scythia, with such a spreading mass of ears that they may cover their entire bodies with them. In the Greek, *pan* means 'all'; *ota*, 'ears.'" Even with the help of Isidore, the syntax of the *ut* clause is hard to construe, since one would expect the transitive verb to be in the singular and the subject to correspond with "a Scythian Panotian."

184　Isidore, *Etymologiae* 14.5.8: "Furthermore, Gaetulia is the Mediterranean portion of Africa."

184–86　Isidore, *Etymologiae* 11.3.23: "Reportedly the people of the Sciopods have a single leg and marvelous speed. For this reason the Greeks call them *skiopodas* ("shadow-feet"), for the reasons that lying on their backs on the ground in heat waves they shade themselves by the massiveness of their feet."

186　Isidore, *Etymologiae* 11.3.17: "It is believed that the Blemmyes in Libya are born having bodies without heads, and that they have a mouth and eyes in their chest." Many codices of Isidore have the reading *Lemnias* or *Lemnas*.

188 Literally, "the limbs of [them] swarthy."

199 The Parthians were famed for riding within bow range and shooting arrows while wheeling away swiftly. See also 2.497.

206–7 The manuscript reads Gothoniel and Gothonieli. Although a person named Gothoniel appears in the Bible (1 Paralipomenon 27:15 and Judith 6:11), the character in the *Eupolemius* corresponds to Othniel, the first judge (Judges 3:9–10). Othniel conquered a ruler identified here as the satrap of the Syrians (but in the Bible as king of Aram-Naharaim), C(h)usan-Rishathaim (the name is written in a marginal gloss, to clarify the remark "a name ponderous to pronounce"), and thereby ended his eight-year oppression.

207 It is not evident whether Othniel is dark with blood, or dark because of his association with death.

208 Doxius, glossed on the basis of the Greek etymon in his name in *B* as "Glorious," correlates to the biblical Aod, who serves as judge after Othniel (Judges 3:15).

211–12 Egon is Eglon, king of Moab (Judges 3:12–17).

220 The gloss in *B* renders *exotica* as *peregrina* (foreign) (not "pilgrim" or "wayfarer," as in 2.215), but Manitius takes the adjective as synonymous with "wicked" or "hateful."

235 In Classical Latin *lageos* designated a cultivar of vine, but here it refers to a type of wine.

254–55 On the one-hundred-year wandering to which the shades of the unburied and unavenged are doomed, see Virgil, *Aeneid* 6.325–29.

264–65 Achelous is the name of a Greek river god (and river) who is endowed with the ability to assume whatever form he wishes. Hercules and he battle to determine which of the two will take Deianira in marriage. Hercules prevails by tearing off one of Achelous's horns, after the god changes himself into a bull.

265 Proteus is a Greek sea god who has the capacity for transforming himself into whatever shape he chooses.

267–68 The wound is awkward anatomically, but less so than would be required by the alternative translation: "piercing the triple-threaded corselet, tore his shoulders from his chest."

271–74 In the book of Judges, Gideon, from Manasseh, leads tribes of Israel to victory over Midianite raiders. On Gideon and the fleece, see Judges 6:36–40.

275–81 On the feats of Samson and his downfall at the hands of Delilah, see Judges 14–16.

279 Samson was shut up in prison by the Philistines: see Judges 16.21.

281–88 The juxtaposition of Samson and Hercules is also found in the *Eclogue of Theodulus* 173–80.

282 Milesian tales were brief erotic tales, probably so called because originally they were set in Miletus (a Greek city of Asia Minor). In the Latin West they were not known directly so much as through passing condemnations of them in late antique writings.

283 For having slain his wife and children, Hercules was directed by Apollo to serve King Eurystheus. During his service, the great hero was assigned twelve "labors" of great difficulty and danger. "the ever-watchful dragon": One labor was to obtain the apples of the Hesperides, three sisters who were assisted in their task by a dragon named Ladon (not here identified). "the three-bodied king": Another labor was to capture the oxen of Geryon, a three-headed and –bodied monster who had the help of a two-headed dog called Orthus or Orthrus (not named here).

284 "the Hydra, which grew more powerful in its loss of a head": Among the twelve labors was to kill this many-headed water snake, which had the capacity to regenerate two heads whenever one was struck off.

285 "daunted the king of the underworld": Another labor was to bring from the entrance to Underworld the three-headed dog called Cerberus. Hercules dragged the monstrous canine to earth and released him. "put the Harpies to flight": The Harpies (whose name means "snatchers" in Greek) were two or three creatures that combined features of women and birds. Virgil placed them at the Gates of the Underworld (*Aeneid* 6.289).

286 "Antaeus who was laying waste to the Libyan fields": Antaeus was a

giant who lived in Libya and made all travelers fight with him. He was undefeatable so long as he kept contact with his mother, Gaia (Earth). Hercules, who encountered Antaeus in Libya while searching for the Golden Apples, choked him to death after lifting him off the ground on his shoulders. "Cacus to the Italian": this Cacus is not the personification of evil who goes by this name elsewhere in the poem, but rather a three-headed son of Vulcan who lived in a cavern on the Aventine Hill. When Hercules rested nearby as he returned with the oxen he had taken from Geryon, Antaeus stole some of them and concealed his crime by having them walk backward to his cave. Eventually the two heroes battled and Hercules won, killing Cacus.

289   Compare Virgil, *Aeneid* 10.428 "pugnae nodumque moramque" ("the battle's knot and barrier"). The metaphor suggests that Crito is difficult to overcome, just as a knot in rope or in wood is difficult to untie or to cut.

293   "a ship": literally, "a poopdeck."

308–9 Nomus could be the object of either *irrident* (mock) or *capiunt* (capture).

320   "in a moan mingled with tears": "mingled" could modify Ramathus rather than "moan"; if so, translate "who was confounded tearfully with moaning."

324   The noun *virtus* is exceptionally difficult to translate in this poem, since its connotations are both epic ("manliness") and Christian ("virtue").

339   Parcae: three Roman goddesses, sisters, who are often designated the Fates and who are depicted spinning thread (as a metaphor for life), measuring it out, and cutting it off.

340   Manitius sees the roots of the name Ermadolon as the Greek noun *to herma* (prop, support) and the Greek verb *doloo* (to beguile, ensnare). Probably the second element is the related Greek noun *ho dolos*, here in the genitive plural: "prop [support] of deceits."

341   "spirits of the dead" (Manes): literally, "the benevolent," so called to avoid giving them offense.

342–44 "from prophetic birds the secrets of the fates": Roman divination included close attention to avian signs. The diviner who observed and interpreted the behavior of birds was the augur, also known as *auspex: avis* (bird) + *-spex* (one who in*spects*). From this form of augury derives the word "auspices."

343 "Assyrian astrology": astrology, or the use of astronomical observations about the positions of celestial bodies for predicting the course of human affairs, was imported into ancient Rome from Babylon, which was included at many times within Assyria.

344 Pleiades: the seven daughters of Atlas and Pleione, who were transformed into a cluster of seven large stars in the constellation Taurus. They were called the Pleiades from the Greek verb *plein* (to sail), because the rising and setting of the constellation marked the beginning and the ending of the season for safe sailing. Orion: a giant in Greek mythology, known for being a hunter and handsome, who was made upon dying a constellation that is supposed to be attended by stormy weather.

345 "a long-haired star, a comet": the word *comet* derives from the Greek word *kome* (hair), in reference to the train or tail that characterizes a comet.

346 "The tripods of Phoebus" refer to the oracle of Apollo at Delphi, where a three-legged stand was used by the Pythian priestess. "quivering entrails": an emendation, preferable to the manuscript reading "purifying entrails" ("tergencia . . . exta"), which would imply cleansing because the animal was sacrificed to exculpate a crime.

347–48 "the harsh threads of the sisters": the sisters are the three Fates, the Parcae.

350–51 "the chilling southeast wind . . . the woods of the Caucasus mountains": Virgil, *Georgics* 2.440–41.

354 Athos: A pyramidal peak at the head of the easternmost promontory of Chalcidice, the triple peninsula that projects from Macedonia. Now known as a holy site for Greek Orthodox monks, in antiquity the mountain was sacred to Zeus (Jupiter).

355 "a priest": Ermadolon. "making three channels": such channels for the blood and entrails of sacrificial victims are mentioned by

Horace, *Satires* 1.8.26–28, and especially by Ovid, *Metamorphoses* 7.243–47.

362   "carves . . . limbs with a knife": although the poet could be describing dervish-like self-mutilation, probably *sua* here refers to the bull ("its limbs") rather than to the priest ("his limbs").

368   "whereas ours moves rapidly": the verb *mico, -are* could refer not to motion but rather to brightness ("whereas ours glitters").

369   Pasithea: one of the three Graces. In *B* the name is glossed perplexingly as "Diana." The gloss could be a mistake prompted by similarity between Pasithea and Pasiphaë, since the latter name in Greek ("all-illumining" or "all-bright") was identical with an epithet sometimes applied to Diana.

372   "Mars": the poet uses Gradivus, a title of Mars.

373   The "grim virago" is the goddess Minerva.

374–75   In Virgil, *Aeneid* 8.435–38, the aegis, not the helmet, is chased with snakes.

395–405   The account of David's duel with Goliath follows 1 Kings 17.

396   "small in body but not in spirit": 1 Kings 16:11, 18, and elsewhere.

396–97 The son of Jesse is David.

407–13 The juxtaposition of David and Achilles is not among the parallels found in the *Eclogue of Theodulus*.

407–8 "bears" and "lions": these feats of David's (but not wolves) are mentioned in 1 Kings 17:34–37 and Ecclesiasticus 47:3.

409   Achilles of Larissa: the great hero of the *Iliad* is credited with deeds similar to the ones of David that have been just mentioned, in Statius, *Achilleid* 1.168–70 and 2.123–25. Larissa (also spelled with a single *s*) was the chief city of Thessaly. The pairing "Larissaeus Achilles" appears at Virgil, *Aeneid* 2.197 and 11.404, probably prompted by the fact that Larissa Cremaste was located within the dominions of Achilles.

410   The word here translated as "cithara" could be put into English as "lyre," "harp," or "cittern."

411–13 See 1 Kings 16:18 and 23.

419   On Jonathan, see 1 Kings 13:2 and elsewhere.

420   Irineus, glossed as "peace-bringing" (*pacificum*) in *B,* may correspond to the biblical Solomon, whose name contains the He-

brew triliteral root for "peace." Adon, on the basis of the Greek *hedone,* is glossed in *B* "that is to say, pleasure" ("s<cilicet> uoluptat"). The form Adonem is attested in both the Vulgate (Ezekiel 8:14) and classical poetry.

422   "Distinguished" *(insignis)* could modify either *illius* or *gloria.*

423   Sarcodomas is glossed "vanquishing the flesh" ("carnem domans") in *B.* The name is a mongrel word that combines an initial Greek element (from the noun *sarx, sarkos* [flesh]) with a second Latin one (from the verb *domo, -are* [to tame]).

423–24   An alternative translation: "from the fierce battle, injured by a wound."

435   "Squint-eyed" here implies "invidious."

443   The parenthesis could mean instead "that miscreant!"

458   "The divine mouth" refers to Oron. In this connection it is worth noting that in *B* the name Orontem is twice written *orantem* (2.428 and 443).

468–555   Politeon makes a long boast in enumerating all the peoples and lands of the earth over whom he holds sway.

471–72   Libra is the sign of the zodiac. The sun is in the sign of Libra at the time of the fall equinox. The son of Hyperion is the sun.

476–80   On the Seven against Thebes, see the note on 2.46–48. The four mentioned here are Adrastus, Tydeus, Hippomedon, and Capaneus. Unnamed are Polynices, Amphiareus, and Parthenopeus. A likely source for the passage here is Statius, *Thebaid* 1.41–45.

481   Laomedon's Troy: the phrase appears at Virgil, *Georgics* 1.502.

483   The Calydonian hero is Diomedes, a Greek hero in the siege of Troy, second only to Achilles in his courage. According to some traditions, he played a key role in restoring the kingship of Calydon to its rightful line.

484   Ajax: another Greek hero in the siege of Troy.

485   "wily Ulysses": the Latin "uarium . . . Ulixem," which appears at Statius, *Achilleid* 1.847, suggest untrustworthiness, but the adjective also carried less ambivalent connotations of many-sidedness that make it a good Latin equivalent to the famous Greek epithet for Odysseus (as Ulysses was known before he underwent Latinization), *polutropos.*

487–52   This long catalog of peoples proceeds from the Far East: Asia,

Egypt, Greece, the northern frontiers of the Roman Empire, Germany, Gaul, Spain, Britain, and the south coast of the Mediterranean, including Africa.

487–88 The tripartite world comprehends Asia, Europe, and Africa.

488 "precious fleece": alongside its basic meaning of "fleece," the Latin *vellus* could denote a lump of unspun silk (Virgil, *Georgics* 2.121).

490 The manuscripts read "Gathmus." Karl Manitius suggests that this name refers to the mountain range Cadmus in Caria, but it could also refer to Phoenicia (with which the mythical Cadmus was associated). Cathippus: a town located between the Hyrcanians and the Bactrians.

491 Nyssa was a city and mountain in India. The offspring of Philip was Alexander the Great (Alexander III of Macedon, 356–323 BCE).

492 The pillars of Hercules are the rocks, one in Spain and the other in Africa, that stand opposite each other at the entrance to the Mediterranean. Now Gibraltar and Jebel Musa, the rocks were supposedly bound together until Hercules sundered them so as to reach Gades (present-day Cadiz).

493 On the Indian river Ganges and its ten great tributaries, see Isidore, *Etymologiae* 13.21.8.

495 Hypanis: the name of two rivers (now identified with the Yuzhnyy Bug and Kuban) that debouch into the Black Sea. The Hypanis was known through various sources, among them accounts of Alexander the Great's campaigns. Gamula: no identification has been made.

496 Theriodes is a Scythian river that debouches in the Caspian Sea. Icosium: originally a Phoenician and later a Roman city, located near present-day Algiers—but this identification does not match with the ethnographic information about the Carmanians that follows.

497 The Carmanians inhabited land to the north of the Persian Gulf at its eastern end.

498 King Ahasuerus is identified in Esther 1:1–2 as having "reigned from India to Ethiopia over a hundred and twenty-seven provinces. When he sat on the throne of his kingdom, the city Susan was the capital of his kingdom."

499   The Araxes (present-day Aras), a river of Armenia.

500   The Hyrcanians lived in a country at the southeast side of the Caspian Sea.

501   Sarmatia was a roughly defined region between the Vistula and the Don.

502   The Heniochi, mentioned by Lucan (*De bello civili* 2.591) in conjunction with the golden fleece, were a people who inhabited the eastern shore of the Black Sea. Phasis was a river of Colchis that flowed into the Black Sea. The fleece of Phrixus is the golden fleece: in Greek myth, Phrixus was to be sacrificed to end a famine but instead fled on a winged ram with a golden fleece. Upon arriving at Colchis, he gave the fleece to the king. Later Jason set out with the Argonauts on a quest to recover it.

503–4 The land lying between two rivers is Mesopotamia.

505   The Hiberians, a tribe south of the Caucasus. The Gelonians, a Scythian people.

506   The Cappadocians, natives of a country in eastern Asia Minor between Cilicia and the Black Sea. The Cilicians, inhabitants of a country in southeast Asia Minor.

507   The Galatians, a Celtic people (as their name signifies) that migrated into Phrygia.

507–8 The Meander, a river of Phrygia that became a byword for its wandering course, is not a tributary of the Hermus, a river of Aeolis.

510–11 The Cadmean peoples are Phoenicians.

511   The Sabaeans are Arabs, of whom Lucan (3.247–48) wrote that they "marveled the shadows of trees did not fall leftward."

512   The Phrygians inhabited a country, most famous for Troy, which occupied the center and west of Asia Minor. Nabataea was a country in northern Arabia. Idume, the country to the south of Judaea.

513   Maeotis, the present-day Sea of Azov, is actually a lake and not a swamp (but see 2.641). The poet's comments on the icing of the lake rely upon Lucan 1.18, which describe the Black Sea and not the Maeotis.

514   A mythic race of female warriors, the Amazons were reputed to live on a river of the Black Sea, the Thermodon.

515   Riphaean mountains, a legendary range in the far north that came
       to be identified with actual Scythian mountains. See Lucan
       2.639–41.

516   The Tanais is the river Don, in Sarmatia.

517   Horace, *Satires* 1.5.100, invokes a Jew named Apella as embodying
       extreme superstition, and Lucan (2.592–93) refers to Jewish wor-
       ship of an "unknown god," presumably partly because of not be-
       ing represented in idols.

518   Meroe, a kingdom of the upper Nile. It is named shortly after a
       mention of Syene in Lucan 10.234–37.

519   Syene, a town (present-day Aswan) on the upper Nile.

521   Thracian Hebrus: the phraseology "Ismariusque Hebrus" is drawn
       directly from Ovid, *Metamorphoses* 2.257. The adjective "Ismar-
       ian," referring to Mount Ismarus in southern Thrace, was often
       applied by poets to characterize anything or anyone Thracian.
       The Hebrus was a river in Thrace.

525   Adige, a river of northern Italy. Caicus, a river in Mysia, which
       was a country in northwest Asia Minor, between Lydia and
       Bithynia.

526–27 The Dacians, Pannonians, and Noricans were all peoples located
       along the northern border of the Roman Empire. The Moschi
       and Alans dwelled between the Black and Caspian Seas.

528   Cynocephali: the name derives from the Greek words for dog and
       head. They were a monstrous race that reputedly had dogs'
       heads and barked. The Swabians were a Germanic nation that
       inhabited the remote north (Lucan 2.51).

529   The Vandals were an East Germanic tribe that moved widely
       across Europe and North Africa.

530   The description "Dana signatis oculis" needs further examination.
       The qualification of the Frisians as rebellious could refer either
       to their wars against the Romans in antiquity or to their restive-
       ness in the Middle Ages. The adjective appears in the same met-
       rical position in Lucan 1.428, in a passage that contributed sub-
       stantially to this one.

531   The Main and the Elbe, rivers in Germany.

532   In antiquity Lemannus designated Lake Geneva, which was

                              373

identified as the source of the Rhône (Caesar, *Gallic War* 1.8; Pomponius Mela, 2.79). In Medieval Latin Lemannus could refer to the Lech, while Manitius took it as signifying the Limmat.

533   The Moselle is a river of northern Gaul. The Ill flows down from the Jura Mountains and along Alsace before joining the Rhine beneath Strasbourg.

534   "wheeling horses": see Lucan 1.425 (and Sextus Amarcius, *Sermones* 4.253–54).

535   Arverni, a people of southeastern Gaul (Lucan 1.427–28).

536   Allobroges, a tribe in the southern province of Gaul, present-day Provence. On their disloyalty, see Horace, *Epodes* 16.6. The Nervians (or Nervii) were a Belgic tribe of the modern Hainaut. The Ruthenians were a Gaulish tribe, located in the region surrounding present-day Rodez in southern France (and therefore not neighbors of the Vermandois). Both the Nervians and the Ruthenians are named in this metrical position in Lucan (1.429 and 402, respectively).

539   The Vascones are inhabitants of present-day Navarre.

540   The river Baetis is the modern Guadalquivir, in Spain (Lucan 2.589).

542   The Balearic were inhabitants of the Balearic islands, Majorca and Minorca. They were famed as slingers.

543   "from the Tyrian nation": this refers to Carthage, the north African coast, or both. "the Egyptian land": the Latin adjective used here, Canopica, refers to Canopus, a town and island on the western mouth of the Nile.

545   Cyrene was a town (and district) of northwest Libya. Two cities on the north African coast had the name Leptis, namely, Leptis Magna in Tripolitania (probably meant here) and Leptis Minor in Tunisia. Hippo Regius was a city in Numidia, a district that extended west and south of Carthage.

546   "tripartite province that is inhabited by black Moors": Mauretania was a country of North Africa where parts of Morocco and Algeria are now located. As a Roman province it was divided first into Tingitana and Caesariensis. Later a third division was

made by splitting Mauretania Caesariensis from Mauretania Sitifensis.

547 The Marmaridae were the inhabitants of Marmarica, a region of north Africa between Cyrene and Egypt. At Lucan 4.679–80 they are mentioned in conjunction with the Garamantes, a tribe that lived in the eastern Sahara. Galaulian: Orosius, a writer of the early fifth century, explains (*Historia e adversum paganos* 1.2.94) that this is the modern name for an African people, the Autololes (see Lucan, 4.677).

548–50 The passage is modeled closely on Lucan 3.253–55. The Ethiops were the inhabitants of Ethiopia.

551–52 Or "which has not been subjected to my dominion and does not continue to serve" (if *ultro* is temporal).

566 The god born on Mount Cyllene is Mercury.

581–86, The Incarnation, meaning "the act of clothing with flesh," is de-
598–99 scribed as an act of cross-dressing.

582 Manitius and Lehmann regard *Parthenie* (glossed "virgo" in *B* and misspelled "Partheme" in *D*) as a genitive. In this case translate as "There is in Bethlehem a poor woman of chaste reputation of Parthenia, whom they call by the byname of wonderful" or "There is in Bethlehem a poor woman of chaste [and] virginal renown, whom they call Taumoto by name." But since the asyndeton seems awkward and since cognomen usually refers to an additional name, *Parthenie* can be taken instead as a nominative modeled on the Greek feminine ending. Taumoto would appear to be a slight garbling of the Greek *thaumatos*, the genitive of the noun *thauma* (miracle).

583 "the stock of David": a quality of Mary's upon which, after the Protevangelium of James (an apocryphal Gospel), it was commonplace to remark.

588–91 A father and a son, both named Publius Decius Mus, became bywords for self-sacrifice in Roman legend. In a battle that took place in 340 BCE at Veseris in Campania, the father lost his life by riding directly into the ranks of his opponents, the Latins. In a battle in 295 BCE at Sentinum, his son sacrificed himself to turn the tide in favor of the Romans.

Another legend held that the Roman consul Marcus Atilius Regulus was captured by the Carthaginians and sent to Rome to negotiate but that he returned voluntarily after arguing against any concession.

601 The good spirit is the Holy Spirit.

604 Pistena, from the Greek noun *pistis* meaning "faith," is said appropriately to come "of Abraham's stock" (Romans 4:16 and 19–20).

607–9 On the fire that fell and the cry of the people to Elijah, see 3 Kings 18:38–40 (as well as Isidore, *Etymologiae* 7.8.4–5).

609–10 On the drought and famine that Elijah predicts, see 3 Kings 17:1 and 18:1–2, Luke 4:25, and James 5:17.

610–12 A son of the sun god, Phaëthon drove his father's sun chariot through the heavens but lost control, singed the earth, and was struck down by a thunderbolt from Jupiter. The parallel between the biblical account of Elijah and the Greek myth of Phaëthon does not appear in the *Eclogue of Theodulus*.

613 In *B* the name Eutropius is glossed "good conversion" ("bona conversio").

614 In the word "six hundred" is glossed "the six works of mercy" ("sex opera misericordie"). On the six (or seven) works of charity, see Matthew 25:34–40.

615 Agapes derives his name from *agape*, the Greek equivalent of *caritas* in Christian Latin theology, and represented charity in a Pauline sense. Like a few other names, it is based on the genitive of the Greek noun. Bethel is explained as "the house of God" in the story of Jacob (Genesis 28:19 and 22).

618 On Jacob's dream of the ladder, see Genesis 28:12–16.

619–20 On Jacob's wrestling match and shrunken sinew, see Genesis 32:24–25 and 32.

621–23 These lines draw a parallel between the biblical story of Jacob and the Greek myth of the encounter that Diomedes had with Venus. The same parallel presentation of the two is found in the *Eclogue of Theodulus* 117–24.

621 Maeonia is the eastern part of Lydia, the country in which Homer is supposed to have originated.

622–23 The leader is Diomedes; the goddess, Venus, who transformed the comrades of Diomedes into birds (Virgil, *Aeneid* 11.272–77; Ovid, *Metamorphoses* 14.456–511).

623–25 David's grief, presumably over not only Abner (2 Kings 3) but also Saul and Jonathan (1 Kings 31:6 and 2 Kings 1:17), and perhaps as well Absalom (2 Kings 18–19).

627 The son of Agatus is Messiah.

628–29 It is appropriate for Leuconous, whose name here is glossed "white mind" in *B,* to ride a snow-white gelding.

629–30 Paton (from the Greek noun *pathos,* which corresponds to the Latin *passio*), a character who embodies the virtue associated in particular with Job (James 5:11).

632–35 Tapinus of Bethany shows some correspondences with the beggar Lazarus (Luke 16:20 and John 11:1).

634 The name Tapinus, from the Greek *tapeinos,* is glossed "humility" ("humilitas") in *B.*

636 Sarcodomas corresponds to Daniel (Daniel 1:8–20).

638–39 The 366 days of an *annus bissextilis,* a leap year in which an intercalary day was inserted in the Julian calendar (Isidore, *De natura rerum* 6.4).

648 On the two springs from which the Jordan arises, and on its debouching into the Dead Sea near Jericho, see Isidore, *Etymologiae* 13.21.18.

659–60 "The prelude of war, the standard-bearer of keen Messiah" would be John the Baptist.

664–67 The virtue Pistena (Faith) battles Politeon (Polytheism: Worship of Many Gods); Leuconous (Chastity), Fuscus (Lust); and Tapinus (Humility), Hiperefanes (Pride). As the text is transmitted, the problem opposition pits Crisargirus against Aelphis. Emendation makes the duel take place between Cresterius (Chresterius, "prophetic"), who would be a good opponent for Aelpton (Greek for "despair" or "hopelessness").

667 Iperfanes (also 1.558), earlier encountered as Hiperefanes (1.364), is synonymous with Superifanes (1.88), who was glossed as Superbia (Pride).

668 "a coat with a fur collar": the concise Latin phrase "pellesque gula-

tas" implies additionally that the fur collar is made from the throats (*gula*, throat) of animals, such as martens. The origins of the fur imply both softness and color (red).

672 "clodhoppers": Isidore (*Etymologiae* 19.34.13) identifies *perones* as rustic footwear.

678 Syntactically Aphilus and Diglossa could be felled by either Agapes or Paton. The text here may be corrupt, since it would make better sense for Agapes to slay only Heretus and for a new character named Apheles (Greek "simple, plain") instead of Aphilus to overcome Diglossa—but note that these four and a half feet appear in exactly the same form and position in 1.557, where they are companions of Fuscus. Since Fuscus could be interpreted as being the opposite of Agapes, there would be sense in having supporters of Fuscus die at the hands of Agapes.

683 Jerusalemite leader: Messiah (or Agatus).

689 The emendation *pristinus* is accepted here in place of *protinus*. Although *protinus* appears in this metrical position (1.79), it is always the first word in a sentence (2.7, 2.69) or at least the first after the particle *nam*.

694 "the sulfurous morass renowned for its bitumen": The Dead Sea.

704–32 In this closing scene Judas represents both the Jews collectively, who mocked Jesus as a carpenter's son, and Judas Iscariot in particular, who betrayed Jesus.

715 Matthew 13:55 (and compare Mark 6:3): "Is not this the carpenter's son?"

727 The meekness of Christ is emphasized at Matthew 11:29. The five penetrating wounds (often called the Five Holy Wounds) of crucified Christ are not mentioned in any canonical source, but they are assumed to be one in each hand, two through the feet, and one in the side where his body was pierced by the lance and where blood and water poured forth.

728–29 On "a sheep to the slaughter" to save the sheep gone astray, see Isaiah 53:6–7. Jesus is styled "the Lamb of God" in John 1:29 and 36.

734–35 The Latin pronouns in these lines are ambiguous.

739 On the various names of Jerusalem (Jebus, Jerusalem, Aelia, and Zion), see Isidore, *Etymologiae* 15.1.5.

740–42 The poet says of the captives who were freed by the self-sacrifice of Messiah that they resemble the Jews when Cyrus II "the Great" brought an end to the Babylonian exile (1 Ezra 1–3 and 2 Paralipomenon 36:22–23).

740–41 Cyrus the Great, who founded the Persian empire in 559 BCE and controlled a vast territory by his death in 530, brought to an end the Babylonian exile of the Jews by an edict that permitted the exiles to return home. Although the figure of sixty-five years is indicated here, the Bible specifies a total of seventy years (2 Paralipomenon 36:21, Jeremiah 25:1 and 29:10).

742 The boughs in question are of willows (a fusion of content from Psalms 136:2 and language from Ovid, *Metamorphoses* 5.590).

743–44 These lines describe the rise of the Pleiades at the entrance of the sun into the zodiac sign Aries in the spring.

746–62 The lament of Messiah's mother (introduced earlier at 2.581–86) shows strong influence from the lament of Euryalus's mother over her son (Virgil, *Aeneid* 9.473–502). It may also respond to religious lyric of the poet's own day in its portrayal of the *mater dolorosa* (grieving mother).

767–69 The sighting of Jesus after Resurrection by eleven disciples in Galilee is recounted in Matthew 28:16–17.

771–72 These lines refer to the destruction of Jerusalem (and especially of the Temple) by the Romans in CE 70, under Emperor Titus (ruled 79–81). Remarkably, the passage does not make mention of the Crusade, which might have been expected if it had been in the air or indeed had already taken place.

772 Jerusalem was renamed Aelia (Capitolina) under Emperor Hadrian (Aelius Hadrianus).

780 The imagery of milk and strong meat was established in the New Testament, in 1 Corinthians 3:1–2, 1 Peter 2:2, and Hebrews 5:12–14. Strong meat is for those who have senses trained to differentiate between good and evil. In medieval exegesis the topos was applied to multiple senses of scriptural interpretation: the literal or historical sense of the Bible suits beginners; the tropological, students at an intermediate level; and the allegorical, advanced scholars. The commonplace appears also in Sextus Amarcius, *Satires* 3.703–4 and 727–32.

Bibliography

Satires

Editions

Manitius, Karl, ed. *Sextus Amarcius: Sermones*. Monumenta Germaniae Historica, Quellen zur Geistesgeschichte des Mittelalters 6. Weimar, 1969.

Manitius, Max, ed. *Sexti Amarcii Galli Piosistrati Sermonum Libri IV*. Leipzig, 1888.

Secondary Sources

Manitius, Max. *Geschichte der lateinischen Literatur des Mittelalters*. 3 vols. Munich, 1911–1931.

———. "Zu Amarcius und Eupolemius," *Mittheilungen des Instituts fur Osterreichische Geschichtsforschung* 24 (1903): 185–97.

Raby, F. J. E. *A History of Secular Latin Poetry in the Middle Ages*. Vol. 1. Oxford, 1934.

Sedgwick, W. B. "Conjecturae in poetas aliquot medii aevi: Amarcius," *Archivum Latinitatis Medii Aevi* 5 (1929–1930): 216ff.

Smolak, Kurt. "Adnotatiunculae ad Sextum Amarcium," *Quaderni del Instituto di Filologia Latina dell'Universita di Padova* 4 (1976): 121–32.

Yunck, John A. *The Lineage of Lady Meed: The Development of Mediaeval Venality Satire*. Notre Dame, Ind., 1963.

Eupolemius

Editions

Manitius, Karl, ed. *Eupolemius. Das Bibelgedicht*. Monumenta Germaniae Historica, Quellen zur Geistesgeschichte des Mittelalters 9. Weimar, 1973.

Manitius, Max, ed. "Die Messias des sogenannten Eupolemius. Aus cod. Dresd. DC 171ª." *Romanische Forschungen* 6 (1891): 509–56.

Translation

Ziolkowski, Jan M. "Eupolemius." *Journal of Medieval Latin* 1 (1991): 1–45.

Primary Sources

Augustine. *De civitate Dei*. Edited by B. Dombart and A. Kalb. 5th ed. Stuttgart, 1981.

Jerome. *De viris inlustribus*. In *Hieronymus liber De viris inlustribus; Gennadius liber De viris inlustribus*, edited by Ernest Cushing Richardson. Texte und Untersuchungen zur Geschichte der altchristlichen Literatur 14/1. Leipzig, 1896.

Manitius, Karl, ed. *Sextus Amarcius: Sermones*. Monumenta Germaniae Historica, Quellen zur Geistesgeschichte des Mittelalters 6. Weimar, 1969.

Theodulus. *Ecloga. Il canto della verità e della menzogna*. Edited and translated by Francesco Mosetti Casaretto. *Per verba:* Testi mediolatini con traduzione 5. Florence, 1997.

Secondary Sources

Babcock, Robert. "Alexander Monachus and Merseburg." *Scriptorium*. Forthcoming.

Borst, Arno. *Der Turmbau von Babel: Geschichte der Meinungen über Ursprung und Vielfalt der Sprachen und Völker*. Vol. 2, pt. 1. Stuttgart, 1958.

Collins, John J. "The Mythology of Holy War in Daniel and the Qumran

War Scroll: A Point of Transition in Jewish Apocalyptic." *Vetus Testamentum* 25 (1975): 596–612.

Curtius, Ernst Robert. *European Literature and the Latin Middle Ages.* Translated by Willard R. Trask. Bollingen Series 36. Princeton, N.J., 1990.

Dinzelbacher, Peter. *Judastraditionen.* Raabser Märchen-Reihe 2. Vienna, 1977.

Dronke, Peter. "Laments of the Maries: From the Beginnings to the Mystery Plays." In *Intellectuals and Poets in Medieval Europe*, 457–89. Storia e letteratura 183. Rome, 1992.

Erdmann, Carl. *Forschungen zur politischen Ideenwelt des Frühmittelalters.* Berlin, 1951.

Forsyth, Neil. *The Old Enemy: Satan and the Combat Myth.* Princeton, 1987.

Gärtner, Thomas. "Zu den dichterischen Quellen und zum Text der allegorischen Bibeldichtung des Eupolemius." *Deutsches Archiv für Erforschung des Mittelalters* 58 (2002): 549–62.

———. "Zum spätantiken und mittelalterlichen Nachwirken der Dichtungen des Alcimus Avitus." *Filologia Mediolatina* 9 (2002): 109–222.

Gröber, Gustav. *Übersicht über die lateinische Litteratur von der Mitte des VI. Jahrhunderts bis zur Mitte des XIV. Jahrhunderts.* Munich, 1974 [Strasbourg, 1902].

Herschel, C. A. "Eupolemius." *Serapeum* 16 (1855): 141–44, 171–76.

Jacobsen, Peter Christian. Review of Karl Manitius, ed. *Eupolemius. Mittellateinisches Jahrbuch* 13 (1978): 304–7.

Jensen, Jens Juhl. 1983. "Das Bibelgedicht des Eupolemius und die mittelalterliche Zahlenkomposition." *Mittellateinisches Jahrbuch* 18 (1983): 121–27.

Langosch, Karl. "Überlieferungsgeschichte der mittellateinischen Literatur." In *Geschichte der Textüberlieferung der antiken und mittelalterlichen Literatur*, 2:80, 169–70n198. Zurich, 1964.

Lehmann, Paul. *Erforschung des Mittelalters: Ausgewählte Abhandlungen und Aufsätze.* Vol. 2, "Judas Ischarioth in der lateinischen Legendenüberlieferung des Mittelalters." Stuttgart, 1959.

Manitius, Karl. "Die Bibliothek des Petersklosters in Merseburg." *Deutsches Archiv für Erforschung des Mittelalters* 20 (1964): 190–209.

———. "Dresdner Handschriften aus St. Peter in Merseburg." *Deutsches Archiv für Erforschung des Mittelalters* 22 (1966): 254–62.

———. "Eupolemius." In *Die Deutsche Literatur des Mittelalters: Verfasser-lexikon*, edited by Kurt Ruh. 2nd ed. Vol. 2, columns 642–646. Berlin, 1978–1979.

Manitius, Max. *Geschichte der lateinischen Literatur des Mittelalters*. 3 vols. Munich, 1911–1931.

———. "Handschriftliche Nachlese zu Eupolemius." *Neues Archiv der Gesellschaft für Ältere Deutsche Geschichtskunde* 28 (1903): 737–38.

———. "Mittelalterliche Umdeutung antiker Sagenstoffe." *Zeitschrift für vergleichende Literatur* 15 (1904): 151–58.

———. "Zu Amarcius und Eupolemius." *Mittheilungen des Instituts für Österreichische Geschichtsforschung* 24 (1903): 193–96.

Orlandi, Giovanni. "Metrica e statistica linguistica come strumenti nel metodo attributivo." *Filologia Mediolatina* 6–7 (1999–2000): 9–31, esp. 31.

Oxford Latin Dictionary. Edited by P. G. W. Glare. Oxford, 1968–1982.

Penn, Stephen. "Latin Verse." In *The Camden House History of German Literature: The Early Middle Ages*, edited by Brian Murdoch, 87–118, esp. 107–8 and 114–15. London, 2004.

Raby, F. J. E. *A History of Secular Latin Poetry in the Middle Ages*. 2nd ed. Vol. 1. Oxford, 1957.

Ratkowitsch, Christine. "Der Eupolemius—Ein Epos aus dem Jahre 1096?" *Filologia Mediolatina* 6–7 (1999–2000): 215–71.

Riley-Smith, Jonathan. *The First Crusade and the Idea of Crusading*. London, 1986.

Rotondi, Giuseppe. "Amarcius." *Convivium* 4 (1948): 929–32.

Smolak, Kurt. "Epic Poetry as Exegesis: 'The Song of the Good War' (Eupolemius)." In *Poetry and Exegesis in Premodern Latin Christianity. The Encounter Between Classical and Christian Strategies of Interpretation*, edited by Willemien Otten and Karla Pollmann, 231–44. Leiden, 2007.

Traube, Ludwig. "Zur Messiade des Eupolemius." *Neues Archiv der Gesellschaft für Ältere Deutsche Geschichtskunde* 26 (1901): 174–75.

Yadin, Yigael, ed. *The Scroll of the War of the Sons of Light Against the Sons of Darkness*. Oxford, 1962.

Ziolkowski, Jan M. "Eupolemiana." *Mittellateinisches Jahrbuch* 26 (1991): 117–32.

Index to Satires

Italicized locators indicate isolated references to subjects named in the translation but referred to obliquely in the Latin text.

Index to Eupolemius

Italicized locators indicate isolated references to subjects named in the translation but referred to obliquely in the Latin text.